FINAL TABLE

FINAL TABLE

A Novel

Dan Schorr

Published by SparkPress, a BookSparks imprint,
A division of SparkPoint Studio, LLC
Phoenix, Arizona, USA, 85007
www.gosparkpress.com

Published 2021
Printed in the United States of America
Print ISBN: 978-1-68463-107-0
E-ISBN: 978-1-68463-108-7 (e-bk)
Library of Congress Control Number: 2021909386

Formatting by Kiran Spees

Part One

1

KYLER DAWSON closed his eyes tightly, breathed deeply, and tilted his head downward in a brief, remarkably unsuccessful attempt to compose himself. Last time, he had been incredibly embarrassed—mortified—and his life and career were savagely disrupted. Now, the consequences would be even worse. If people believed what was currently being said about him, he was finished.

He felt the chaotic rush of people around him, scrambling to their boarding gates and dashing to the ride-share station. Carts loaded with the elderly and disabled careened through the crowds as their *beep beep beep* warning noises ordered the able-bodied out of the way.

Most of those who were not moving through the busy airport were standing or sitting, looking at their phones and tablets—posting on social media, checking bank accounts, responding to emails, video chatting, texting, sexting, reading the news, playing mindless games, so absorbed and seemingly oblivious to those around them. A few were probably even playing poker, trying to win a few dollars before boarding time.

He desperately wanted time to pause, to give him a chance to collect himself and decide what to do. But the latest news about him was spreading online with merciless speed, and he needed to act fast. He knew all too well how savage an online hit job could be. He had experienced it before when it incinerated the last strings holding together his relationship with his then-wife. And that time he learned a big lesson: passively ignoring the issue and hoping it would fade as the next social media news scandal emerged was a huge mistake. Without a real response, the allegations would become indelible. He couldn't let that happen again.

This time he would respond immediately—clearly, forcefully, and without reservation. But what should he say?

With every second, the story gained more shares, more retweets, more comments, and thus more credibility. So he steadied the phone in his trembling hands and began to tap out his answer to the world.

Be assertive. But don't sound angry or defensive. Stay positive.

As he had been preparing to board his first-class seat, the online world had just been told that he had no money—that he had, unfathomably, lost it all. If true, it would be a stunning development. Blowing through all the money could only mean that he'd be perceived as a complete failure, a colossal loser. And in his world, that kind of perception quickly became reality. No opportunities to earn. Severance of all available roads to make a living, pay his bills, live his life, and provide child support—including the crucial opportunity that was awaiting him at the other end of his flight.

He didn't want to be cast away as a failure. He didn't want to be a dead-beat dad. This was not about just preserving his reputation and avoiding embarrassment. This was about survival.

So he tweeted:

"I can't believe I even need to write this, but I am NOT broke. Please don't believe lies of a jealous blogger. I'm so grateful and happy with my life and success. #blessed"

He read it a few more times, wondering if each phrase and sentence carried the meaning and nuance that he intended. It didn't matter that it was already forever in the public domain now—he still questioned every word as his stomach rumbled, his chest rose and fell quickly and repeatedly, and his head struggled to focus.

Was it clear enough? Strong enough? Positive enough? Maybe he shouldn't have acknowledged the anonymous blogger, giving him or her or them unnecessary attention and driving more readers to the story. Was the capitalization of "not" too much? Tweets in all caps were annoying—but this was just one upper case word, so it was okay. Right?

#blessed

He liked that hashtag. There was a time when he really, really had been #blessed, and hopefully he would be #blessed again very soon. One thing he knew for sure: he should NOT look at the Twitter replies (yes, NOT in all caps).

His phone quickly populated with a flood of retweets and comments. He knew that social media was ready to mock and desecrate him, and reading brutal comments by a bunch of terrible people hiding in the shadows would serve no purpose. It certainly wouldn't help him calm down and concentrate.

But there were so many of them . . .

What were they saying?

Were any positive? Maybe there was a pocket of support for him. Maybe that would give him the strength to board his flight and, after landing, emerge as if nothing was wrong.

"Final boarding call for American Airlines flight 5282 to Washington, DC . . ."

He needed to put the phone away and get moving.

But wasn't there time to look at just one response?

@vegaslife1968: "I don't care if ur broke or not. I care that ur fellow poker pro is missing & shes maybe dead and ur just selfish AF thinking about urself #sixofdiamondsontheriver #ezpass"

Of course, he recognized the two hashtags, but he had no idea anyone was missing. He would have to look online and see what he could learn. Beyond that confusion, he just felt fury.

He fantasized slamming @vegaslife1968's head into a wall. Kyler was a big guy. Maybe not as muscular as he used to be, but he was strong enough that odds were he would win a physical fight against an anonymous tweeter.

He thought about reading one more comment—maybe the next one would be supportive—but instead he shut down his phone and boarded his flight to Washington, hoping that his first ever trip to DC would save his life.

2

Three days earlier.

In her thirty years as a local television news reporter in the nation's capital, Tori Kinum had covered too many horrific stories to count. The nursing home fire that resulted in twenty-five assisted living residents burning to death. The mentally ill man who stabbed his six-year-old neighbor twenty times and then drowned him in a swimming pool because the kid had accidentally kicked a soccer ball through the man's glass window. The combat veterans returning from service with missing limbs and other physical and mental wounds.

Local news lived in tragedy, and she reported it daily. How many times had she been yelled at by a grieving family member?

"Get that fucking camera away from my home. My child is dead! Are you inhuman?"

None of that experience with the dreadful and grotesque prepared her for the sight of her sister's murdered body.

"Emily . . ."

Her lungs heaved, and she released a scream of agony. Scars covered Emily's body, bruises darkened her face—the face that in so many ways had been her face, too. The short black hair, the hazel eyes, the self-assured, commanding smile. Now the right eye area was swollen and disfigured. The once-perfect teeth were each now broken, crooked, or missing.

Her sister was her hero, her inspiration for being a journalist and so much more. Emily's content went way beyond the local tragedies that Tori was stuck in. Her sister traveled the world and lived in the most repressive and dangerous societies. Her journalism was world-renowned—winning countless awards and, more importantly, helping to expose corrupt, brutal leaders and governments. As she risked her life to uncover and document oppression, her investigative journalism about the barbaric treatment of women, child slavery, religious persecution, human trafficking, torture and murder of opposition figures, and so many other human rights issues galvanized the free world time and again to support local activists who brought about real change. Her writing shone a light on the world's cruelest practices, and, because of her work, countless people lived better, freer lives.

While most of humanity threw up its hands in exasperation about the impossibility of helping improve "hopeless" situations, Emily faced unthinkable risks, wrote shocking truths, and never viewed a human life as expendable.

Now Tori needed to muster her sister's strength and determination. Tori's lifelong symbol of strength, vitality, and justice lay dead before her. But she was not going to be hopeless. She was going to fight back, in every way that she could.

She ran her right hand over her sister's forehead.

"I love you so much, Emily," she sobbed. *They tortured her*, she thought, agonizing over what she imagined her sister went through during her final hours.

As a journalist, Tori chased down every hot tip and relished the opportunity to obtain a precious nugget before the rest of the pack, especially when she successfully scooped her national media competitors. Now she had ultimate insider access to the most explosive, confidential story of her life—but this time she and her journalist sister were the *subjects* of this soon-to-be media feeding frenzy.

She looked around the small, dark room, which contained no

furniture except for the table that supported her sister inside a zipped open body bag. There was one other living person in the room, and she turned to face him.

"You can't let them get away with this," she ordered as her voice cracked.

Bryce Kirkwood gave her a sensitive nod. He appeared to be about to reach out to provide a hug or some other physical display of compassion but then paused uncomfortably. Thirty-one years old, he looked twenty-six at most, way too young for the job. He was handsome and determined in a youthful way, like a former college athlete now working his ass off as a junior associate in a prestigious law firm.

But this was no newbie attorney sentenced by a senior partner to hours and days and weeks of document review. This young man had rapidly risen in the cutthroat world of DC politics and now stood before her on his third day as White House chief of staff.

"They won't," he replied with assurance in his eyes. "We won't let them."

"*Look* at her!" she exclaimed, even though she now barely could. "They tortured my sister! They murdered her because she was going to expose them. Promise me you won't just respond with more bullshit sanctions. They need to pay with their lives."

"Tori, we're 100 percent going to get vengeance. The people who did this don't deserve to live another second. But we don't know for sure who killed her yet. We don't know how high up this goes. The crown prince is saying he knew nothing about it and that he's doing his own investigation—"

"You're not going to trust—"

"Of course not. Whether he was involved or not, and he probably was, he'll do whatever he can to cover it up, find a scapegoat. We're using our own sources, but our intel in the Kingdom is weak. We don't have all the facts yet."

She looked back in the direction of her sister, unfocused so that she could avoid revisiting the heart-wrenching details. *I can't handle what they did to you. And your killers aren't suffering real consequences yet, so I'm already failing you. But I will be relentless.*

She stared back at Bryce, the man who spoke for the president.

"You should be telling me how you're going to use the mighty power and reach of the United State of America to kill the people who did this," she instructed. "That's what I want to hear."

He looked back at her with understanding.

She added, "And that's what the American people are going to want to hear. Promise me you won't just throw economic sanctions at them. This was a murder, not some trade infraction."

"I want what you want," he said with seemingly sincere compassion. "Sanctions never accomplish anything. They just make us look weak. But between you and me, some in the administration will want them. Brad Connelly is already pushing for that. I'm doing my best. I'm on your side."

"The president listens to you. I'm counting on you."

"I promise, Tori. As long as the president still takes my advice, once we have the evidence we need, you'll get the military response you're looking for. Anything less would be a disgrace. Now that her body's been returned, we'll learn a lot more about how she was killed and who's responsible. But we're not there yet. And remember, they're probably a nuclear power now. It makes this a lot more complicated than if it was just some shitty third-world country that we could bomb."

"Well, I'll be *very* vocal about what the US needs to do. And I'll shame anyone continuing to invest there. She was an expert at that," Tori explained, glancing at her sister. "And I watched her carefully. So I know how to do this."

"I support you completely, Tori. I know there's nothing more excruciating than what you're going through. I'm so sorry. The president and I and the whole country are on your side."

"We'll see. When does the public find out?"

"Whenever you're ready. Do you want more time? I can step out."

She leaned back down and softly kissed her sister's battered forehead. Then, full of resolve, she turned back to the young man in front of her.

"I'm ready."

3

"I KNOW UR VERY BUSY but we need to talk about what happened last week"

Maggie Raster lay on her apartment couch and stared at the text she had sent her former boss the night before. The message showed that it had been read, but there was no reply.

She was still sorting out what had happened, second-guessing her actions and decisions. She hadn't confided in anyone about what he had done, fearing that others thinking of her as some kind of "victim" would be worse than the act itself. And as she wrestled with finding the right words to describe it, her ruminating sometimes led to extreme terms that she knew were absurd. Her life would be so much easier if she could just move on.

But even a week later, she couldn't.

There was a lot of drinking by the group that night, although she'd been relatively sober. She remembered how handsome he looked, how excited they all were to celebrate his new position.

And she recalled the moment in the midst of it all when everyone was toasting and laughing and their eyes met and he smiled and she thought with building excitement and curiosity, *Hmmmm . . . I don't work for him anymore. We're both single. There's really no reason this can't happen.*

Then they were in the Uber together, heading to her nearby apartment. Her skirt had risen a little, and her bare leg rested against his perfect suit pant. It was a tantalizing physical touch with someone she had been so professional with for so long. She tilted her head up to his face and started to lean in for a kiss, but his hand met her shoulder as he gently guided her away.

"Wait wait wait. We're not alone," he whispered. He saw the disappointment that she couldn't avoid expressing and offered her a little smirk. "Yet . . ." he added flirtatiously with a quick wink from his right eye.

They simultaneously giggled, and he took her hand in his as the car cruised through the beautiful Washington winter night.

A few moments later, he released her hand and began lightly stroking the inside of her left thigh, and she took the cue to place a hand on his knee and then slowly start moving it up his pants. He exhaled as she got higher, and for the moment he wasn't stopping her, so she playfully moved two fingers farther and farther up the inside of his leg and then seductively over his crotch.

"Wait wait wait," he then said for the second time.

"You don't like that?" she asked with a mischievous tone, as two fingers turned into a whole hand that caressed his dick through his pants.

"Oh my God," he sighed. "Wait, stop. Really." He moved her hand away. "We need to be able to walk out of here in a few minutes. What if someone recognizes me?" he said in a hushed voice, indicating the now noticeable bulge in his pants.

"Maybe they'll be impressed?" she asked with a grin.

"No, really . . . I can't have that happen. We'll be there soon."

"Okay," she whispered, and kissed his neck.

Finally, the ride ended. They hustled to the elevator and then rode up to her apartment. Once they were inside her place with the door closed, his reticence vanished. He kissed her passionately and quickly unbuttoned her cream-colored blouse. She placed her hands around his waist and then began to unbuckle his belt.

There was nothing wrong with them being together, but their previous ultra-professional relationship added another degree of excitement and the illusion of taboo, which helped flare their passion.

Soon they were having sex on her bed, and it was such a welcome, needed escape. Even at the point when she felt like he was fucking her for just a little too long, and she was hoping he would come soon, she felt more blissful than she'd been in a very long time. The terrible stresses of her life seemed to recede, if only for a short while.

The consulting business she was struggling to set up. Her financial problems now that she no longer had a salary. Her parents' medical issues and skyrocketing health care bills. The growing fear that she'd made a terribly stupid career decision and ruined her future.

For the moment, she tried to allow herself to feel content. He was behind her as she lay on her stomach with a pillow under her waist, and the sex still felt pretty good, but she couldn't wait until it was over so they could experience the afterglow together.

Then, finally, it arrived. And for about seven seconds, it did not disappoint, as he wrapped his arms around her chest from behind and held her close to his body.

Now she wasn't just back to reality—she was confronting a whole new reality, and she didn't know how to begin to acknowledge or tackle it.

And she still had her other problems to fix. So many people had warned her not to leave her enviable position in government. "Just wait a couple more years, until the end of the term. Then you'll be really marketable. Everyone will want to hire you."

But she didn't want to wait. She sensed this was her moment, when she could take the experience and connections she had made and begin political consulting on her own. She truly believed in her own ability, and she very much wanted to be her own boss and gain independence from all the assholes in government.

Maggie Raster Consulting, LLC.

When the name was official, she was excited and proud. She did everything she could to network and spread the word, and she was even quoted in a few news articles about current events.

But no clients. A few teases here and there as people inquired about her services, but she couldn't close a deal. She had saved enough to live for three months without an income, but now nine months had passed, and she was paying the rent through credit-card loans with soon-to-be exorbitant interest rates. "0% Intro APR on purchases and balance transfers for six months! A special offer just for you!" She now had five of those.

And then there were her parents' issues . . .

It was at the promotion celebration for her former boss, right after she reminded the group that she was now building her own political consulting business, that she was told for the umpteenth time what she needed to do.

One of the guys there, a balding, middle-aged staffer named Brad Connelly, pointed his finger and declared, "Hey, well, you need to get on TV. You're *definitely* cute enough to be a political talking head. I'd fucking watch if you were talking about *anything* . . ." There was an awkward pause, so he exclaimed with intoxicated exuberance, "Fuck! I hope I didn't just commit some fucking MeToo violation!" and then burst out laughing.

The rest of the assembled chuckled along. Maggie, half-heartedly pretending to be amused, wondered if anyone actually thought it was funny.

Connelly had always acted this way. Maggie and other women who had been staffed with him elsewhere were familiar with his penchant for creating an uncomfortable work environment, full of sexualized comments and awkward invasions of personal space. Nothing had changed, as he continued making ridiculous, immature observations all night.

"Why is it called doggy style anyway? Why not just *dog* style? I mean, what adult calls a dog a *doggy*? There's no other situation when we do that!"

"Well, what about leftovers in a restaurant? We call it a doggy bag," a woman interjected.

Connelly looked at her sternly and explained, "Well, I don't. I just say I'm taking it *to go*." Then he erupted in laughter again.

Getting away from people like him was one of the reasons she wanted to leave government employment, one of the reasons she didn't want to join someone else's consulting firm. She understood politics as well as any of these people, and if she could just break into the consulting world, she knew she'd be great at it.

But how?

The continual advice was that she needed to get on television. National television.

It wasn't as if she hadn't tried. She'd reached out to every booker and producer she could find a connection to, through phone calls, emails, and social media, telling them all about her career credentials and availability—and noting her television experience that she in reality did not have. Most ignored her. A few sent polite responses. "Thank you for your email. We will certainly keep you in mind for future segments."

She was well aware that in the political consulting world, and in many other worlds, people thought that if you were on television, you must know something. And people wanted to hire someone who knew something. Plus, people liked seeing their consultant on television, so they could feel as if they were connected to someone with a modicum of celebrity.

She had never been interviewed on television, but she had watched countless political news segments with the same formula: two consultants debating some hot topic. She was as knowledgeable as any of them. She was as well-spoken as any of them. And yes, she was as attractive as any of them. They were mostly just more polished than she was, but she could get there over time. She just needed to get in the game.

Meanwhile, still no reply to her text message.

"I know ur very busy but we need to talk about what happened last week"

At four in the morning, she had woken up on her apartment sofa, where she had slept every night for the past week, and she'd lain there awake and virtually motionless for the next four hours. She wondered what she would do that day. At what time would she finally get off the couch? Would she ever venture outside? She had no clients and nowhere to go, and she was increasingly anxious and distressed.

When her phone suddenly beeped with the sound of an incoming text message, Maggie shocked herself by how quickly she moved to seize it. She was both hopeful and fearful that it would be from him. But it wasn't.

"Hey Maggie. Kinda last minute but have u been following Kinum murder? Can u do 11:30a hit on possible government response? Pls let me know ASAP thx!!"

It was from a recent college graduate named Natalie Ellison who was now booking segments for a national cable news network—a young woman who was a friend of a friend, who she had emailed a few weeks earlier and had gotten no response.

Maggie was in no state, physically or mentally, to have her television debut in just over three hours, but that was irrelevant. To make things worse, she'd cut herself off from all news for the past day or so and had no idea what the Kinum murder was or what kind of government response would even be considered. But that didn't matter either. And she certainly wasn't going to delay her response to look less desperate and then hear that the network booked someone else in the interim. So she texted back immediately:

"Absolutely. I've been following it closely. Thanks for reaching out."

"Great! Just email me some talking points for producers in the next half hour, ok? And send me address for car service pickup thx!!"

She quickly googled "Kinum murder" and a flood of articles popped up. Emily Kinum, American citizen and prominent international human rights journalist, had been murdered in the Kingdom earlier that week, and news of the killing had broken the previous day after her body had been returned to the United States. There weren't many details available, but the White House had issued a statement praising Kinum's life work "on behalf of the oppressed around the world." It also had called for an independent international investigation and declared that there would be "serious consequences" for those responsible for her death.

Meanwhile, the Kingdom also issued a statement condemning the murder, vowing that government officials knew little about its circumstances but were conducting a "prompt and thorough" investigation.

Maggie had read much of Kinum's work and greatly respected her. For years, Kinum had risked her life to report from unstable, war-torn countries, and now she had been horrifically killed. Maggie immediately felt an emotional connection to the case, and she wanted the murderers identified and punished.

She knew that this was a very tricky and serious situation. The United States ceased formal diplomatic relations with the Kingdom a few years before. Although a relatively small nation, experts believed that the Kingdom had become a nuclear power two years earlier and that they'd perfected long range missiles only a few months prior. Summits, threats, condemnations, and sanctions hadn't deterred its leaders from becoming more and more dangerous, and they could now potentially reach the United States with a nuclear warhead. Despite the murder of a revered American journalist, she knew the United States would have to tread carefully and not let this situation become a full-blown military conflict.

On social media and in online op-eds, many were calling for a complete boycott of the nation, with significant commentary on the upcoming Goodwill Poker Classic, a prominent international poker tournament that the Kingdom was planning to host the following week. As she read more, she learned that the event was apparently the brainchild of the Kingdom's crown prince, an avid poker player, in order to "promote goodwill to the world and highlight the Kingdom's ongoing modernization and liberalization."

Maggie didn't know anything about poker or this event, but she was sophisticated enough to recognize an insincere public relations attempt by an immoral, repressive government.

The online consensus was clear—poker players from all countries should boycott this tournament. There were also many people calling for the administration to issue an executive order banning any US citizen or resident from traveling to the Kingdom for any kind of business.

One more key fact caught her eye: the invitational tournament, which would feature one hundred players, had a $20 million winner-take-all prize.

She quickly typed her talking points for the television segment and then emailed them to Natalie:

"The Kingdom is a brutal dictatorship where little happens without the knowledge and approval of its leadership. It's hard to fathom that a prominent journalist would be murdered without the government's involvement. It's also a government that maintains heavy surveillance of its citizens' activities, so they surely already know what happened to Kinum, regardless of who's responsible. The United States must demand immediate and full transparency for an international investigation. The president should immediately issue an executive order instituting strong economic sanctions and prohibiting all American participation in the upcoming Goodwill Poker Classic. Additionally, all poker players worldwide should boycott it. The United States must also strongly consider an appropriate military response once more information is obtained."

She showered for the first time in three days, going over in her head what questions she might be asked, how she would phrase her answers, and the potential clients who would hopefully come her way from this and future television appearances. It was a huge opportunity, and she needed to focus, put everything else outside her mind, and make it successful.

When she emerged from the shower and wrapped her wet body in a towel, she glanced at the mirror to see her long brown hair falling over her shoulders as her eyes still looked weary but now also just a little hopeful.

She then glanced down at her phone and read a text message from Natalie:

"Hey Maggie. Sorry, just found out producer wants to use guy who wrote column for WaPo calling for tournament boycott, travel ban, and sanctions."

Her heart sank. She was getting bumped. Should she throw her phone against the wall? Crumble back onto the sofa? Beg to return to her government job?

Then she saw the text dots indicating that Natalie was still writing. She scratched her cheek while nervously anticipating the follow-up message. Then the dots vanished. Then they appeared again. Finally, the text came through:

"Want to book you for other side. Ok?"

"Fuck . . ." she muttered.

She knew news stations loved to have one person on each side of the issue, so they could create "good TV" by getting two commentators to hurl emotionally charged arguments at each other while the host pretended to play peacemaker. Now she had been informed what part she was being assigned in today's performance.

She would be arguing against sanctions and a military response, and saying that the president should not ban travel to the Kingdom. She'd also have to contend that poker players should be able to participate in the tournament. She would have to assert all this with conviction, despite the fact that a legendary American journalist was just murdered there, quite possibly at the instruction of the nation's leaders.

Could she make an argument for that side while staying true to her principles? She concluded that somehow she could and would. She just had to figure out how.

But would appearing for that side hurt her credibility so much that it would undermine the benefit from appearing on television? Possibly, and it really depended on the tone of the segment's writers and anchor, but she couldn't control or predict that.

Should she pass on this opportunity for her first national television news segment, with all the opportunities that might come her way as a result? Absolutely not.

She typed back:

"No problem. Looking forward to the segment."

4

TODAY WAS Jacques Bouchard's sixty-fifth birthday, and after decades of fascinating adventures throughout the world and meaningful service to his nation and the globe, he now found himself consumed with grief, loneliness, and trepidation on this milestone day.

He was in mourning but lacked a body to bury, a tomb to visit, or anyone to tell about it. The woman he loved was dead, and there stood a decent chance he soon would be, too.

"Emily . . ." he gasped, holding his phone and looking at a photo of the two of them. It was a sloppy selfie, typical of his lack of tech skills. But the image was proof that they'd been together—proof that he would savor for the rest of his life, even as that proof might lead to a death sentence. Deleting the photo would break whatever was left of his heart, and he had no doubt that those monitoring him had the photo already anyway.

He gazed at his phone, as he and Emily, off centered and tilted, smiled back at him. Well, he smiled at least. She had that confident grin that she would often display—the one that, without looking arrogant, said she knew something important that no one else did yet. And that was usually the case.

In the photo, his thick gray hair and crow's feet revealed his age, while she radiated with timeless grace. They were roughly the same age, and both had divorced many years earlier. They'd each had a life filled with eventful international travel, and in all his life he'd never strongly connected with anyone as quickly.

An assortment of birthday emails from friends and family back home in Canada and around the world spilled in, as well as the "secure" communication from his home country that his request to leave his current assignment had to be rejected for now. Of course, no message in the Kingdom was ever actually secure.

His official title was "ambassador," but the position was more challenging than any of his many previous foreign missions. Although Canada had once had full diplomatic relations with the Kingdom, a decade ago a number of its "aggressive and militaristic actions" led his country to impose tight restrictions on the relationship.

Canada then announced the adoption of a Controlled Engagement Policy, under which bilateral contact with the Kingdom's government would be limited to subjects concerning "regional security concerns, human rights, and humanitarian issues."

He had precisely worded his request to leave the Kingdom, careful not to reveal his sense of urgency. After a long career, he wanted to retire effective immediately, he wrote, or transfer to a less demanding assignment. The response informed him that, with the growing nuclear threat from the Kingdom and the increased tensions resulting from the murder of Emily Kinum, his experience was very much in demand and irreplaceable, at least in the short term.

Canada telling him that he was too important to leave during this turbulent time in fact meant that the United States had told Canada that he was too important to leave. The Americans had no formal diplomatic relations with the Kingdom, not even a Controlled Engagement Policy. In reality, they unofficially had the Canada Engagement Policy, which meant that back channel diplomatic contact generally went through the Canadian ambassador. And now, more than ever, the United States thought they needed him.

He had first met Emily about six months ago, when she was

planning to visit the Kingdom for some general research. She had sent him a formal email, explaining that she was an American journalist—which he of course already knew, having been very familiar with her high-profile work. She was planning to be in the Kingdom for a few days and wanted to get the insight of the Canadian ambassador while she was there, as there was no United States representative with whom she could connect.

Would he agree to meet and discuss the current state of affairs? It could all be off the record, she noted. She wrote that for now she was just looking for a better understanding of the nation and its government and people, not pursuing a specific story.

Their first meeting in the Canadian embassy had been scheduled for a half hour, but after talking in his office for fifteen minutes, he suggested they continue the conversation while strolling the streets of the Embassy District. They weren't discussing anything confidential—just the general lay of the land in the Kingdom—but he thought it would be beneficial if they speak outside where monitoring by the government was less likely.

She asked about the Kingdom's key players and the dynamics in the country and the surrounding region. As he gave her information, she appeared to take mental notes, no doubt unable to jot or type anything that might be seized before she left the country.

There were a few other people walking outside that day—not a heavy crowd, but he and Emily weren't alone either.

"You think they hear everything we say, Ambassador?" she asked.

"Not outside. Less likely, at least," he replied.

"Then tell me—"

"Still off the record?"

"Of course," she reassured. "Off the record. What's your biggest concern here? What keeps you up at night?"

"The Kingdom launching nuclear missiles," he said.

"And what about human rights issues?" she inquired.

"Well, my government has been clear in its condemnation of the human rights abuses here for many years. And they are quite disturbing . . ."

"But?"

"But they don't threaten the existence of all life on this planet as nuclear missiles do."

They walked and talked a little longer, and then she thanked him with a handshake and departed by car service.

He stood there in the street for a few minutes, frozen in place. In his life he had mingled with world leaders, captains of industry, and movie stars, and now he had just spent an hour with the most extraordinary woman he had ever met. It wasn't anything she had said while they talked—their conversation itself had been unremarkable—but knowing her history, her achievements, her body of work, made every word she spoke in his direction exhilarating. She was so smart and accomplished. He quickly began thinking about every sentence of their conversation. Had he sounded knowledgeable? Appropriate? Sophisticated?

He wondered if he would ever meet her again and very much hoped so.

A month later, she sent another request for a meeting, and he was thrilled. She would be back in the Kingdom for twenty-four hours, and he arranged a dinner in the Embassy's private dining room. While they ate together, she asked some general questions about the nation, but the conversation mostly centered on the many fascinating places and experiences that had shaped their very international lives.

When she returned a few weeks later and suggested a late evening walk outside, he felt a growing personal connection and greatly desired more.

"Welcome back to the Kingdom," he said as they strolled through a nearby park. "It seems you either like me a lot or you're working on a pretty good story."

"I'm working on a pretty good story," she replied deadpan, then added a light-hearted raising of her eyebrows.

She asked about the crown prince—his background, how he rose to power. But he knew that she was already well versed in all things crown prince. She was after something else.

"Emily," he said. "I very much enjoy talking with you. But I sense this isn't what you really want to discuss with me."

She leaned close to him.

"Where can we talk?" she whispered.

He signaled his driver, and the two slid into the back seat of the dark sedan and headed deep into the capital. The city at night revealed very little apparent activity, with occasional figures drifting down the sidewalks in front of governmental structures and office buildings that rarely exceeded ten stories. Soon they passed by a residential area, consisting mostly of dilapidated apartment buildings with dim lights occasionally illuminating objects and people existing on the other side of the windows. Everywhere they looked were images of the crown prince and his royal family—on billboards, posters, and the sides of buses, sometimes posing with schoolchildren, on others looking determined while surrounded by military figures. Along with the images, there were enthusiastic messages promoting the nation's supposed compassion for its citizens, economic development, military strength, and general prosperity.

Finally, they arrived at their destination. On a lively block lined with shops and restaurants, they entered an establishment he had visited only twice before. Over the narrow door was the image of a lion's head and above it a sign that read in all caps, "THE DEN." They exited the car, he guided her inside, and they were immediately overcome by loud pumping dance music. The place was crowded, but they were quickly ushered to a table where they sat next to each other, just a few inches apart, looking out at the packed dance floor. The youthful inhabitants were moving to the music while imbibing large amounts of alcohol, some throwing back multiple shots of various colored liquids while others swigged directly from large bottles of champagne, all amid a variety of public displays of affection—kissing, fondling, licking, grinding. There were a few people at the Den that night who looked a little too old to be in that crowd—and Jacques and Emily were about a quarter century older than those people.

The club was so loud that it was challenging for two people to carry on an extended conversation unless they were very close, so she simply mouthed to him, "What the fuck?" Before he could respond, he was able to barely hear her say, "If you're trying to charm and impress me, you've failed spectacularly."

He leaned closer and said, "No one can hear us talking now."

She nodded to show her understanding, and then glanced toward a nearby table where a group of friends were snorting white lines. "I guess the Kingdom isn't always as repressive as its reputation," she offered matter-of-factly.

"There are 95 percent expats in here. As long as they stay in their expat world and don't advocate for democracy, the government doesn't really care what they do."

"I've seen this elsewhere," she replied, her mouth moving a little closer to his ear. "Locals suffer while Westerners safely indulge their little *Casablanca* fantasies—pretending they're running from something, while having wild, profound experiences in a dangerous, exotic land."

"Exactly. Should we ask the DJ to play 'La Marseillaise'?"

Emily smiled. "You come here a lot?" she asked.

"No, rarely," he replied, looking around and taking in the scene. "If I was twenty-seven, I suppose I'd be here every night."

She shook her head. "No, I don't think you would."

He considered the accuracy of her comment as a waitress came by to take their order of a couple glasses of wine. The drinks came quickly, and he took out his phone to capture the moment.

It took a few seconds for him to figure out how to open the camera app. “May I?” he asked.

She shrugged and raised her voice to be heard above the music. “I don’t mind being in a photo with you. I just want to be able to deny that I was ever in this place,” she replied with a charming eye roll.

He reached out and clumsily took the selfie, and then leaned even closer toward her.

“So,” he said, his mouth inches from her ear as the noise raged around them. “What can I really tell you?”

She pulled away a little to look at him, but they were still close enough to barely hear each other and for him to secretly bask in their proximity. “Is this like one of those cheesy TV moments when the music stops just as I’m saying something sensitive?” she asked.

“No, the music never stops here.”

“Okay, Mr. Ambassador. Tell me. What’s the real story here?”

“Besides the nuclear threat?”

“Yes.”

“And the reported human rights abuses?” he asked

“Tell me something the rest of the world doesn’t know,” she commanded.

“This government is far less stable than people think. There’s more opposition to the crown prince than the international community knows. There are people who want to kill him and his family and seize control of the government. Some of these people put themselves out as reformers, but most are hard-liners. And the crown prince is terrified of them.”

“Does the American government know?”

“To a limited extent. They see *him* as the potential reformer and know that the next leader could very well be worse. So they don’t want this government to fall.”

“And what is the crown prince doing to stop them?”

He looked at her seriously and then moved in even closer. “He’s having them murdered in brutal, barbaric ways. Anyone suspected of being a part of any opposition. Torture. Drowning. Electrocution. Decapitation. Burning alive. And not just his opponents—also their spouses and children. Murdered. The true extent isn't known outside the Kingdom. But, Emily, the world needs to be told. It's a human rights catastrophe."

He knew that she had reported on atrocities around the world for decades. No doubt she was appalled, but none of this shocked her. She sat there in thought, quietly taking it in. "You'll connect me with witnesses?"

He shook his head. Several people had told him about the killings, but he couldn't reveal their identities without putting them even more at risk.

"Will you go on the record about this?"

"Unfortunately, my government would never allow that."

She gave him a disappointed look but then changed her expression to one that reassured him of her gratitude. "Thank you for this. Now, let's get out of here."

They departed the club and entered his waiting car, which dropped her off after a silent ten-minute ride to her hotel. He exited the vehicle and held the door open for her. She stepped out onto the street and said a quick goodbye while firmly shaking his hand. Then she entered the hotel, and he headed back to his residence.

He didn't hear from Emily for months, but she was constantly on his mind. Each day, he yearned to receive a new email or call from her. He heard from others that she returned to the Kingdom a few times, and he assumed that she was conducting further investigation based on what he'd told her.

What was she learning? When would he be able to see her again?

If he didn't receive any communication from her soon, he would reach out. The waiting was becoming unbearable. Was she *ever* going to contact him again? He vowed that the next time he saw her, he would tell her how enamored he was. Based on how little actual contact they had shared, he feared this might sound crazy and creepy, but he had to say something.

And then, four days ago, his assistant told him that Emily Kinum had just shown up at the embassy without an appointment. He was in a high-level staff meeting but of course said that he would see her right away.

He walked to the waiting area, trying to conceal his excitement. There she was, standing quietly beneath a Canadian flag.

"Emily, hello," he greeted her warmly. "Please come with me."

She followed him into his office, he closed the door, and he gestured toward a seat on the plush sofa. She sat down, and he sat next to her.

"I'm sorry for coming without an appointment," she said.

"No problem at all. I'm glad to see you."

"This is my last visit to the Kingdom, so I just wanted to say thank you for your hospitality. I'm very grateful."

He understood her message. His information had been helpful to her. She wouldn't say that explicitly because of government monitoring, but he was thrilled nonetheless. He wondered what else she had learned and what she would ultimately be reporting.

He gave her a smile, and she kind of smiled back. His mind raced as he tried to read her face, gauge her true feelings. He wanted so badly to put his arm on her shoulder, look her in the eyes, and kiss her. If she responded favorably, it would be one of the most exciting moments of his life with the most remarkable woman on the planet. He could soon leave his post and meet her outside the Kingdom, where they would be free from political restrictions and government surveillance, able to really talk and begin to share their lives together.

But maybe this potential affinity for each other was all just in his head. Was there any evidence of a real man/woman connection, of her having actual affection for him, besides the powerful belief in his gut? It was so hard to read her, and if she wasn't receptive, it would be a humiliating disaster and possibly an international embarrassment—an ambassador trying to proposition a serious journalist as she conducted research in a dangerous country. She could find it offensive and at a minimum laughable. Would she include the anecdote in her next article? Or mention it as a brief aside during a television interview? Or maybe just tell the story on social media, about the old ambassador who tried to hit on her while she was reporting on unspeakable murders? He had had such a dignified, successful career. And now it was might end like *this*?

"Emily, it's been my pleasure. I hope we can stay in touch. It would be great to meet again when we're both outside the Kingdom."

"Of course," she responded, extending her hand for a final shake.

And then she was gone.

A day later, he received an urgent, supposedly secure message from his government. The Americans needed his assistance. One of their journalists had been murdered, and they wanted help on the ground to find out what happened and who was responsible. He needed to meet with the Kingdom's officials and demand answers and their immediate cooperation with an independent investigation.

"Who is the journalist?"

He wrote these words while already sensing the answer, as his soul crumbled and he sobbed with rage while alone in his office. The response came quickly:

"Emily Kinum."

In his mind it actually read: *"The woman you love: Emily Kinum."*

He told them that he needed to be re-assigned, that he was no longer the right person to serve as ambassador to the Kingdom. But his request for leave was rejected. He was needed now, more than ever.

He wanted to tell the Americans what had happened, that Emily had been researching a story on the Kingdom's brutality right before her murder. They needed to know. The world needed to know. But any message he sent would also likely be read by the Kingdom.

He desperately wanted to contact Emily's sister, a local journalist in Washington. She deserved to learn the truth about her sibling. But how, when he couldn't call or email her?

And while he mourned Emily, he thought about her phenomenal life—how vibrant she was and all she'd accomplished. Selfishly, he wondered if she might have wanted him to be part of that life. Meanwhile, he agonizingly obsessed over how she might have been killed. What had they done to her? Had she suffered?

And he was afraid for his own safety. No doubt the Kingdom knew that he had spent time with her, and even though he'd been careful, they might figure out his role in helping to expose the Kingdom's cruelty. There was no solace in thinking that they wouldn't murder a diplomat—they had just killed a renowned journalist, and they had been thwarting the world's norms and conventions for years.

Should he flee? How could he possibly get across the border without being taken?

And then there were additional fears that escalated his terror.

First, the Americans would be tempted to respond aggressively to this killing. Tensions with the Kingdom were already high, and they would no doubt quickly escalate as the United States sought retribution against what was now a nuclear power with intercontinental ballistic missiles. Even if he got the truth to the right people and the public, would that help prevent a nuclear war? Or would it further inflame the situation and therefore cause one?

And then there was the information he gave Emily. If he hadn't told her what he'd heard about these brutal murders, maybe she wouldn't have set off on a path that led to her death. Of course the Kingdom didn't want a reporter exposing its evil practices. Certainly they would try to silence anyone seeking to tell the truth about them. He should have known that.

Then there was the fear that might eat him alive. Her murder seemed to confirm that she was investigating a legitimate story, but what if the details he gave her weren't accurate? He'd heard from several sources about the killings of children and families and believed the world needed to know. But he hadn't seen them himself, nor had any of the people who had supplied him with these allegations. His information had made her a target and led to her death. What if his intelligence had been wrong? Yes, the regime was terrible and clearly murderous, but what if *these* allegations had been incorrect and he'd been too quick to believe them and pass them on to her?

What if the woman he loved had her life brutally ended because he relayed incorrect or exaggerated stories in a misguided attempt to assist and impress her? If that turned out to be the case, he wasn't sure how *he* could continue to live either.

5

IN THE MOMENTS before the news alert about the murder of a journalist popped up on his phone, Kyler had been staring at a photo on the screen. The image showed the stunning piece of jewelry that was the fantasy of every remotely serious poker player.

The bracelet contained seemingly countless diamonds and colorful depictions of the four suits—hearts, diamonds, clubs, and spades—each surrounded by gold. Large, bold letters glittered brazenly with pride: WSOP Champion.

People around the world viewed the bracelet and dreamed of winning it or maybe coming close. For some, the hope was simply to compete for it one day. But Kyler was a little different. He wondered how much the bracelet itself was worth or, more specifically, what it could be sold for. And how could one sell it discreetly?

Poker could be the source of tremendous fortune, excitement, fun, and camaraderie. It could also cause extreme heartbreak, aggravation, and sorrow. He had been at a very low point in his life almost two years earlier—having nothing to do with poker—when his friend Nolan Campbell texted him.

"Hey buddy. Checkin to see how ur doing. Know it's tough now but keep ur head up!"

Nolan was a friend from a local basketball league that Kyler played in. "Keep ur head up"? Such a tone-deaf thing to write when Nolan knew how miserable his life was then.

"Thanks Nolan. More counseling with Mia while I live in this shitty apt. Still won't forgive me for the money I lost. Kids r taking her side w/ everything. No job still. Ridic bills every day can't pay. Will keep head up tho . . ."

"Sry dude, where u at?"

"Just home"

"U need to get out. Guys from bball league having another poker game tonight. Wanna join?"

Yes, he did want to join. Any kind of wagering—cards, sports, horses—could give him at least a few moments of adrenaline and entertainment. But there was one problem.

"Buy-in?"

"$600 tourney"

He considered how much cash he could scrape together and whether any of his credit cards would let him take another cash advance. He *really* wanted to play.

Kyler didn't respond for a few minutes, so Nolan wrote again:

"I know $600 a lot. I can stake u and put up $300."

So he'd have to come up with the other $300 in order to play in this tournament. Somehow he'd figure that out, and hopefully he'd leave with a lot more.

"OK in. Thanks. Where?"

The tournament was in a decent-sized gathering room at a local country club. As he entered, he saw a few unfamiliar faces along with a bunch of guys he recognized from the basketball league. They milled around, eating from a buffet of food, some drinking beers or scotch. They talked and laughed—this was similar to the jovial, pre-game atmosphere at other poker games he'd been part of, with one big difference: tense excitement filled the room. Tonight's game seemed to be a bigger deal than most.

And he quickly found out why. Nolan grabbed him soon after he entered, stuffed $300 into his hand, patted him on the back, and guided him to a desk where one of the organizers sat collecting the $600 buy-ins. Kyler handed over the $600, and the guy collecting the cash looked up and began affably explaining the rules as he gave Kyler a card designating a random seat assignment at one of the three poker tables in the room.

"Hey, Kyler, good to see you buddy! So we have thirty spots, $600 each, total pool 18K. Winner gets 10K buy-in to the Main Event, plus $2,000 travel expenses to Vegas," he quickly explained. "Tonight, $500 goes to food and drinks, and second place gets the remaining $5,500 cash. 10,000 starting stack. Twenty percent of any Main Event winnings is shared by the rest of tonight's final table. Good luck!"

Kyler received a few warm looks and verbal greetings from around the room, and he knew why. Yes, he was a fun, friendly person whom most of them liked to spend time with, and some felt bad for him because of his marriage, employment, and financial woes. But more importantly, as they each competed to win a seat at the Main Event of the World Series of Poker, he was the very player they wanted to see. A guy who could play well at times, but who could also let his emotions get control of him, go on tilt, and make bad decisions at key moments. In poker and in life. A great opponent for them, he was the donkey who had just tossed $600 in dead money at their dreams of WSOP glory.

"Thanks, Nolan," he whispered to his friend. "I appreciate it."

"No problem," Nolan replied. "I know you need to get out and enjoy life again. Don't take this the wrong way, but for a good-looking guy you really look like shit."

It was true. He was tall, with a decent build, and just a few years earlier he had been considered handsome. But that was back when he took better care of himself—back when his life wasn't full of reminders of his failures and incompetence.

"You don't like the beard?" Kyler asked, rubbing his fingers through the unkempt mass of black hair. "Beards are really cool now . . ."

“Not that beard,” Nolan replied, shaking his head. “Okay, we’re about to start,” he added right before heading to his seat at Table 1, with Kyler assigned to Table 3. “See you at the final table!”

After devouring a few chicken wings and grabbing a beer, Kyler sat down in his assigned seat—Table 3, Seat 8. His nine other table-mates also found their chairs. A white round disc with black letters spelling out “dealer” sat on the green felt in front of Seat 1, and it would move around the table as they took turns dealing. He counted out his chips to make sure they indeed added up to 10,000. Each person would play until they lost all of those chips, and by the end of the evening one of them would have all 300,000 chips in play and be off to Vegas. In two months, that player would be one in a field of over 7,000 at the WSOP Main Event with a first prize of over $8 million.

The tournament started, and the guy in Seat 1 dealt the first hand, giving each player two cards face down. A couple of people called the big blind, and then Kyler looked down at his cards—ace of clubs, king of clubs. Ace king suited. Pretty nice start.

“Raise,” he announced, placing the chips in front of him. “One fifty.”

There were two callers, and the dealer placed three cards up in the middle of the table. The flop missed his ace-king: three of clubs, seven of diamonds, ten of diamonds.

Two players checked to him, and he put in a decent size bet. One called, the other folded.

The turn card: jack of clubs.

Just one other player was left in the hand, and that guy slowly tapped the table twice to indicate a check. Kyler bet again and hoped the other player would fold.

“Call,” the man responded, tossing chips in front of him.

Kyler knew he needed some help with the final card—the river. A club would give him the nut flush. An ace or king would likely give him the best hand, too.

Ace of diamonds.

Again, the player checked. With the pair of aces, Kyler bet again, and his opponent was silent and still for about thirty seconds before declaring "raise" and pushing in a large bet.

Kyler looked at his cards again—the ace of clubs was still there, pairing the ace on the board. Did the other guy have a flush, two diamonds in his hand and three on the board? If so, what a terrible card the ace of diamonds was for him, giving him top pair while simultaneously completing his opponent's flush.

He thought for a few moments, knowing a re-raise was out of the question but wondering if he should call. Instead Kyler sighed and shook his head before tossing his cards into the muck to fold.

"I fucking hate this game," he announced with an exasperated smile before taking a sip of his beer. The table responded with supportive laughter and knowing looks, and the player in Seat 2 soon began to deal the next hand.

This was not going well, and he could already feel himself getting frustrated in a way that usually meant his play was going to suffer, big time. For the next hour he made a few bad calls and a couple of ill-timed bluffs. He knew his head wasn't in the right place for smart decision making. His personal life was a mess, he was in crippling debt, and he urgently needed to win some money. Kyler was very aware that this was the completely wrong mind-frame for winning poker. He needed to be calm and logical. He had to make the right decisions for each hand. But with every bad move, with each unfortunate card, he grew more agitated and less competent.

Soon there were twenty-four people left in the tournament, and he was down to 4,000 in chips. There was a raise in front of him when he peeled up the edges of his starting cards and saw two black queens.

"All in," he announced as he pushed his short stack forward.

"Call," the raiser declared and turned over ace-king.

The flop, turn, and river were dealt and his pair of queens won the hand, doubling him up to over 8,000. A couple of hands later, he played pocket fives, flopped three of a kind when another five appeared, and won a large pot with his set. He was back in it.

That little run of good luck made him a better, less antsy, and smarter player. He felt focused as he continued to observe the playing styles of the other participants and factor what he learned into his strategy.

This guy always folds to a re-raise unless he has a monster hand. That dude bluffs on the river whenever he misses his draw. This woman only raises with premium hands and checks the flop whenever she misses it. The man in Seat 3 usually calls another player's river value bet with the second-best hand.

As he continued to build his chip stack, more and more players were eliminated. The blinds continued to increase and the play got more aggressive—around midnight there were six people at his table and five at the other remaining table. He heard a man's voice at the other table declare "all in!" and a woman quickly reply, "call." There was a tense silence for a few moments, and then the man roared, "Fuck! You gotta be fucking kidding me! I had a billion outs there. Straight draw. Flush draw. Overcard. Fuck!"

And just like that they were down to ten players—the final table.

There was a break in the action as the remaining players took their new seats. There was also new, unmistakable tension in the air. While he had earlier been the recipient of friendly, benevolent looks and easy conversation, the better he did, the more he was surrounded by disgruntled whispers and disapproving glances. And now that he'd reached the final table, many of those remaining in the room looked at him with frustration and disdain.

Nolan, who had long since been eliminated, was in the corner having an animated conversation with a guy named Jared, an accountant in his late twenties and one of the tournament organizers. Occasionally, the men would glance over at Kyler. Then, in a burst

Jared declared, "Well, if he wins, it's *your* fucking problem to fix," and stormed out of the room.

Kyler wasn't an easily angered guy, but as the final table progressed and he continued to do well and eliminate competitors, the growing annoyance of those around him began to raise his blood pressure. Yet he couldn't let that derail him. He was close to winning, and he needed money, badly.

Around three in the morning, a short stack moved all in with ace-ten. Kyler called with ace-queen, eliminating another person, and the tournament was down to three. This was the big bubble of the tournament—first prize would win the WSOP entry, second prize would take home $5,500, and third place had to settle for the remaining cold chicken wings and another beer.

There was a break in the action, and the other attendees kept their distance, unwilling to stand near him, make eye contact, or in any way acknowledge his existence. Kyler walked up to Nolan and pulled him aside.

"This is bullshit," he said. "I'm winning fair and square. They're acting like a bunch of dicks."

"They don't want you to win, and you know why," Nolan replied. "You can't really blame them."

"I don't even want to win," Kyler exclaimed. "I want to come in second. I don't give a shit about that WSOP entry. I want the cash. I want the $5,500. Once we're heads up, I'm losing on purpose. Then everybody goes home happy."

Nolan shook his head. "Don't say that. This is an amazing opportunity. Go for first. Remember, I get half a vote here."

Half a vote.

That's when Kyler realized that if he won the $5,500, Nolan would expect half because he'd fronted him $300. The value of second place had shrunk dramatically. *Screw it,* he thought. He'd go for the win. Go big and watch all these pricks go home.

His two remaining opponents were a middle-aged woman in a hooded sweatshirt—the wife of one of the basketball players—and an older guy he didn't know who was wearing jeans and an untucked long-sleeve green button-down shirt. Kyler was in second place with approximately 110,000 in chips, and the man was the chip leader with about 130,000. The woman had 60,000.

Kyler quickly folded a weak starting hand, and his two remaining opponents built up a decent sized pot, which the woman ended up winning, pulling all three players close to even. Then it was Kyler's turn to face off with her in a hand that quickly escalated. After a lot of betting, he found himself facing an all-in bet on the river. It was an ugly board—three of clubs, eight of diamonds, jack of spades, four of diamonds, three of diamonds. He tried to figure out what she had.

Did she hold a three? Unlikely—she'd raised pre-flop and been betting strong the whole way. Had she paired the board? He sensed she hadn't. A diamond flush? Possibly, but he didn't think so, especially with the final two diamonds coming on the turn and the river.

He merely held ace-ten of spades—ace high. If he called and was wrong, he'd be almost eliminated. If he folded, he'd be left with a pretty short stack and in real danger of coming in third with nothing to show for the night.

Nine-ten. A straight draw.

That was the only hand that made sense. She'd flopped a straight draw, kept betting it, and then bluffed all in on the river when she missed. He could be wrong, though. Was he on tilt? Was his critical need for cash, the late hour, and all the negative looks and energy from others directing him toward a monumentally poor decision? She also might have a pocket pair, in which case he'd be toast.

"Call," he said.

She was silent and still for a few seconds and then slowly shook her head in frustration.

"Nice call, Kyler," she muttered, as she tossed her cards face up on the table—nine-ten of hearts.

Kyler turned over his cards and heard an immediate wave of displeasure sweep the room as he began raking in the chips.

"Ace high. Oh my God . . ." said a man behind him, vocalizing everyone's shock that Kyler had made a winning call with such a weak hand.

With just two players left, they stopped rotating who was dealing and an eliminated player sat down to distribute the cards. In an attempt to simulate the millions of dollars placed on the table at the World Series of Poker and other major tournaments for the final two combatants, one of the tournament organizers placed $12,000 in cash for the first prize WSOP entry and travel expenses on the green felt.

It was three-thirty but over twenty people remained, standing around the table, and no doubt all but Nolan were rooting for Kyler's green-shirted opponent.

They went back and forth for over an hour—betting, raising, bluffing, folding—and Kyler slowly developed a decent chip lead. Then, after a flop, his opponent moved all-in on a 10-high board, and Kyler called. The opponent showed ace-ten and the group looked aghast as Kyler turned over a pair of jacks. The tournament was Kyler's as long as an ace or ten didn't fall on the turn or river. Both men stood to watch the final cards.

Turn card: seven of spades.

River card: king of diamonds.

Kyler pumped his fist in victory. A wave of satisfaction, relief, and excitement swept through him, and he felt Nolan pat him on the back while the rest of the room remained quiet and looked at each other uncomfortably.

Kyler reached for the prize money on the table, but before he could get there, Jared's hand slammed down on the stack of cash.

"No," Jared declared. "No fucking way."

There were a bunch of slow nods from the tired group.

He's right, they were saying. *It's sad that's it come to this, but he's right.*

"What the fuck?" Kyler exclaimed. "I won! Give me my money."

"He won," Nolan added. "Let's not go crazy over this."

"Every year we hold this tournament so one of us can play in the World Series and the rest of the final table shares any winnings," Jared responded. "You and I both know that he'll never use this money for that. He's going to just gamble it away and it'll be gone within days."

"Hey!" Kyler interjected, stepping close to Jared. "I'm right here. If you have something to say, look at me and say it."

"I'm saying," Jared began, not backing down, "that you'll quickly lose all this money like you always do, and you'll never use it for the Main Event. That's what this money is for."

"Who the fuck cares?" Kyler exclaimed. "I won. It's mine."

Nolan put his arm between the two and gently nudged Kyler back.

"Guys, please. This is a friendly game—"

"Friendly?" Kyler cried incredulously. "You think this is friendly? Look how I'm being treated."

"Kyler, tonight's final table is owed 20 percent of any Main Event winnings," Nolan explained. "We've been doing it this way every year for a decade. One of us goes to the World Series, and the rest of the final table has a stake. They don't believe you're going to use the money to enter the tournament. They think you're going to blow it somewhere."

They were right about one thing. He wanted—*needed*—the cash, not the tournament entry fee.

"So how about I give you guys 20 percent of the 12K back right now instead? $2,400 right? Fine. I'll just take $9,600."

"No," Jared snapped, then looked at Nolan. "This is your fault. You need to fix this."

"Okay everyone," Nolan said to the group. "It's really, really late.

We're all tired. Let's not end a fun night this way. I'll make sure Kyler enters the Main Event. If not, hold me accountable, alright?"

There were a few grumbles and shrugs from the exhausted men and women who remained, and some started heading for the exit.

"Fine, and we *will* hold you accountable," Jared answered. "Plus one more condition: he doesn't play here ever again."

There was a pause and then Jared stared at Kyler before continuing. "Sorry, you asked me to look at you when I talk about you so I'll rephrase that: *you* don't play here ever again."

Kyler was furious and ready to lunge, but he forced himself to stay composed. He had played well. He had won. And he didn't want to now go on tilt.

6

MAGGIE STRUGGLED with a whole host of uncomfortable emotions, including being extremely nervous about her national television debut, but felt that she was holding it together really well on the outside. And since this was television, wasn't that what really counted?

Black pencil skirt. Rose, silk boatneck blouse. Showered, clean, and looking confident.

She walked into the lobby of the network's office building, slid her driver's license to the security officer, and then waited until a female intern exited the elevator bank, greeted her, and escorted her upstairs.

She was taken into the hair and make-up room where cosmetic experts prepped her for the cameras. Then the intern brought Maggie into the green room, which had a couple of televisions on the wall, machines for coffee and water, and a few pastries. She'd heard that green room spreads were much more elaborate before recent budget cutbacks, but that didn't matter—there was no way she could get food down in her current state.

She was excited but very stressed—such a huge opportunity, one she couldn't afford to waste. Over half a million people would watch her segment live, and then hopefully many more would view it via social media. A good clip would reveal that she was, indeed, a television-quality political analyst. This would be invaluable for new business.

She didn't love that she'd be arguing against immediate sanctions, a travel ban, and a boycott of the poker event. But she didn't feel as if she had an option at this point in her life. In the future, if she was successful, she could be more selective. For now, she'd just have to remember what she'd been told was the main rule for successful political talking heads: have a strong opinion and back it up. To make for good television, a consultant had to be a solid, articulate fighter. The subject of the fight was often irrelevant.

She went over and over in her head how she would phrase her arguments and what subtle and not-so-subtle looks she would display during the segment.

Just concentrate on nailing this. Don't think about anything else. While you're on television, nothing else exists.

"Ms. Raster?" a young male assistant producer asked her. "I just want to confirm how we'll identify you on air: Maggie Raster Consulting and former special assistant to the White House chief of staff? Is that right?"

"Yes, thank you."

"Okay, please make yourself comfortable. Your hit time is in about twenty-five minutes, so a few minutes before that we'll mic you up and bring you into the studio."

"Sounds great."

A few other people were milling around the green room. She recognized a couple of network regulars, well-known television analysts. She sat on a couch and reviewed the notes she'd quickly drafted on her phone. With the segment growing closer, her nerves escalated and she felt an acidic surge in her stomach. She turned to look out a window that overlooked the city and drew in long, slow breaths.

You can do this. You'll be great. You know what you're going to say, and you'll say it well. Yes, the murder of Emily Kinum is a horrible tragedy that must be answered for, but imposing sanctions and boycotting a major goodwill event in the Kingdom will simply escalate tensions with a nuclear power while most of the key facts about the murder are still unknown. It's a reasonable, defensible position. You can argue this successfully and come off really well.

She felt a slight easing of her panic, but this modest relief was quickly interrupted by a man's voice near the doorway. "I'm so sorry for your loss," he said softly.

"Thank you," a woman answered, full of strength, conviction, and sadness. Then into the green room walked a late-middle-age woman with short black hair, wearing a conservative business suit—local television journalist Tori Kinum.

One of the famous consultants gave her a long, sympathetic hug as he said, "I'm so sorry Tori. Your sister was a spectacular woman. I hope everyone stays firm so there can be some justice here, although I know nothing can bring her back."

"Thank you," she said as the hug ended. "You know, the outpouring of support has been tremendous. It's come from all over the world."

"I'm really glad to hear that."

"And then of course there are people who just don't give a shit and want to appease her killers no matter what. Like helping a bunch of brutal murderers sell a bullshit nice guy image in a propaganda poker tournament."

"I heard about that. Goodwill Poker Classic. Do they even see the irony in a name like that? I saw one poker champion was full-out condemning it. A young woman."

"Priya Varma," Tori clarified. "Never met her but she's very impressive."

"Absolutely. It's unbelievable that anyone would support this thing now. But of course there are always people who will for a price."

"That's why I'm here," she said defiantly. "In a few minutes I'm going to expose this abomination to the world."

Maggie had heard the entire conversation, frozen in panic. Her trepidation was so all-consuming that it barely even registered that she recognized that poker woman's name from somewhere.

Oh God no . . . please no. Tell me I'm not about to go on air with her. I'm going to come off like a monster.

She grabbed her phone tightly and raced to text her booker, who she assumed was somewhere else in the large building.

"Am I on same segment as Tori Kinum?"

Within a few seconds she received the young woman's response:

"Yes!! We were just able to book her last minute. Really excited about it! Replaced other consultant w/ her but we def wanted to keep u!!! ☺"

Horrified, she quickly tapped out her answer:

"I don't want to be the opponent of a woman whose sister was just murdered . . ."

But she didn't press send—yet. With her pulse accelerating and her head pounding, she speeded through her options. She could send the text, pushing back on the booker and producers, but they weren't going to change the segment now. She could refuse to go on air under these conditions, but she had no bargaining power and would certainly be blackballed, at least at this network. And what other network was even considering her for anything?

She could also just do the live segment but fail to take the position that they had booked her for. She could take a more nuanced, even-handed position. That, too, would certainly anger the network, possibly even more so. And she would be seen as wishy-washy, which would make her completely unappealing to networks and potential clients.

And then their eyes met. Tori, standing strong, a couple of feet away. Maggie, hoping she didn't look as scattered and petrified as she felt. Tori glanced at her with thoughtful skepticism.

You need to say something, Maggie told herself. *You need to say something NOW.*

She jumped up and extended her right hand. "Hello Tori. I'm Maggie Raster. I'm so sorry about what happened to your sister."

Tori slowly reached out and shook Maggie's hand and then dropped it in thinly veiled contempt.

"Nothing *happened* to my sister. They *murdered* my sister."

Maggie nodded sadly, with sincerity. "I know."

"And what are you here to talk about?" Tori inquired.

There was a tense, awkward silence as Maggie tried to find the right words.

"I'm . . . uh . . ."

"You're taking the Kingdom's side in my segment?" Tori interrupted.

"No, not at all. I would never do that. I'm discussing the possible travel ban and the complexities of dealing with a nuclear power . . ."

Tori put her hand up, palm facing Maggie, silently ordering her to stop talking.

She instantly complied.

"Well," Tori said with a knowing, disgusted smirk, "I guess some people will do *anything* to get on TV." And with that, she dismissively turned and walked toward the other side of the green room, where she was greeted and comforted by other well-wishers.

Maggie stood there, completely deflated and more terrified than ever. She was lost in a million racing thoughts until the short guy with the headset repeated his question and snapped her out of it.

"Ready to be mic'd up?" he asked. "We're heading into the studio in a few minutes."

"Sure," she responded weakly, her mind battling to stay focused.

He clipped a small rectangular battery pack to her waist, and as he did so, his hand momentarily rested on her left hip. She flinched involuntarily, sending the pack and the attached microphone wire tumbling to the ground.

"I'm sorry," the technician said, kneeling to pick up the electronics.

She was shocked and troubled as she considered her own unconscious reaction. But she couldn't deal with that now. She would need to consider that later, when she could really think. One truth, though, was viscerally clear—she did not want to be touched.

I need to keep it together. I can't lose it now. Not here. And certainly not live on the air.

He placed the microphone pack back on her waist, then reached to clip the microphone itself to her blouse. She concentrated hard to be stoic as his hands hovered inches from her right breast and felt a small wave of relief when he was done.

"Which ear do you prefer?" he asked, holding an earpiece.

Do you see the hell I'm in right now? You think I give a fuck what ear that goes in?

She was about to say either was fine, but she did realize that a precise answer might make the resolution of this process come sooner, and also make her appear more experienced with television, for whatever that was worth—almost certainly nothing.

"Left," she said decisively.

Meanwhile, one of the television screens showed the broadcast that she would soon be part of. A series of still images of Emily Kinum now filled the screen.

"Coming up," the perfect male anchor voice said with authority. "The tragic murder of renowned journalist Emily Kinum shocked and horrified people throughout the world. Who is responsible and what should the United States government do to get justice? You'll hear from her sister, Tori Kinum, who is advocating for immediate, strong measures against the Kingdom, and a former top government official who cautions against a rush to judgment. We'll debate—next!"

Maggie cringed. Not only was she being set up to be the villain, but in her first television appearance she'd be facing someone with decades of on-camera experience. It was a complete mismatch, and she needed a miracle.

The engineer gestured for her and Tori to follow him out the door. Maggie paused so that Tori could walk out first, and then she trailed the two of them down the hall toward the looming disaster that awaited her reputation, career, and future.

They entered a large television studio that was shockingly cold, and she felt her hands start to stiffen as a woman guided her and Tori to a white anchor desk where the host was looking down at his papers while scribbling notes.

She and Tori were both seated at the desk facing the anchor as a few production people scurried around during the commercial break.

"Maggie," she heard a male voice call for her through her earpiece. "Please count to five for me."

Mic check. Her confidence had been crushed to such an extent that she wasn't sure that she could successfully comply.

"One . . . two . . . three . . ."

As she said "three" she felt her throat clog up, and when she uttered "four" it came out garbled. She forced herself to cough roughly, and then finished with a "five" that sounded relatively good.

"Perfect," came the voice in her ear. "Thank you."

Perfect.

The anchor looked up from his notes and gave a polite smile from his handsome, television friendly face.

"Thank you both for joining us," he said.

"Sixty seconds," she heard in her earpiece.

There were three cameras positioned around the desk, and she could see the first words for the anchor displayed in one of them. Maggie silently read the teleprompter introduction: "Welcome back. It's been twenty-four hours since the world learned that journalistic icon Emily Kinum was murdered in the Kingdom, and the debate about how to respond is raging throughout the country and the world . . ."

Ever since she started her own consulting firm, Maggie had tried desperately to get on television, and now that she had succeeded, she wanted to be anywhere but here. And then came a sudden sign of the miracle she had hoped for.

The anchor glanced at both of them after listening intently in his ear, and said, "We're told the president is going to make a statement about this momentarily. Please stand by. We need to take this live."

And in seconds the anchor was on the air, talking directly into one of the cameras, as Maggie remained still as an awkward statue next to the very icy Tori.

"Breaking news! We've just been alerted that the president is going to issue a statement from the White House Briefing Room about the murder of Emily Kinum. We now take you there live . . ."

He tossed to a reporter who was standing in the Briefing Room, facing a camera with her back toward an empty lectern with the White House seal behind it. As the reporter started to speak, a new female voice sounded in Maggie's earpiece.

"Sorry Maggie. Really bad timing. Promise we'll book you for another segment if yours gets bumped."

She perked up and looked at the time displayed on one of the screens in the studio. Ten minutes to the hour. In ten minutes, this show would be over, and a new program with new producers and new bookers and segments would begin. Her appearance would be cancelled if it wasn't on before then.

For four minutes, the reporter talked with the anchor, and Maggie silently and intently counted along with every passing second that ticked away on the digital clock next to one of the cameras.

Six minutes left. Please. Six more minutes.

She was almost home free when the reporter turned to the side, nodded, and looked back at the camera.

"We're now being told the president's statement has been delayed about an hour," the reporter said. "Of course, when the president is ready, we'll bring his statement to you live."

The anchor thanked her, paused momentarily, and then began reading the teleprompter as Maggie's heart sank. She was about to face a television buzz saw, now with enhanced ratings because of all the people tuning in to see the president.

"It's been twenty-four hours since the world learned that journalistic icon Emily Kinum was murdered in the Kingdom," the anchor read, "and the debate about how to respond is raging . . ."

7

KYLER'S FIRST TIME on television occurred on a sweltering July day in Las Vegas, eighteen months earlier when he was midway through Day 1 of the Main Event of the World Series of Poker. Almost 8,000 entrants with a buy-in of $10,000 each competed in the tournament, all starting with a 60,000 chip stack. To make money, he needed to survive until 15% of the field was left—about 1,200 people. Everyone who made it to that point was guaranteed at least $15,000, with the payouts increasing as more were eliminated, all the way to a first prize of $8.8 million and the title of World Champion.

True to his promise, Nolan had taken the cash and traveled to Las Vegas with Kyler to make sure he entered the tournament—and to be there for support. To Kyler, the scene in the cavernous convention hall that housed the event felt surreal, with poker tables spread out as far as the eye could see and the faces of past world champions staring out from banners displayed along the walls.

The room vibrated with excited energy as the players milled around and found their seats while various poker journalists spoke into cameras, took photos, conducted interviews, and scribbled notes. Many of the players were like him—regular guys from a local home game, no doubt in over their heads, trying to live out a fantasy and hit it big. And seated all around were the famous poker players he had seen on television and the movie stars who had flown in from around the world.

The competitors were dressed in a wide array of attire—casual T-shirts and shorts, a few suits, some cowboy hats, a lot of sunglasses, and various lapel decals advertising online poker sites. Some entered the tournament while engaged in elaborate and creative cosplay featuring medieval characters and masked superheroes.

It was quite an international field, even including a royal family member who was garnering a lot of attention. He was a tall, handsome young man with a close-cropped beard, stylish slacks, and form-fitting gray shirt. As he walked the room, the place buzzed about who he was. At the time, Kyler understood only that he was royalty from some foreign country. The thing that struck Kyler the most was that some of the Hollywood celebs were coming over to shake the man's hand and ask to take a photo with *him*.

Meanwhile, Kyler felt as far from royalty as one could. In the two months since he had won the entry, his financial situation had gotten even worse. No real job prospects, more bills coming due, and continual demands for money from his estranged wife—supposedly on behalf of their three children. Then there was some particularly bad luck betting on the NBA playoffs.

One game was particularly galling, and he was having a tough time getting past it. He had bet the under in a game where the over-under was 220. With just *fifteen seconds left*, only 200 points had been scored and one team was leading by six. It seemed like a lock. Then the trailing team hit a tough three-pointer. Then stole the ball. Then banked in a crazy three-pointer at the buzzer, sending the game into overtime. Final score after overtime: 113-109. Total points: 222. Over.

Five thousand dollars lost. Five thousand that he didn't have.

His life was in crisis, but he couldn't let that disrupt his play. He didn't seek this opportunity, but he was determined not to waste it. He needed do everything possible to leave this event with some prize money.

After everyone found their seats, there were a few short speeches, and then the famous "Shuffle up and deal!" pronouncement signaling the start of the Main Event. Kyler recognized one poker pro he had seen on YouTube at his table, and a B movie actor who hid behind dark sunglasses. Kyler's plan was to play smart, not be too aggressive early, and try not to get eliminated.

Right away he saw that this was a different level of poker than he'd ever experienced. The players were highly skilled and creative, their decisions so much more aggressive and sophisticated. Within a couple hours, he had raised with decent hands four times and had been re-raised pre-flop by someone else at the table before folding. On a few other hands, he called raises and then folded to a bet after missing the flop. His stack had already shrunk to 37,000. He gave a discouraged glance to Nolan, who watched supportively from the side.

The tournament required players to be at least twenty-one years old, so even though the player next to Kyler looked no more than eighteen, Kyler assumed that he was older. The kid was in a hand with the famous pro from across the table, and after the younger player made a large post-flop raise, the pro took a while to consider his next move. "Clock," the youth said calmly.

The pro stood up and bellowed, "Are you fucking kidding me? *You're* calling the clock on *me*? I bust idiots like you all day, every day. Who the fuck are you?"

The kid just sat there and stated matter-of-factly, "You were taking a really long time."

Two television camera operators dashed over to cover the unfolding scene, and action ground to a halt at a few surrounding tables. Meanwhile, the clanking of chips continued from other tables across the huge room.

"Fucking unbelievable," the pro exclaimed, as he folded by tossing his cards face down with disgust. "You know who I am? You have a lot to learn about how to act at a poker table, son."

When Kyler watched the coverage later, he saw himself on television looking at the young player with a bemused expression on his face—a brief respite from the tension of the tournament and his life.

Later that evening, he started to catch some good cards that resulted in nice sized pots—aces, kings twice, two flopped sets, and a huge flush on the river for a big pot. Then at 1:00 a.m., after thirteen grueling hours of poker, play ended for the day. Tournament officials distributed bags to the surviving players, and Kyler filled his with 155,000 before sealing it for the night. He was exhausted, numb, and still far from winning any money.

Nolan had stayed throughout, conferring with Kyler about key hands during breaks, giving his own analysis about other players, and offering encouraging words.

"Nice job, buddy!" Nolan exclaimed as he gave him a hug. "On to Day 2!"

"Thanks," Kyler replied, trying to see through bleary eyes. "Pretty crazy, huh? Can't believe I'm still here."

"Awesome, dude. You need some sleep."

"Yeah, but a beer first."

"You got it!"

They drank together while discussing various hands of the day, assessing the merits of different reads and decisions, and brainstorming tweaks to his game that he could implement when play resumed.

The following day, the tournament continued as a wild ride for Kyler: winning big hands and losing others; getting moved to new tables with different players, famous and unknown; seeing person after person eliminated, sometimes uneventfully, sometimes in excruciating fashion that sent players to the door in tearful distress.

But by the end of Day 2, as the field continued to shrink, Kyler remained alive. And after lasting through Day 3 and receiving another exhausted hug from Nolan, he began to feel the thrilling surge of possibility that he might actually end up with some of that prize money.

"The money bubble will hit early tomorrow," Nolan advised. "You're doing great. You have enough chips to just fold into the money. Guaranteed 15K."

Kyler nodded. If he just folded for an hour or so on Day 4 as others were eliminated, he would easily have enough chips to reach the final 15% and win at least $15,000. Amazing.

The next morning, Nolan reminded him, "Just fold until the money. Don't do anything crazy. No risks right now, okay?"

"Got it," Kyler replied.

"Seriously," Nolan emphasized. "You've played fantastic poker. You've come so far. You've made it to day four of the fucking Main Event! Don't go home with nothing after all this."

And the unspoken corollary was, of course: "If you're stupid enough to ignore this advice, definitely don't go up against a big stack now, since they have enough chips to eliminate you in one hand."

The final 1,182 players would be "in the money." When about 1,200 players were left, one of the large stacks—a heavy set, middle-aged guy wearing a gray sweatshirt and black baseball cap—was raising almost every hand. His strategy was clearly to be aggressive and take advantage of all the now-timid players such as Kyler who were anxiously hoping to make the money. It was the time when good players, especially those with decent chips stacks, could gain a lot.

Meanwhile, Kyler was still intent on folding, as Nolan supportively watched from the rail. The big stack raised again, and Kyler looked down and internally cringed when he saw ace-king.

Fuck. I can't fold this hand.

Normally he would re-raise here, but maybe he should just call and see what happened on the flop. He considered that the guy was raising virtually every hand to take advantage of the money bubble situation—some of those had to be with weak cards. Maybe if Kyler just re-raised, the guy would fold because someone had finally pushed back.

"Re-raise," Kyler declared and shoved a healthy stack of chips in front of him. While he maintained a steady poker face, he noticed that Nolan did not, as his friend's eyes widened and mouth opened with concern.

"Call," came the response from Kyler's opponent.

The flop was king of hearts, ten of clubs, eight of hearts, giving Kyler a pair of kings with an ace kicker. Pretty strong hand. But when the opponent bet big, Kyler had to think hard. Was his hand good enough to risk it all? Maybe the other guy had hit a set—three of a kind. Maybe he had a pair of aces. Maybe, maybe, maybe.

But Kyler sensed that the big stack didn't have an especially strong hand. His instincts had been serving him well, so he decided to trust them.

"All in," he declared, hoping for a fold.

"Call," came the response that Kyler absolutely did *not* want to hear. After Kyler nervously showed his cards, his opponent turned over jack-nine of hearts. Kyler had the made hand with the pair of kings, but any heart on the turn or river would give the guy a flush, and any seven or queen would complete his straight. Any of these cards would eliminate Kyler and send him home with no money to show for all he had been through.

Kyler stood to watch what came next, his stomach in knots, as Nolan looked extremely concerned from the rail. The dealer tapped the table and then dealt the turn card—three of clubs.

One more card to dodge. Please, just one more card. No heart. No seven. No queen. Please. Please! Please!!!

Four of spades.

Kyler won the pot—more than doubling his chips and giving him one of the bigger stacks in the tournament. While the black-hatted opponent shook his head in disappointment, Kyler rushed over to Nolan.

"Oh my God," Kyler declared. "I almost had a fucking heart attack."

Nolan was shaking his head in disbelief. "I think I'm having one now."

"You were supposed to stop me from doing crazy shit like that!" laughed Kyler.

"Seriously?" Nolan replied with a chuckle. "When have I *ever* been able to stop you from doing crazy shit?"

Soon the money bubble burst, and the remaining players congratulated each other with cheers, handshakes, high-fives, and fist bumps. At the next break, a reporter for an online poker site asked Kyler about making the money and his prospects for the rest of the tournament. At first Kyler thought it was just an informal question, but as he started to answer he saw the reporter recording the audio of his response on her phone.

A reporter is actually interviewing me? Someone cares what I have to say? Is this real?

He continued to find friendly cards and cruised through the rest of Day 4. Once play ended, he and Nolan went to the hotel bar for a beer that had quickly become their daily tradition. Only 310 players were still alive, and Kyler had a little over 2 million in chips. The payout for people eliminated now would be $37,000, with that number continuing to climb.

They clanked their beers together.

"This is unreal," Kyler said. "The last year of my life has been so unbearably shitty. I forgot what it felt like to have something go right."

"I know it's been really tough," Nolan replied. "Mia still giving you a hard time?"

Kyler nodded slowly as he thought about the separation and all the pain he had experienced. "A couple months ago she sent me some texts that were just . . . I'm not even sure the word for it."

"What did she say?"

"They were just so nasty, but not normal nasty. Like, really hurtful . . . personal . . . angry. Just wanting to devastate me. And it worked."

"Like what?"

Kyler looked away, trying to avoid getting too agitated. No way could he share specifics. And he didn't want to tear up, not now. "I . . . I'd just rather not really go into detail."

"No problem," Nolan quickly answered. "Hey, let's just think about positive stuff." He raised his beer up in the air. "To your incredible poker playing for four long days!" Nolan toasted.

Kyler lifted his bottle, drank a few gulps, and smiled. "Thanks. I've been feeling really locked in. I've never played this well before. But oh my God, I'm getting ridiculous cards. Just totally hit by the deck."

"I think you're going to make us a lot of money this week, Kyler. Don't mean to jinx anything," he added as he knocked on the table, "but that's what I think."

Us.

Kyler considered that word, trying to show no visible reaction, just as when he was in a high stakes poker hand. Yes, Nolan had paid $300 of his original tournament entry. Correct, Nolan had been very supportive and encouraging and at times even helpful analyzing specific hands.

But what was his expectation for the prize money? Kyler already supposedly owed 20% of any profits to the other participants in the home game final table. What would Nolan be looking for when this tournament was all over? He wished he knew but was certain there was no benefit in raising the issue now.

"Man, I'm exhausted," Kyler said. "I'm gonna crash. See you in the morning."

"Get some rest, Kyler. Great job," Nolan replied. And as Kyler walked off, he heard Nolan exclaim from behind him, "Day 5!"

8

JACQUES STOOD in front of the Canadian embassy as a strong gust of wintery air cut through his bones. It was just past dawn, and he knew that the makeshift memorial wouldn't last for long. He bent down and picked up a photo of Emily Kinum. This one was approximately 8" x 10" and appeared to be affixed with glue to cardboard. It was a headshot, showing her looking thoughtfully into the distance at some unknown object in some unknown place.

There were various photos of different sizes, about twenty-five, mixed together with an assortment of flowers and several small United States flags. In a brutal land devoid of public dissent, those items alone bordered on subversive. The fact that there were also a few photos of the crown prince strewn about, each with the words "murderer" scribbled in red across his forehead—that was revolutionary.

Who was brave—or foolish—enough to do this? Did they know what they might face if caught? Torture, execution, or both—there was no tolerance here for anti-establishment expression.

He went inside and had his security officer pull up overnight footage from the front of the embassy. He saw that around two-thirty in the morning, four or five figures clad in black from head to toe appeared seemingly from nowhere. With speed and precision, they erected the memorial display within sixty seconds and then were gone.

He noticed nothing identifiable about the individuals involved, but he was no investigative expert. No doubt the Kingdom would be requesting this footage soon, if they didn't already have access to it. They might be able to detect something subtle about one of the individuals that would lead to an identification.

"Erase everything from last night," he instructed. "And make sure it's not recoverable."

The security officer paused for a moment, and then nodded to show his understanding and compliance.

An hour later, there was activity outside. He threw his coat on and hurried back to the street outside the embassy. Three military policemen, wearing camouflage and holding machine guns, stood guard as a street sweeper devoured the remnants of the display.

He watched as the truck mechanically sucked up photo after photo. Again and again he saw Emily's precious face look up toward the gray sky and then disappear. The flowers and flags and crown prince images also quickly vanished. Soon, all gone.

He wanted to take his own photo from his phone and wave it in the faces of the soldiers. Or he could quickly print it out, find something to mount it on, and produce a new monument to Emily's exceptional life and beautiful spirit. But that would accomplish nothing. And he was already no doubt suspect here. In reality, there was no diplomatic immunity in this land—he could disappear or die in an accident or be violently murdered by assailants whose identities were "unknown" pending an official investigation. There was no safety for him.

So he just stared, keeping his mournful feelings inside, viewing the soldiers and the truck go about their work. He wondered if the men would try to speak with him, but no—soon they were gone, too, and there were no signs remaining that anything of note had ever been there.

9

ON DAY 5, Kyler continued to play smart, make correct reads, and receive some lucky help on the occasions when he blundered or when, through no fault of his own, he found himself in a bad situation. Like the time he flopped a set of kings and then called the huge all-in bet of a player who turned over an inferior pocket aces, and the opponent ended up walking away distraught and disgusted.

With every elimination, the playing field continued to shrink, and more and more tables were removed. Nolan was no longer the only person on his side watching—a bunch of people from home, some from the basketball league, and a few from other parts of his life had made the journey to Vegas, too. The media presence increased, and at times Kyler's table was actually live on television, with a small camera broadcasting his cards and microphones picking up the table conversation.

It wasn't until near the end of that day, when the tournament was down to ninety people sitting at ten tables and they were each guaranteed at least $77,000, that he found himself sitting at the same table as poker pro, international activist, and rising media star Priya Varma. She was placed in Seat 4, with him right next to her in Seat 5. There she was with that larger-than-life aura, movie-star poise, stylish clothes and hair, and intoxicating confidence.

He gave her a friendly nod to welcome her to the table.

"Congrats on your win earlier this year," he said. "I'm definitely folding any hand against you if there's a six of diamonds on the board."

She responded with a polite smile, and he realized with some embarrassment that she'd probably been hearing some version of this line from a lot of people since the beginning of the tournament.

As with virtually everyone else who followed poker, Kyler had seen the YouTube videos of her January tournament victory at the Borgata in Atlantic City—an event with a first prize of about $500,000. When it had come down to two people, Priya had a huge chip lead on her opponent and was heading toward the win. Her opponent was all in with pocket tens, and Priya had called with ace-jack of diamonds. The flop included a jack and two diamonds, which gave her a commanding lead with a pair of jacks and the nut flush draw, but then an unlucky—for her—ten fell on the turn.

The crowd had rumbled in disapproval, as the spectators were virtually all rooting for her victory. She was the rock star there, and they wanted to be able to celebrate her win. Priya stood next to the table, seemingly unfazed by the unfortunate ten. She turned toward the crowd, appearing bold and charismatic.

"Six of diamonds on the river," she commanded.

And then the dealer revealed the final card—astonishingly, the six of diamonds.

Priya clasped both hands over her mouth, shocked by the accuracy of her prediction and thrilled by her tournament victory. The audience screamed in amazement and delight, and the television announcer declared, "Six of diamonds on the river! Can you believe it? Priya Varma has won the tournament by calling the exact river card! Incredible!"

Priya had had a huge chip lead at the time and most likely would have won anyway, but the moment went viral in the poker world. Still unknown to the public at large, she gained instant fame and deity status among those who followed the game.

The videos quickly amassed hundreds of thousands of views and social media posts and shares, with such YouTube titles as "Poker Pro Calls Exact Card to Win Tournament!" "Queen of Diamonds Priya Varma Predicts Winning Card!" and "Hot Poker Chick Wins Big with Six of Diamonds!"

Two months later, a documentary that had been filmed the previous year was released. It followed a small group of activists from an international human rights organization as they crossed from Turkey into Syria on foot over barbed wire in the middle of the night and then proceeded to risk their lives to document and expose human rights atrocities. Kyler had never actually seen the movie, but he had read some of the effusive online praise for the daring group, which had included a young poker player named Priya Varma.

Now, four months after the release of the film, she was deep in the Main Event, and people well beyond the poker world were abuzz with excitement. Because she had been moved to Kyler's table, he had even more cameras and reporters indirectly following his progress, but he tried not to let that disrupt his rhythm.

When play ended for the day, leaving seventy-seven players remaining, poker journalists swarmed Priya to get her reaction.

"Only one woman has made the Main Event final table and that was back in 1995," a reporter began. "Do you think you can reach the final table? And what would that mean for you and women in poker?"

"My goal isn't to make the final table," she replied smoothly. "My goal is to win the tournament and become world champion."

"First female world champion?" another replied.

"Well, first lots-of-things world champion."

The next day, when a man at another table was eliminated in seventy-third place, the prize money jumped to over $100,000 for the next people eliminated, with the first prize of $8.8 million still in the distance but now tauntingly visible.

Kyler grew more and more excited with every pay jump but also kept wondering how much of it would really be his. Despite the fact that Nolan had helped him enter the satellite tournament, and even though he and others were now enthusiastically cheering for him with every hand, it was *his* play that had gotten him this far, and it was *he* who was by far in the most dire financial situation.

As the sixth day of play continued, the pay jumps became even more dramatic—with fifty-four players left, $156,265. With forty-five left, $189,165. And when only thirty-six players remained across four tables, they were each guaranteed $230,475. He continued to amass chips thanks to more great reads and some phenomenal luck. At the end of the day, he flopped a straight against a player who had a set. He called an all-in and then prayed that the huge pot would be his—he just needed the turn and river to not pair the board and give his opponent a full house.

When the final cards were dealt and he won a massive amount of chips while eliminating another player, his chip count was over 15 million, and he was guaranteed over $282,000.

"Nice hand," Priya said as the surviving twenty-seven players began bagging their chips for the night, with the final table of nine now really in sight. Priya and Kyler had played at different tables earlier in the day but had spent the past two hours again competing at the same one.

"Thanks," he replied. "I'm on the run of a lifetime here. It's so crazy. The most I've ever won playing poker before was a couple thousand dollars."

She put one finger to her lips. "Shhh . . . you're going to give yourself away as an amateur," she mock-warned.

"Ha! Well here's one more amateur move . . . could I get a picture of us?"

"Sure," she responded politely, as she stepped closer to him, and he reached out with his phone to take a selfie. Her shoulder brushed lightly against his as he snapped the photo, and he couldn't believe what had happened to his life. He was competing on television for millions of dollars and interacting with this famous, highly accomplished, magnetic woman.

"Thanks," he said as he looked at her. *She's amazing. Maybe if I took better care of myself like I used to. And wasn't nearly-divorced with three children. Possibly if I wasn't such a fucking loser, there would be a small chance that she would be with me.*

He imagined all sorts of dream scenarios, each of which he knew was pathetically unrealistic—as unlikely as it had seemed a week ago for him to be this close to making the final table at the Main Event of the World Series of Poker.

10

TWENTY-FOUR hours later, when the tenth place person was eliminated and Kyler had improbably, unbelievably made the final table, his small group of supporters surrounded him with congratulatory hugs and cheers. Was this real? He was guaranteed to win at least $1 million for ninth place and as much as $8.8 million for first.

He and the other remaining players were mobbed by journalists looking for interviews and insights about the journey to this point and plans for the last stretch. The fact that, for the first time in over a quarter century and only the second time in history, a woman would be playing at the final table resulted in even more public attention and unprecedented coverage in mainstream, non-poker media.

"You're an amateur with no experience in major tournaments," one reporter said to Kyler while her cameraman pointed a lens at him. "Now you're up against eight experienced professionals. How can you compete and win?"

"Well," he replied thoughtfully, "I know I'm the ninth best player left. If we played for a lifetime, or a year, or even a few weeks, they would all destroy me. But I just have to be the best for one final table. Just one. If I have some good luck, I know I can do that."

Meanwhile, Priya took part in interview after interview with national news outlets, who were enthusiastically covering the return of a woman to the WSOP final table and the possibility of the first female world champion, as well as her exemplary activist credentials.

"Winning is *very* important to me," Priya told the interviewer who had asked her what it would mean to win it all. "But it's not just about the money or about poker. If I win, I'll have an invaluable platform from which to help others around the world—to support people who are really suffering, people who don't know anything about poker but know that they're in a lot of hurt and need an advocate."

The video instantly went viral, as people around the world began showing online support for her with the hashtag #sixofdiamondsontheriver.

The next day's final table occurred not in the large convention hall but in the nearby theater that usually was home to music, magic, and other Vegas-style entertainment. The poker table was on the main stage, with supporters of the nine remaining players and other poker fans filling the spectator seats.

Kyler concentrated on pushing back every instinct that told him this world was too big for him and that he was liable to make a stupid mistake that would cost him millions. The $1 million prize for ninth place was tremendous, but the difference between that and the $8.8 million first prize was mind-blowing. He was starting the final table in third place, with Priya close behind in fourth. He could afford to be patient and wait for good cards and opportunities. And maybe while he was playing it cool, a few other players would be picked off.

There was tremendous excitement in the room as the time to begin approached. Nolan looked at Kyler with admiration and gave him a big supportive hug. "I'm so proud of you, buddy. What you've done here is beyond astounding. You can win this. I know you can."

"Thank you. I really appreciate it," Kyler answered.

"Just one thing," Nolan added. "We're fifty-fifty on all this, right? I know it's been a little unspoken, but I gave you half your buy-in and just want to make sure we're on the same page. This is a *ton* of money we're looking at."

Kyler glowered at his friend. This was beyond outrageous. "*Now*? You're fucking kidding me. Right *now* you want to talk about this?" He pointed around the room with all its majesty and continued, "I'm about to start the final table, and you want to haggle with me *now*?"

"I just want to make sure there's no misunderstanding. It's a *lot* of money."

"No shit it's a lot of money. A lot of money that I've earned. You have no idea how tough it's been to get this far. Fifty-fifty? What the fuck!"

"Hey, Kyler," Nolan fired back. "You wouldn't be here without me. Don't fuck me over now. Okay? Don't do that to me."

"In thirty minutes I'm playing for *eight point eight million dollars*," Kyler explained angrily. "You gave me *three hundred*. You'll get what you're owed." His blood was boiling. All the focus he had worked to bring about was now evaporating, right when he needed it most.

"And how much is that?" Nolan asked.

Kyler shook his head in disgust. First the rest of the home game final table would want their 20%, then Nolan would want half of the rest? This was out of control. "I'll pay your $10,000 buy-in next year, Nolan. Then let's see how much *you* can fucking win."

He stormed away, his chest heaving, and then forced himself to take slow, deep breaths. But there was so much noise, activity, and excitement around him, it was almost impossible to decompress and concentrate. He wished he could be far away for just a moment.

However, there was no escaping now. And he wasn't the only final table participant stirred to anger right before the most pivotal poker event of the year.

The good-looking royal he had seen on Day 1, now long ago eliminated in the tournament and today wearing an expensive gray suit and red tie, walked amidst the area that had been cordoned off for final table participants, close family and friends, tournament officials, and other VIPs. He was strolling around, shaking hands while displaying a big smile, and congratulating each member of the final table.

"Mr. Amateur!" he exclaimed after catching Kyler's eye. "Congratulations!" He grabbed Kyler's hand and shook it with a particularly firm grip.

"Thanks," Kyler replied.

"Listen," he continued. "I don't know how much you've heard about me and my country. Westerners generally refer to it as the Kingdom. Despite our many strengths, in numerous ways we've failed to really enter the twenty-first century. I'm working to change that, and I'm spearheading a major reform campaign."

"I really apologize," Kyler responded, "but I'm not the most informed about the international world. Or the national world, for that matter."

"No apologies! And you have too much important work today to listen to me ramble. But I want you to know that, despite my terribly poor play in this tournament, I am a huge poker fan and believe it has an unparalleled ability to bring people together. So as a symbolic part of my reform program, I'll be organizing a Goodwill Poker tournament in a little over a year's time in my country. And I'm very proud to say that the event has been designated as that year's official International Poker Federation championship competition. Something like this is unprecedented in my county. Hopefully with exciting players like you, it will be very successful! But more on that another day. Most importantly, I just want to say: congratulations on your inspiring run here and good luck today!"

Kyler nodded with appreciation, and the royal turned toward Priya, the next target of his outreach. She'd been listening from about ten feet away, but now, instead of displaying radiant charm, she wore a caustic glare.

The oblivious royal approached her, beaming. "Priya Varma!

Congratulations! What you've accomplished here is an inspiration to women all over the planet! And, let me add, an inspiration to the reform program I'm leading in my country, which is striving to better the lives of women and girls."

"Your country helping women and girls?" she replied coldly. "Your women aren't allowed to drive."

"Well, that's absolutely a needed reform that I—"

"Or have real careers. Or have free speech. Or vote."

"Priya—"

"Although those last two things, men don't have either in your country, so I guess in that respect there is equality."

He raised a hand and lowered his head slightly in an attempt to defuse the escalating situation. "I'm certainly not here to argue with you," he explained. "I'm a relatively young person trying to reform my country. If I only followed what my nation wanted, I certainly wouldn't be here now. Please give me a chance to show you."

She looked at him with the self-assured mercilessness she used so deftly at the poker table. "Look, I know more about your country than probably anyone here, besides you. I mourn for any girl—or boy for that matter—who grows up there now. You may be a crown prince back home, but you're not one in this room. I see how all these celebrities kiss your ass and treat you like some great reformer, while your people are treated with such cruelty. They suffocate and die under your oppression. I'm not fooled like everyone else, and I love this game too much to allow you to use poker to ingratiate your appalling regime to the world. What the hell are you doing here anyway? Didn't you get knocked out on *Day 1*? Get the fuck out of here."

And with that, she turned and walked away, leaving him standing there awkwardly.

Kyler took the opportunity to step away, too—he certainly didn't need to be in the middle of any additional conflict. He was already riled up by his conversation with Nolan, and with only a few minutes until the final table started, he needed to get his mind right.

Fortunately, he then received a friendly text message from a surprising source—Mia:

"Hi Kyler—I know things have been really bad between us and I deeply regret some of the hurtful things I said recently, but I want to let you know that I'm very impressed with what you've done and wish you very good luck today."

Her financial motive for reaching out wasn't lost on him, and the pain she'd caused him had been severe, but he appreciated the apology.

"Thanks Mia. Crazy scene here. And Nolan saying I owe him half of winnings b/c he gave me $300 a few months ago! We NEVER agreed to that. Such unbelievable BS!!"

"Don't worry about that now. Just stay calm and do your best. The kids and I are rooting for you."

11

"SHUFFLE UP AND DEAL!"

The previous year's champion made the ceremonial declaration, the crowd applauded, and the dealer began to distribute the cards to Kyler and eight other final table participants. This was no poker table in someone's basement or a rented room at a local club. Kyler was playing on center stage in the most important poker event in the world, surrounded by television cameras, journalists, and fans who were ready to cheer and chant as with any other major sporting event.

He was the only amateur, surrounded by eight experienced pros. It would be very easy to get caught up in the excitement, panic, and make a mistake. The game was no limit Hold'em, so one major error and he could be gone, costing himself millions of dollars. He was guaranteed at least $1 million—but how much of that would he actually keep? The first prize of $8.8 million was tantalizingly close.

In order to play his best poker, he told himself to treat it like another neighborhood tournament.

Just play your game. Make smart decisions. Don't go on tilt. Don't let the bright lights and huge amount of money change how you play. It's the same game you've been playing for years. Fifty-two cards. Four suits. Be patient. Let others get eliminated first. You can do this.

He was in Seat 3, and the first to act in the first hand. He looked down at his hole cards, trying not to think about the fact that as he viewed them, they were being broadcast to the world.

Ace of hearts, king of hearts. He soaked in the cards with both excitement and trepidation—they could win him a lot of chips, but they also had a good chance of getting him in significant trouble, which he knew too well from experience.

"Raise," he said.

The three guys after him folded, and then Priya, sitting across the table in Seat 7, looked at her cards and then straight ahead for what was probably only ten seconds but felt like a lot longer.

"Re-raise," she announced, pushing forward a large stack of chips and clearly not taking Kyler's bet very seriously.

The next few players folded, so it was back to Kyler. Should he call? Or four-bet with another raise? If he did that, what would she do? Would another raise get her to fold pre-flop? Or would she just re-raise again or even move all-in?

"Call," he answered, taking the conservative route. This was only the first hand, after all.

The flop: seven of spades, eight of spades, two of hearts.

Not what he was hoping to see at all. Nothing that helped his ace-king.

But as he looked at Priya, who was usually stoic and unreadable during a hand, he sensed that she didn't like that flop either. It was something subtle, a tiny movement of her bottom lip and momentary change of direction in her eyes. The flop had clearly missed her, too.

"Three point six million," he stated firmly, indicating his bet as he moved the corresponding chips in front of him.

She was quiet and still, taking her time as the once-boisterous audience was silent in tense anticipation. Thirty seconds passed, then a minute, then almost two.

"Eight," she finally said, and pushed 8 million in chips in front of her. The crowd cheered in support of her aggressiveness—she was by far the fan favorite. And it wasn't just a woman thing. It was her. Smart, charming, media savvy, entertaining. A force for progress in the world. She was a heroine almost everyone could get behind as she fought for poker's ultimate prize.

But Kyler needed to shut all of that out, not think about how many people were rooting against him, and just concentrate on the hand. He knew that Priya was an aggressive player, using position and betting to push others around, especially amateurs like him. She didn't necessarily have a strong hand, and he grew increasingly convinced that she didn't. He considered every detail of how she bet and how she looked, and he knew that she didn't have much. Possibly some kind of draw, maybe a small pair, maybe ace-king or ace-queen. If he raised he might be able to force her out and take down the large pot.

"Twenty," he heard himself say, and the crowd rumbled, shocked by the quick acceleration of action on the first hand of the final table. He had now committed almost half his chips on this hand.

Right away he could tell that Priya was not thrilled by his re-raise. Again, it was something almost unnoticeable that he picked up in her demeanor, posture, and gaze.

She stared straight ahead for three minutes, seemingly thinking hard about what to do next. Then she began moving her chips around with her slender fingers, putting out two small stacks and with one hand merging them into one. After five minutes she slowly separated enough chips to match Kyler's bet, and then counted what she would have left after a potential call.

Meanwhile, Kyler knew that as weak as her hand might be, he was in a bad position with just ace high. Against a top pro like Priya, he needed to be still as a statue as she contemplated her next move and intensely observed him.

His heart was beating heavily. Was she able to notice this? He felt some sweat develop on his forehead, but of course he dared not move to wipe it off. But wouldn't she see that it was there? It was agony, with millions of dollars and his financial future at stake. Why had he gotten himself into this mess so soon? As her contemplation reached almost ten minutes, he yearned for this torture to end. Where was that kid from earlier in the tournament to call the clock?

He desperately wanted her to fold—a desire stronger than just about any he had experienced in his life. It was such an overwhelming, all-powerful wish that he wondered how long he could keep the intense emotion from being obvious.

Or possibly it already was. Because when she finally spoke, she offered two simple, devastating words.

"All in."

His heart sank in profound disappointment as the crowd erupted in a loud, supportive cheer, thrilled by their star's boldness. Some chanted her name, while others screamed words of encouragement. Many times in his life, Kyler had irrationally felt as if virtually the whole world was against him, but now it really seemed true. Except for a few supporters in the audience, he was forced to play the villain here, and no one wanted him to prevail.

He told himself that he needed to ignore all that and just make the best, most correct poker decision. He had to forget all his personal debt and the millions of dollars the wrong decision here might cost him and his children.

So many chips were already in the middle. If he called and won, she'd be eliminated in ninth place and he would be the chip leader with eight players remaining—an incredible position that would make the $8.8 million more attainable than ever. But if he called and lost, she would be the chip leader, and he'd be virtually gone—barely enough chips to continue playing. And if he folded? He'd already given up about half his chips on this hand. He would still be alive, but greatly damaged, and in a much weaker position going forward.

Now she was the statue—staring straight ahead, motionless—while he tried to figure out what to do. She clearly didn't have a great hand. He had sensed unmistakable weakness as she deliberated. He still thought she probably had a draw or a small pair—in either case, he'd either be ahead or would still have outs with an ace or king on the turn or river giving him the win, or maybe even runner-runner hearts bringing him a flush.

She had no doubt detected that he was uncomfortable before the all-in bet. So maybe she was bluffing simply based on her read that he wanted her to fold. And as cool and professional as she usually was, maybe now *she* was on tilt after that fiery altercation with the crown prince.

He had gotten this far—inconceivably far—by trusting his instincts. And he had some great recent history of successfully calling with ace high in a big hand. He thought back to that one hand at the home game final table where he won his WSOP entry. He had showed the winning cards and then heard one of the watchers cry out: "Ace high. Oh my God . . ."

He looked right at Priya, their eyes met, and he knew exactly what he needed to do.

He was, and had always been, for better or worse, a gambler. And right now he wanted to gamble on the fact that he was right.

With his eyes still locked with hers, he announced the biggest decision of his life:

"Call."

12

THE WORD had barely escaped his mouth when Priya flipped over her eight-seven of clubs and confidently sprung up from the table. He saw her two pair that had his ace-king crushed and felt as if a dagger had just been thrust into one of his lungs. The crowd's roar was deafening, thrilled by her powerful hand as everyone waited for him to reveal his.

For a moment he sat there, stunned and apoplectic, and for the millionth time in his life, furious at himself for making a terrible, ruinous decision. She had played him perfectly—sucking him in, making him think she was weak, springing her trap, and inducing a disastrous call for virtually all his chips.

He looked at her eight-seven and then stared again in disbelief at the flop of seven of spades, eight of spades, and two of hearts.

Who was I to think I could read her? She's a top professional poker player. I'm a fucking idiot. Calling here with ace high? I'm not in a damn neighborhood poker game anymore. I'm at the final table of the Main Event.

He wished he didn't have to show his cards, knowing the mockery and delight that would shoot like electricity throughout the crowd. Over the past week he had become an amateur star, and now he would be the laughingstock of the poker world, the guy who started the final table in third place and got virtually eliminated on the *first hand* with an inexplicably bad call.

"Sir, please show your cards," the dealer commanded. Mortified and devastated, he slowly and uncomfortably revealed his ace-king and then stood up from the table. As expected, the crowd exulted in his poker incompetence, gasping in shock and then cheering relentlessly.

Priya's eyes narrowed in surprise as she fixated on his cards. She wasn't acting—there was no longer a need to. She was genuinely stunned by the weakness of his hand.

The crowd continued to celebrate, as the dealer tapped his fist twice on the table and then revealed the turn card: king of spades. It paired his king, giving him new life, and sending a groan of anguish throughout the audience. Priya exhaled deeply and her shoulders slumped just a little, as Kyler momentarily emerged from his despondency.

"It's never easy," one of the other final table participants interjected.

The board now read seven-eight-two-king. Priya had two pair with her seven-eight and he had one pair with ace-king. He could still win this hand with a helpful river card. After the final card, one of them would be the chip leader, while the other would be destined for ninth place.

"No ace! No king!" screamed a Priya supporter from somewhere in the back of the room. "No ace! No king!" another quickly echoed imploringly.

Maybe that was why, when the dealer revealed the river card to be the two of clubs, there was a small eruption of excitement from some of her fans.

Priya, of course, knew better. Her face was instantly aghast, and then she closed her eyes in disbelief. Once the initial cheers subsided and everyone had finally realized that Kyler's two pair, kings and twos, had defeated her two pair, eights and sevens, an eerie silence fell over the room.

Her eyes opened and she stared at Kyler, her eyes searing him.

Your stupidity has destroyed my dreams, torn out my heart, and cost me a place in history and millions of dollars, her look said. *I would have been able to do so much with this opportunity, and now your incompetence has destroyed it all.*

Simultaneously, Kyler was absorbing the stunning reality that he had been granted a last-minute reprieve from a horrible fate. Somehow, he had not only won the hand, but he was now the chip leader with eight people left. Relief and elation swept over his mind and body, and a big smile involuntarily stretched across his face as he shook his head incredulously.

"Brutal . . ." he heard another final table participant interrupt the stunned silence.

"How do you call with ace-king there?" Priya lashed out from where she was standing on the other side of the table.

"I . . . I thought you were bluffing," he answered honestly and defensively.

Besides the two of them, the room was quiet, with everyone still absorbing the shock of the hand, and watching this new brewing confrontation that was being broadcast and streamed throughout the world.

"*Bluffing*?" she exclaimed with contempt. "How am I bluffing there? I raised you every step of the way. What the hell do you think I'm bluffing with?!"

He didn't know what he was supposed to say. He had made a major mistake . . . and nevertheless won.

"I know, Priya. It was a bad call," he acknowledged, trying to look solemn and apologetic, though he felt neither.

She nodded, still glaring at him. "Yeah. It was a bad call. It was an *absurd* call."

This is so fucking unjust, her look cried out. *This is so wrong.*

Awkward silence returned for a few seconds, and then the tournament director spoke enthusiastically into his microphone.

"Please join me in congratulating Priya Varma for her remarkable performance and ninth place finish! The first woman at the Main Event final table in over a quarter century! Let's hear it for her!"

The entire crowd and all the remaining players stood and applauded for over a full minute as she stood there motionless. Then one player stepped over to hug her, and she apparently decided that to appear gracious, she would need to circle the table, bidding farewell to each of the remaining eight.

When she arrived at Kyler, he put his arms around her back and leaned in for his turn to hug. He felt her body against his, and for a moment put the tournament and her anger at him aside, acutely aware that undoubtedly he would never be this physically close to her again.

"I'm sorry," he muttered weakly into her ear.

"Good luck," she replied, with the same level of insincerity as his apology.

And then, after fifteen more grueling hours of play, when the final cards were dealt, and Kyler had won the tournament and was the new poker world champion, his small group of supporters rushed the stage and embraced him wildly. He dropped to his knees, covered both eyes with his hands, and began to sob uncontrollably with immense joy and relief.

A few minutes later, his tearstained face beamed for the cameras as he sat at the poker table, showing the winning cards from the final hand, with the beautiful main event bracelet sitting on $8.8 million in cash in front of him.

His phone of course blew up, with messages from virtually everyone he knew, and even more from people he didn't. One in particular deeply resonated with him when he saw it a few hours later. It was a video message from Mia, with her and his nine- and seven-year-old daughters and eleven-year-old son, all looking at the camera.

"We love you Daddy! Congratulations!" his beaming children squealed.

And then from his estranged wife, who throughout their marriage had relentlessly pleaded with him to stop his destructive wagering on sports, poker, craps, horses, and everything else: "Good thing I always encouraged you to gamble!" she declared with a sarcastic wink.

It was probably the happiest moment of his life, and he wished he could go back and press pause right there. In fact, if he had died later that night, it would have been the perfect time to go. But who wants to die when things are great? Instead, he was so excited to live and enjoy the greatness, to ride the exhilarating rush of happiness and success. Why would there be any desire to stop? Better to live and revel in his newfound wonderful life, at least until the inevitable time came when all signs of greatness were gone again.

13

". . . AND ALSO JOINING us is a woman who is urging a more cautious response to this brutal murder, former state department official Maggie Raster," the anchor informed his audience. "Thank you both for joining us today."

State department official? What the fuck. Didn't they just confirm with her in the green room that she worked for the White House chief of staff? Should she correct him?

"Thanks for having me," Maggie replied graciously with her best attempt at a tone that communicated both *happy to be here* and *I take this tragic killing very seriously, so therefore I'm not really that happy.*

The anchor turned to Tori and sadly nodded his head. "First of all, our hearts are all broken by the brutal murder of your sister," he said. "As a journalist and as a human being, she was someone I've always greatly admired. She was a hero to so many around the world, and I can't imagine how painful this must be for you and your family."

"Thank you, Jon," she replied with the perfect mixture of sorrow and strength. "Many people know my sister from her exceedingly brave and influential reporting. She was an inspiration to me and countless others. But I also remember the kind, wonderful older sister I grew up with, who taught me so much, who protected me as a little girl, and who throughout my life has been my best friend. Her loss, especially in this manner, with no consequences so far for those who murdered her, is really unbearable."

"And you're now calling for a complete ban on travel to the Kingdom?" he followed up.

"Yes, but much more than that. This is a brutal regime that in addition to torturing and killing its citizens, just murdered an American journalist. Those responsible must pay the ultimate price. Nothing less is satisfactory. And no one should engage in economic activity with the Kingdom until justice is served here. As you know, the crown prince has a duplicitous public relations campaign to pretend that the Kingdom is on the path to liberalization and modernization, which is completely false. The crown jewel of that campaign is a major international poker tournament that takes place next week. We can't allow any Americans to be used as props in this obscene spectacle. I'm calling for the president to issue a travel ban to prevent any American from attending, and for all good people who believe in freedom and justice around the world to boycott this travesty. History's worst dictators have long used large public events as powerful propaganda to keep themselves in power and mask their true barbaric nature. We must not permit that to happen here."

"Now Maggie," the anchor said, turning toward her, "You're arguing against a forceful response, against a travel ban. Your position is that there's nothing wrong with this tournament. So US poker pros should just participate as if nothing has happened? Doesn't that send a terrible message to the world about American resolve?"

Jon, I can't stress enough how I don't give a fuck about this poker tournament or a travel ban. Your booker forced me to take this side, then pitted me against a grieving sister without warning. The only reason I'm still sitting here is that I'm desperate to be on television. Not desperate like all those news and reality show wannabes who will do anything for the slightest bit of fame. I don't care about that at all. But I'm trying to build a real, independent business based on experience I've accumulated through some tough years of grueling work. I have a lot to offer, I have an urgent, critical need to make this financially viable, and I've been told over and over that I need to be on television in order to be successful in the political consulting world. So I'll reluctantly play this game. I'll act like I care about this side of the issue so people will think I'm a strong, knowledgeable advocate, while I try not to appear like a heartless villain. Okay? Now, what was the question again?

"First, let me also extend my condolences—" she began.

"Spare us the obligatory condolence line," Tori interrupted.

"I sincerely mean it. I—"

"If you meant it, you wouldn't be here, spinning for a tyrant. You'd be joining the fight *against* the people who murdered an American journalist and so many others."

Maggie knew she was swimming in perilous waters in which she had little experience. For a variety of reasons she was in a vulnerable state, and there was a strong likelihood that this was going to be a calamity for her. But she wasn't going to grovel for respect, and she wouldn't passively let herself be torn apart. She was determined to stand firm.

"Tori, with all due respect, you don't know me. And what you just said is contradicted by my years of government service dedicated to making this nation stronger and fighting for our citizens. I want your sister's murderers to be found. I want *them* to be killed. But we don't know who they are yet—"

"You have to be quite naïve to think anything like this would happen without the crown prince's knowledge and blessing—"

"Well, there have been far too many rash, disastrous actions taken by our country throughout history based on incomplete information. Let's not make that mistake again. I don't want us to unnecessarily inflame a tense situation with a nuclear power that now has intercontinental ballistic missiles. We're one escalation away from nuclear conflict."

"Aren't you arguing for appeasement?" the anchor interjected.

"Don't forget what history has taught us about the consequences of *that*."

"No one is talking about initiating nuclear war!" Tori exclaimed. "Don't create some fictional extreme situation to justify what you have to know is an unjustifiable position. We can't let Emily's murder go unanswered. And we can't allow our citizens to embolden the manipulative, dangerous disinformation campaign of this regime by supporting this event. For starters, the president needs to ban travel to the Kingdom, *now*. And the international community needs to similarly ban and boycott any support there. That's not going to result in nuclear war, and you know it!"

The anchor nodded in agreement and looked right at Maggie. "It's a good point," he said. "Throwing around the idea of nuclear war to justify playing poker with a despot? That sounds like a pretty weak argument. And also insulting to all those who have been tortured and murdered . . . and their families," he finished, with a knowing glance toward Tori.

"Look," Maggie pushed back. "Wars often start with small steps which neither side initially thinks are significant enough to lead to the death toll that ultimately results. But fine, put aside that risk for a moment. Let's also consider that *we don't know all the facts*. We have to push for an independent investigation, not controlled by the Kingdom. Once we find out the truth, then we can decide how to respond."

"But we can't contribute to frivolous entertainment that helps legitimize and prop up this regime!" Tori responded as she shook her head in exasperation. "Even before they murdered Emily, significant people in the poker community like Priya Varma were condemning this tournament because she recognized it for what it is. We need everyone to follow her example, but some will just see the $20 million first prize and won't care about morality. That's why our president has to act, and stop all travel there immediately! Allowing the

Kingdom to grow more powerful through manipulative theatrics is the real threat to decency, justice, and our security. If the president doesn't issue an executive order for a travel ban today, it will be a monumental undermining of America's strength and moral authority in the world."

Priya Varma, Maggie thought. Yes, she recognized that name from years ago. And now she realized why. But was it the same Priya Varma?

"Restricting the freedom of Americans to travel based on unproven assumptions is never a good idea," Maggie explained. "Plus, there are plenty of countries with tyrannical governments to which Americans are free to travel. Russia. China. Iran. Should we ban travel to all of those places? Let's get the facts and be smart about this, and then we can make sure we get justice for your sister. Let's not change government policy over a poker tournament."

Then their time was up, with the anchor mercifully ending the segment by thanking both Tori and Maggie for participating. Maggie rose as a technician began to remove her mic and earpiece. She couldn't wait to escape, but before she turned for the exit, she saw Tori still seated, staring at her with scorn.

"I really *am* very sorry for your loss," Maggie said contritely.

Tori barely moved as she replied, "I don't know how you sleep at night."

Maggie knew that no response could mitigate this situation, so she quickly fled the studio, retrieved her belongings from the green room, and darted past security as she left the building. In the car service back to her apartment, she received a text from Natalie.

"Thank u for joining us today!! Nice hit! Will follow up later to get ur availability for next week! ☺"

It was good to get this positive message, but was Natalie happy because Maggie had been a strong guest or because she'd been willing cannon fodder? Maggie hadn't seen the segment yet, and she didn't know if she'd be okay with how she came off. She received a few positive texts from friends about how great it was to see her on television and how nice she looked, but of course her friends were going to be positive no matter what. And nobody mentioned whether she'd made any sense, whether she'd appeared reasonable and smart and not immoral and all the other things she wanted to believe herself to be.

She turned to social media to see the public's reaction. Her Twitter already had many mentions, and she anxiously started reading. The first one:

"Awesome job. I want to fuck your face!"

And the next:

"What an embarrassment. Who put this annoying cunt on tv? #sixofdiamondsontheriver"

She read a few more, dropped her phone to the floor of the car, and stared out the window as the buildings of downtown Washington, DC flew by. Tears began to roll down her face as she cried, really cried, for the first time since she brought her former boss back to her apartment.

Why is this so difficult? Why has everything become so impossibly difficult?

14

EIGHTEEN MONTHS after his seismic win, Kyler still took time every day to open his photos and stare at the picture of the championship bracelet. Fortunately, he had found a poker superfan who wanted to temporarily and discreetly—hopefully discreetly—hold onto the actual bracelet and pay Kyler $250 a week in cash for the privilege. He remembered the first time the guy held it, and how he stared in awe as he placed it on his wrist.

Supposedly winning $8.8 million had opened up a lot of options for credit, but many were now either maxed out or no longer active. His newfound fame also led to a slew of paid personal appearances at poker events and free buy-ins to major tournaments. But after a year and a half of poor results in tournaments and cash games, he was becoming old news. Add to that his new luxury travel lifestyle, child support payments, terrible litigation strategy and attorney fees, and very unfortunate gambling luck including a brutal football season, and he was on a major downward trajectory with crisis-level cash flow problems.

Eight point eight million dollars. If only he had *really* won that much . . .

He could still garner some appearance fees, but the number and value had already been undermined by the mortifying information that had been publicly disseminated about him. He was paid because people wanted to meet and greet and play poker with a real winner, but every public indication that he was no longer a winner weakened future opportunities.

He was hanging off a ledge, fearful every day that his financial problems would become obvious to everyone. Public disclosure would be a catastrophic hit to his earning potential and ability to borrow funds. If the world knew about his money woes, he would lose any remaining street cred with poker and creditors. Then it would all be over for him.

Yes, he had fucked up, but it wasn't all his fault—far from it. He vowed that if he could just get back into a solid, sustainable financial position, he'd never let it get away from him again.

But how could he find his way there? It seemed there was only one way.

Half a year earlier he'd answered a call from a foreign number.

"Mr. World Poker Champion!" the voice on the other end exclaimed.

He hadn't heard that voice since the night of the final table, but he recognized it immediately as the WSOP royal who turned out to be the crown prince from the Kingdom. So why was he calling now?

"Good evening," Kyler answered. "Or is it morning where you are? And what do I call you? Your highness?"

"My friends call me Prince," he said warmly.

"Well, Prince . . ."

"I have a special invitation for you. Do you have a few minutes?"

"Sure. Of course."

"As you may know, I'm leading a *major* reform program in my country to better the lives of our people. To celebrate and promote our very important efforts, I am hosting a gala, unprecedented, world class poker tournament in six months. It will be called the Goodwill Poker Classic and will be this year's championship event for the International Poker Federation. It will promote not only the improving lives of my citizens but our renewed efforts at international collaboration on a wide variety of important issues, from nuclear nonproliferation to economic cooperation to combating global climate change."

"That sounds amazing," Kyler responded.

"Yes, *amazing*. And as they say on your TV, 'but wait, there's more' . . . This tournament will be winner-take-all with a $10 million prize to the victor! Participation will be invitation only, and I am honored to invite you, Mr. Champion!"

"Well, thank you," Kyler answered. But how much would it cost him to play? And to travel there? "Prince, what's the buy-in?"

"Buy-in? No buy-in. You and the other invitees, who are the stars of the poker world, business people, and other celebrities, will all be our guests. There will be only one hundred participants. We will pay for all transportation and you will be staying here in luxury for this magnificent event."

Ten million dollar prize. No buy-in. Small field. Free travel. And a great humanitarian cause. Was he dreaming?

"Please let us know in the next couple of weeks if you'll grace us by participating," the crown prince continued.

"I'm there," Kyler said quickly. "Count me in, absolutely. I'm honored to be a part of it."

"No, no, no. The honor is *ours*. Thank *you*, Kyler."

Ten million bucks. And this time, if he won, the prize would be all his. Unlike before, he could use it all to live his best life and support his children, and never stress about money again.

A month later, the Goodwill Poker Classic was publicly announced, and Kyler felt a rush of excitement. This was really going to happen. It would be a challenge to win, but what an opportunity. At the Main Event, he had survived a field of nearly 8,000. Now it would be just one hundred, with a potential $10 million prize.

It was a lifeline thrown to a drowning man. But the world decided to cut the lifeline, while he still flailed about in the current, fighting for air.

A small amount of public criticism followed the initial announcement of the event, which some characterized as being part of a heartless dictator's propaganda machine. A handful of top poker pros announced their refusal to participate, and there were some online petitions and social media posts demanding people boycott.

The pressure continued to mount, and then the prestigious International Poker Federation announced a month ago that it "deeply regretted" its decision to hold its annual championship "in a nation so tragically unwilling to provide more than lip service to remedy its appalling record on human rights." The IPF pulled its name from the event, and all signs suggested that Kyler wouldn't need to decide whether to attend the tournament, as it would surely be cancelled.

But the crown prince wasn't about to fold. Instead, the Kingdom increased the prize the following week, promising $20 million to the winner. News sites proclaimed *Crown Prince Doubles Down on Poker Event* and other similar headlines, showing that much of the media didn't know or didn't care about the difference between poker and blackjack terminology.

And this growing criticism of the tournament was all *before* the murder of Emily Kinum. As soon as her death became public a couple of days ago, just over a week before the start of the tournament, worldwide denunciation exploded, particularly in the United States, with opponents portraying participants as traitors to decency and human rights. The same Hollywood celebrities who took selfies with the crown prince in Vegas now scrubbed their social media accounts and joined the chorus of outrage. More top pros announced their refusal to take part, as participation went from being somewhat criticized to facing intense condemnation.

But Kyler knew that he just couldn't back out. He couldn't afford to. This was his only shot at winning a staggering amount of money and resuscitating his existence.

Now the fury was at a fever pitch, and Kyler was very aware that the boycott by major poker players actually *increased* his odds of winning because of the depleted talent at the tournament. But if he played, would he be blacklisted from major events in the United States? Maybe, but his prospects for affording or being invited to them were quickly dissipating like vapor anyway.

He would have to play. He hated to be a part of something so many found objectionable, but his disastrous financial circumstances left him no choice. And then he saw news that threatened to dash his plans. The president was considering issuing an executive order banning all travel to the Kingdom. Kyler's flight was scheduled to leave in three days, but would he even be allowed to take it? He marveled at how preposterous it was that any decision of the *President of United States* would be directly relevant to his life, but that's where he now found himself.

He scrolled through his phone, looking with trepidation for news coverage of what the president might decide. Would he seal Kyler's fate or grant him an opportunity at a restored life? Kyler had never been a huge consumer of news, but he now read every online article and watched every news video he could on the topic. He came across one from the previous day, with the sister of the slain journalist on television imploring the president to issue the travel ban and to impose even more extreme consequences.

But there was another woman on that video, too. A young woman, who was smartly and deftly advocating for . . . him. Well, not *specifically* for him, but she was forcefully and articulately arguing for what he needed.

He googled her and quickly found her website—Maggie Raster Consulting, LLC. Former *White House* official. Providing "expert communications and political advisory services." Wasn't that *exactly* what he needed? Someone who could help change the public narrative and stop the executive order. This woman clearly had the connections, experience, and skills to save him. She was perfect, and she was already on his side.

15

IT WAS NIGHTTIME, and Jacques stood in his embassy study reading the breaking news stories on his tablet about small protests on the border and about how a handful of participants who may or may not have attempted to cross into the Kingdom's sovereign territory were now missing. He had no inside information and had heard nothing further from his government back home. And neither were there any messages from the Americans.

He had a meeting scheduled for the following afternoon with the Kingdom's foreign affairs minister, officially to discuss how the Kingdom's "investigation" into the death of Emily Kinum was proceeding but also to confer about escalating tensions with the United States. He would be the diplomatic intermediary, a role he had successfully undertaken many times in his career.

But this felt different. He was more personally involved than he was comfortable with, he didn't know if he was in jeopardy himself, and he had never actually been responsible for coordinating between two nuclear powers while they might be headed to a cataclysmic conflict.

And now there were some people potentially missing, with at least one being an American human rights activist. He knew that when people disappear here, it rarely ends well. The Kingdom, of course, denied all knowledge and declared in an official statement that no Americans were in custody.

He was scheduled to receive a "secure" briefing the following morning with instructions on how to proceed. That night he knew he wouldn't sleep much, if at all. So he was still awake and at work in his study at about two in the morning when a male security staffer alerted him to an unexpected visitor.

He headed down to a private, windowless conference room near the main entrance.

"She's an American," the security officer said. "She came right up to the gate and asked for you."

He entered the room, and saw a tall woman standing beside the table, her face full of determination. She was dressed all in black and held a black mask in her right hand—the same or similar attire as those who had placed the photos of Emily outside the embassy. He recognized her immediately, although they had never met.

"I'm Jacques Bouchard," he said, extending his right hand, "Canadian ambassador to the Kingdom."

"Priya Varma," she replied as she shook his hand.

"I've watched the Syria documentary. That was very dangerous. And inspiring."

"Thank you. We have to do whatever it takes to shine a light on the world's atrocities. That's the only way they'll end."

"I understand you're American."

She nodded. "Born and raised."

"I'm glad to see you're alive. I was just reading some online reports saying you're missing."

"I had to leave my phone behind so I couldn't be tracked. So I don't know what's being reported."

"You illegally crossed the border."

"I've been pretty critical of the Kingdom, so getting a visa wasn't an option."

"Would you like to sit down? Can I get you something to drink? Or eat?"

"Not right now."

Jacques considered how to proceed, and decided a low whisper was most prudent. "Look, Ms. Varma, please tell me what you're doing here. I have much respect for you, but you're putting yourself and this embassy at great risk. You know this government murders people who threaten them in any way."

She paused for a moment and then whispered back, staring at him forcefully. "What's happening here is unacceptable. The murder of Emily Kinum can't be whitewashed. I'm going to show the world what they really are."

"I understand. And I saw what you and others did outside the embassy. It's not brave. It's foolish. You can't get a message to anyone this way."

"We're not trying to get a message to *anyone*. We're getting a message to you."

He broke eye contact and looked toward the door, wondering if he should leave and direct a subordinate to continue the conversation. Then he turned back to her. "What message? And from whom?"

"The message is from me. And many others like me. Millions probably. The message is that you need to do more here. You're now the only one in this country with the position and authority to expose these atrocities. You need to do more. And I'm here to help and make sure that you do. When this is all over, history will judge you on how you handled this humanitarian crisis, and right now you're failing."

16

"I NEED TO TALK with u. I know things are hectic now but I'm having a v tough time with what happened. Please don't ignore me."

Maggie had still received no response from him. She had called twice but hadn't left a voicemail. Instead, she texted him again and continued to wait alone in her apartment as night fell and then a new day began.

She wasn't eating much and could still barely sleep. She tried to find something on Netflix to divert her thoughts. Even though over twenty-four hours had passed, she still hadn't watched her television segment, afraid of how bad it might have been and unable to deal with seeing herself just yet. And she certainly hadn't looked at any more online comments.

Then her phone rang. An unknown number. Normally she wouldn't answer, but she hoped it might be him. "Hello?"

"Good afternoon," a nervous male voice responded. "Can I please speak with Ms. Raster?"

"Yes . . . this is Maggie Raster. And who is this?"

"My name is Kyler Dawson, Ms. Raster. I saw you on TV. I . . . um . . . I'm sure you're very busy. But I was hoping you could help me with a very time-sensitive matter. That I could . . . um, maybe hire you . . ."

Holy fuck. Did this television thing actually work? Is this guy legit?

She talked with him further, telling him to call her Maggie. He said that he was a professional poker player who had been invited to participate in the Kingdom's upcoming poker tournament, and he very much wanted to play. But he was quite concerned about potential presidential action to block travel and about how playing might hurt his public image going forward. He saw her advocate so well for this issue on television, and he needed her assistance. He sounded like a real person, with a real need, who wanted to retain her.

She broached the topic of payment, and he was quickly reassuring.

"Don't worry about that," he said. "Have you heard of the World Series of Poker?"

"Well, I've heard of *poker.* And I've heard of the World Series. But not—"

"It's a huge poker tournament. I won it a year and a half ago. First place was *eight point eight million.*"

"Wow. Congratulations . . ."

"Thank you. My point is . . . money is not a problem."

Eight point eight million.

A six-figure consulting fee could very well be obtainable here. What a difference that would make for her.

The communications consulting would be challenging but relatively straightforward. The influencing of presidential executive orders, not so much. She remembered the words of her former boss, whenever there was a very sensitive topic they needed to discuss. He'd said it so many times: "Not over text. Not over email. Not over the phone. Meet in person."

She found out that Kyler was living in the Midwest.

"We should talk about this in person, not over the phone," she directed. "Can you come to DC?"

"I can fly there tomorrow morning," he replied. "As you know, this is an urgent situation. I'm scheduled to fly to the Kingdom in three days."

And just like that, one day after her television debut, she had set up a major client meeting. How would she actually pull off what he was asking for? She didn't know, but she felt she had the skills to try. And she could worry about the details after she was officially retained. Maybe this was the first step toward escaping all the difficulties within which she was currently trapped.

She poured herself a glass of wine and sat on her couch, where she had been spending so much time lately. There was real hope here. Maybe things could work out after all.

She began reading about Kyler on her phone, scouring various news articles. It was true—he really did win $8.8 million playing poker the July before last. She then saw what a turbulent and horribly embarrassing time he had had since then. Poor guy. Maybe she could actually help him here—do some good while jumpstarting her business and resurrecting her life.

As she continued her online research, she saw that there was news from the Kingdom. While the president was officially still considering the executive order to ban travel as well as potential military action, there were growing protests on the Kingdom's border. Some might have tried to cross in, and a few individuals were reported missing. Details were sketchy, but among the missing was American poker pro Priya Varma.

The photo of Priya within the online news article showed her sitting at a poker table, looking stylish and in command, wearing earbuds with a lot of poker chips in front of her. Yes, this was the same person Maggie had known, and she felt terrible for her now. Hopefully she was okay.

She told herself that whatever she did for Kyler or any other client, she would never minimize or justify inhumane conduct by evil regimes such as the Kingdom. But there was an important role to play in shaping US policy and public opinion, and that would be her job. Her task would be even more difficult because of this latest news. Would it make Kyler want to back out? Or would it just make her work more complex and therefore more lucrative?

She set up Google alerts for the Kingdom and Kyler Dawson and was actually successful in sleeping for about three continuous hours on her couch—her longest consecutive stretch in a week.

When she woke at about six thirty, with daylight streaming through the cracks in her wood shades, she picked up her phone and saw the alerts. Plenty more news about the Kingdom and the protests, but not much clear detail.

And then an alert delivered a new blog post about Kyler:

"Kyler Dawson Broke!! Amateur Poker Champ Blows Through $8.8 Million in 18.8 Months!!!"

It was posted on an amateurish-looking site called pokernewz.net, by a blogger with the screen name fullhouseparty1999.

"I've been told by a VERY RELIABLE source that poker champ, amateur legend, E-ZPass Kyler Dawson has LOST IT ALL and gambled EVERYTHING away!!!!"

There were a few more sentences, and a lot more exclamation marks. No specifics on the source or how he supposedly lost his fortune. She wanted to scream. She needed to punch something. But instead she just continued to stare at the screen.

Could this be accurate? Could her big, rich, potential savior client actually have *no money*?

Of course. Of course, he has no money. That's my life right now.

She looked elsewhere online for more information, but aside from snarky social media comments, she couldn't find anything noteworthy. And then she saw that Kyler himself had tweeted about fifteen minutes ago:

"I can't believe I even need to write this, but I am NOT broke. Please don't believe lies of a jealous blogger. I'm so grateful and happy with my life and success. #blessed"

She only had two seconds to consider the potential veracity of the tweet when her phone rang, with the caller ID proclaiming: "Bryce."

Seeing the name as her phone sang and shook sent a fresh pulse of apprehension throughout her body. She had waited so long to speak with him, and yet she felt so unprepared to say anything. She forced herself to answer while maintaining an anxious silence.

"Maggie?"

"I'm here."

"Listen Maggie, whatever's going on, you can't—"

"I know," she cut him off. "I'm sorry. I know. Not over text, not over the phone. But we need to talk about . . . you know. I'm having . . . a lot of trouble with it. I'm not okay with what happened."

"I have no idea what you're talking about," he replied firmly.

She knew that this was false, and she understood that he felt he needed to deny all culpability while speaking on the phone. He didn't want to acknowledge anything, especially during an unsecure conversation.

"And you looked fine when you were on TV," he continued skeptically.

Should I say thank you? No. Of course not. "I need to talk with you," she implored. "We need to meet." There were a few moments of painful waiting, so she added, "Please."

And then she received her reply. "Okay. Late this afternoon. Just the two of us."

First she was relieved, and then the relief was overwhelmed by the fact that she was terrified. She decided to keep her response simple.

"Thank you, Bryce."

Part Two

17

"I PROMISE I won't come inside you," he whispered with a tone of confident reassurance. And quite possibly Bryce kept that promise, although Maggie couldn't be sure.

A few moments earlier, the two were mostly undressed and on her bed. He was kissing her neck while she ran one hand through his thick brown hair and the other over his back. Her bra was already off, and as his right hand slowly worked its way down her abdomen, he simultaneously pulled down her green panties with his left.

"Are you on . . ." he started to ask.

She shook her head no. And then came the promise. A promise she had heard from guys more than once before, and she had always found it woefully insufficient.

"I promise I won't come inside you."

"No," she replied, as she put her hand under his chin and tilted his head up to look her in the eyes. "You have a condom?"

"I don't," he told her. "I'll pull out. I'll be really careful. I promise."

Again, not the first time she had heard a version of that.

She gently pushed him off her and then outstretched her right arm toward the small wood table next to the bed. She opened the drawer, reached in, and then came back to face Bryce, now silently offering a bronze condom wrapper that she held firmly between her right thumb and forefinger.

Of course, she could have just taken it out earlier, and maybe she should have, but she sensed that guys weren't necessarily thrilled by a woman effortlessly grabbing one from her own stash, and that men no doubt preferred to use their own if they brought one to the party.

But Bryce said he hadn't.

He looked at her for a moment, maybe a little taken aback. Was that a slight look of disappointment? Or possibly, hopefully, he was actually somewhat impressed, or at least intrigued.

"Okay then . . ." he responded with a smile, playfully snatching the item from her grasp and then moving down to start kissing her breasts.

Later, when he lay next to her, holding her protectively from behind as her back pressed against his comforting chest, she kept her eyes closed for a few seconds to savor the moment. In hindsight, she should have kept them closed. Because when she opened them, she saw it.

There it was, cast onto the floor a few feet from the bed. Seemingly torn, with its useless carcass lying lifelessly on her baby blue area rug.

She thought she'd seen it all from guys, but this was a new one, and she tried to understand its meaning. She had watched him put it on before he started having sex with her. Why was it now on the floor? How had it gotten so far away? And why was it ripped?

She was still facing away from him, and he still held her in his affectionate, post-coital embrace. But she could feel how tense her body suddenly became, and it would be at most only seconds before he noticed, so she knew she might as well speak now.

"When did you take it off?" she asked as calmly as she could, hoping for an answer that would ease the increasing panic building inside her.

No response came immediately, so she pulled away from his grasp, and turned around to look at him. The movement made her right hand become suddenly aware of what was no doubt his cum on her sheets. And she could feel it on the inside of her left thigh. Where else? Why not in the condom? And why wasn't he answering?

She looked at him, and he delicately stroked her cheek.

"It's okay," he said. "I was really careful."

She sat up quickly, pulling her head away from his touch, her naked body covered from the waist down by her new, white satin bed sheets. Her mind was racing with anxiety and a little bit of anger. But most of all, she was consumed by confusion.

What the fuck just happened?

"What happened to the condom?" she asked.

It was now increasingly obvious to her that at some point he had intentionally ripped it off. The tear didn't look like an accidental breakage during sex.

Now he sat up also, facing her at eye level. Across the room, his phone was buzzing angrily, and he glanced in its direction for a moment, clearly wanting to find out why it was blowing up. "Maggie, it's okay. Just don't get upset, alright?"

And then he rose and walked over to the dresser where he had placed his phone and began scrolling and reading intently.

"Fuck. Fuck fuck fuck . . ." he muttered. And then she watched as his fingers whipped across the keyboard and he appeared to fire off a quick message or two. Or three.

He looked up at her and lightly bit his lower lip for a moment before telling her, "I'm sorry, I have to go," and then began collecting his clothes from around the room and putting them back on.

She didn't need him to remind her that he was the White House chief of staff. He was busy. He was important. He was dealing with a million different fires all the time. He probably thought that she should consider herself fortunate that he had spent some of his valuable time with her. And she hated to admit to herself that, quite possibly, she would have felt that way a little if it had all ended differently. But she certainly didn't now.

"Just tell me what happened," she said solemnly. "Please don't leave without telling me."

He looked at her, then again at his phone, then toward the door, and finally back at her. He climbed back on the bed, he now clothed, she still completely undressed, and wrapped his arms around her in a tender, intended-to-be-soothing hug. And for a few seconds she let him hold her, hoping he would speak soon and answer her query as her left cheek pressed against his chest.

Finally, he did.

"I wore it almost the whole time. I promise. I just . . . it's hard for me to come with a condom on. Especially if I've been drinking."

She was trying to process this, to understand what this all really meant. He released his embrace and she looked off into the distance while she felt his gaze still on her.

"So you just ripped it off? How long were you having sex with me without it?"

"Just a couple of minutes," he answered, and she knew that really meant *at least a couple of minutes.*

She rose, picked up a light bathrobe from a nearby chair, and wrapped it around herself tightly as he also stood. She folded her arms across her chest. It was suddenly cold in her apartment and she needed to turn up the heat.

"I told you to wear a condom," she said pointedly.

"No, you *handed* me a condom," he replied. "And I wore it almost the entire time. Except just at the very end. And I pulled out before I came. I promise. Maggie, I swear I was careful."

She was growing increasingly angry at Bryce but even more livid at herself. Why had she allowed this to happen? Why hadn't she been clearer about what she wanted?

And she was concerned about the possible consequences for her. She would need to get Plan B. And STI testing. Would that be all? She was already dealing with so much—she couldn't handle any more.

She needed to tell herself that this was not a big deal. Yes, it was wrong—clearly, undisputedly wrong. But guys had done sleazy things before, and those instances hadn't disrupted her life. This felt like it might be different, but she couldn't let it be.

She wanted to take a shower and wash those sheets right away, as soon as she could get him out of her apartment—something he was clearly itching to do anyway.

"Just leave," she instructed, still looking away from him.

"Maggie, don't do this. You're making a big issue out of something that's not."

"I'm just telling you to leave. You said you had to leave. So now I'm saying 'leave.'"

He sighed with frustration as his phone resumed a relentless buzzing. For the moment he wasn't looking at it.

"Okay," he finally said. And then he put his arms around her again, and kissed her lightly on the forehead. She looked up at him and saw that he seemed to be sincerely concerned that she was upset. Or at least he did a fine job of displaying the appropriate facial expressions to appear as if he was—slight serious frown, narrowed focused eyes, furrowed brow—while gingerly stroking her back.

And then he was gone.

There was no communication either way between the two of them for days until:

"I know ur very busy but we need to talk about what happened last week"

Now, they were finally scheduled to have that talk in a few hours. She knew she urgently needed to speak with him, but she couldn't figure out what she wanted from the conversation. An apology? An explanation? She was looking for something that would enable her to put this behind her and not have it infect her life anymore. What she really needed was for him or someone else to tell her that it never happened.

At least she would have a distraction before their scheduled meeting so she couldn't entirely dwell on it all day. First, she would meet

Kyler, potentially her first consulting client (also potentially a broke-ass gambler with a life maybe even more fucked up than hers, who might be completely wasting her time).

And then her phone buzzed. She grabbed it from atop her bedside table, the one that faithfully stored her condoms, and saw that there might be even more to this day than Kyler and Bryce.

18

"HEY MAGS!! U around this afternoon? Bunch of stuff in flux but may need u on air later today if you're available thx!!"

"Mags"? Where had her young booker gotten that from? Maggie never used that nickname and disliked the few times anyone called her that. On another day, in another situation, during her former life, she would have been annoyed, but now she didn't have the luxury or the energy.

"Bunch of stuff in flux"? *Yeah*, she thought, *I have a bunch of stuff in flux too . . .*

She responded quickly, considering and then rejecting the impulse to call her "Nats."

"Hey Natalie! I have a few client meetings scheduled today but happy to try to move them around. When is approx hit time?"

She felt that her text hit all the right notes. It made her look busy and in demand (client meetings—plural!) but also flexible and available, and prompt with her response.

But it was also ridiculously unrealistic. No fucking way could she try to reschedule with Bryce—she absolutely needed to see him and he *was* the White House chief of staff. He was reluctantly meeting her anyway and probably would never agree to another meeting if she cancelled or tried to postpone.

And Kyler Dawson? Maybe there was a little flexibility there, but his matter was urgent and she didn't want to risk losing her first potential client. Or maybe he'd be impressed if she changed the time because of a national television appearance?

"Not sure yet but will get back to u shortly thx!! Crazy news day here, everyone scrambling bc Kinum story and now Priya Varma stuff. Producer also trying to put together segment in 8p block with someone who knows Varma. Personal, non-political angle."

Eight that evening. Prime time. Much bigger audience, potentially huge exposure. It could put her in a totally different strata from being an inexperienced daytime analyst. She knew that prime time hosts and bookers often refused to use anyone who was appearing during daytime and it was so hard to get in the door with them.

Her day was already beyond daunting, and for a moment that kept her from texting the response she wanted to send. Could she really do a major prime time television interview right after meeting Kyler and Bryce? What emotional shape would she be in after the latter discussion?

Yet she knew that she had no choice. Her life might be headed toward failure—all available evidence suggested that it was a real possibility. But she was determined not to crash and burn for lack of effort to seize every opportunity.

So she stood in the middle of her apartment, tossed the hairbrush she had been holding onto the sofa, and texted back:

"We were actually college friends. We went to Penn together."

She waited a few moments, and then a reply popped up:

"Omg!!! That's so perfect! I had no idea. U available tonight??"

The day had just gotten even more challenging. Maggie wondered if she would ever again feel a sense of peace and quiet and happiness. Maybe on a beach somewhere having a few cocktails while the sun was still up. Possibly at a nice spa without her phone, totally unplugged from the world. Or just lounging around in her apartment, reading a book or bingeing some show, passing time without a care in the world. Would she one day have a sense of security and positivity again, the way she used to? Or would she now forever be in crisis mode, attempting to avoid failure and financial difficulty, while struggling to come to terms with a brief nonconsensual sexual experience with a former boss?

Either way, her response was obvious:

"Absolutely ☺"

And her booker quickly answered:

"Great!! Forget this afternoon—will pass ur info to tonight's producer. She'll b in touch shortly!"

Maggie soaked in the significance of what had just happened. If she could survive this day—if she could make it to the evening in one piece—she would be a prime time guest on national television.

Through it all, she would need to somehow find the time, energy, and concentration to get up to speed on the Priya Varma and Kingdom news and figure out what she should say on the segment. She would have to square her comments with both her sincere sympathy for Priya and the position she had already staked out on her last segment, which was clearly at odds with what Priya was advocating for.

How would she do this? And when? She felt a renewed surge of anxiety as she acknowledged that she really didn't know.

But if her prime time appearance was somehow successful, who knew what else was possible.

19

AS KYLER marveled at the abundant beauty and history of the nation's capital, he was filled with regret that he had never been able to afford to take his children there while his family was intact. It would have been so nice to stroll with them on the breathtaking National Mall, to visit the Air and Space Museum, the Lincoln Memorial, and maybe even the White House. It would have inspired his children and been a powerful bonding experience.

But it never happened. Flying five people to DC would just have been too expensive, not to mention the hotel, the meals, the overpriced souvenirs. And by the time he did have the money, his family life had been so ravaged that a Washington vacation was unthinkable. So the memory he so much wanted to have of a wonderful few days together in Washington would now exist only as a taunting reminder of what might have occurred if he had lived a better life, if he hadn't been laid off, if things had just broken his way when he needed them to.

Now he was finally there, right near the awe-inspiring white Capitol dome, walking toward the Regus office address on North Capitol Street that Maggie had texted him. It was a frigid day in DC, and he wore his charcoal gray coat over worn jeans and a thick tan sweater. He entered the building a few minutes before their scheduled noon meeting, checked in with a young desk receptionist, hung his coat in a guest closet, and sat on one of the chairs in the waiting area as people shuffled past.

He forced himself to avoid his phone, especially social media. He needed to be undistracted and professional for this to go well, for this successful former White House official to agree to work with him. He couldn't be rattled by what was no doubt a plethora of people eagerly devouring his reputation online. Hopefully Maggie would agree to help fix that, and to enable him to reach the ultimate goal—being able to participate in the Kingdom's tournament and take home the $20 million prize.

"Kyler," a female voice said warmly and energetically. "It's nice to meet you."

He looked up and saw the woman from television, there in front of him, dressed in a sharp gray business suit with a lavender blouse. Her light brown hair fell over her shoulders and a friendly smile graced her beautiful face as she extended her hand toward him. Their age difference was probably seven or eight years, as she looked to be in her late twenties.

He jumped up and happily accepted her touch, taking her hand in his and then, after what he assumed was the appropriate amount of time, letting go.

"Ms. Raster, it's great to meet you," he said.

"Please—just Maggie," she replied and then motioned for him to follow her. "Let's talk in my office."

He walked with her down a hallway and then into an office with a desk, sofa, and a few chairs. A painting of a river reflecting a colorful sunset hung on one of the beige walls, and a window revealed a few snowflakes starting to fall outside. She closed the door behind him and then gestured toward the navy sofa. He took his seat as she sat in one of the nearby chairs, a few feet away from him.

"Would you like something to drink? Coffee?" Maggie asked.

"No, thanks. I'm good. And thank you for meeting with me. I know you're very busy."

"Well, thank *you* for reaching out to *me*," she answered amicably.

"You were really great on TV," Kyler gushed. "Are you on a lot? Sorry, I don't watch much TV news. When I do, I just see people shouting at each other about things I don't care about." He instantly realized he'd probably just offended her—he was already messing this up. So before she could reply he clarified, "But I don't mean you, of course!"

"No worries, Kyler," she said with a sweet laugh and wave of her hand. "And thank you. Yeah, I've been on a few times lately. Actually, I'll be on tonight in the eight o'clock hour."

"That's awesome. I'll definitely watch."

"Thanks. So . . ." she transitioned. "Tell me about this poker tournament."

"Do you know how poker tournaments work?" he asked.

She shook her head.

"Okay. Well, tournaments can operate in different ways, but in most of the big ones, like this event in the Kingdom, everyone starts with the same number of chips. You keep playing until you lose all of them, which means you're eliminated. Usually the last 10 to 15 percent of the players remaining win some prize money, with the most going to the final person surviving. But the Kingdom is just having one huge prize which will go to the last player standing. Does that make sense?"

She nodded. "It makes enough sense for what I need to know now. So in this case the grand prize is—"

"Twenty million," he interrupted. It was exhilarating hearing it emerge from his own mouth, and he loved how the number instantly made her adorable brown eyes widen just a bit.

"And did I read correctly that there are one hundred players?" she asked while looking at him and no doubt trying to assess his potential as a worthwhile client. "So basically a one in a hundred chance to win $20 million? Not bad. Definitely better than any state lottery."

"Well, yes, one hundred players. But you have to understand

who these players are. The top pros are basically all boycotting this event, especially the Americans. The tournament will be filled with minor celebrities and rich Eurotrash guys who have business connections to the Kingdom and think they can play poker. I'm far from the best poker player in the world but I *will* be one of the best at this tournament. I really believe that. It's an incredible, *incredible* opportunity."

"Does it really matter who these people are?" she asked. "Doesn't it come down to what cards you get?"

"There's absolutely luck involved. You can do everything right and lose. You can do everything wrong and win—for a little bit. But ultimately it's a game of skill, and playing smart maximizes your chances of winning, while doing things wrong increases your chances of losing. If I can play in this tournament—"

"You're going to play smart. And you believe you have a very good chance of winning."

"Exactly." It was so easy to talk with her. So comfortable to sit with her, to look at her. He was so fortunate to have her undivided attention, and he needed to get the point while he still had it. The president could act at any moment. "So if the president issues an executive order banning travel to the Kingdom, I'm . . ." Kyler resisted the urge to end the sentence with "fucked."

"You lose this opportunity," she finished for him.

He wanted to jump up and scream that it wasn't just losing "this opportunity"—it was losing his last chance to ever be successful, to have a comfortable life, to overcome nearly insurmountable debt and stress and guilt. But he couldn't look desperate. She wouldn't want to work with a loser. God, she already surely knew so many embarrassing things about him just from basic online searches. She was treating him with such respect, professionalism, and kindness—what a switch from all the disparagement he received elsewhere.

"It's an opportunity that will never come again for me," he said.

"One tournament. No buy-in. Twenty million dollars. I just need to be able to play. I need your help."

"Listen Kyler," she replied, looking him directly in the eyes. "I know the people who will be influencing whether this executive order happens. I can't promise any result of course, but I think if we worked together and started right away we'd have a decent shot at stopping it and making sure you have that chance to enter the tournament."

"That would be amazing," he told her.

"But this won't be easy. And even if we're successful getting you over there, the public backlash against you will be fierce. So much more than what you're already seeing."

"I know," he replied soberly. The animosity directed his way was getting worse, and this tournament would greatly exacerbate that. But if he won $20 million, would it matter?

"I can help you with that, too, Kyler. We'll present your story to the world in a way that stops this nasty narrative that you're a bad person. I've read about you, and now I've met you, and I don't think you are. I think you're a good man. Other people need to know that, too."

He let this soak in, and sensed that his eyes were on the verge of tearing up. But he couldn't allow himself to look weak in front of her. *It's true. I'm not a terrible person. I want my kids to have a happy life. I don't want them to hate me. I don't want them to grow up seeing me as a failure. As a fucking joke.* "Thank you, Maggie. I would love that."

"Great," she replied. "I have my standard contract for you to review. It's nothing too complicated. I know the tournament begins in less than a week and we need to get started right away. I also ask for a paid retainer before I work with a new client."

The past year and a half had given him a crash course on the importance of contracts, or lack thereof. The mere mention of it now brought forth a flood of painful memories and emotions. But a contract with Maggie wasn't really a concern. A paid retainer? That was a separate issue, and it made his head start to throb.

How was he going to pay her? He'd hoped she would bill him after it was all done, and he could compensate her from his extensive winnings from the Kingdom. And if he didn't win, he would be so devastated financially that one more invoice he couldn't pay wouldn't matter. It would be a problem for later and maybe he could just figure it out then, like he often did. Or didn't.

"How big of a retainer?" he asked as calmly as possible.

"Fifty thousand dollars," she answered. He hesitated in responding, so she added, "When we spoke on the phone, you said money is not a problem."

"It's not a problem," he tried to assure her. "I just have funds tied up in a lot of things right now. I'd have to figure out what to liquidate. It would take some time. We don't have that time because this situation is moving so fast."

He looked at her, and saw the benevolent, enchanting smile began to fade. He detected a hint of disappointment in her eyes as her expression moved from excited and ingratiating to something more distant and unapproachable.

She hadn't responded for a few seconds, and he considered what additional explanation he could provide. But it was probably of no use. People who didn't really know poker often talked about great players being able to read other people. But what was often even more important, Kyler knew, was being able to tell whether other players were correctly reading *you*. And Kyler saw that she now completely saw through him. She had no doubt read the blog posts. She had just seen his deep hesitation to pay a retainer. Of course, she now knew he was full of shit, and it was only moments before she would kick him out of her office in disgust.

"How much can you pay now?" she asked with an impatient tone that implied that she already believed she knew the answer.

He considered her question, looked down at the cream-colored carpet, and then directed his eyes back at Maggie. "You may have seen a blog post—"

"Yes. I did."

"I want you to know that it's full of lies. I'm not broke. Not even close. I won *eight point eight million dollars* a year and a half ago, and I'm all set financially. But I just can't pay a retainer now. I'm sorry."

She leaned back in her chair, took this in, and nodded in thought as her tongue briefly moved across the inside of her upper lip. He could tell she was frustrated. He could see that she was considering a variety of responses.

Finally, she spoke.

"So what do you want to do here, Kyler?" she said with exasperation. "I'm not a *pro bono* shop. And I'm not relying on an invoice being paid after this is all over."

"I . . . I totally understand. I'm not here to waste your time. I'm very grateful that you've agreed to meet with me. That you're considering helping me. I've read about your stellar background and experience. I saw you on TV. I see you here. I know you're the one who can get this done. And then I'm the one who can win this tournament."

"Kyler, I appreciate that. And of course, I've done my research on you."

"What's out there on me is full of lies. Let me explain the truth."

"I don't need to know. Really."

"There's so much bullshit out there. And the stuff with my wife. It's so embarrassing. And I just want to say it's *totally* not true. She—"

She held up her hand. "And I *totally* don't want to hear about that," and then added for emphasis, "Really."

"Okay. Sorry. Look, it's obviously been a tough year for me. Really tough. But this opportunity is very real. And very big. And without your help I probably lose it. So how about . . ."

He trailed off, considering his next words. He needed her. He needed her help.

"How about what?" she asked with an odd blend of hope and annoyance.

"Ten percent of my winnings. Two million dollars."

She considered this for a few moments, with her thumb gently grazing her chin. Finally, she shook her head.

"If you lose I'll get nothing. I'll have utilized a lot of personal and professional capital to make this happen. And I don't need to understand poker to know the odds are against you. I have a business to run, and I just can't agree to that."

He summoned all the confidence he could. "I'm going to win," he told her. For once, no part of him was faking. He really believed it. If he could just get there . . .

She stood, turned her back to him and walked over to the window. It was still snowing outside on a scenic winter day in Washington. He couldn't see her face, but he could tell she was deep in thought.

After a minute, he rose, too. He wanted to approach her, or say something, or both, but he did neither and just stood there in silence. He could now see her reflection in the glass. Her eyes were wide open, vacantly looking out into the distance. Her face was somber and still.

Another minute passed and then another, and Kyler continued to wait. With each additional second, his stress level rose.

Call the clock.

Finally, she turned back to face him, with a new look of determination and purpose that startled him and sent a wave of nervous energy through his body

"Fifty," she said simply.

At first, he didn't understand. "Fifty?" he asked.

"Fifty percent," she clarified. "Ten million dollars."

Kyler thought about how he had gone through hell because of Nolan wanting half of his winnings last time. Now it was supposed to be all his, for him and his family. His World Series of Poker fortune had been progressively taken from him by all sorts of vultures, and he had been determined to do things right this time. He promised himself that these winnings would be his, with no significant claims by anyone else. And now already, before he even departed for the tournament, she was telling him that he would need to give up 50 percent.

Ten million dollars. A tremendous amount of money. Life-changing money. And he saw that Maggie looked empowered at the idea of laying claim to it.

The executive order decision was probably imminent. She had worked for the president. She knew him, knew his people, knew this complicated Washington world. He needed her. Now.

Clearly, he couldn't stay with 10 percent. That would be insulting to her, and he would lose everything. She would cast him away and turn her attention to her real clients, the ones who could actually pay up front. He couldn't let that happen.

So what should he counter with? Twenty-five? Would that be enough?

"How about 30 percent?" he suggested. "Halfway between our two numbers. That's $6 million for you."

"No," she replied immediately and firmly. "Fifty percent. I believe I can help you, Kyler. No guarantees of course, and it won't be easy. The whole situation is escalating quickly, and we don't have much time. But I think I can make this happen. If you commit to 50 percent, I'll work with you. I'll do my part, you'll do yours, and maybe together we can pull this off."

Kyler wondered what would happen if he told her that 50 percent was too much, and that he was prepared to walk out. Was she bluffing? She had said she didn't know poker, but she had risen high in the world of DC politics at a young age, so she was no doubt highly skilled at negotiation and manipulation.

She was a successful young woman and in general didn't need to be working for his loser ass, but even for her this had to be a lot of money. What were the chances she would really let him leave without an agreement if he told her the highest he would go was 35 percent?

He also considered what he might win if he left right now without retaining her. Possibly all $20 million. More likely nothing at all. And it wasn't lost on him that they were wrangling over a crazy amount of money that wasn't theirs. A high-stakes negotiating session for money that might never exist for either of them.

"And I'll need it in writing," she added. "Last time you offered someone half it didn't go very well, so let's avoid that situation this time."

"Now wait a minute!" he exclaimed, taking a step toward her, suddenly fired up by her unnecessary, inaccurate, and insulting characterization of events that were so fresh and so painful. She had been controlling the conversation, but now it was time for him to stand up for himself. "First of all, I *never* offered him half. And he ended up more than fine, so you're doubly wrong!"

Her expression and tone softened and she also took a step closer, bringing back the warm demeanor he'd basked in earlier.

"I'm sorry," she said. "That was unfair. I apologize. I do need our agreement in writing, though. That's my policy for all clients."

"I have no problem with that."

"Look, Kyler, whatever happened to you over the past year, whatever happened to the money, none of that can change the fact that you've shown you can be a winner in an *unbelievably* huge way. You won *eight point eight million dollars* in a fucking poker game! This happened. So I want to help you be a winner again. Let's work together and make that a reality. Fifty-fifty is fair. You'll be winning a major poker tournament. I'll be working to steer the policy of the *President of the United States* and protect your reputation."

Her message was clear. She was peeling away his façade and calling him out for what she believed he really was—a loser now who probably had no money. He didn't like that at all. But she was also saying that she knew he could be highly successful when given the chance. She was saying she believed in him. And didn't she? If she thought he couldn't pull this off, why would she ever bother joining forces with him, calling in favors with important people, merging her reputation with his?

He wasn't leaving the room without making a deal. But could he suggest 40 percent? Would she really walk away if he told her he couldn't go higher than that, which would potentially earn her $8 million? Unlikely, but possible. And he didn't want to risk it at this point. He didn't like giving up so much, but there was no better option right now.

He took some solace in the fact that he wouldn't owe her anything if he failed to win the tournament. But that was actually a small detail, considering his existence would be on life support then anyway.

So 50 percent it would be. "Alright," he said with exaggerated resignation. "Fifty-fifty. I just hope you appreciate it when I win you ten million fucking dollars."

She flashed him a smile. "I just hope you appreciate it when I win *you* ten million fucking dollars," she replied.

He laughed. This was exciting. On a lot of levels.

"So," he said, "Where's this contract?"

She took a document from the nearby desk and then they both sat back down. She paged through it, filling in a few blanks with a black pen, and then handed it to Kyler.

He looked through the seven-page contract. The key points were clear enough: he was retaining her for confidential consulting services, there was no guarantee of success, and in lieu of a set fee she would be entitled to half of any tournament winnings at the upcoming Goodwill Poker Classic in the Kingdom.

Some parts were more opaque, such as sections on limitation of liability and indemnity that might as well have been in a foreign language. But there was no time to consult a lawyer. And the lawyers he knew best had already taken enough of his money.

Kyler signed and handed it back to her, and then she signed. She left the room for a couple of minutes, then returned and handed him a photocopy.

"Thank you, Kyler," she said, reaching out for another handshake. "I'll get to work on this immediately. I'll keep you posted."

"Good luck," he replied as he took her hand. "And thank you."

He was just turning to leave when she started talking again.

"One more thing," she said. "There's a lot of criticism that playing in this tournament is tacitly supporting some really bad people, and this public sentiment may only get worse. But even though that opinion is greatly overblown, of course there's a kernel of truth there. So why don't we agree that if you win—if we pull this off—we both devote a significant amount of the money to helping people in need. Maybe here, maybe elsewhere. Maybe even in the Kingdom."

"Absolutely," Kyler replied immediately. "That sounds perfect."

Because *she* was perfect. So engaging, so smart, so successful.

She'd probably make a really good poker player, Kyler thought. *Maybe one day she'll let me teach her how to play . . .*

20

LIFE IS FULL of gambles. Maggie's biggest had been stepping away from a coveted job in the White House, one that so many aspiring politicos would kill for, in order to start her own consulting business at a time when she had no real savings and no waiting clients.

But in the sense that most people used the word—*gamble*—that activity had never been for her. Sure, there was the bachelorette party in Las Vegas over a year ago, her first time in the city, when she won $40 at roulette. But putting $20 on black a few times while her intoxicated crew laughed and cheered as they killed some time before hitting the clubs—that was the most insignificant part of that weekend. She had nothing against people who gambled, but it just never really appealed to her, never gave her that exciting rush that others received.

Vegas. That was back when life was fun. Remember that? Before she was drowning in stress and debt and parental medical concerns. And before she brought Bryce back to her apartment. Before he . . .

Would life ever be fun again? She had been surrounded by great friends, grateful for a dream job on the other side of the country, imbibing and partying and happy. Her group had all been cool enough to be crazy for the weekend, but smart and professional enough to be highly selective with photos and social media.

Now, so abruptly, the idea that she could ever be in the frame of mind for something like that again seemed impossible.

But back to gambling . . .

Somehow, her predominantly non-gambling existence now had $10 million riding on a poker game and on her ability to help a broke, divorced father of three play in it. Kyler had said that luck was involved but that poker was generally a game of skill. Could he summon the necessary skill to achieve their joint goal? Could she?

And now she was cold, so cold, as she walked with her stylish light blue winter coat hugging her body to the secluded park Bryce had designated as their meeting place. Snow had stopped falling but covered the ground. The sun had set, and a few park lights illuminated the area. Her brown Dolce Vita boots made a *crush crush* sound as she stepped through the white-covered grass.

Before she headed over, she read on her phone that the White House was expected to reach a decision regarding a potential executive order banning travel to the Kingdom "very soon." As White House chief of staff, Bryce would have the power to influence whether the president would sign. With the tournament five days away, this was Maggie's one shot with Bryce to urge him to stop it.

But of course, that's not why they were meeting. Her original purpose remained crucially important to her. She needed something from this conversation regarding that night, but she was still unsure exactly what that was. Some kind of explanation, some kind of closure. Most of all, she needed to gain control over a memory that was controlling her, and she hoped that talking with Bryce might accomplish that.

Her fear was that the growing feeling of violation was here to stay, that ten years from now it would still be a significant fixture in her life, casting a shadow over all her personal and professional interactions.

And there was Bryce, standing across the park by a tree whose branches had long shed its leaves for winter. He was wearing a dark coat and gloves, his breath visible as he exhaled amid the winter air.

It was the first time she'd seen him since he left her apartment, and she felt a flood of both sadness and anger. Maybe this was a mistake. Maybe seeing him again would exacerbate her fraught emotions instead of providing healing. But she couldn't leave now.

"Hi Maggie," he said as she approached him. And before she could respond, he added, "I need your phone."

The command jolted her. She didn't like this beginning at all. She had come here to regain control over her life, and he was issuing orders.

"I'm not recording you," she answered.

He extended his right hand, palm facing toward the sky. His eyes were firm, unwavering in their stare and message that she needed to comply in order for this conversation to proceed.

She reached into her purse, withdrew her phone, and handed it to Bryce. He looked at the screen, and then at Maggie.

"What's your code?"

"I'm not giving you my code," she replied, feeling slightly emboldened by her ability to push back.

"Fine," he said, handing her back the phone. "You unlock it."

She knew this wasn't worth fighting over, so she took it and did as commanded, and then handed it back to him. She watched as his fingers flicked across the screen, his eyes carefully reviewing what was in front of him.

Then, apparently satisfied, he thrust the phone into his coat pocket. Maggie wondered if she should demand it back immediately but decided not to—there was too much else that she needed from him right now.

There was an awkward silence as each waited for the other to talk about the real reason for their meeting. Finally, Maggie decided to proceed. She had asked—repeatedly—to speak with him and she knew time was short.

"Thank you for meeting me, Bryce," she said calmly, intending to sound as nonconfrontational as possible. "We need to talk about what happened the other night."

He nodded. "I'd like to give you a hug, but I don't know if you want that," he said with a sympathetic look.

"I don't want that."

"Okay, I respect that."

"Thank you," she said, and then immediately cursed herself for again uttering that phrase, now twice in the past minute. Yes, she was trying to be conciliatory in order to hopefully have a more healthy and helpful conversation. But he had callously disrupted her existence and he didn't deserve her thanks for anything. She needed to stop saying those words and acting like he was doing her a favor.

"Bryce, I'm having a very hard time dealing with what you did. I'm barely sleeping. I can't eat. I'm constantly thinking about it."

"I didn't *do* anything," he answered with a sigh.

"Please don't say that. I don't want to play games. And I'm not here to attack you. I want to have a real conversation about what happened. We've known each other for a long time, and I know we can do that. I need us to do that."

"Maggie, I don't know what you're talking about," he said, almost robotically, not as if he really believed it.

She was growing increasingly aggravated. Maybe it would be best if she just explicitly described his transgression out loud. It might help him really understand, just as she sought to understand it herself.

"We both know that's not true," she said. "Please don't make this even more difficult. We both know what you did."

"Maggie, don't try to pull some crap about me doing something to you, like I *made* you do something. You were all over me and you know it."

"Bryce—"

"You kept grabbing my dick in the Uber and I had to *repeatedly* tell you to stop."

She glared at him. "First, that's an exaggeration. Second, it's totally irrelevant."

She was about to continue, and then it occurred to her that his statements were too crafted. Maybe she wasn't the target audience.

"Bryce, are *you* recording this?"

"Fuck no, I'm not recording this! You think I want a recording? You think I'm an idiot?"

The conciliatory portion of the discussion was clearly over. She needed to just get to the point before the whole conversation disintegrated.

"Look, obviously I wanted to have sex with you. Also obviously, I wanted you to wear a condom. That was important to me. You knew that. And you took it off and had sex with me without one anyway, when you knew I wouldn't be able to tell. That was wrong, Bryce. That was really fucked up."

"I *didn't* know that," he shot back. "And it was for less than a minute."

"Now it's less than a minute? That night you told me it was a couple of minutes!"

"Well, I didn't time it precisely! Oh my God, you're fucking crazy!" he exclaimed, as if he had just realized this fact in a tragic epiphany. And he gave her a patronizing look that said: *Oh, I see—you're one of those insane girls who seem normal but then go batshit nuts after having sex with a guy.*

She started to question whether she was making too much out of something that didn't merit it. Nothing that was happening here was making anything better. Was it possible she was overreacting? Was this conversation even worth the added grief? Then she checked herself before she went too far down that road. She needed to confront him about what he did, about what it had done to her. That alone was enough to make this meeting a necessity.

"I had to get Plan B. And STI testing."

"Why would you do that? I didn't come inside you. I told you that. I said I wouldn't and I didn't. And I don't have an STI," he responded, as if just the mention of the acronym was deeply insulting, and foolish of her to utter.

"Well, you had unprotected sex with me. How do you know I don't have one?"

"I know you don't," he said decisively.

"How do you know?"

"Do you?"

"No."

"Exactly."

She glanced down at her boots, which were covered with snow as her toes started to freeze. She shifted and flexed her feet in an attempt to reboot their circulation.

"Bryce," she said, looking back up at him. "I don't know why you're being like this. I'm upset about what you did. I'm having a very hard time with it. I thought talking with you, in good faith, would be helpful for us."

"For *us*?"

"Okay, for me."

He was silent for a few seconds, seeming to search for the right words that would get him out of this conversation. "I'm sorry if I did something to make you feel bad, Maggie," he finally stated.

Yes, it was a non-apology apology, used so often in their political world, acknowledging absolutely no transgressions. But at least those two words were in there. That was a start, and it meant something to her, albeit just a little.

Nevertheless, she reminded herself: *Don't say "thank you" . . .*

"I just don't understand why you're doing this," he continued. "I see you're upset. I'm taking that seriously, but . . . come on. Can't we just both move on?"

Move on.

"I want to," she replied. "That's *all* I want."

"Look, most people in this world never get a real chance to live a good life, to be successful, to make a difference, to be happy. We both have the opportunity for all that. To have everything we've ever wanted. Let's not fuck it up by getting derailed with minor issues, okay?"

Maggie fervently wished she could receive an objective, authoritative answer from some divine all-knowing being as to what was wrong or right here. Was she blowing this out of proportion? She didn't think so, but how could she be sure? She wasn't ready to share this experience with others, she couldn't trust Bryce's view, and unfortunately she now felt that she couldn't trust her own either.

Later she would need to wrestle with all this and attempt to sort it out, but she needed to face the fact that her time with Bryce was probably almost up, and she had something else to discuss with the White House chief of staff. She was in no mood to talk with him about the Kingdom, and there was no easy transition, but she had to make one. This was her one chance to help her first client. To maybe earn $10 million. To change her life forever.

"Bryce, can I ask you about something completely different?"

"Of course," he said, appearing to welcome the change in topic.

"It's about the Kingdom's poker tournament and the potential EO."

"Yeah, I saw your segment. You're good on TV, Maggie. Keep doing it, and it'll definitely help your business."

"Thanks."

"Just one minor suggestion," he said gently. "If I were you I'd steer away from debating people whose family members have just been murdered. Not the *greatest* positioning for you because to some viewers you'll appear—"

"Yeah yeah, no, I get it," she interrupted. "Noted."

There was a silent pause, and she could tell he was about to announce his departure.

"So . . ." she began. This was awkward and uncomfortable for so many reasons. She needed to just plunge forward. "I have a client who wants to play in the tournament," Maggie explained.

"Isn't it invite only?" he asked.

"Yes. Yes, it is. And he's been invited. He's American. And I think he should be allowed to participate."

He ran his right glove through his hair as he considered what she said, then directed an unsettlingly cold look at her. She felt her pulse rate increase as she braced for what he was about to say or do.

"And what do you want to ask me about it?" he said slowly. "You said you wanted to ask me something, right?"

"I wanted to . . . wanted to ask you to oppose the EO. I think it's a mistake. It's understandable that the White House would want to take a tough stand against the Kingdom, but it's unfair and counter-productive to ban travel there. I just wanted to be able to discuss it with you."

He nodded as he considered her remarks and then grimaced. "You're a disgusting person, you know that?" he charged.

"What?!"

"Now I see what's going on here. None of this made sense, but now I understand."

"Wh-what are you talking about?!"

"You bring up this ridiculous MeToo shit, hold it over my head, and then tell me to use my position to help one of your clients!"

"No, no, no Bryce. No, no, no. No. That's not what I'm doing. Please," she implored. "Let's just talk about this. I swear I'm not doing that."

"So you'll go public unless I help you?!" he said, his voice rising, his eyes full of fury. "You fucking bitch."

"Bryce, no! I swear. You know that's not me. I would *never* do that to you."

This was now a catastrophe. Of course, she would never threaten someone like that. Her issues with Bryce were deeply personal, and very troubling, and it would be a nightmare to release them for public consumption, so she could be lampooned and harassed and defined forever by one to two minutes of her life. And as angry as she was at Bryce, as much as she yearned to secure this $10 million prize, she would never use what he did to her for leverage. It was against every fiber of her morality. Plus, she was smart enough to understand the laws of blackmail and the real prison time that could very well result. No, this was absurd, and she needed to quickly convince him of that.

Then she saw something beyond rage in his eyes. It was terror. The normally poised chief of staff to the president of the United States was now nervously moving his hands together, and darting his eyes around in fear. She could tell he was full of trepidation, and realized he must be thinking of all the high-profile men whose reputations and careers and lives were snuffed out recently because of public allegations of sexual misconduct. It was a new world in which a near-universally praised person could be instantly turned into a pariah, where a man with an extraordinary career could quickly become unemployed and unemployable, and she saw that he now seethed and squirmed as he considered that this might be his fate.

This was not what she wanted at all. And suddenly her primary goal was to find a way to comfort the man whom she had come to the park to confront.

"Bryce! Listen to me, please! I will never, ever, ever make a public allegation against you. I swear! No matter what. Never. *No matter what.* Understand?"

He shook his head in anger and there might have been the beginning of a tear forming in his left eye, and then he turned and began briskly walking away.

"Bryce!" she called after him. "Please, Bryce!"

She considered running after him, but was frozen by not only actual cold but also a complete lack of confidence that she could do anything besides make things even worse.

"Bryce!" she yelled again, while he ignored her and kept moving. And then she remembered . . . "My phone!"

As he continued walking, he reached into his coat pocket, withdrew her device, and tossed it with contempt over his shoulder.

It landed silently a few feet in front of her and vanished into the snow.

21

JACQUES WAS getting nowhere with the two Kingdom officials who were doing a very effective job of providing no useful information while appearing to be collegial and earnest.

They sat around a large wood conference table in a top floor office looking out at the capital. At the head of the room, high up on the wall, a framed headshot of the crown prince watched benevolently over the assembled.

Of course, his photo was there. It was everywhere.

Both men had stylish cropped beards and expensive tailored suits, with one man shorter and stockier than the other. They listened to his questions and pretended to be responsive, but Jacques knew it was all a game to them, toying with the Canadian ambassador and subtly rebuffing his questions. For Jacques, this couldn't get more serious.

"Gentlemen," he said, "With all due respect, you're not really answering my question. The international community is seeking an independent investigation into the murder of Emily Kinum. Will your nation cooperate and allow investigators unfettered access to the relevant locations, witnesses, and evidence?"

"It's not a simple question, Jacques," replied the taller one, who was the foreign affairs minister. "Of course we want to assist in finding the killer or killers. But we have our own investigation that's very active, and we have issues of sovereignty and logistics that have to be considered before allowing foreigners to conduct a criminal investigation on our soil."

"We all have the same goal," the other man responded. "We want to bring those responsible to justice. We're all on the same team here. There's no disagreement about what needs to be done."

"Just to be clear," Jacques said, his frustration growing, "I want you to understand that I'm going to report that you are stonewalling an independent fact-finding into Emily Kinum's murder. The international community is unwavering in its demand—"

"You mean the United States," interrupted the foreign affairs minister. "America is demanding."

"No, I certainly do *not* mean that. Canada joins in this call, as do many others."

Before they could respond, both men abruptly rose and stood straight in response to the door opening and another gentleman entering—tall, handsome, slicked back hair, dark gray suit, red tie and pocket square, perfectly put together.

"Mr. Ambassador," the man said, extending his hand.

Jacques rose and shook hands, not the first time in his career that, for diplomatic reasons, he had to press the flesh with an authoritarian tyrant. But on this occasion, because of Emily, it felt different, more personal, and thoroughly sickening.

"Prince," he said in return.

"Have my men been helpful?" he asked cordially.

"No, of course not," Jacques responded. "Let's be direct, shall we? The international community wants to conduct an independent investigation into the murder of Emily Kinum. Are you going to cooperate?"

"Ambassador, we're doing our own investigation. *Very* thorough. And I believe we're close to finding those responsible. Once we've concluded, we'll share that information publicly, of course. This is an extremely serious matter for us."

"That's not what the international community is asking for. The world wants transparency and accountability. You know there will be serious consequences if that's not achieved."

"Serious consequences? Let me please just explain a few things to you, okay? And you can deliver what I say back to your nation, or the United States, or whomever else you want. First, I want no conflict with you or any other country. Yes, we have problems here. I acknowledge that, and that's why I'm leading a huge reform program, but I don't want to be told how to run my country. Canada has problems. America has problems. I would never instruct those nations how to run their internal affairs."

"If you had a prominent citizen who was murdered in one of those countries, you might."

The crown prince looked at him sternly. "Ambassador, I understand your point, but I think you're really the wrong person to deliver this message."

"How so?" Jacques answered evenly, without revealing his growing concern.

"You're not necessarily innocent here. Weren't you with Ms. Kinum right before she was murdered? Weren't you escorting her to some seedy 'off the radar' locations? Maybe *you* killed her. Maybe the investigation will conclude *that*."

Jacques took in this outrageous statement and considered how to respond. He couldn't show how furious he was. He also knew that there was a real threat here. Evidence could be manipulated to show anything. Or they could simply kill *him*, just as they had murdered Emily. "I'm not going to take such outlandish comments seriously," he replied, trying not to appear distressed.

"That's fine," the crown prince continued. "And I'm certainly not saying you killed her. Possibly you are a suspect, yes. But it could be many other people, too. Plenty of men would have a motive here because I understand that she was about to publish a lot of nasty things about many people here. But you already knew that, right, Ambassador?"

"No, I *didn't* know what she was going to publish. But based on her life's work, how she exposed corrupt and brutal practices throughout the world, I would suppose it's possible she was about to write some damaging things about *you*."

The two officials gasped at such a disrespectful comment being directed at their leader. Jacques knew he had crossed a line, but at this point he didn't care. Nothing positive was coming out of this meeting nor out of his time as ambassador to the Kingdom. After a career of diplomatic successes, it was all ending with failure and the sickening murder of a remarkable woman whose death was probably going to go unanswered. He needed to leave this place while he could, but who then would fight here for Emily?

Meanwhile, the crown prince looked as serious as ever as he stared back at Jacques. He then turned to the men and motioned with his right hand toward the door. They promptly left the room, and Jacques was now alone with the crown prince. He thought about his military training and how if he was younger, he conceivably could have grabbed the royal and broken his neck before help arrived. But instead he just stood there and listened as the object of his assassination fantasy spoke again.

"Maybe she was going to say damaging things about our government. I have no idea. But let me explain something very important to you, something you should already know. Information that undermines my government is very dangerous for the world. Because there are radical, treacherous factions here who hate America and its allies. They want to overthrow this government and kill me and my men. Some of them were outside your embassy recently conducting illegal, disruptive activities—and we are tracking them down. Obviously, this type of threat is aimed at me, but it's also not beneficial for you if our nation is led by crazy men who despise you while possessing nuclear weapons. None of us want that, correct?"

Jacques nodded. Of course, that would be a terrible situation. But the present state was intolerable as well.

"Unlike them, I admire America," the crown prince continued. "My reforms are inspired by America. My Goodwill Poker Classic is inspired by America. I love America . . . and Canada, of course."

"Of course. I'll convey all this, Prince. They'll be very disappointed that you're not cooperating with an international investigation. I don't know how they'll respond. That's beyond my control. But they *will* respond. They'll have to."

"Understood. Just one more thing about 'how they'll respond': If the fear of having me overthrown by treacherous madmen isn't enough and they're still considering some military option, I want to be very clear about something. Too many wars are fought because of misunderstandings about the other side's intentions and capabilities. You're a smart man and a great ambassador, so I know you'll accurately convey what I'm about to say."

"And what is that?"

"I would never be foolish enough to threaten the United States. I want no conflict. I want my nation to prosper and thrive without causing problems for any other. But it's well known that we now have intercontinental ballistic missiles capable of delivering thermonuclear warheads. *These are purely for defense and deterrence.* I can't emphasize that enough. We will never strike first without being provoked. But if we are attacked by America, we'll launch these missiles. It's true we don't have many, but two of them are ready to be used immediately. They're currently aimed at Washington, DC and New York. Those cities, obviously, would then no longer exist."

This is what Jacques had feared for years, what the world had been desperate to avoid but unable to prevent. A repressive dictator who could and probably would annihilate millions if his power, and therefore his life, was ever threatened. This is what he had tried to explain to Priya when she appeared in the middle of the night at the embassy, demanding more action in response to Emily's murder and myriad human rights abuses.

"You've put us now in a really bad situation," he had told her. If the Kingdom found out she was there, wearing the same dark attire as the protestors, she would become a prime target. But without the world knowing her whereabouts, online rumors about her death or disappearance in the Kingdom circulated aggressively. And if Canada was seen to be harboring someone actively opposed to the crown prince's regime, that would be the end of the fragile diplomatic relations that already existed. Or worse.

"Bullshit," she had responded. "You were already in a really bad situation. If you can't get something done now, I'll take matters into my own hands."

What a fucking mess. He had allowed her to stay at the embassy—what choice was there? He couldn't expel her now, and he knew it was probably useless to try to stop a young activist niche celebrity with a large Twitter following. She and her minions were fired up, and an aging diplomat probably wasn't going to be able to dissuade her. Yes, she was standing up for a just cause, but by doing so she was recklessly inciting people around the world in a way that might result in an apocalyptic conflagration. He would continue trying to explain the real perils here, but he knew that he most likely wouldn't sway her. His message for her when he returned to the embassy would have to be:

Try not to get us all killed, Priya. Try not to start a nuclear war.

22

"I LOVE YOU all so much," Kyler said with a smile while lying in his hotel bed and gazing at the iPad screen that he cradled in his right hand.

His three children stared back at him, slightly nodding in response to his statement.

"Where are you?" eight-year-old Britney, his youngest child, asked.

"Washington, DC," he answered.

"What are you doing there?" came her follow-up question.

Before he could answer, Mia's voice jumped in from off-screen.

"Kids, I need to talk with Daddy, okay? Give me a few minutes."

They each muttered their own quick version of "bye" and then they were gone. Mia's face soon appeared and stared back at Kyler, looking older and more tired than he had expected. Not that he should judge. He didn't look his best either.

They had once been such an attractive couple, the envy of friends and neighbors, running half marathons together and posting perfect family photos on Facebook.

"Hey, Mia."

"Kyler . . . I saw the blog post. Are you okay?"

He shrugged. "Not really. Not sure how this got out there. Too many people knew about my problems. Now all these fucking online people want to tear me down. They're so brave when I don't know who they are. Who the fuck's gonna pay me to promote their poker event if people think I'm broke? They want someone who people will see as a winner. Winning poker players aren't broke."

He was stuck in this excruciating situation—if people thought he didn't have money, it was harder for him to make money. He needed to appear as a winner in order to be a winner. He looked at Mia, and she appeared numb. Obviously, he didn't need to tell her about online cruelty.

"What about the Kingdom tournament?" she asked.

"I'm trying. That's why I'm here."

She paused before speaking again, and then began delicately, "What about . . ."

His body tensed in irritation. He knew where she was going and didn't appreciate it.

"What about . . .a real job? I can help you try to find one."

He wanted to explain again how unrealistic that was, how he wasn't qualified for anything that would earn a decent amount of money. The thought of reporting every day to some office or some construction site again and have another arrogant boss control and berate and torture him was nauseating.

"Let's talk about it after this Kingdom tournament," he replied. "Let's see what happens with that."

"Okay," Mia said. "But we need to discuss your child support payments, Kyler. We can't keep pushing that back. The kids and I need them."

"You're the one with the fucking money, Mia," he said, his voice growing more agitated. "Why am I being hounded here? If I had it, I'd pay it. Of course, I want to pay. I don't *have* it!"

Even though she had been prodding him during this conversation—to get a job, to meet his child support obligations—she had done it with a gentle and supportive tone, clearly prioritizing being productive over venting her frustration. But now that he had raised his voice and turned more confrontational, it was unavoidable that she do the same.

Her eyes widened and her face appeared larger as she leaned into her tablet.

"You mean you shouldn't have to support your children because you gambled away your money again? Is that what you're saying!?"

"Mia, after taxes and everything you ended up with like a million dollars. Please just get off my back right now. I'm trying."

"Don't act like we're somehow set for life Kyler! That's our nest egg and all we have. You know how much the school pays me. I'm supporting our three kids here, and my salary can't cover that. We want them to all go to college, right? Will what's left even cover that by then?"

"I'm just saying, you have *a million dollars* because of me. You're not about to be thrown out on the street. I'm trying."

"How is gambling away your money while you have three children to support trying?!"

"Well, I'm always *trying* to win . . ."

What was he supposed to do, other than what he was doing now? He was working to set them all up, to win enough money so that they would never have to argue about finances again. She knew that, yet was still obsessed with side issues that weren't helpful. The reality was that this opportunity was all or nothing. There was no backup plan. If he failed here, he was destroyed.

When the conversation finally ended, he lay in bed thinking about all the other times they had argued, before and after the end of their marriage. One conflict of course stood out from all the others, the clash that still hurt so much and ended up crippling them. It occurred almost two years ago, right after his win at the satellite tournament Nolan brought him to, when he was still thinking about how he could use the cash winnings and avoid playing in WSOP.

He had gotten some beers with Nolan at a local bar to celebrate.

Three months earlier, at Mia's request, he had moved out of their family home to a dilapidated apartment—all he could afford. Their "trial separation" was potentially temporary, the guidelines undefined. But they had been constantly bickering and they agreed that at least a short break was best for everyone involved.

Late that night, he found himself pretty sloshed and sitting with an equally intoxicated woman in a booth at the back of the bar. Was she attractive? Hard to remember, but in his memory he decided to believe so. She had been talking with him for over an hour, laughing at his stupid jokes, ordering round after round of beers with him.

Finally, she said she had to leave. He asked for her number and she gave it, and then leaned in to kiss him.

He froze. The separation with Mia had felt like it might be short-lived. Theoretically they could work things out and be a happy family again. Most importantly, they had never really discussed the rules of their separation. Could they see other people? He suspected that she wouldn't approve of that, but it had been three months . . .

So he kissed her, for maybe thirty seconds, her tongue plunging deep into his mouth with drunken abandon. Then she was gone. Over the next week, he called her a couple of times, texted her a few more, and never got a response.

For all his faults during their marriage, he had never been with another woman. Therefore, he hadn't as much as kissed another female in almost fifteen years, and he didn't feel great about it now. Had he "cheated"? He wasn't sure. He figured the best course of action was to be honest with Mia, so there would be no misunderstanding about what the expectations were.

It was at their next weekly therapy session, with each of them far apart on opposite ends of the leather couch, both staring ahead at their brown-haired female therapist who sat across the small room, that he decided to raise the topic. This was supposed to be their safe space, where they could talk about anything.

"We've been separated for three months now," he began gingerly. "And obviously we're working on things and hopefully we can figure this all out . . . but we've never talked about whether we can see other people during this time. I think we should . . . talk about that . . ."

The therapist looked at Mia, whose face twitched with discomfort as her eyes shifted with discontent.

"I thought we . . . were working on our marriage here . . ." she said softly.

"Of course we are," he responded.

"Then why are you asking about dating other people?"

"Kyler," the therapist said, "This is something you've obviously been thinking about—"

"Is it just thinking?" Mia jumped in. "Or have you done something?"

There was silence as the two women waited for his reply.

"I . . . I just kissed a woman. In a bar. Just a little bit . . ."

Mia began crying, and the therapist handed her a fresh tissue.

"I come here every week and pour my heart out," Mia said between sobs. "I work so fucking hard at my job for a shitty salary. I raise our three kids. I'm so *exhausted*. I try and try and try some more to figure things out so our family can be together again, so our children can see their father every day . . . and you're fucking hanging out at bars looking for women to hook up with!"

He was sorry that he'd hurt her, and as their eyes met, her upper lip quivered with anger and betrayal. He sensed that it wasn't just the kiss that hurt her. It was no doubt apparent and painful to her that he also felt a little piece of satisfaction in her distress. Satisfaction from knowing that the woman who had made him leave his home and children and suffer alone in a depressing apartment was now facing consequences for her decision. Satisfaction from showing her that, without her in his life, he could still be wanted by a woman (well, sort of).

He couldn't sleep that night, as he was wracked with guilt and fear that their problematic relationship had taken a giant step backwards. So when he received Mia's first text at 2:37 a.m., he was already wide awake on the studio apartment's sofa bed, sipping his fourth bottle of Bud Lite and thinking about how messed up his life was.

"Fuk u kyler"

He decided to ignore it for now. Let her vent. Don't make things worse by responding. And then two more texts followed a few minutes later.

"Fuc u kyler"

"Now I have smthing to tell u bout"

He should have just shut off his phone, but he didn't. "What?" he texted back.

"Fuck u kyler . . . FUCK YOU!"

"Ur drunk right?"

"Yea now my turn to tell u something"

"What?"

"Better than u kissing sum bitch . . . bet she thru up after. I always wanted to"

He knew that she was furious with him and that alcohol could sometimes accelerate her anger. He told himself not to take her comments personally. She was clearly trashed. She wrote for the third time:

"So now I can tell u shit, my turn"

"Ok what?"

He waited tensely as the text message box showed that she was writing. He couldn't imagine what she had to say, and, at almost three o'clock, it couldn't be anything good. Finally, he received her response.

"Now ur not only one to b with someone else"

He hoped this didn't mean what it seemed. Had she kissed another guy? Or worse? The idea of some other man touching his wife, the mother of his children, the woman he still loved, was torture. Even though he'd thought it would eventually happen if they didn't reunite, he had known that when she moved on physically to someone else it would be very painful for him. And he certainly wasn't ready to hear about it now, alone late at night in a dark, sad, cramped, strange studio.

Instead of asking for more details, he became quickly defensive.

"I just kissed one woman one time that's it"

"Don't try to take credit bc she didn't want to fuck u! Omg she didn't want to fuck pos loser unemployed broke gambler asshole . . . shocking!!"

Now his blood started to boil. Where had they gone so wrong that she wanted to hurt him this much? And then there was the fact that he suspected that she was somehow right, that this woman had never responded to his outreach for all the reasons she outlined.

He was completely certain that the smart thing would be to leave the conversation at that point, as it was headed in a horrible direction. Plus, he was very aware that hearing details about whatever drunk hookup she had would possibly devastate him. But he just had to know now. He just had to find out how bad it was, or else he'd be left to imagine the worst-case scenario.

"What did u do?"

"Thsome"

Then she followed up with:

"Threesome"

The word hung there, staring at Kyler, and he quickly longed for what would previously have been his mind's worst-case scenario. This was the woman who had slept with only one other guy before they met. This was not Mia. Hopefully she was just making shit up in a drunken stupor.

"Guy and girl or 2 guys?" he typed. He quickly wondered why he had even asked, why he cared. For some reason, he wanted to know, and then he considered which option would be worse. He imagined that a male and a female would mean she teaming up with some other woman to give another man (who was *not* him) incredible pleasure—a highly disturbing image. Two guys would involve them treating her like a piece of meat, defiling her in all sorts of sordid ways, as he had watched a few times on Pornhub. He couldn't handle *his wife* being subjected to that.

"Why not 2 girls and me?"

He didn't like that either, but it would certainly be the best option . . . by far. Before he could respond, she wrote:

"But no kyler sry"

"Sex with 2 guys"

And this killed him. Just destroyed him. The idea of two men having sex with her, taking turns with his wife, she probably blowing one while the other fucked her from behind, both coming all over her, sent him into an apoplectic fit. He leaped up from his bed and screamed with agony, and then picked up the Bud Lite bottle and heaved it against the wall, sending beer and shattered pieces of glass flying around the small room. One pierced his right forearm and lodged there as blood began to trickle out.

His phone buzzed again and his whole body shook as he picked it up to look.

"U want to know more?"

"No," was all he could manage to type.

"Well too bad u caused this so ur gonna hear more rn"

Far too late, he decided then that he was done texting with her for the night. Maybe he would never speak with her again. He collapsed onto the floor, shedding intoxicated blood and tears, the phone cruelly lying next to him. He wouldn't reply again to her texts, but unfortunately he couldn't bring himself to turn off the device, so he lay there in emotional torment, staring in depressed dismay as her crushing messages continued to fill the screen:

"It was awesome"

"So fun"

"The things they both did for me . . . stuff u never cud"

"So hot. Can u picture us? I let them both do anything they wanted. Everything they wanted. Fingering myself now just thinking about them touching me."

"Real men kyler"

"Not like u"

"So great, neither had to apologize for cumming in 2 secs"

"Like u do kyler"

"Not fuckups like u"

"Incompetent fuck"

"Can't fuck, can't provide for family, fuck u kyler!!"

"Fuk u kyler!!!"

23

*D*ON'T GET *overwhelmed. Don't let your problems distract you. Put aside the disastrous conversation with Bryce and all the thoughts about what he did to you. Don't think about the false hope provided by Kyler. Just be good—or at least passable—on TV for one segment, lasting just five or six minutes at most. Until that's over, nothing else exists. Focus!*

But first Maggie needed to thaw.

"Can you turn up the heat?" she snapped at the driver as soon as she had closed the car door. Then, for some inexplicable reason she thought about her Uber rating and added, "Please."

She had originally planned to return home after meeting Bryce, where she could maybe change her outfit, fix her hair and makeup, prep for the segment, and then head in the network-provided car to the studio. But when she pulled up Google Maps she saw that she had greatly underestimated the DC traffic back to her apartment, and there just wasn't enough time for all that. She would have to head straight there.

She sat in the back seat and looked at her phone, which fortunately still functioned despite its belly-flop into the tundra outside. She frenetically searched for any news on Priya, the Kingdom, the Goodwill Poker Classic, and anything else that she might be asked about on her first prime time television segment. Staring intensely at her phone in the moving car while under such stress started to make her feel nauseated and light-headed, so she quickly opened her passenger window.

"Is it too *hot* now?" the driver asked. "Want me to turn the heat down?"

"No thanks," she replied, and pushed the button to close the window most of the way, leaving a little crack of icy air blowing onto her face.

She needed to figure out what she was going to say. She was being interviewed as a college friend of Priya's, whose location was now unknown. Priya's last public comments had been about the Kingdom's cruelty and the moral bankruptcy of anyone who would support the poker tournament that she called "propaganda for a tyrant."

Maggie was on record opposing a presidential ban on travel there, and was now working on behalf of an American who wanted to play, although the network surely wouldn't know that latter fact. She also had a $10 million stake in said American's potential participation and victory. Fortunately, there was no way the weak fact-checkers would be able to uncover that either.

But what if somehow they did? How would she square her work with Kyler, or at a minimum, her statements on the last segment, with the fact that she was going on air as someone supportive and sympathetic to Priya? Which she was, in the sense that she hoped Priya was alive and well, although not successful in blocking this poker opportunity.

Online, she didn't find any significant new developments from the past few hours, but Maggie took note of the swelling online movement in support of Priya Varma and Emily Kinum—and in opposition to the tournament. #sixofdiamondsontheriver was still trending, as was #kingdomboycott, #justiceforemily, and #executiveordernow.

One thing she knew for sure: she wasn't going to look at her Twitter mentions after *this* segment. *No fucking way.*

She arrived and went through the hair and make-up experts who, fortunately, were very skilled at their jobs. She ended up looking pretty camera ready, despite her appearance when she arrived and how she felt inside. She looked in one of the make-up room mirrors and adjusted her medium-length black skirt and cream-colored blouse. She made sure her necklace was centered and that it still worked with the hoop earrings that she had bought as a birthday gift to herself the previous summer.

Then she waited, in a different green room this time—larger, with a couple of sofas and a few chairs around a coffee table. Junior producers typed at desktop computers on the far wall. Two United States senators, one from each party, talked amicably near the coffee and drinks area, and some of the recognizable big-name prime time hosts breezed in and out quickly, giving warm hellos to guests and staffers.

It was a friendly atmosphere, but soon they would transition from enjoying cordial chat in the green room to enthusiastically throwing out the red meat. For the moment, they were friendly like football players greeting each other during pre-game warmups before three hours of ruthless aggression and bruising hits.

The system certainly had its faults and phoniness, but it was in many ways the place to be—preparing for a national prime time television audience with Washington's movers and shakers. She felt like a trespasser in an exciting world. Any moment they might look at her, tell her she didn't belong, and escort her out of the building. Or, she might crush her segment and be a frequent guest on a whole variety of issues, as her consulting business boomed . . .

Stay calm. Don't think about Bryce.

As she continued to review news articles on her phone and hurriedly craft some decent soundbites, she kept a careful watch for the mic person so that she wouldn't again be startled. Finally, he showed up, and as his hands fumbled around her body to hook up her mic and earpiece, she made sure to ignore how uncomfortable she now felt with strange hands around her body.

When she was mic'd and all set up, a producer ushered her into the cold studio and placed her at the anchor table, surrounded by cameras, lights, and screens. Men and women raced about, placing new copy in front of the host, adjusting cameras, making sure the teleprompter was accurate, and handling other assorted tasks that were beyond Maggie's understanding. It was a whir of activity as she was asked to conduct her mic check and then told it was ninety seconds to air.

"How do you pronounce your last name?" the female host asked matter-of-factly. Maggie had watched her on television numerous times. She was a tall, blonde-haired ex-prosecutor who had rapidly transitioned from daytime talking head to prime time talking head to daytime host to prime time host. The new American Dream.

"RAH-ster," Maggie replied.

"Thank you," she said, and then returned to silently reviewing several papers in front of her and scribbling a few handwritten notes.

"Sixty seconds," warned a female voice in her ear.

The host suddenly looked up and squinted her eyes as she appeared to receive information being told to her through her earpiece.

"Wow," she said. "Okay, wow. Are you sure it's legit?"

She listened intently for a few more seconds and then continued to talk to someone Maggie couldn't see: "Well, you all better fucking confirm it's for real before we go on air with it. We can't have another fuckup . . . okay . . . okay . . . just get it right . . . don't make me look bad here."

The person on the other end must have said something humorous or complimentary because the host started to laugh and then responded, "Exactly. Don't forget it!"

With the seconds counting down to the beginning of her prime time debut, Maggie urgently needed to know what this was about. Did something newsworthy happen that she would be asked about during her interview? Her phone sat useless back in the green room.

She wanted to ask the host, but would it be bad form to start chatting when the segment was about to begin, and the host surely needed to concentrate?

"Did something happen?" Maggie forced herself to say.

"Thirty seconds," the voice chimed in.

The host looked at Maggie. "Potentially some tweets from Varma, if they're real," she said quickly. "She tweeted that—" And then she stopped, listening to the voice in her ear again. "Wow . . . okay . . . she really wrote that? . . . okay, just fucking confirm that before we go with it."

Maggie looked at her, waiting for more information. She had already been nervous enough. She didn't want to now be responding to something significant on the fly, with no time to prepare.

"What was it?" she whispered.

The host waved her right hand, indicating that the time for talking was over. Instead she was now locked in on the camera in front of her, ready to return from commercial and speak to her audience of roughly 2.5 million viewers.

"Ten seconds. Nine, eight, seven . . ."

And then they were live.

"Welcome back to Prime Time Politics," the host read from the teleprompter as Maggie sat across from her and uncomfortably followed along. "Thanks for watching. Now, for our Impact Segment. Priya Varma. Poker superstar. Human rights advocate. A leading voice against the Kingdom's crown prince and what she has called his 'phony modernization.' Now, reports of her disappearing near the Kingdom's border have led family and friends to fear the worst. For the human side of this story, we bring in Maggie Raster, founder and CEO of Maggie Raster Consulting and a former White House official. More importantly, she's Priya's best friend from college."

Best friend? Maggie recoiled inside. She had *never* said that. Hadn't she merely texted that they were college friends? For the second time in as many segments, she considered whether she should start her appearance by correcting the host. Surely, that wouldn't be very well received.

"Maggie, thank you for joining us."

Maggie nodded politely.

"Thanks for having me on," she replied.

"We may have some breaking news soon," the host said. "But as our team works on that, I know you and many, many others have been very concerned about Priya Varma. For those who don't know her, or who only know her from her public persona, what can you tell us about the real Priya?"

"Sure," Maggie began to answer. "I knew her best in college. She was an extremely smart, kind, outgoing, witty woman who was very well-liked across campus. Those of us who knew her were not surprised at all that she became such a success and force for good in this world. And everyone is hoping and praying that she's okay and somewhere safe, and that we'll hear from her very soon."

"Definitely. We're all praying for her safety. Now, as a very close friend of hers, do you find it difficult to be so opposed to the human rights advocacy that she has championed?" the host asked.

Maggie felt as if someone was suddenly squeezing her throat, as she fought with every fiber to remain unflustered. There was so much wrong with that question. She *wasn't* a "very close" friend of hers. She *wasn't* opposed to her advocacy. She, too, was for real reform in the Kingdom and around the world that would result in healthier, freer, and fuller lives for all, especially subjugated women and girls.

But besides all that—wasn't this supposed to be a lighter segment about Priya's personal side? That's what Natalie had implied and Maggie had hoped. But, as with everything else lately, her hopes had been unrealistic.

"I'm not opposed to her advocacy at all," Maggie asserted, firmly but professionally. "Priya Varma is a hero for what she's done and what she stands for."

"Yet you were on our network yesterday defending the Kingdom, a brutal dictatorship that she's been so critical of."

Maggie was now more conscious than ever of the cameras surrounding her and the fact that millions were watching her every word, every breath. How many more would see this later and tear her apart on social media and various political blogs?

Obviously, this segment wasn't going to be a success. Clearly, she wouldn't be proudly and prominently displaying the video on her Twitter and company website. Instead, she was going to have to think fast and fight in order to leave without an irreparably scarred reputation.

Maggie made a quick, tactical decision that she would no longer be concerned with insulting the host. She couldn't allow herself to become network roadkill and another entry on the host's video resume of unpopular guests she had destroyed while her audience cheered at home.

"That's a complete mischaracterization of what I said. I condemned Emily Kinum's murder and called for an independent investigation, as the international community has. I merely explained that we can't rush to judgment here and risk escalating this situation into a nuclear conflict."

"Rush to judgment? Is there any doubt that the crown prince leads a repressive, cruel regime?" the host asked aggressively. "Even without the Kinum murder, how can America justify allowing its citizens to assist in a propaganda spectacle poker tournament? Your *good friend* Priya was opposed to it even *before* Emily Kinum was butchered there. She didn't need an investigation to know the difference between right and wrong. Why do you?"

I never wanted to take this fucking side, Maggie thought. *How did* *this escalate so much, so fast? If they only knew I now have $10 million riding on it, I'd be flayed alive.*

"Your characterization of my opinions is completely unfair and inaccurate—"

"Before you answer that," the host interrupted, "we have very important breaking news."

Maggie saw a huge "BREAKING NEWS" icon appear on the studio's monitors, all capital red letters starting small and then spinning and growing in a matter of three seconds until they filled the screen, all while a dramatic drumbeat increased in volume.

The host looked directly at one of the cameras and spoke in an urgent tone.

"We can now confirm that the following two tweets were just posted to Priya Varma's verified Twitter account in the last few minutes. We will put them on your screen momentarily. We can't yet confirm that she herself posted them, but they appear to be a strong sign that she is alive, she is well, and she is escalating her fight with the Kingdom and those she believes support it."

The monitors filled with one message, alongside the light blue Twitter bird logo in the upper left portion of the screens. The host read along with the text.

"@officialpriyavarma: To all my fans—thank you for your invaluable support. I'm in the Kingdom now, continuing our fight against oppression. I'm safe, but so many others are not, and we must NEVER accept that. If you support the Kingdom in ANY way, you are supporting it in EVERY way. #justiceforemily"

The monitors then shifted to a new tweet, and the host continued:

"@officialpriyavarma: We need YOUR help to win this fight. Let our nation's leaders hear your outrage. They are failing us! Tell them to finally confront these atrocities. DM me any info that will help the cause! Send anything that will take down those appeasing injustice! #sixofdiamondsontheriver"

The host then turned to Maggie and sternly said, "She tweeted, 'If you support the Kingdom in any way, you are supporting it in every way.' She's talking about you, isn't she? People like *you*?"

Maggie was flabbergasted at how direct and personal this attack now was. With all her stress, all her weariness, she could tell that the strings holding together her composure were quickly fraying. While the host salivated over her prey, Maggie was outraged, and now nothing was going to hold her back.

"What you're doing here is highly deceptive and manipulative, and I'm pretty sure you know that," Maggie began, keeping her voice steady and assertive. "It's irresponsible and inflammatory to take my comments about cautiously confronting a nuclear power and falsely twist them to sound like I'm promoting some immoral coddling of terrible—"

"Well, I'm just asking the question, Ms. Raster. Our audience can decide for themselves what the truth is."

"Just asking the question? I was invited here to talk positively about someone who I knew in college and is missing. I'm elated that she appears to be okay. And now you're turning this segment into a cynical, dishonest attempt to destroy me with false allegations."

"Now, *that's* dishonest. You're experienced in politics, so I would think you wouldn't have such thin skin, Ms. Raster. I would have expected you to be able to defend your prior comments without whining about this show."

"Apparently you think it'll help your ratings to attack and smear me. Whether you're correct about that, one thing's for sure: it's wrong. We can have a substantive discussion about a complex topic, or you can make simplistic attacks that make you look tough and may help you get a viral video."

The host glowered at Maggie and she stared right back, not backing down.

"That's *highly* offensive. No wonder the White House didn't want you there anymore. I'm sorry being interviewed is too difficult for you, but at least you won't have to be concerned about that anymore because you'll never be on this network again, and I can't imagine any of our competitors will care what you have to say either."

"I left the White House under very good terms and for you to suggest otherwise without any basis in fact just further shows that to you, facts are meaningless."

"Cut off her mic!" the host ordered, and as Maggie tried to continue speaking, she heard that indeed her audio was now silent.

The host now turned to the camera, with her best prosecutor face, full of serious justice-seeking and determination.

"Well, ladies and gentlemen," she said, shaking her head in disgust and disappointment, and then displaying a knowing grin, "this is what the people of this country and around the world are up against. People who say one thing, then when confronted either change their story or start hurling insults. But Prime Time Politics will never back down. We're committed to always asking the important, tough questions that get *you* the information you need. And if that makes the so-called power players uneasy . . . that's *their* problem, not *ours*. We'll be right back . . ."

And in a flurry of expeditious movements, before Maggie could totally process everything that had just happened, network tech people unhooked her earpiece and microphone, escorted her out of the studio, returned her green room possessions, and walked her to the hallway elevator.

At least they hadn't cancelled her car service, which waited by the curb outside. She entered the black vehicle's back seat and the car began moving into the DC night.

She couldn't escape fearing that instead of boosting her sputtering consultant practice, this segment may have just delivered her career a mortal wound. But as she considered that, her thoughts also turned to Priya. Now that Maggie was off air and basically alone, she could really soak in the messages that Priya had purportedly tweeted.

Oh my God, is she crazy? Tweeting opposition to the Kingdom while inside its borders? After what they did to Emily Kinum? Doesn't she realize that they'll fucking kill her?

From her work in the White House, she was very well informed about the Kingdom and the sensitive, high-stakes diplomacy that was primarily conducted via the Canadian ambassador on behalf of the United States. She had met Ambassador Bouchard once—a well-meaning, experienced man with decades on the international scene. He was someone who prized stability and accountability, not rash, inciting statements that could jeopardize a fragile peace.

Priya's statements, and her presence in the Kingdom, just made his very difficult job so much more challenging and dangerous. No doubt Bouchard would be livid when he learned about them.

She powered her phone back on, and it blew up with text messages, emails, and notifications about social media mentions. She would stay away from the online mob for now, and maybe forever.

There was a text from Kyler.

"Thank you so much for meeting with me today. Please let me know when there is any update. Great job on tv tonight!"

Great job? What the hell was he watching?

And, to her surprise, there was a text from Bryce.

"Saw your segment. POTUS announcing EO decision tomorrow morning. Meet me 6am, same location."

The man had sexually assaulted her and then chastised her when she had sought some understanding about what had transpired. Now he was ordering her next move. No part of her wanted to again brave the freezing weather and painful memories in just over nine hours. But the lure of $10 million meant that she had no choice.

"Copy. See u there."

24

DESPITE KYLER'S tweet declaring that he was not in fact broke, the news about his alleged staggering financial collapse was captivating the poker world, and mainstream news sites were getting into the action with clickbait headlines:

"The poker champion who reportedly lost $8.8 million in months"

"$8.8 million ALL IN: what it takes to lose everything"

"How might Kyler Dawson have lost $8.8 million in a year? Poker pros and gambling experts discuss how it could happen"

Everywhere, the unifying spin was that he was an irresponsible, clumsy gambling addict with no common sense, a pathetic creature who in about a year blew more money than most people would see in several lifetimes.

No one would ever again pay him to promote a poker event or casino. No normal tournament would ever give him a comped seat just so they could announce his appearance. No mainstream person or entity would ever benefit from associating with him.

He had turned off his hotel room's television after watching Maggie's interview, encouraged that such a fighter was in his corner. He believed that if anyone could save him by navigating today's complex political realities, it was she.

But as he continued to scroll through news and social media comments about his situation, he wanted to scream to the world, "I did not lose $8.8 million!"

But no one seemed to care about the truth. And what was the truth, anyway? The reality was a blur by now, a painful year-and-a-half-long saga that started with an impossible WSOP championship and ended with . . .

What was the ending, anyway? Had the ending happened yet? Was *this* the ending?

The downfall hadn't started with a bad beat or an unwise bet or an out of control late-night gambling bender. For thirty days, he was on top of the world, an instant celebrity, the everyman who conquered the poker world, starting from a sleepy home game and culminating on the biggest stage. He was an icon of good luck and success, in demand by poker promoters, journalists, and talk shows.

Then he received the legal demand in the mail, followed by a copy via email. From Nolan. Or, more accurately, from Nolan's attorney. The letter outlined how Nolan had provided half of Kyler's original entry fee, and that Kyler had allegedly confirmed numerous times, "including explicitly right before the start of the WSOP final table," that Nolan was therefore entitled to receive half of his winnings. Kyler had had to pay 20% to the participants in the home game's final table, as per the rules of the satellite tournament, so that left about $7 million. The lawyer's letter concluded with an instruction that $3,520,000 be paid immediately to her client, or else she would be forced to seek relief in court.

He should have contacted an attorney, but instead he dismissed it as a frivolous claim he could simply ignore. He was too successful, too happy for once in his life, to allow something this meritless to drag him down and divert his attention. $3.5 million because Nolan paid $300 of his buy-in at a home game? It was beyond insanity.

Then a second demand arrived, both in physical and electronic forms, which he also cast aside. But when he was signing autographs at a casino's poker event and one of the purported autograph seekers actually served him with formal notice that he was being sued, he knew that this wasn't going away, and he would need to find a lawyer immediately.

He asked around for referrals and was told to contact a contracts lawyer named Dorothy Blatt. He looked at her law firm bio and photo and saw that she was in her late 60s, with short gray hair, and supposedly had handled all sorts of contract negotiations and litigation for over thirty years.

He met with her in a large corner office of her downtown law firm, and explained his story. He had been broke, and Nolan had given him half of a $600 buy-in for a local poker tournament. He had never promised Nolan a cent at any point. He had miraculously turned that $600 into $8.8 million.

"You never put anything in writing?" she asked.

"Never."

"You never promised him a portion of your winnings?"

"Absolutely not."

"But it's customary in the poker world that if someone pays for part of an entry fee, that person would receive a share of any prize money?"

He had to pause before answering this question. Yes, Nolan was probably entitled to *something*. But $3.5 million? From $300? When Kyler did all the hard work and actually won? Absolutely not.

"A share, maybe," Kyler responded. "But not half. Not even close to that."

Dorothy nodded.

"Well," she said, "This case screams out for a settlement. He probably just wants some money to go away, so he's trying to scare you with the $3.5 million demand. We'll have to arrange a meeting with him and his attorney, and we can make a settlement offer."

"How much?" Kyler asked.

"I'd suggest 5 percent. $352,000."

"No," he replied instantly. "He doesn't deserve that. Maybe $10,000?"

"Listen Kyler, if this goes all the way to trial, you're facing hundreds of thousands in legal fees, plus all the headaches and aggravation of being sued, in addition to the possibility that even with the best defense you could end up *losing* and pay $3.5 million, plus *his* legal fees. I don't think he deserves that, but juries can be crazy. Judges can be crazy. You don't want to gamble with the legal system if you can just make this go away. Trust me. Let's offer him a quarter million, and be willing to come up to $352,000. Let's make this disappear so you can return to enjoying your millions."

A week later, he was sitting at a conference room table at Dorothy's law firm with his attorney, Nolan, and Nolan's attorney—a woman named Angela Paterson, who seemed to be a longtime professional associate of Dorothy's. The two of them interacted cordially, as if they had been through the drill countless times.

Meanwhile, Kyler and Nolan alternated between glaring and ignoring each other from across the table.

"Angela, we don't believe your client is entitled to anything here," Dorothy explained. "There's no written contract and no evidence of any agreement at any time. My client was hugely successful without your client ever playing a hand. There's really no basis for his claim, but we also don't want to go through the time and expense of litigation. So we're willing to make a settlement offer of $250,000 to fully satisfy all claims by your client."

Angela shook her head.

"My client was a 50 percent investor in a venture that earned $8.8 million, minus 20 percent for the home game finalists. It's pretty straightforward. He's entitled to half of what's left. And my client will testify that your client repeatedly *confirmed* that he would be entitled to half, including right before the beginning of the final table."

"That's bullshit," Kyler grumbled.

"You told me I would receive half," Nolan quickly responded. "You said it on the day of the final table. And many times before."

"Look," Angela said. "At worst, it's my client's word against your client's word. That's certainly worth more than $250,000."

"Well, what's your proposal, Angela?" Dorothy asked. "And don't say $3.5 million."

"Forty percent. That's about $2.8 million."

"No, we might as well take our chances at trial then. We can do at most 5 percent. $352,000."

"He promised me half!" Nolan burst out.

"I did not!" Kyler shouted back.

Both attorneys turned toward their clients to de-escalate the situation, with Dorothy looking at Kyler and then at the door to suggest they step outside the conference room. In the hallway, Kyler looked at his attorney with the intense frustration of someone being shaken down by a con artist.

"He's lying!"

"He's going to testify that he's not."

And that's when Kyler had an idea. He grabbed his phone from the front right pocket of his jeans, and spent about thirty seconds scrolling and searching. Finally, he found what he was looking for and showed the screen to his lawyer.

"Does this help?"

She peered at the phone and read the text message he had found:

"Thanks Mia. Crazy scene here. And Nolan saying I owe him half of winnings b/c he gave me $300 a few months ago! We NEVER agreed to that. Such unbelievable BS!!"

"Is that from the day of the final table? The last time that he alleges you made the promise?"

"Yup."

"That's good, Kyler. It's contemporaneous documentation that supports our position. I think it can be very helpful."

They walked back into the room, and saw that Nolan and his attorney were now standing and conferring toward the back of the room. They stopped talking with each other upon seeing their adversaries, and then Dorothy spoke.

"Angela, I'd like you to look at something. Kyler, please show her what you shared with me."

Angela approached them and Kyler held out his phone with the text message displayed on the screen.

"Why would he be texting his wife that he never promised half if he had just made such a commitment?" Dorothy asked. "That would make no sense."

Angela silently read the text while Nolan looked concerned from the other side of the room.

"Why don't you send me a copy of that to review and then I'll get back to you," Angela suggested. She was too experienced and professional to look deflated, but she clearly considered this a setback.

Two days later, Kyler returned to his lawyer's office for a follow-up meeting. He was feeling good and still impressed with his memory and how it had helped him. Just like remembering how another person at a table played a certain hand and using that information to win a huge pot later in a tournament. He could recall important and helpful information and that could lead to success, as it hopefully would here.

He sat down in a chair in Dorothy's office as she shut the door and then sat across from him at her desk.

"Any update?" he asked.

"Yes, they just filed a motion. Based on the text message that we produced, they want to subpoena all text messages between you and Mia from the date of the neighborhood tournament to the evening of the final table. They're arguing that they need them in order to see the full extent and context of any texts about paying Nolan."

Kyler's whole body immediately convulsed with horror and alarm.

He leaped from his chair and began wildly looking around the room and breathing heavy. He grabbed his face with his left hand, which slid down from his forehead to his neck and then dropped to his side.

"No!" he exclaimed, vigorously shaking his head. "That can't happen!"

Dorothy rose and raised a hand out with her palm facing him and moving slowing back and forth in an attempt to calm him.

"Hold on, Kyler. Don't freak out here. Let's discuss this, and then we'll deal with it together. I'm your attorney. I work for you. Talk to me."

"No one can *ever* see those messages!" he cried out.

"Do they undermine our case?" she asked.

"No," he replied. "But there's a lot of personal shit between me and Mia in there. We'd been separated for a few months and were going through a really bad time. He can't get those, can he?"

He looked at her fearfully, franticly hoping that this expert in the law would deliver a verdict that would save him and his family from cataclysmic mortification.

"Well," she began to answer. "Like a lot of legal questions, the answer is 'it depends.' But I'll do everything I can to stop that from happening."

Kyler thought back to his conversation with Nolan at WSOP, when he had foolishly confided in someone who at the time was supposedly his good friend.

"I know it's been really tough. Mia still giving you a hard time?"

"A little over a month ago she sent me some texts that were just . . . I'm not even sure the word for it."

"What did she say?"

"They were just so nasty, but not normal nasty. Like, really hurtful . . . personal . . . angry. Just wanting to devastate me. And it worked."

"Like what?"

"I . . . I'd just rather not really go into detail."

And now Nolan was going after the detail. Kyler was no lawyer—he was as far from being a lawyer as one could be—but he knew the argument about wanting other relevant texts or seeking "context" was complete bullshit. Nolan was looking to embarrass him, or to use the threat of embarrassment to get a better settlement.

"What if we say that we don't want to use any texts in our case anymore?" he asked. "Then he can't try to get the other texts, right?"

"Unfortunately, it doesn't work like that, Kyler. But he doesn't have them yet, so hopefully we can keep it that way."

What followed over the next month was a series of motions and court appearances. Dorothy filed an objection to the subpoena, arguing it was a fishing expedition with no realistic chance of finding relevant material. The judge denied their motion, but said that she would examine the text messages herself and redact any necessary information.

He wondered if he should share with Mia what was happening, but decided it was better not to. Their lawyers were working out a divorce in a surprisingly amicable manner, and this would only scare her and inflame the situation. So he went on with his new life as a poker celebrity, traveling, attending casino events, and spending large, all the while secretly living every second in fear that he was headed off the edge of a cliff. What should have been a fantasy existence turned into a life of constant foreboding.

Then he was back sitting in Dorothy's office. She had a grim look on her face, as if she was about to deliver unfortunate news, and Kyler feared the worst.

"Kyler, I just received the redacted text messages. The judge took out some personal information and a few texts, but . . . I'm sorry, I see there are texts in there from your wife, about the men she was with, and the stuff she said to you. I assume those are the ones you were concerned about?"

"Does Nolan have those now?" he asked with apprehension.

She paused before answering, and that short silence felt interminable as Kyler knew it meant that the situation he dreaded was now a reality.

"I'm sorry. I did everything I could. I'll file a motion to preclude him from questioning you about them at the deposition, and from using them at trial. So maybe we can keep them private to some extent."

He pictured Nolan, gleefully reading those texts with a refreshing beer in his hand, laughing at Kyler and planning how he would use them to destroy him. Kyler's newfound celebrity status would mean that they would go viral instantly, and he could barely conceive of a more horrifying nightmare.

He didn't want to look Dorothy in the eyes again, now that he knew she had read them. She was the first person besides Mia who knew about these messages with whom he had to share the same room, and it was now so uncomfortable. Was she secretly laughing at him, too? Would she share with others her crazy work tale about a client's outrageous text messages—an entertaining legal war story relived at cocktail parties while listeners snickered?

What would happen if the whole world knew, and every inch of this country and cyberspace was laced with people who would be sneering and mocking? What if there was nowhere for him to hide from it all while he still lived? And what would happen to his earning ability if he was suddenly an object of ridicule instead of admiration?

The next day the four of them were back in the conference room for another settlement discussion. Nolan sat next to his lawyer while displaying the enthusiasm of a Cheshire cat.

"We're willing to come to up to a million dollars," Dorothy announced.

She and Kyler had discussed making this offer, and being open to increasing that to $1.5 million. He needed this to be settled. No way could he risk these texts being publicly referenced at a deposition or trial.

"Angela, my client won't settle for anything less than $3.5 million. That's half, and that's what he was promised and what he deserves."

Kyler maintained his poker face but inside he felt the alarm of being re-raised all in after bluffing with a weak hand in a huge pot.

"Three point five?" Dorothy asked with confused annoyance. "Your previous offer was two point eight. You know that's not how this works."

"Sorry, Dorothy. With the recent discovery, we believe three point five is fair."

"What discovery in *any* way supports your client's case?"

The answer, of course, was nothing. But that was irrelevant now. They didn't need information to support their case. They had his life in a vice, and he was at their mercy.

"We'll see during questioning of your client what ends up being relevant," Angela replied. "What ends up being *significant*."

"This is crazy," Kyler decried. "Nolan, you gave me $300 and I'm offering you a *million dollars*! Just be reasonable about this."

"I was there for you at your worst!" Nolan responded. "And this is how you treat me? Trying to rob me of millions of dollars? If it wasn't for me, you wouldn't have *any* of this money."

"I'm offering you a million dollars! For Christ's sake, three hundred turned into a million!"

"It's *three point five* or we proceed toward trial," Nolan's attorney interjected. "Please consider that and get back to us."

The meeting ended moments later, and now Kyler knew that he would have to tell Mia. With everyone out of the conference room, Kyler stood alone by a window overlooking the city and nervously placed the call.

"Kyler?" she answered with some surprise. Their recent communication had been only through their attorneys, except for his visitation times.

"Mia, I need to talk with you."

"What's wrong? Are you okay?" she asked.

"No," he said, his heart thumping. "Nolan's attorney subpoenaed all of our text messages. My attorney tried to stop it, but . . . he has our text messages."

There was a disturbing silence for few seconds, and then a female voice full of panic. "The ones I sent?"

"Yes."

"How? How can he get to look at them?!"

"Because I sent you a text about not promising half to Nolan, so the judge is letting him look at the other messages between us from around the same time."

"Please tell me you're fucking with me, Kyler. Please! If you're doing this to scare me, to get back at me, you got it, you did it. Just please tell me it's not real!"

"I'm not fucking with you. He's using it as leverage. He wants half. Or else I'll be asked about them at a deposition or trial. In public."

"That's blackmail!" she yelled.

"I know! I don't know what to do, Mia."

"Kyler, you fucking settle this now!"

"But he wants half! *Three point five million*!"

This was very real money to her, too, as once the divorce was finalized she would be entitled to a huge share of what he had won. The more Nolan got, the less she received, too.

Her voice grew louder and less steady, as he heard her breathing become heavier. "Kyler, our kids are going to see those messages! Everyone at my school will read them! You have to settle this!"

"I know! But *three point five million*, Mia . . ."

"Then get a better fucking deal. Get the best deal you can, but fucking settle this. Stop this! Don't do this to me, Kyler!"

"Do this to *you*?" he asked incredulously. "What did I do to *you* here?! These are your messages. You did this to me!"

"Kyler, these are going to make me look like some crazy sex-crazed shrew, just some nasty insane bitch saying horrible things, when you've said so many hurtful things to me for years . . . some so much worse!"

"Worse? What the hell have I said that's *worse*?!"

"Kyler, listen to me," she said, her voice suddenly firmer. "Things have been really bad between us for a while, and we haven't felt like we're on the same team for a long time. But let's agree that the most important thing right now, maybe the most important thing we do in our entire lives, is make sure our kids don't see those texts. Let's not make them live with that. I don't want to live with that. Oh my God, I *can't*."

It was so much money to give up. But a horrible fate if he didn't.

If it was just his wife fucking two other guys, would he be able to live with it then? It would be horrible for her, and for his children, and of course for him, too, but would it be worth giving up millions?

But that wasn't all she had written. The rest of the content, what she had texted about him personally, was what really terrified him when he thought about how the outside world would respond. And yes, living while knowing that his children had seen those texts was a fate worse than death.

Back in his lawyer's office a few minutes later, he tossed his cards into the muck. "Please just settle this. Get the best deal you can and make it go away."

She nodded, and he saw pity in her eyes, the same shameful, disrespectful pity that he feared the whole world might soon have for him.

For the next week, she kept him apprised of negotiations, while he funneled his anger and distress and fear into a continuing escalation of bets on craps, blackjack, and football. At first this was a much-needed diversion, but then he realized that the more he won, the less painful it would be to have to pay so much to Nolan.

Except that, after the first day, he generally didn't win. Spending hours and hours at the high-limit blackjack and craps tables, he found himself running pretty badly, and it didn't help when he began increasing his bet size to overcome the losses. Instead of trying to compensate for what he would lose to Nolan, with increasing concern he worked to earn back what he had already donated to the casino over the past few days. At times he had a short string of luck that made a dent in his losses, but that would soon be followed by heartache as the dice and cards returned to cruelly falling against him.

He was now betting on credit—a luxury afforded him because of his Big Winner status as WSOP champion and his swollen bankroll. The credit was more than covered by his current holdings, except that his bank account would soon be raided by a settlement payment to Nolan. Did he have enough to cover it all? It really depended on what the settlement amount was, and how well he did on the games that weekend.

But an array of football bets—college football on Saturday and NFL on Sunday—were disastrous, and he tried to make it all good by betting Detroit plus one and the over at forty-seven on Monday Night Football. When the Lions missed a last-second 45-yard field goal and lost 24-22, he was eight beers in and watching alone in his dark apartment, aware that he had lost both bets but too numb to calculate the week's total damage.

In the morning, hungover and exhausted with a pounding headache, he realized he was stuck for approximately $1.8 million for the week.

"They've agreed to settle for $2.8 million, Kyler. I'm sorry, but I can't get them to budge any lower," Dorothy told him on the phone a couple hours later. "The settlement contract will have strict non-disclosure and confidentiality provisions that prohibit Nolan from sharing any information obtained during litigation."

"Thank you," was all he could say at that point, feeling slight relief while being engulfed by a feeling of complete and utter defeat.

Two days later, he signed the contract in his lawyer's office and arranged for the wire transfer of $2.8 million.

For two weeks, he somberly lived his life, mostly alone, mostly at home. He needed to take a break from gambling and for two weeks he was successful. Then, on a Wednesday morning, he had a noon flight to Los Angeles to attend a poker room event for which he was the guest of honor and would be paid $17,500.

He woke up early and looked at his phone, and there it was. It was everywhere and his heart nearly stopped. He saw the original story, posted on pokernewz.net, which started with the cruelly enthusiastic headline:

"WSOP Champ Kyler 'E-ZPass' Dawson and His Ex-Wife's Taunting Threesome Texts!!!"

Followed by the sadistic, gleeful, and attempting-to-be-clever sub-head:

"She Done Two Guys, He Done (in) Two Seconds!!!!"

They were all there, every text from that fateful exchange, with a mocking article that salivated and celebrated over every salacious detail. The blogger, identified only as fullhouseparty1999, referred to Kyler each time with the "E-ZPass" nickname, referring to how quick he allegedly finished ("speedier than the E-ZPass lane!!"), as per Mia's texts. And now #kylerdawsonezpass was trending.

"No!" he screamed in panic and agony. "Fuck no!"

Despite all his efforts, this terrifying nightmare was coming true, and he was helpless to stop it now. The sordid story had posted earlier that morning and already seemingly proliferated throughout the entire online universe. The consequences for him, his family, and all of their existences were incalculably disastrous. He was furious, he was petrified, and he was consumed with sadness.

Later, when he talked with Dorothy, they discussed how all of this probably, obviously, came from Nolan. They could sue him for breaching the settlement agreement if they could prove he was responsible, but how could they do that? It could also, theoretically, be explained by a leak from a phone company employee, some disgruntled court personnel, or a hacker who had penetrated his or Mia's devices.

As hours went by, he intensely wanted to respond, to address this madness. But what would he say? That these texts were actually fake? That they were untrue? He wanted to say that this nickname and everything that cyberspace was enthralled with was not only mean and demeaning, but also unfair and inaccurate.

He decided that if he just ignored it and remained silent, maybe in this age of short-term memory and a viral moment every hour it would soon go away with the next online scandal and news cycle. In hindsight, he should have gotten out there right away, putting out his version and showing that he wasn't cowering in silence. Maybe he could have owned it, responded with a self-deprecating humorous comment that would have salvaged his reputation. But he made the unfortunate, fruitless decision to never acknowledge it at all, and as a result it ended up ballooning beyond anything he could have anticipated and defining him to the world without his rebuttal.

But before the call with his attorney, before he considered responding and decided against doing so, in the moments right after he first saw the online assault on him and his family, he first called Mia.

How would he break the news to her? There was no easy way.

But it turned out that he didn't have to. When she answered the phone, instead of hearing her voice, he found himself listening to her sobs. Despite all of their conflicts, he desperately desired to protect her and felt completely inadequate in his failure to do so.

"Mia . . ."

The crying continued, and then turned to wailing, the wailing of a grieving person as if a life she loved had just tragically ended.

"I want to die," she finally said mournfully. "I want to die because we have children and I can't bear facing them. But I can't die because we have children and *someone* needs to be there for them."

"We can tell everyone these texts were fake," he suggested weakly.

"No one will believe that . . ."

"Well, maybe we can say they were all a joke, Mia," he said in another grasping-at-straws attempt to soothe her. "We can say none of that really happened. Like, I don't even know if it really *did* happen, you know? . . . I mean, *did* it?"

She was silent for a few seconds, and then responded with disgust.

"Does it really matter? What the fuck does that matter now, Kyler? You're such a fucked up idiot asshole to ask that now."

25

WHY HAD she not slept?

Maybe because she had just been sliced up on national television in front of millions and then cast off and banned from future appearances. Maybe.

Or was it because the man who had taken advantage of her and then vilified her was waiting to see her in a few hours? Was it because she was completely incapable of quelling her mounting anxiety about the future while she endeavored to make sense of a violation for which there clearly would be no accountability?

And then it could be one of the issues that predated all of that—a failing business, serious financial problems, and ailing parents with out of control medical costs.

But an optimist could also credit the tantalizing excitement of a highly improbable but still possible $10 million payday. Would that solve all of her problems? Definitely not. Would it greatly help with many? Absolutely yes.

Before she worked at the White House, Maggie had never been a morning person. But she'd quickly gotten used to the early morning starts and long, merciless hours. After a few weeks there, 6:00 a.m. meetings weren't shockingly early anymore—they were routine.

And now, unable to sleep, and agitated by uncertainty about what would transpire, she welcomed the crack-of-dawn appointment. The waiting was brutal.

After last night, it was very possible that she was finished, in every way. The real fallout, how the rest of her world would react to the events, was still unclear. Considering the prominence of the show, the low number of encouraging messages she received from friends afterwards was disheartening. They probably didn't know what to say, and she understood. Plus, there was no follow-up text from Natalie this time.

She did take solace in one victory: even though unable to sleep all night, she had completely stayed off social media. She didn't need to read a bunch of strangers calling her a pathetic, stupid bitch in order to feel low about herself and her life—she could handle that on her own.

At five minutes to six, she exited the Uber at the same park and bundled up again in the freezing DC winter, the streets and paths now cleanly shoveled and the snow covering the grass and painting the trees. In the distance, she saw Bryce, wrapped in his dark coat and blue scarf.

She trudged over the white lawn to reach him, just feet away from where her phone had landed as he fled the scene the day before.

"Good morning," he said innocuously, as if it *was* a good morning, as if their last meeting hadn't ended the way it had, as if he hadn't had unprotected sex with her without her consent.

He silently extended his gloved hand toward her, palm up. She responsively reached into her bag, withdrew her phone, plugged in her passcode, and handed it to him. He took a quick look at the screen and then placed it in his jacket pocket.

"I'd appreciate it if you just hand it back to me this time," she said.

"I promise," he replied.

Another promise. Way too many promises.

"I think I figured out who you're working for, and I looked him up. The E-ZPass guy, right? Quite a character," he said with a condescending chuckle.

She was still sorting through a variety of conflicting feelings, but for the first time she was sure that she hated him. And therefore, she hated herself for voluntarily being in his presence again and hated life for requiring her to be there.

"By the way, quite an appearance last night, Maggie," he added. "Everyone's talking about it."

She wasn't looking to discuss this topic, especially with him, so she changed the subject by asking, "What's the president's executive order decision?"

He didn't seem bothered by her redirection. After all, it was why he'd summoned her for a morning meeting on a bone-chilling day.

"It's complicated," he said at first. "Those Priya Varma tweets are galvanizing opposition to the Kingdom and this tournament. So you know her from college?"

"Yes," she answered. "What's the decision?"

"The situation over there is very difficult, as you know," he said. "We want to find out the truth about the Kinum murder. We don't want to tacitly assist an authoritarian leader's propaganda after they tortured and killed an American journalist. We want there to be consequences and accountability. But we need to navigate all this tactfully and smartly so we don't have an armed conflict."

"Of course."

"At ten o'clock this morning, the president will strongly condemn the Kingdom for blocking an independent investigation into Emily Kinum's murder. He'll also say that until the Kingdom cooperates with the international community, Americans should not travel there and should certainly not help promote or participate in any high-profile activities or competitions that the crown prince is leading."

"And what about an executive order banning travel?" she asked.

"There's a lot of sentiment within the White House for him to issue one. Most forcefully from Connelly. He's been pushing hard for powerful economic sanctions, too, which I oppose for these types of situations. But he has a lot more leverage now with his new title, and the president seems to really listen to his opinions."

"How the hell did Mr. Dog Style get promoted to deputy chief of staff anyway?" she asked. "He was such a clown at your promotion party. That guy's terrible." She really didn't want to divert from the main topic, but she couldn't help pointing out how preposterous this was.

"The president likes him," Bryce said, shrugging. "And he's very smart. Very hard worker. I know he can be over the top sometimes, and we certainly have our disagreements, but I appreciate what he brings to the White House."

She realized she shouldn't have bothered to ask the question. It could have spared her the explanation of why one highly objectionable person was seen as valuable by another. In the end, not really a surprise. "Bryce, what about the EO? And why did you ask to meet? Obviously you didn't summon me here just to tell me what will be on the news in a few hours."

Bryce nodded. "Absolutely. I need something from you. The *president* needs something from you, Maggie."

She looked at him skeptically, trying to figure out what manipulation game he was working. The president barely knew who she was and probably hardly remembered her now that she was outside the White House. What could she possibly help him with?

"The president was going to issue the travel ban," he continued. "But your segment last night provided us an idea. We have no reliable American working for us on the ground there. The Canadian ambassador is supposed to be our official liaison, but he's currently pretty ineffective. And now Priya Varma, your friend, is stirring up all sorts of shit from inside the Kingdom. We need someone there we can trust. Someone smart and discreet who understands these issues. And, as we learned last night, someone who's friends with Varma and can try to talk her down. She's making this all even more difficult and, whether she appreciates it or not, her safety is very much at risk. We need *you*. Unofficially. Working for us. So no travel ban, and your client goes and plays in the tournament, and you travel with him as his consultant as your cover story."

"But I'm really working for you," she replied. "And what do you want me to do?"

"For now, learn what you can, and we'll be in touch with further directions. We may ask you to try to connect with the ambassador and Varma. But be very careful with your communications there. Surveillance is everywhere. Officially you don't work for us, but if you get in any trouble, head to the Canadian embassy and we'll extract you right away. It's a real opportunity for us. If you agree, we won't issue the travel ban."

"So you condemn anyone participating, and then I secretly work for you while supporting a participant?" she asked.

"Do you feel uncomfortable with that?" he asked.

Uncomfortable. Did he really dare ask if something he did made her uncomfortable?

She probably should have focused on the fact that she was being asked to travel to a dangerous nation that was hostile to women at a time when an American female journalist had just been murdered. She could have thought more about the reality of being an unofficial quasi-spy in a place where there was little if any protection. But after all the frustration and heartache and disappointment in her life recently, she decided to embrace this as extremely good news.

Maybe she *could* help her country here. Even making a small difference in this difficult, challenging situation would be very rewarding and satisfying. And she could strive to do that while successfully delivering in a huge way for her first client—a client who now would have the opportunity to win her *$10 million*.

She had been asking herself over and over when she would ever be able to appreciate any aspect of life again. Now, she made the conscious decision that she was going to appreciate *this*, and that emotion felt good, and so strangely unfamiliar.

"No, it's okay," she replied. "I would never turn down a request from the president."

"Thank you," Bryce responded, full of gratitude and relief. He then reached into his coat pocket and gently handed Maggie back her phone.

26

"I KNOW a magician doesn't reveal her tricks," Kyler said in a hushed tone as he looked at her with admiration, his right hand gesticulating with enthusiasm while clenching a beer bottle. "But how did you do this? It's amazing."

When Maggie first called and explained that in a few hours the president would announce that there would be no executive order banning travel, his response was one of delirious relief and excitement. She wondered if she had ever before made another human being so happy. He was ecstatic as she told him he could head to the Kingdom and enter the tournament, which was then scheduled to start in four days' time.

"Thank you! Oh my God. Thank you so much, Maggie. I-I . . . oh my God . . . This is . . . unbelievable."

When she told him that she would be traveling there with him, it was clear that this new wrinkle took him by surprise and further added to his elation. She didn't tell him the real reason, and he didn't ask for one.

"That's awesome. You're obviously very good luck, so I'll certainly need you to bring me luck there!"

Twenty-four hours later they were waiting to board their flight in the airline's premium lounge, the Kingdom having provided tickets for him and guest. They would have a short stop-over in London and then continue on to their destination. The venue was full of activity, with business travelers and a few vacationers enjoying the top-shelf bar and enticing food spread.

Kyler looked quite out of place, wearing a pair of battered blue jeans and a black sweatshirt from some casino she had never heard of, his hair askew and short beard unruly. She was wearing jeans and a comfortable scoop-neck long sleeve olive T-shirt, both relatively new and in good shape. She and Kyler were each dressed casually for the long travel ahead, but appeared remarkably different, she attired in a stylish and thoughtful way, he blissfully not concerned with such issues. What an odd traveling pair they made.

Maggie noted that Kyler was tall and decently built and probably would be handsome if he paid any attention to his physical presentation—which he clearly did not. She wondered if he had always been like that, or if his disregard for how he looked stemmed from all of his recent heartache and humiliation. Would this ultimately be her fate, too?

She was still trying to feel positive about this opportunity, but she was wrestling with increasing nervous reticence about where they were going and their actual prospects for success. It didn't help when Kyler handed Maggie her boarding pass at the airport and she saw her seat assignment: 2A. She then glanced at the one he was holding and tried not to show her exasperation when she saw his labeled 2B.

Such a long flight to London, and then another one to the Kingdom. Nothing against Kyler, but she really didn't want that much face time with anyone right now. Meanwhile, she could sense he was even more exhilarated by having her as his traveling companion in an adjacent seat.

They took a couple of sofa-type chairs in a far corner of the lounge, trying to avoid unnecessary contact with other people. In the airport she had already received a few unusually strange stares, as if people were trying to figure out if they recognized her from somewhere.

He was on his third beer, and she was still on her first glass of sauvignon blanc, taking a couple of sips. She would probably need to start drinking if this flight was going to be bearable, but she really didn't want to imbibe at the moment. Meanwhile, was it okay that he was drinking so much already? Shouldn't he be getting his mind right before a competition that would require immense concentration and high-level thinking?

Maybe it would at least make him fall asleep quickly on the plane and save her some interminable hours of conversation. Otherwise, she would just have to pretend that she was asleep while listening to some music or podcasts. She knew that actually sleeping, something she had been struggling to accomplish in the "comfort" of home, was very unlikely on the plane.

"You gotta tell me—how did you pull this off?" he prodded again.

"I can't really get into details, unfortunately," she replied in a whisper. "These things are complicated."

His eyes twinkled with admiration. "Okay, I get it. You must be so tapped in, having worked for the White House chief of staff. Nice to be that close to someone with so much power," he replied.

"We're not *that* close," she answered.

"I've seen him on TV. What's he like? Good guy?"

"No, definitely not a good guy," she replied way-too-fast and instantly regretted it. This was as far as she was going to take this part of the conversation. She really didn't need her mind to go there now, even though in one form or another it was heading there constantly. "But I can't talk politics here," she added, looking around at the travelers milling about in this DC airport lounge.

"Okay, no problem," he replied, lowering his voice. "I know nothing about politics. Although I once met my city councilman when he was campaigning outside a Chick-fil-A."

He drank his beer for a few seconds, and then they were silent for a minute, both looking out the far wall that was all window, revealing the planes taxiing, taking off, and landing. Kyler then glanced back at her, as if there was something serious he needed to share.

"Hey, Maggie . . . I really owe you an apology," he finally said.

"For what?" she asked.

"I told you I had a lot of money to pay you. When we first spoke. That wasn't true. And I'm really sorry."

"Well, if you win this tournament, all will be forgiven," she said.

He nodded. "That's my goal. I was in a bad situation when I called you, but that's no excuse. It's just that sometimes you're in a position where it's impossible to be honest if you want to be successful. Hell, it's hard to be honest sometimes if you just want to *survive*. It's like, tell the truth and you're done."

"Like having bad cards in a big hand, and the only way to win is by bluffing," she responded.

"I thought you didn't know poker," he said with a smile while still keeping his voice hushed.

"I don't. I really don't. But I get the general concepts. Listen, Kyler, don't worry about that now. We've all been there," she said, and then added, "although of course not after winning $8.8 million."

"Okay, okay," he said. "I want to explain that."

"No, really, Kyler, it's not necessary."

"No, I really want you to understand. Look, I 'won' $8.8 million," Kyler started, using two fingers on each hand to make air quotes. "But I immediately owed 20 percent to a bunch of guys who played in the tournament where I won my entry. So then I'm down to a little over $7 million. Next, this fucker who gave me $300 for the original tournament sues me for half, even though I never promised him a cent. We end up settling for $2.8 million. Big mistake, and that's another story, but that takes me to $4.2 million. My divorce gets finalized and my ex-wife gets half, so now I have about $2 million. I pay taxes and then I'm at just over $1 million. Then I have legal fees of about $150,000 for the suit I settled . . ."

"Oh God," she said sympathetically. "I'm so sorry."

"I made some decent money in personal appearance fees after my win, but I also had a really bad run of luck and lost . . . way too much. More than I had left. So there's a lot of debt now, too. But people think I gambled away $8.8 million. Even I couldn't lose that much. But the appearance fees were already slowing down before I called you, and no one wants to hire someone who's broke to promote their casino, so once that got out there . . . I know I won't get any more promotional events. No more comped tournament entries. And I can't afford the ones with any real prize money. It's pretty hopeless."

"But this tournament . . ."

"Yeah, *this* tournament . . ."

"You make up everything and more if you win," Maggie said.

"Right. Except my reputation. Can't make that back because of those bullshit texts from my ex-wife. Meanwhile, she's a 37-year-old middle school teacher and deals every day with being slut-shamed by a bunch of fucking 12-year-olds. I know, I know. You don't want to hear about that. But the media . . . and those online trolls . . . they can be so savage. So gleeful as they destroy someone's life. It's the twenty-first century but people still love a public execution."

"Well, all that I totally understand. I've experienced a lot of really nasty media behavior recently. Live and online."

"It's really depressing. A lot of times I feel like I don't even want to leave my apartment. I can't face the world anymore. But at least I'm not one of those MeToo guys who are *total* outcasts . . . The ones who go from superstar to supervillain overnight. I get so much ridicule and hate for playing in this tournament and everything else, but at least *some* people will still talk to me."

"Well, unlike you, those guys deserve it."

He appeared to be in thought for a few moments as he quietly sipped his beer. "Is it true every woman has dealt with it?" he asked.

"Dealt with what?"

"The whole MeToo stuff. Seems like it's everywhere all of a sudden these last couple of years, but what do I know? I read it happens to all women to some extent. Is that right?"

Another conversation she didn't want to have. If this was a prelude to what the flight would be like, she was in huge trouble. Hopefully, hopefully, hopefully this would all be worth it. "I can't speak for all women, Kyler. Like you can't speak for all men, right? But let's just say powerful men sometimes think they can get away with just about anything. And in my experience, with some I've worked with, unfortunately they're often right. Even now."

27

IT WAS ONLY Kyler's second time traveling internationally. Fortunately, he already had a passport for a tournament he attended in Toronto the previous year. United States, Canada, Kingdom. So limited. So much more of the world to see. Maybe. One day. If he was still around to see it.

Traveling for hours and hours and hours with Maggie was the most intense experience he had had with someone he barely knew. And as he spent all that time close to her, with every word and gesture shared, he grew more and more enamored. So smart, so attractive, such a successful woman who knew how to make things happen.

Of course, he would love to date her. He would be insane not to welcome that. But he recognized that most likely she wouldn't be into him, especially in his current broke, pathetic state. Maybe he could change that soon. In any event, with every new moment with her, he gained more and more appreciation for the idea that it would be a windfall to have her in his life in any capacity. Not a girlfriend? Well, simply having her as a friend, someone who occasionally spent time with him—that would be wonderful, too.

They talked about so many different topics during their travels, sharing their backgrounds and outlooks on the world, and he explained some of the theories and nuances of poker.

"You made that comment about needing me to bring you luck. But you also told me when we first met that it's a game of skill, not luck," she said while they were eating at a Heathrow restaurant during their stopover. "So which is it?"

"If you play well," he explained, "you're often betting with the odds in your favor. So that's different than any other casino game. In the long run, luck is irrelevant, because good luck and bad luck even out. Over time, skill is everything, and great poker players will always do better than others in the long run."

"Are you one of those great players?"

He thought about this. He wanted to give an honest answer, but he wasn't sure what the truth was. He could play so well at times, but also like a total donkey on too many occasions. "I can be. It really varies unfortunately. I'm certainly not a *bad* player . . ." He saw that this answer didn't inspire confidence, after she had devoted so much and traveled so far based solely on a promised share of his winnings, so he added, "But I intend to be a great player for this event. Just like I was when I won the world championship."

"I wouldn't be here if I didn't believe in you, Kyler. I know you can win this."

"Thank you. That means a lot to me," he said. "The thing is, even though luck evens out over time, that's only if there's *time* for it to even out. If there are opportunities for it to even out. But sometimes it all comes down to one hand . . . one turn of a card . . . and then luck can really save you."

"Like getting a two on the river?" she asked.

"Oh, you saw that, huh?" he asked enthusiastically.

"YouTube."

"Yeah, that was something, right? Wow. Too bad it came at the expense of your friend. I saw on TV that you knew her."

"In college," she said, with a wave of the hand, indicating that that was a long time ago.

"I've seen her at poker events since then and . . . she's not my biggest fan," Kyler explained.

Before they boarded their connecting flight, he looked through his phone, including social media mentions such as:

“Broke @kylerdawsonpoker now reportedly heading to goodwill dictator poker classic bc he is known loser in every free country #ezpass #sixofdiamondsontheriver #kylerdawsonisover”

And:

“There’s financial rock bottom & then there’s moral rock bottom. Congrats @kylerdawsonpoker u achieved both in same week! #bankylerdawsonfrompoker”

Followed by someone else’s succinct response:

“Factsssss”

A bunch of tweets linked to the change.org petition “Ban Kyler Dawson From Poker!” which urged casinos and poker tournaments to announce that he, and anyone else who played in the Kingdom, would be permanently banned from their facilities.

78,328 signatures so far. If there had been any doubt that he had no other future prospects, this confirmed it. The mass outrage and condemnation would only swell once the tournament started. There was only one shot left for him.

“You’re looking at Twitter?” she asked with annoyance. “Jesus, stay away from that this week! Please. And don’t you dare tell me about anything you read about me.”

Soon they were back in the air flying to the Kingdom, Maggie sitting next to him on the plane, listening to music or something else through her earbuds, while he thought about what was next. When he had entered WSOP, he started with no expectations and little hope for success. Just making the money and a small profit was a dream then. It didn’t even occur to him that he could potentially win it all, so there was zero pressure to take it all down. Now, it was different. There was no simple “cashing” in this tournament. He had little to go back to if he couldn’t conquer the whole field. The pressure on him was immense, and he had serious doubts about whether he was up to it.

They landed in the Kingdom that evening, and he envisioned a map of the world and thought about where he currently was. So surreal. Maggie and Kyler were greeted by a suited driver who helped with their bags and then whisked them out of the airport and toward a small downtown area with a few modest office buildings. They were taken to their hotel, a majestic twenty-story white structure with large marble columns abutting the grand entrance. Soon he was in his spacious room, where he barely took in his surroundings before collapsing into the king bed, exhausted.

He woke up, the day before the tournament was to officially begin, after an unconscious ten hours. Light shone past the expensive burgundy curtains, and he lay alone in his large bed. Everything he had read suggested that it was unwise to venture out alone in this strange place, but he had no interest in sightseeing anyway. He ordered food to his room and hoped to play some low stakes online poker to pass the time and warm up his poker muscles. But he quickly learned that online gaming was prohibited and blocked. Instead, unfortunately, he was left alone with his thoughts.

At about seven o'clock, he showered, put on a clean pair of jeans and a blue striped buttoned shirt, and then took a long look in the mirror. He actually appeared much better than he usually did—fresh, hair combed, beard groomed, clothes not looking like articles from a donation bin. Hopefully Maggie would notice the difference, although it was all superficial. No shower and presentable clothes could alleviate the tension, concern, and anger that continued to eat away at him.

What had he done so wrong in his life to be in such a messed-up situation? He knew he had made some poor decisions, and that was at least a small part of his marriage and life unraveling. But he also felt he was a well-meaning guy who *wanted* to do the right thing, even if he often failed. And yet, so many people now reviled him. People he had never met. People all around the world.

He thought back to Maggie's words when they first met: "*So why don't we agree that if you win—if we pull this off—we both devote a significant amount of the money to helping people in need.*"

Absolutely, he thought. *Then I'll be free to show people who I really am.*

Minutes later, it was time to head downstairs for the tournament welcome reception. As he prepared to exit his room, he saw a white letter-size envelope that had been slipped under his door. On the front, there were only the typewritten words "Kyler Dawson." He opened it and read the single-page letter.

As he and Maggie had arranged, he met her downstairs by the lobby elevator. She was looking refreshed and beautiful in a maroon dress.

"I got a letter—" he began.

"I did too," she jumped in. "Under your door?"

"Yeah. Can we ignore it?" he asked.

"I don't think so. We shouldn't. We can do it together after this thing."

They walked down a long hallway and toward the hotel's grand ballroom, presented identification to uniformed security at a table outside the door, and then entered.

It was magnificent—ornate chandeliers, gold-plated high ceilings, and expensive-looking portraits around the walls showing what appeared to be leaders of the Kingdom, past and present. The only one Kyler recognized was the biggest image of them all, depicting the crown prince he'd first met almost two years earlier in Las Vegas. In the painting he looked everything a leader should be—powerful, wise, benevolent. The nation's flag—red bars at the top and bottom, blue in the center, and two white swords crossing in the middle—hung large and high in the front of the room behind a wood and metal podium. There were a couple hundred people around the room, and food was being passed around on trays by tuxedo-wearing servers. Extravagant bars were set up at three locations.

Video screens showed a variety of poker broadcasts from around the world. The other individuals in attendance appeared just as international, their looks and clothes suggesting they originated from around the globe. His eyes searched for people he recognized, either from tournaments he had played in or online videos and poker coverage that he had seen. A few second-tier European pros were there, but the others appeared unknown and unremarkable. For certain, he was the only former world champion in attendance, and he wondered if he was also the only American.

"Can I get you something to drink?" Kyler asked Maggie. "I'm just having club soda. I need to be sharp tomorrow."

Before she could answer, a middle-aged man wearing a suit with an open collar shirt and holding a glass of red wine called out to Kyler. "Hey, is that you? Mr. E-ZPass!" he shouted with an Eastern European accent.

Maggie, standing beside Kyler, shifted uncomfortably, probably embarrassed for him. Meanwhile, a couple of other men in the surrounding area—there were very few women in the room—snickered, with one adding in an accent that was unrecognizable to Kyler, "Listen, man, don't give E-ZPass a hard time. At least his shit works. That's more than I hear about you!"

"Oh, your wife just told you that to make you feel better after I finished with her," the Eastern European answered with a laugh. "Trust me, she was so happy to finally be with a real man. Not like you and E-ZPass!"

"Don't let them get to you," Maggie whispered.

They weren't. It was difficult for Kyler to be embarrassed now after all the demoralizing brutality he had already experienced. And he was too close to his goal and salvation to get rattled by junior high school name calling.

Instead, he observed the lack of top poker pros in attendance and the less-than-stellar nature of the others he had glimpsed and heard from so far. These were, for the most part, B-level players at best—people who had connections to get invited here and compete for $20 million, as the crown prince tried to assemble the most accomplished field he could for the event he had been promoting and planning for two years. With all the backlash, all the boycotts, this was now the best he could do. It was passable, but it wasn't impressive to those who really knew the game.

"Not a chance," he replied to Maggie in a low voice. "They're a bunch of fools and I've never been more sure that I can beat them."

The lights dimmed, and a spotlight appeared over the podium in the front of the room. A well-dressed bearded man walked up to the podium and smiled at the crowd.

"Welcome all of you, to the first Goodwill Poker Classic!" he proclaimed, as the audience cheered. "Tomorrow morning we'll begin an historic international display of friendship and competition, all leading up to the awarding of our unprecedented $20 million grand prize! I now introduce to you, the man responsible for phenomenal leadership, visionary reform, and breathtaking compassion . . . our wonderful crown prince!"

Triumphant music blared as the crown prince entered from a side entrance, wearing a sharp pinstripe suit with a teal tie. He shook a few hands on his way to the podium as the attendees gave him a thunderous ovation, while Kyler and Maggie contributed more subdued but still polite clapping.

"Good evening, friends!" he declared. "Two years ago, I was taking a break from a hectic schedule to do something that many of you do all the time—play poker. And I realized that the game provided unparalleled comradery, brotherhood, and unity. So I thought, how can I bring those same qualities to our fractured world? Our planet has too much war, too many misunderstandings, so much hate, and endless conflict, some of which are shockingly petty but still profoundly destructive. The next few days will not solve those problems, but I hope they will play a small part in showing that the world can come together as one great human race. I look out on this room and see participants from around the globe. You are here not only to complete for a great prize, but to show that it is possible for us all, despite our differences, to be one unified brotherhood of mankind. You are making history. You are standing up for a better world!"

The room cheered again—for him, for themselves, for the benevolent stand that they appeared to believe they were making.

"And while people try to undermine and delegitimize this event and all we are working for, they have failed. The International Poker Federation may have caved to a bunch of nasty, hate-filled activists, but I have not. And you have not. This event is actually far stronger than I could ever have imagined, with so many accomplished and celebrated and important people before me. In particular, I want to recognize an individual from the United States of America—world poker champion Kyler Dawson!"

Kyler held up his right hand in acknowledgment as virtually everyone turned toward him and applauded. Even the E-ZPass hecklers joined in the salute, although Kyler could see that the Eastern European was subtly smirking. Despite all he'd been through, he was still an American citizen and a former world champion, and therefore no matter how tarnished he was, in this room, for this audience, and for this leader, he was an asset.

"Before I leave you to enjoy the rest of this evening," the crown prince continued, "I have two major announcements to make. First, as you all know, one of the central missions of my leadership, and my life, is to make this nation and this world a better place for women and girls. I am therefore announcing the next step in our historic reform program. Beginning immediately, female citizens of the

Kingdom will no longer need to obtain the permission of a male relative in order to work or travel. Yes, that unfair burden is hereby lifted!"

The crowd yelled in support, a few whistling their enthusiasm, as the sounds of approval swelled and lasted for thirty seconds.

"I didn't even know that was a thing," Kyler muttered to Maggie as they both slowly clapped along.

"Oh, it's a thing," she responded with not-so-subtle disdain. "One of *many* things . . ."

When the noise began to ebb, the crown prince continued. "Unfortunately, there are many in this world who don't want progress. Instead, they choose to defame us and undermine our efforts—to spread lies about me, about you, about all of us. Some would rather stoke petty grievances and anger in order to sow the seeds of more conflict. But as I see this great gathering and I look forward to the next two days of collegiality and sportsmanship, I have no doubt when I say, 'They have failed!'"

More enthusiastic noise from the crowd followed, and as Kyler repeated his respectful clap, he considered that he was watching what so many had cautioned against—propaganda from a third-world dictator. He didn't like being a part of this, but if that was as bad as things would get, he could survive it. Then it was on him to win the tournament and get the fuck out of there.

After a few seconds, the crown prince raised a hand to ask for silence.

"But wait. I have one additional announcement, and it is a very important one. As you all know, we have been conducting a very aggressive, professional, and thorough investigation into the tragic murder of American journalist Emily Kinum. Many have tried to say otherwise, but this investigation has been our highest priority since that horrible slaying. Now, I am able to share with you momentous news. Two vicious killers who are responsible for her murder were captured last night. They have confessed to their twisted crime, and have been justly punished in a very appropriate manner. Because of what they did, they have paid the ultimate price, and the world will not suffer their atrocities again!"

The people around him erupted, and instead of pausing, the crown prince raised his voice and continued, "Finally, this horrible matter is now closed, but we will always remember this magnificent woman. Therefore, this tournament will now be played in Ms. Emily Kinum's honor!"

And now the crowd was in raptures—singing support, shouting, clapping, standing on chairs with hands raised in adoration. Kyler didn't know what to think, what to believe. He perfunctorily clapped for a moment, saw that Maggie wasn't, and then stopped, too. He glanced at her next to him, not wanting to stare directly and draw attention to the fact that her hands remained defiantly still at her side. She returned a short, disapproving stare.

Maggie then stepped even closer to Kyler and said, under her breath, "Are we the only ones here who recognize how fucked up this is?"

Her opinion was strong and clear, unlike his, which was muddled and confused. But he decided to play along, proceeding with the assumption that her experienced take was probably correct. "I'm sure we're not the only ones," he replied quietly.

"This is a good time to take advantage of that invitation," she suggested.

He nodded, and they both slipped out a rear door as they heard the crown prince proclaim, "So I say to you all, please enjoy this evening and our entire goodwill event. I wish very good luck to all our great poker competitors when our wonderful competition begins tomorrow!"

In the hotel lobby they were able to get a car service and both entered the back seat of the black sedan.

“Canadian embassy please,” Maggie instructed the driver, and they were soon passing through the capital’s sparse downtown.

Kyler pulled the folded letter out of his back pocket and read it again. The stationery was from the Canadian embassy, and the short letter, signed by Ambassador Jacques Bouchard, asked him to visit the embassy that evening.

"I know you are here for an important event and are surely very busy,” the letter read, “but I would greatly appreciate if you could make the time for a short but important discussion this evening.”

Maggie and Kyler rode in silence, and then arrived at the gated complex about fifteen minutes later. They exited the vehicle and pressed a white button on a call box.

“Please identify yourself,” a female voice sounded through the device.

“Maggie Raster and Kyler Dawson,” Maggie replied. “We have an appointment with Ambassador Bouchard.”

They heard a buzzing sound, and then the gate opened. They walked up the concrete path to the front door, which was slightly ajar. Kyler pushed it open, and the two entered a gray lobby with the Canadian flag displayed along one wall.

In front of them stood a young woman, eyes red, face flushed.

“Priya . . .” Kyler began.

“Kyler . . . Maggie . . .” she replied, looking at each of them, appearing firm while holding back some concern. “Come in. The ambassador’s not here. But I sent you both that letter because it’s essential that we talk tonight. I have an important proposal for both of you.”

28

TORI SEETHED with fury—fury directed at both the Kingdom and the White House. And at the entire world, which was full of injustice and so many pathetic, weasel enablers who fostered it.

The news had just broken that the Kingdom was claiming to have found her sister's murderers and had "brought them to justice" by swiftly killing them. This was no doubt a fraud and a lie. She knew from the beginning that the crown prince himself had to be responsible for Emily's death. Then he revealed his guilt by stonewalling any type of objective, independent fact-finding. Of course, they were releasing little actual confirmable facts. And they were taunting and mocking her sister's memory by claiming to "honor" Emily in the type of authoritarian strongman display that her sister would have detested and then eloquently exposed in her journalism.

She immediately called the personal mobile phone of the White House chief of staff. And he answered.

"Tori—" he began.

"What are you doing about this?" she demanded. "No more spin and false promises. What are you doing about this?!"

"Tori, I was going to call you. I agree this is unacceptable. Where are you?" he asked. "Can you come see me? We should talk in person."

Forty-five minutes later she was sitting in his office in the West Wing of the White House. The walls showed photos of the president in assorted scenarios and Bryce with the president and other world leaders and dignitaries. It was a smaller office than she would have imagined for someone so powerful. On another day, in another time, she would have appreciated where she was and all the history and significance the building commanded. But right now, she was consumed with getting justice.

She refused his offer of a seat and stood facing him, not caring if he viewed her uncontained anger as disrespectful or inappropriate.

"All I see is the most powerful nation on Earth appeasing this butcher!" she exclaimed. "You don't issue an executive order to stop travel for this propaganda show. There's no military retaliation. There's just a weak-ass suggestion that there should be an independent investigation, which of course he ignores!"

"We have reasons for everything we're doing," he said defensively. "It's a complicated situation because—"

"I know. They're a nuclear power. Does that mean they can do anything they want? They can murder my sister and others without consequence? Are you going to do anything? Are you going to do *anything*?"

"Please sit down. Let's discuss this."

"No. I'm not sitting down. Tell me how you're going to respond to them murdering my sister. An American journalist. Tell me something real. No more bullshit."

"There are things that I just can't discuss. Please understand that. I promise we're taking this situation very seriously."

She realized that her message wasn't getting through. Nothing was going to happen unless she made her position crystal clear.

Throughout her life, as a reporter covering countless tragedies, as the sister of a journalist exposing worldwide atrocities, she had seen too many times that it often seemed random and arbitrary who gets punished and who doesn't. One person may spend decades in prison for a minor crime, while another may be responsible for the death of thousands—or *millions*—and become an exalted leader, an icon celebrated with respect throughout much of the world.

But from her experience, she knew that in truth it often really wasn't all that random. The ones who are punished generally had relentless people going after them, people with enough power and influence to hold them accountable or convince others to do so. Without that tenacity, it was likely that nothing would happen, and the world would just move on to the next inhumane incident and then the next. So she needed to stay firm and tireless and strong. She must stay absolutely committed to not giving up until those who killed her sister were held responsible.

While she was consumed with grief and rage, he was dignified and steady. So handsome, successful, in command—dressed in a trim gray suit with a crisp white shirt and stylish tie, his brown hair perfectly parted and combed. Helping to run the world when many his age were still figuring out what they wanted to do for a living.

This issue was probably just a small blip in his life, one of many issues to handle and make go away, while Emily was dead and Tori would never recover. She needed Bryce to feel her urgency. She needed to convince him and the man he worked for of how high these stakes were for her, and therefore for them.

"You know I'm not a passive person," she began.

"I don't think anyone has ever accused you of that," he responded.

"And I'm not shy about speaking out in the media and galvanizing people and doing whatever it takes to get justice for my sister. You understand that, I hope."

"I do," came the solemn reply.

"So I want to be very careful how I word this, because it's important that you comprehend exactly what I'm saying. If you and the president are the ones standing in the way of justice . . ."

"We're not, Tori."

". . . if you're the ones standing in the way, then that is the message

I'm going to deliver. And if that destroys your career, if that costs the president re-election next year . . ."

"We're on your side. The president is your greatest ally on this."

"Then prove that to me right now. Give me something specific. Some real action that you're taking. And not some meaningless financial sanctions. I need you to tell me something now. Not in a month. Not in a week. Now."

"There's a lot happening that's highly confidential. But I swear to you. A lot is happening."

"No one is being held accountable, except for some sham arrests and executions of some other probably innocent people. So many immoral individuals every day are not being held accountable around the world for horrible, cruel things, and I'm not going to allow that to happen here. I'm not resting until I change that. Even if you end up being one of the people who also needs to be held accountable for your inaction."

When she was finished, he released a quiet sigh. He was probably used to being surrounded by sycophants all day, so this had to be an unfamiliar experience.

"I'm pushing hard for something significant to happen," he said with a serious look. "Very significant."

"And what is that?" she replied skeptically.

"I want to tell you, Tori. But if you reveal it publicly, or to anyone at all, the consequences will be disastrous."

"I won't. I promise."

He continued to watch her as he calculated how to proceed.

"On my sister's memory," she added. "On Emily's memory. I swear I won't repeat what you tell me."

He considered this response for a few seconds. "Okay, here's the truth. The Kingdom is threatening us with nuclear weapons—"

"We all know that. So that means they can do whatever they want?"

"Please let me finish. We recently received some new intelligence showing that their missile program is not as far along as they want us to believe. We now have a small window to do something about that. We can take military action and hopefully remove their nuclear capability and maybe decapitate their military leadership."

"A pre-emptive attack."

"To save all of us from being hostages to their nuclear power forever, yes. The president hasn't made a final decision, but I'm pushing very strongly for this action, and I think that's how he's leaning. I believe it's going to happen."

"When?" Tori asked.

"I can't get specific," he said. "But very, very soon. Or we lose this opportunity."

Should she believe him? She certainly didn't fully trust him, but he appeared to be earnest. And he was taking a big risk by telling her of such a plan, whether it was true or not. If this was real, she could understand why they hadn't taken action earlier through an executive order or otherwise. They would want to hold off on being aggressive until the moment was right to strike.

She imagined the arrogant face of the crown prince, her sister's killer, watching as his military strength and then his own life were snuffed out in a forceful show of moral vengeance. That wouldn't bring back Emily, but that would be justice.

Tori nodded, acknowledging the significant secret that Bryce had just entrusted in her.

"The administration is going to need you on its side while we're planning this. *I'm* going to need you. You won't have to wait long, but your public support may be crucial to buying me the time to convince the president to proceed."

"Okay," she answered. "If you and the president are deceiving me, then I'll—"

"We're not. I'm not."

29

PRIYA GESTURED for them to follow her into a room at the end of the hall, and both Kyler and Maggie reluctantly obeyed. The invitation had said that the Canadian ambassador was requesting their presence for an urgent meeting, but they now knew they'd been deceived.

Kyler could leave, but part of him wanted to hear her out. She said she had a "proposal"—maybe it would be something that could help him. He surely needed assistance in his mess of a life. She was a powerful, smart, successful woman, and if there was an opportunity to join forces with her in some form, he needed to at least consider that option.

She led them into a medium-sized reception room, and then Priya closed the door behind them. Flames crackled from a warm fireplace in front of two couches adorned with maple leaves. Framed documents and photos filled the walls, and a lush red rug and wood coffee table lay between the two couches by the fire.

"This is one of their secure rooms," Priya said. "It supposedly jams outsize monitoring."

"Where's the ambassador?" Kyler asked.

"He's not here right now. He's dealing with other business."

"And you're now running the place?"

"It's a long story," she replied. "They're not thrilled I'm here. But they don't want to kick me out because of what the government here would do to me."

Kyler observed that Maggie looked uncomfortable as she silently stood near them, glancing around the room with an unfocused gaze. She hadn't really greeted Priya, and he wondered why. Sure, there was plenty to be stressed about for both of them—but Kyler noted something that went beyond the concerns related to the reception they just left, the upcoming high stakes tournament, and general Kingdom safety issues.

"Would you like to have a seat?" Priya asked them both.

"No, thanks," Kyler answered, while Maggie continued her silence. "So what's this proposal?"

"Kyler, I'm asking you to withdraw from this tournament. But before you answer—"

"I'm not quitting—"

"Before you answer, just hear me out. Okay?" she implored, her voice starting to rise. She then paused, closed her eyes for a second, and then proceeded more calmly. "Just listen to me for a couple of minutes. I'm in touch with some very brave people here who are trying to change this country so there's real reform, not disingenuous show-reform. Real modernization, a real movement to giving liberty to an oppressed population. I just learned that two of those people, a man and a woman, two people I have gotten to know well, were dragged out of their homes today."

Her face revealed increasing distress. She paused, pursed her lips, and then looked at Kyler before continuing.

"His name is Jonah. Her name is Madeline. They provided information to the outside world about the true story here. They gave information to journalist Emily Kinum. She'd been planning to write about the atrocities they shared with her."

"And what happened to them?" Kyler asked.

"They were locked in a small shed, and then, on orders from the crown prince, government soldiers lit that shed on fire. They slowly burned to death while struggling to escape. Screaming and slamming their hands against the walls, begging for mercy, all of this ignored. And now, the crown prince announced that they were executed because they were Emily Kinum's murderers. And he's declaring the case closed."

She was now breathing deeply, her right hand in a clenched fist.

But this was Priya Varma. Master poker player. An unreadable statue under intense stress. Now she was unable to stay in check? Kyler had serious doubts about her story. "How do you know this happened? Were you there?" Kyler asked.

"No," she answered. "But I know."

"How do you know?"

"I have very good sources. Here and elsewhere. People tell me things because they know I'll use the information for good."

Kyler walked over to the fire and looked deep within the dancing flames. He turned and made eye contact with Maggie, who clearly wanted to leave. Then he glanced back to Priya.

Poker superstar Priya. Six of diamonds on the river Priya. Bad beat at the WSOP final table Priya. Human rights activist Priya.

"That doesn't sound convincing to me," he replied. "Everyone has an agenda here. Who knows who's telling the truth about anything in this place? So you think that if I play in this tournament, I'm helping those who supposedly killed these two people."

"Not *supposedly.* They murdered them. And you are."

Kyler sighed deeply and shook his head in frustration. For all he knew, "Jonah" and "Madeline" weren't even real people and had never existed in the first place. "I'm just playing in a fucking poker tournament that may give me the ability to support my family for the rest of my life. That's all I'm doing."

"They're horrible people, Kyler. You're just one person, but you add a lot of credibility to this farce."

"Me?" Kyler scoffed. "Please."

"You're the only American in the field—the only former world champion they have. If you withdraw and condemn this whole charade, you'll be a hero. A worldwide hero."

"Oh, come on, Priya. You've never played in a poker game run by bad people? That's how all the poker legends grinded for decades! Going from game to game, facing down thugs and thieves and murderers. Shady houses hosting illicit action. Taking down big hands and then figuring out how to escape with the winnings. That's poker. So now you want me to give up my shot at $20 million so you and a few other people can maybe say I'm like a nice guy for a few days before you forget about me? What does that do for my life? Does that pay off my markers? Support my kids? I'm leaving, Priya. Right now. This tournament starts tomorrow, and I'm going to be well-rested and ready. And I'm going to win."

He began to walk toward the door, but Priya blocked him by standing in his way.

"Wait! Just listen to me. Here's my proposal, Kyler. I'll help you. I know you're in a bad spot right now—"

"You have no idea what I'm going through."

She couldn't possibly understand. An attractive woman, single, popular, no dependents, revered by adoring fans. She surely read the poker blogs and news articles. She knew about the sordid allegations, true and false, and the mortifying details that blanketed him every day. But what did she really know about his plight? Trying to maneuver worldwide embarrassment, a contentious divorce, evaporation of millions of dollars, three children who relied on him. Sure, she looked as if she was risking it all by being here, surreptitiously entering another rogue nation after her previous documentary foray into Syria. Again taking supposedly bold stands against obvious heels. But in the end she would emerge stronger than ever, more glorified than before. She didn't have to face a world that basked in vilifying her, and she never would. She knew nothing of his pain.

"Whatever you need, Kyler, I'll help you. I'll work with you to rebuild your life. The odds of winning this tournament are not great anyway. You can leave and be a hero. And then I'll work with you to get you whatever you need. Paid personal appearances, financial backing for big tournaments, endorsements, you name it. I'll vouch for you as a great advocate for human rights who took a brave stand here. We'll resurrect your reputation, your life, your finances. I'll help you!"

Kyler looked toward Maggie who was still strangely, silently standing off to the side. Surely she would want him to play, right? She had utilized important connections to get him here, and had a potential $10 million windfall in sight. Maybe he should ask her.

As for his own opinion, he thought two things about Priya's offer. First, even if she intended to follow through on all her promises, could she really deliver? How much would one person's support, albeit someone as prominent in the poker universe as Priya Varma, really help him? Maybe he could earn some money with her assistance and cash in a few tournaments. But even though her persona was large and she had a devoted fan base, she might also flame out as so many stars do. How durable and effective would her support really be? The truth was that if she had won the Main Event, her status would be infinitely more elevated and her offer much more valuable. But with a two of clubs on the river, she hadn't.

Plus, there was his other concern. Her words were just words, and thus virtually meaningless. He had learned from Nolan the devastating, crippling consequences of relying on a promise that the giver never intended to keep.

"And if you don't?" he asked.

She looked at him quizzically. "Don't what?"

"If you don't do any of that. If I withdraw and then you don't . . . do any of that."

She slightly angled her head to the right and viewed him thoughtfully, exuding the perfect balance of showing sympathy without being patronizing. “Kyler, if I say I’m going to do it, I’ll do it. I promise. I’ll be indebted to you for the rest of my life for the stand you take here, and I’ll always, always be grateful. I’ll help you. Whatever you need, I’ll help you. Always.”

He was calculating the pot odds of all this in his head. Thirty-five percent chance she actually follows through, then 50 percent chance her help is meaningful, so that’s a 17.5 percent chance she backs him in an actually helpful way. What does that earn him at most? A couple hundred thousand dollars? And then there was this tournament, where he could take away half of $20 million. What were his odds of winning that? There were one hundred players, but he felt as if he was one of the best there. The value far exceeded anything she could provide, even if she was sincere, even if she was capable of delivering a little fleeting salvation.

“I actually think I have a great shot at winning $20 million here,” he replied. “I just can’t walk away from that. I just can’t. I’ve come so far to get here. If I quit now, it would be a meaningless gesture that would accomplish nothing and be quickly forgotten. People want a certain type of person to be their hero, and it’s not me. Maybe you and others say some nice things about me for a few days. Maybe you help me get a few personal appearance fees. Then after a short time, no one will give a shit. Everyone will move on. That’s how this stuff goes. I can’t do that. I’m close to a $20 million payday, and you want to negotiate a chop where I get basically nothing.”

“You’re wrong, Kyler,” Priya answered. “Your stand against these horrible people will be monumental. You’ll be praised around the world. It will change your life.”

“I just don’t see it that way. No one will care what I do. And it won’t help anyone in the end, except maybe you. Right, Maggie? You know how these things work. What do you think? She’s your friend . . .”

With Kyler’s last comments and his rejection of the proposal,

Priya's outward show of compassion and support quickly melted away. Her demeanor was changing, her warmth receding. Yet she appeared firmly in charge, as she usually did.

Maggie didn't immediately answer Kyler's questions, and, as he and Priya turned toward her, he saw that there was something about his last comment that troubled her. After a short silence, Priya spoke directly to Maggie for the first time since they arrived at the embassy.

"Do you want to tell him?" she asked accusingly. "Or should I?"

"Tell me what?" Kyler asked.

Priya responded to him while her eyes trained directly on Maggie, who stood a few feet away in the corner of the room. "She's not my fucking friend. I've never met her in my life."

Maggie shook her head slowly in protest, but she didn't voice any disagreement. Kyler took this in and tried to make sense of it. *Of course*, they were friends. He had seen Maggie discuss Priya in detail on television. She had told him about their friendship herself. Hadn't they attended college together?

"Maggie, is that true?" he asked.

But Priya jumped in before Maggie could respond, again addressing her with an intimidatingly directness that Kyler hoped would never be trained on him. "So when I was reported missing and people thought I might be dead . . . when I could have been dead, for all you knew . . . you went on television and lied about how you were my 'very close friend.' And college 'best friend.' And then you used our fake friendship to try to publicly undermine my efforts to help people here! I mean . . . It's unbelievable. It's just *unbelievable*. What the fuck?"

"I never said those things," Maggie finally spoke.

"I watched it!" Priya quickly answered. "Now you're going to lie to me about what I saw with my own eyes!?"

"Watch it again. I never said those things. The anchor did. Not me. And I never told them to say that."

"Well, you didn't correct them!"

"It's really tough on air. It moves so fast . . ."

"That's ridiculous. And my God, don't they vet this shit before airing it?" Priya said with exasperation.

"I assume there's some light vetting . . ." Maggie replied meekly.

"You lied and said we were friends in order to undermine what I'm working for here. If people only *knew* what a horrible person you are . . . And you talked about how outgoing and popular I was. All lies! I was a total fucking loner, basically playing online poker in my dorm room 24/7. Did we even go to school together?"

"Yes, we did," Maggie said sullenly. "I was a year behind you. We met once, at a small off campus party."

"I wonder if *that's* even true."

"It is. And I'm sorry, Priya. I really am. But it's not what you think. It's still wrong, and I'm very sorry, but it's not what you think."

"Not what I think?! You didn't lie on TV about being friends with me?"

"No, I did . . ."

"And you did it to undermine all of my work to help people here?"

"No, No . . . that's where you're wrong. I've been doing television to promote my business, and one of the producers figured out I went to Penn when you did, and asked me if I knew you for a prime time segment. I thought they were just looking for positive, personal comments about you. So I just said yes because I thought it would be harmless—"

"And good publicity for you."

"Yes, good publicity for me. But I never meant to hurt you. To undermine you. That wasn't why I did it."

"But you *are* doing all that! Not just with what you said on TV but by supporting this regime. By being here. By helping *him*," she said, pointing to Kyler.

So Maggie *did* lie on television about her relationship with Priya?

What else had she fabricated? She had seemed so proficient, so . . . flawless. Was it all an act? Or was she just someone who stretched the truth one time because she needed to in order to be successful? Because Kyler certainly had done that, too. If he were to condemn her, he would have to condemn himself.

"So, I have a question for you," Priya said to Maggie.

Maggie clearly didn't want to hear what came next, but felt she had no choice. "Go ahead," she said simply.

"Anyone who digs into your background with any competence will quickly figure out your deceit here. So maybe you'll get lucky and no one will ever care enough to dig. But what would happen to your credibility, your consulting business, your ability to be on TV, your whole career . . . if I publicly revealed that you went on television while I was missing and lied about being my friend in order to promote yourself?"

Maggie's face was crestfallen, ashen. She was breathing heavily, and her eyes showed real fear. "Please don't do that," she whispered.

"What would happen to your life then? If I did that . . ."

"I'd be ruined," she replied despondently. "Done . . ."

"No one would hire you. No one would book you. You'd be finished. Right?"

Maggie nodded in capitulation, and her voice shook as she beseeched Priya for mercy. "Please, Priya. I'm so sorry. Please don't do that. I beg you. I'm so sorry. Whatever I can do to make it up to you, I'll do it. I promise. I'm not the bad person you think I am. I'm really not."

Kyler watched as Priya allowed an extended moment of tense silence to fall over the room, while she basked in the power that she now held over Maggie's existence. He intensely wanted to help her, come to her rescue, find some clever way to be her savior. And even if he wasn't successful, he knew he needed to try, so at least she would know that he made an attempt.

"Please, Priya," he interjected, "Don't be cruel about this. It's not right. She's a very good person, and you're not being fair."

Priya turned to Kyler with fire in her eyes. "You want to help her? Don't play tomorrow. My offer still stands. Withdraw and I'll help you rebuild your life. And you'll have my silence about this fucked up thing that was done by your . . . your . . . *partner* here, whatever she is to you." She then faced Maggie and continued. "You want to make this up to me? This is how you make it up to me. Get Kyler to end his participation in this travesty and we'll be even. If he withdraws by tomorrow morning, the world won't have to know exactly who you really are."

"That's not right!" Kyler proclaimed. "You're not being reasonable."

"Oh, really, Kyler? What the fuck do you know?" Priya lashed out. "You've got the worst judgment of anyone I've ever met, and you're going to say what's right and wrong here? You're the guy who thought it was the right play to call off all your chips on the first hand of the final table with ace high."

"But I won," Kyler needlessly reminded her.

"And because your horrendous judgment worked out one time, you think you know anything about anything? You took my fucking title, and you lost all the money! Then you come all the way here to try to get more money while ignoring all the people around you who suffer in oppression!"

"You're still mad at me for calling there?! You *tricked* me into calling! You *wanted* me to call! I fell for your trap, and you're still angry at me for doing exactly what you *wanted* me to do. So I sucked out on the river. You've never put a bad beat on anyone?"

Priya waived her left hand dismissively. "Whatever, Kyler. Keep playing your game, and we'll see how quickly you're felted tomorrow."

Before Kyler could respond, Maggie was speaking again. "I want to make this up to you. I really do. I know I need to. But I can't control if Kyler plays. You know that."

Priya took a step closer to Maggie and quickly transitioned her demeanor from fury to one of kindness and support. “I should despise you, Maggie. And part of me probably does. But I also have a lot of sympathy for you. For what you’ve gone through.”

“What are you talking about?” she asked, as Kyler wondered the same thing.

“I remember when I got knocked out of the Main Event,” Priya began. “By your friend here. Have you ever seen what happened?”

“I have. After I met Kyler, I watched it online.”

“Do you know poker?”

“Not really.”

“Okay,” she began to explain, “so when all the chips were in the middle, when Kyler called me for basically everything he had, and the winner of the hand was going to be in first place with a dominant position to win $8.8 million, I had a 93.8% chance of winning. Now, we know I didn’t win, and that was beyond devastating. That title, world champion, and all that money, would have transformed my life, and I would have used all that to then transform the lives of so many others. It was an extraordinary, once-in-a-lifetime opportunity that was savagely ripped away, and I’ll never get over that.”

“I’m sorry,” Maggie replied, and Kyler could tell she did it out of obligation more than true compassion. The other woman held her life in her hands and Maggie needed to placate her.

“So then I get this patronizing standing ovation, saluting me for coming in *last* at the final table, and it just rubs salt in my wounds and reinforces all that I had just lost. I only wanted to get the fuck away from there. You can’t imagine how much I needed to just disappear. But then one of the other players decides to hug me, and it’s not just a pat on the back with an air kiss. It’s a sweaty guy holding me too tight for too long on a worldwide broadcast, acting as if by playing at the final table together we just shared some formative experience that will bond us for eternity. And then the hug finally ends, and there’s this moment when I see that all the other players are now standing and I realize I'm going to have to repeat that with every single one of them."

"And they were all like that?" Maggie asked with what Kyler detected was a pretense of compassion, a desperate and understandable attempt to sound sympathetic.

"No. A couple were fine. But most were lingering too long with wandering hands, pulling me absurdly tight against their bodies and whispering bullshit niceties so unnecessarily close to my ear. I've never felt so defeated, and all this is happening while millions around the world watch this pathetic walk of shame around the table. It was mortifying, and unbearable, and it seemed to last forever."

"You couldn't walk away," Maggie said, and Kyler first heard it as a question but then realized it was a statement of fact.

Priya shook her head. "I was crushed. So broken. I wanted to just get through it for whatever period of time was necessary so I could then escape and really melt down in private. So I went with it all, all the way around the table, and I was . . . appropriate."

Kyler tried to recall his hug with Priya, but it was hard to remember details. It was such a blur. A wild moment on an incredibly surreal night. "I didn't do that, did I?" Kyler asked.

Priya looked at him with stern disapproval. "You really want me to answer that?" she said scornfully.

Kyler thought for a moment. "Actually, yes," he replied. "I do. If I did something wrong, I want to know."

Priya rolled her eyes and then looked back at Maggie. "I'm sure in politics you've experienced a lot of fucked up situations," she said.

Maggie nodded knowingly. "Absolutely."

"I know you have," Priya added. "And I know that what I just described is nothing compared to what *you* experienced recently."

Kyler saw in Priya's focused eyes that she wasn't just talking generalities. There was something specific, something very real and important that she was citing. He observed that Maggie noted this, too, as her eyes narrowed and a surprised confusion crept across her face.

"You don't know anything about me," Maggie replied, and Kyler caught that her bottom lip subtly twitched for half a second. No doubt Priya saw that, too.

"You've had it much worse. By a man you trusted. A man who violated that trust."

Maggie closed her eyes for a moment, and when she opened them Priya was still in front of her, and Kyler watched as his consultant worked to summon some inner strength in order to compose herself. "What are you trying to do here?" she asked. "What kind of fucking game are you playing with me? I said I'm sorry for what I did. And I am. I deeply regret it. But what you're doing now is . . ."

"I'm not playing a game with you, Maggie. I told Kyler earlier that I had a proposal for him. A proposal in which I'd be on his side and help him. So I have similar proposal for you. I can be on your side and help you. Because I know what someone did to you, and I know it's eating you up inside that he's getting away with it."

Maggie looked away at the crackling fireplace and then down to the ground and then finally back at Priya. She opened her mouth as if she was going to speak, but then exhaled and closed it. There was no doubt that Priya had struck a nerve, and Kyler tried in vain to figure out what her angle here was. If her goal was to just rattle Maggie, she had clearly succeeded. But that alone couldn't be Priya's endgame.

"We'll go after him together," Priya offered.

"There's no one to go after," Maggie replied unconvincingly.

"Yes, there is," Priya said with certainty. "You don't think I really know? You think this is just some bluff? I know, Maggie. I know what Bryce Kirkwood did to you."

Kyler watched as Maggie responded to the name drop by closing her eyes once again as her chest began to involuntarily rise and fall with her deepened breaths. She squeezed her eyes tighter and ran her right hand across her nose, and Kyler closely tracked the tear that trickled down her right cheek and onto her breast.

Finally, she opened her eyes and shook her head in mournful outrage. “I don’t know what you think you know,” Maggie said. “But I’m sure it’s wrong, and it’s none of your business.”

Kyler very much wanted to learn the truth here. What had Maggie experienced? Obviously, there was some truth to whatever Priya was referring. But why was she being so insensitive about an issue that clearly involved raw, emotional pain? “Stop fucking with her, Priya! This is wrong. Just stop—”

“No!” Maggie declared in anger, raising a hand toward Kyler to silence him. “I can handle this myself!”

Kyler crumbled back into silence, as Maggie proceeded to turn her ire on Priya. “Tell me right now what you think you know. Tell me!” she commanded.

“I know he’s a predator, and that you’re one of his victims.”

“You have no way of knowing that!”

“Obviously, I do. And you’ve just told me that I’m correct.”

She shook her head vociferously. “I haven’t told you *anything* . . .”

But Kyler knew, as Priya of course did, that she had. Priya was a master at baiting others to involuntarily provide key information, and the response here had been well beyond a faint tell that only an expert could decipher. Maggie’s reaction had been visceral and overwhelming, and despite her wishes she had unwillingly revealed some deeply held, dark truth.

“Bryce Kirkwood isn’t just someone who mistreated you. He’s a very powerful man who’s currently the point person for appeasement here. He’s the one who killed the executive order banning travel here. I have very good contacts who tell me he *personally* greenlit Kyler coming over.”

“Coming over here?!” Maggie exclaimed. “*You’re* here!”

"I'm on a humanitarian mission, not trying to profit from this horrible place. People all over the planet placate the world's most despicable barbarians when their financial interests are at stake. Some of us need to fight back. The world needs to know the truth about what Kirkwood did to you, and I want to stop him from guiding our president into a feckless foreign policy that cowers at instead of confronting oppression, censorship, and murder. It would be really helpful for everyone to know that the main person in the White House supporting this regime is a sexual predator. It's time for him to be taken down. It's overdue."

"This story that you're creating is not true," Maggie shot back. "It's fiction. And I won't be a part of it."

"Well, that's your choice. But once this gets out, and on my word it will, you know that everyone will be seeking your comment."

"Where is this coming from? I don't even understand what you could be basing this on. Whatever you think you know, it's wrong. And even if there was any truth to it, which there's not, it wouldn't be your story to tell!"

"Please, Maggie, after what you've done, you're the last person who can make a moral claim about accuracy and controlling your own personal narrative. You went on national television and lied about—"

"I know what I did! I'm sorry. I said I'm sorry, and I am. But this is so different. You know it is. You're acting like you're this noble freedom fighter but you're in the wrong here. You created a dishonest ruse to draw us here, and now you're threatening my life. It's not right. Please realize that!"

"I want you both to listen to me," Priya instructed and then turned to Kyler. "I want you to withdraw from this tournament before it starts tomorrow morning and say you've decided you can't support this repressive government. I'll then work with you to rebuild your reputation, your life, your earning potential, all of it." She then looked toward Maggie and continued, "And I'll leave it to you to decide what to do about Kirkwood. I still think you need to come forward. You owe it to yourself, if no one else. But if Kyler plays tomorrow, then the information I have will be released publicly. Maybe I'll put out a statement that you went on television and lied about knowing me while I was missing. Your career couldn't survive that. Or maybe social media will suddenly have an anonymously sourced article about you and Bryce Kirkwood. Of course, I can't both call you a liar and have you named as a credible victim here, so I'll have to choose one. Which would you prefer?"

"You're blackmailing me," Maggie responded.

"No, I'm fighting back. And now it's up to you two to figure out by morning how to proceed. We can all work together on this and do the right thing. Your call."

"Just tell me," Maggie pleaded with agonized helplessness. "What is it you think you know about Bryce Kirkwood and me? I truly don't understand what you think you know!"

Priya just looked back at Maggie and shook her head. Kyler wasn't surprised. He knew Priya wasn't the type to show her cards when she didn't need to. How much and what kind of information did she really have? Maybe they would both find out later, but at this point it didn't really matter. It was clear to all three of them now that Maggie had inadvertently confirmed that Priya had, to at least some extent, referenced the truth. And soon Priya might reveal some version of that truth to the world.

"It looks like you've been off social media recently," Priya said to her. "If Kyler plays tomorrow, you'll want to get back on."

Kyler felt sorry for Maggie, and he wanted to help her. But she had just rejected his lame attempt at assistance, and he didn't know what else to do. Would she want him to withdraw from the tournament? He wasn't sure. But he couldn't imagine doing so. The prize was far too large.

He knew that if he played and Priya followed through on her

threats, Maggie was in store for a miserable, life-altering few days, and a possibly ravaged existence after that. He would do whatever he could to be there for her, to support her as much as she would let him.

And he hated himself—truly detested what a fucked up human being he was—for considering that if Maggie's life took a tough hit, if she was really knocked down and struggling to survive the way he constantly found himself, there was a greater chance that she would be with him. Maybe then she'd be in a position to settle for him, and over time he could make her glad she did. And if he could somehow win a $20 million prize for them to share, he could *really* be her hero.

Part Three

30

Pocket aces.

Two red aces, to be more specific. One with a small red "A" above a diamond in the top left corner, and the same A/diamond pairing upside down in the bottom right. A single large red diamond filled the middle of the card. The other, the ace of hearts, was nearly identical except for red hearts substituting for diamonds.

They were a beautiful sight, especially when playing poker with your life on the line.

It was the sixth hand of the tournament. His cards, the best starting hand in Texas Hold'em poker, contained so much promise. He could raise, get some callers, and begin building a large pot. He might greatly increase his chip stack, maybe double up. Possibly even do better than that.

But of course, besides the excitement and hope that Kyler felt while he remained perfectly still on the outside, the two cards also brought their own special foreboding that disaster might just be a few streets away. With some bad luck and unfortunate play, the best hand could inevitably be cracked by a small pair hitting a set on the flop, a cruel two pair, or a flush or straight made against long odds on the river.

Once he had so many chips committed, while holding those two wonderful aces, would he be able to get away from the hand if needed? Would he know when he was beat and fold, or make a terrible crying call and lose a bulk of his remaining chips, or even all of them? Or maybe he'd sense that tragedy was just in front of him, convinced that he was beat, and make a carefully considered fold, only to then be shown a bluff and learn that he was a fool.

There was much more comfort in looking at hole cards and seeing a pitiful three-eight off suit and knowing that there was no decision to make, that a fold was automatic, and that nothing bad could possibly happen on that hand. With those cards, he would know beyond any doubt that he would still be alive to see the next hand.

Not so with pocket aces. This might be the hand that would change the tournament for him. Or end it. But as Kyler considered how much to raise, he learned that there was yet another possibility for how this hand could play out.

"Hey, you gave him three cards."

It was the Eastern European guy from the reception, the one who had mocked him. Kyler had since learned that his name was Sacha. He again wore a nice suit with open collar shirt while most others wore casual attire. He was three seats to Kyler's left, and Kyler had winced when he saw the man take his seat at the same table.

Sacha had displayed a wry smile and proclaimed, "Well, hopefully *this* one isn't done in two seconds for *any* of us."

Don't let him get under your skin, Kyler had told himself. *Don't let him put you on tilt.*

Now, everyone turned to the player in the small blind, four seats to Kyler's right. Instead of the normal two starting cards that everyone received each hand, three face down cards lay in front of him. The dealer, a young man with a buzz cut, wearing the same loose-fitting royal blue shirt as the others, looked quizzically at the three cards, trying to figure out what had gone wrong.

These dealers were terrible. Kyler had heard from another player that most or all had never dealt poker before, as there were no actual legal casinos in the Kingdom, but they had all received crash-course training before this event. During the initial hands, the shuffling and dealing were sloppy and the management of the blinds and subsequent bets was less than precise, with players having to advise the dealers on correct counts for blinds and change. God help them the first time a side pot would have to be calculated.

On an earlier hand, a guy bet big on the turn and another folded. The player who took down the pot showed one of his two cards, an ace of spades, leaving the other one tantalizingly face down until the dealer turned the other one over, too, revealing a ten of hearts.

"Show one, show all," the dealer explained robotically, as the players at the table looked on in confused disapproval.

"That's not what that means," one finally explained. "Show one, show all means . . ." and then he dropped it. It wasn't worth it, he apparently concluded.

Now, as Kyler saw the three cards in front of the player in the small blind, and thought about the exhilarating pair of aces in front of him, he badly wanted to suggest a solution.

Just use the third card as the burn card, he thought. *Then we can proceed.*

But if he said it out loud, he knew it would probably be too clear that he was desperate for this hand to continue, that he liked his cards too much. He couldn't allow it to be that obvious. So he waited a couple of seconds, hoping for another player to speak up, while the dealer continued to glance at the three cards and then around the table to figure out the mix-up.

And then it was over.

"Misdeal," the dealer muttered unapologetically, and then he swept his hand around the table, securing everyone's starting hands, ripping away Kyler's heart and diamond aces.

Then there was the appalling blind structure. Unlike the World Series of Poker, in which blinds slowly rose over days and days, giving players plenty of chips and time to be patient for decent cards, get a feel for the players at the table, and make a few minor mistakes without being eliminated, the Goodwill Poker Classic was a turbo tournament looking for a quick resolution.

One hundred players, divided evenly among ten starting tables. All but nine would be eliminated during a frantic day one, with the final table taking place the next afternoon. They each started with 12,000 in chips with the starting blinds at 50/100. Just 120 big blinds each—low for any serious tournament, and an appallingly small number for what billed itself as a major event.

As he called a pre-flop raise from Sacha with queen-jack of spades, Kyler took a quick glance at Maggie, who stood by the far wall of the large room—the same one where the reception had been held the night before. She looked back at him for a moment, and her drained face and heavy eyes revealed the toll that everything was taking on her. Priya's threats had the potential to publicly drop at any moment, and Maggie quickly went back to nervously looking down at her phone. She was waiting in fear, and the fact that she was still waiting showed Kyler that nothing had been unleashed yet.

"So if I asked you not to play, I assume you'd play anyway?" she had said the night before, seated on the sofa in his hotel suite.

"You know I have to," he replied. "Why, do you want me not to?"

"Well," she said, pausing dejectedly to consider what he asked. "Once again, it doesn't really matter what I want. It's all just going to happen."

He had wished he could reach out and touch her. Not in a sexual way, but to soothe her. A supportive hand on the arm. A brush of her hair. A hug, holding her close in a firm embrace. Rubbing her back to provide comfort as she leaned her head down on his shoulder. He would feel her body against his, and she would look up at him with affection and gratitude, and their eyes would lock and she would smile, a smile that said that despite all this stress, all the obstacles and misery that they both faced, she was glad that they were in it together. She would kiss him, first on the cheek, and then on the lips, and then within moments they would be undoing each other's clothes and . . .

But wait, this was about soothing her. Nothing sexual.

"Of course it matters what you want," he replied. "I'm only here because you wanted me to be here. I wouldn't be here without you making it happen."

The flop came down eight-nine-seven rainbow—each card having a different suit. Sacha made his continuation bet, and Kyler decided to call. He didn't really have much, but with two overcards and a gut-shot straight draw, he wanted to see the next card.

Turn card: ten of diamonds, the second diamond on the board.

Kyler stared dispassionately at his opponent as his mind exulted at this miracle card. With the board showing eight-nine-seven-ten, he now had a straight with his jack-queen. And if Sacha held a jack, he, too, would have a straight, but an inferior one.

"Fifteen," Sacha declared, tossing a few chips that totaled 1,500 in front of him.

Kyler waited a few moments, considering how much he could raise here with his monster. Too much might scare him off, so he wanted to be smart and careful.

"Raise," Kyler stated. "Four thousand."

Sacha turned his head to the right to stretch his neck and then cracked his knuckles as he appeared to be considering what to do next. With each player starting with 12,000, a bet of 4,000 this early in the tournament was a lot.

"Call," finally came the answer.

The dealer dealt the river, a four of diamonds.

"My man here came up with a good number—4,000," Sacha explained. "Let's do another 4,000."

He pushed 4,000 out in front of him.

Kyler tossed 4,000 in chips to call, and then turned over his jack-queen to show his straight. The other players and the dealer turned to Sacha who stared silently at Kyler's cards.

"A queen?" Sacha finally asked with intense disappointment in his voice. "Not only do you have the straight with the jack, but you also have the queen?" He shook his head and muttered with annoyance, "My straight's not as good," while turning over the jack of diamonds.

A warm rush ran through Kyler and he looked at the chips in the middle, almost enough to double him up, a great start to this tournament. It was added satisfaction that the chips came from this jackass who would now be teetering on elimination.

"But," Sacha said before the dealer could push the chips to Kyler, "I do have a flush."

And he revealed his other card, the ace of diamonds, completing the diamond flush and beating Kyler's straight.

Kyler leapt up from the table in rage as a feeling of sickness and disbelief enveloped him. He turned toward his opponent who was three seats away.

"You fucking slow roll me like that? Are you fucking kidding me?!" he exclaimed.

His opponent's etiquette was atrocious, breaking so many unwritten poker rules as he acted as if he'd lost before showing the winning hand. The consequences for Kyler were even worse, as it would leave him nearly crippled, with a short stack of just over a thousand chips, almost eliminated in the early minutes of this tournament.

Sacha stood up, too, and snapped back, "Hey man, you better relax. This is a friendly tournament. Can't start screaming whenever you lose a hand."

So many times Kyler had let his emotions get the best of him during a poker game and he had really strived to avoid that happening here. But if there was ever a justified time to not hold back, with all the pressure and the terrible position he suddenly found himself in and all the horrendous events of his recent past, it was now.

"That's really fucked up!" Kyler yelled. "That slow roll . . ."

"Hey, just calm down man. Wow, you really *do* get too excited very, very quickly."

Sacha was a little taller and in better shape than him, but at this point Kyler didn't really care. He was in full fury and ready to throw down.

"How about I knock you out very, very quickly?" Kyler asked as he stepped toward Sacha.

A few uniformed male security officers immediately surrounded the table, and one of them blocked Kyler with a stiff arm while another stepped in front of Sacha. Sacha just raised his arms in the air with his palms face up.

"I'm just playing poker guys. This loser's the one causing trouble and making threats," he explained.

As blinded as he was by the anger of the moment, Kyler was nevertheless aware that Maggie was no longer pensively looking at her phone and instead was walking rapidly toward his table with an open mouth and eyes full of concern. Play had momentarily stopped at the surrounding tables as players throughout the hall stood to look at the commotion, some in shock, others in bemusement.

Kyler stepped back from the table and the security officers and made his way toward Maggie. She grabbed his right arm firmly—no affectionate touch here—and glared at him. She kept her voice low but it was full of intensity.

"What the fuck are you doing?" she asked, her eyes both accusing and pleading. "You can't do this here. Not now. You need to stay—"

"He just . . . he just slow rolled me and—"

"How much do you have left?"

"Not much . . . I'm almost done."

Maggie looked fiercely at him as she released her grasp.

"You better not be done," she commanded. "My life's about to be torn apart for this tournament."

He nodded and wondered whether if he got knocked out soon it would leave him enough time to reach out to Priya and beg her to hold her fire. Maybe he could still save Maggie, if not himself.

"Look," Maggie said, "I need to leave to deal with . . . my stuff. But I'm not abandoning you."

"Where are you going?"

"I can't say. I'll be back in a couple hours. I'm expecting you to still be alive when I return."

He sighed in deep frustration and disappointment and in fear of what was about to come for both of them.

"I'll do everything I can," he replied. "But I'm really short-stacked now."

Her lack of poker knowledge probably helped her believe this was salvageable, as she responded, "Kyler, you can do this. I need to go, but I know you can win. If I didn't believe that, I wouldn't be here."

And then, a few moments later, she wasn't.

31

EVEN IN THE early afternoon, the dance music was pumping and the mostly under-thirty crowd was filling the tables, booths, and dance floor. Were they getting an early start on a party that would go into the night? Or still raging from last evening, oblivious or indifferent to the fact that the sun had risen? Probably some of both.

"Good to hear from you again," it sounded like the man said as he leaned into her ear, although she couldn't completely tell over the cacophony. But, of course, that was the point. "I see you've raised your profile since I last saw you," he added.

Just wait a few minutes. This is nothing. "Is this where the ambassadors hang out?" Maggie asked sardonically.

He shook his head. "This is where the young expats spend their parents' money."

One thing Maggie shared with the all-nighters around her was a lack of sleep. She was exhausted and wondered if and when she would ever have a real night's rest again. Meanwhile, there was an unmistakable sexual energy among the congregants who were drinking, dancing, talking, kissing, and fondling sporadically around the club. For a fleeting moment, she uneasily noted that this or any other kind of sexual energy now seemed so foreign to her.

Her phone was out on the table in front of them, face up, as she and the ambassador sat next to each other in a small booth in a corner of the club, looking out onto the main floor. For now, the device was still, but she braced for the moment when it would explode and her already charred life would be engulfed by flames.

She kept trying to comfort herself by seizing on the fact that Priya didn't really, *couldn't* really, know anything about her and Bryce. But she clearly had some basis for her threat, and in the world of Washington, DC and social media, vague accusations of impropriety could very well be enough to capture the public's imagination and forever shadow the lives of those involved.

And then there was the possibility of Priya exposing her misrepresentations about their friendship. Maggie had always prized honesty and integrity, and she prided herself on having a strong moral compass, even when dealing with so many unsavory people in her career. At the time, it had seemed like a meaningless exaggeration, a white lie, the kind of spin almost everyone engaged in at some point. Now it might sink her.

How she wished she could undo that last TV interview. How she wished she could undo that flirty, devilish look she exchanged with Bryce at his promotion party. How she wished she could undo . . .

Kyler's last hand.

Turns out, a flush beats a straight. She hadn't known that before, but she certainly did now.

Could he recover? Was he already knocked out? No, he would have texted her if he was eliminated. Wouldn't he?

But as so many thoughts raced through her head, she knew she had very little time and couldn't afford to waste any.

"I need your help," she said succinctly.

"And I need yours," Jacques replied quickly. He was probably three times the age of some of the revelers. He was so out of his element in this place with his dark suit and blue tie, his gray hair and small bags under his eyes. But this was where he had wanted to meet when she reached out to him early this morning—so their conversation couldn't be overheard.

Maggie's mind had contemplated all night what she could do to forestall or at least mitigate what might come from Priya at any moment. She considered pre-empting her—publicly stating exactly what had transpired through a series of tweets outlining how Priya had misled them and threatened them. But then Priya would just respond, at a minimum, by revealing Maggie's dishonesty on national television, and her reputation would be destroyed. And maybe Priya didn't really intend to say anything publicly. Perhaps it was just an empty threat. In that case, it would be a huge mistake to be the first to launch a public attack.

"Can you get me a secure line of communication to Bryce Kirkwood?" she asked. "It's urgent." She had finally decided that she needed to warn Bryce in a confidential way about what was looming for both of them. And she wanted him to know that this wasn't coming from her. The Canadian ambassador, who she had met once a couple of years earlier, was her best hope.

"Nothing is totally secure in the Kingdom," he replied. "But I can give you the closest thing we have in the embassy. Can I ask what you're speaking with him about?"

A waitress came by the table, and Maggie impatiently waived her off, and then leaned in closer to his right ear. "Yes! You have an American at your embassy who pretended that she was *you* last night in order to lure me and a client over there and blackmail us. Are you aware of this? My God—she said she's going to release all sorts of lies about Bryce Kirkwood and me if—"

"If your client plays today?" he interjected knowingly.

She nodded.

"And he did, I understand."

"Yes."

"What information is she blackmailing you with?"

"I'd rather not say. Is she still there?"

"For now. I'm working to get her safely out of the country. The

Kingdom figured out where she is and wants her turned over to them. Of course, I've refused. So they've demanded that my government replace me as ambassador."

"And will they?"

"With my consent, yes. I want . . . I need to leave here, too. Both of our lives are in danger here."

"Are you aware of what she's doing? You need to stop her."

"I don't have the ability to control her. I don't condone her tactics, and I don't have all the specifics anyway, but I do know that she's fighting to make things better here. That's sorely needed."

"She has you fooled then," Maggie replied sharply. "She's threatening to destroy my life. She's not a good person."

"I'm not here to argue with you, Maggie. Right now I'm working on getting her—and me—out of this country, safely as soon as possible. And I would suggest you and your client do the same."

"Why is that?" she asked.

"Because the United States is planning an imminent attack to take out the Kingdom's nuclear capability and to exact revenge for the death of Emily Kinum. But the crown prince says that he has a nuclear arsenal that will be launched at the start of any attack, with intercontinental ballistic missiles that will reach the United States. I don't want to sound unsympathetic, but whatever she's threatening to say about you and Bryce Kirkwood . . . you won't have to worry about it getting much media attention once nukes start falling."

"How do you know his threat is real?"

"He told me himself, and I can tell he wasn't bluffing."

"What kind of bullshit is that, Jacques? That's how we're gathering intelligence these days?"

He stared out at the club as he considered how to reply. He then nodded a little and gave her a look that said, "Fair point, but still . . ." before explaining, "I'm trying to stop a war. I, too, need to speak with Bryce Kirkwood because I understand he's the main presidential advisor urging military action. I need your help to convince him to get the president to hold off on any attack. I want justice for Emily, too. There *needs* to be justice, but not in this way. It won't work. The president listens to Kirkwood, and he's the main person standing in the way of a non-military solution. I need your help to convince him we can find a better way that still holds the crown prince accountable, without starting a war."

"So he did have her murdered?" she asked.

Jacques leaned in closer as he answered. "I believe so. I was actually close to her and this is quite personal for me. I think at one point he did want to be a reformer like everyone believed, but who knows. He probably saw that with reforms came open dissent, which really threatened him and his family. A change in government would mean that they have all their wealth stripped away, they're prosecuted for crimes real and imagined, and maybe even killed by new leaders who are potentially far worse. I'd be fine with the crown prince and his regime wiped off the face of the planet, but it will come at a horrible price. We have to convince the White House to find another path."

"When is this attack supposed to happen?"

"Any day now. Maybe within hours."

"How do you know?"

"I have good sources. I've been doing this my whole life. And can I ask why you're here, Maggie? Just to watch your client play poker?"

She recognized that her dire situation required that she be fully open with him. "I was asked to be a liaison for the president here."

The ambassador looked surprised and confused. "If that was true, I would know about it."

"You think I'm lying—"

"No, no, of course not! But it's strange because I'm the eyes and ears for the US here. To send someone without telling me makes no sense. But it's not important now."

"Sounds like we both need to speak with him immediately," she said.

"Okay. My car will take us to the embassy right away."

The music was still loud, the club full of activity with pockets of near-chaos. Her phone had remained still throughout the conversation like a well-trained lapdog. There was no way she would hear it over the noise in this place anyway, but just before they rose to leave, it began to move ever so slightly. Within moments, the vibrations were constant as the phone lit up with a seemingly endless stream of messages and notifications. She could even feel the device's silent howls all the way down the table leg that pulsed against her right knee.

As the ambassador began to rise, her body wouldn't move, so she instead sat and stared in dismay and fear as the music thumped and the phone kept rocking.

32

MAGGIE WAS GONE, security had withdrawn, and Kyler hurried back to the table, returning just as the dealer began to distribute the next hand. He sat down and quickly counted his chips while hearing Kenny Rogers lecture him in his head.

"You never count your money when you're sittin' at the table . . ."

Thirteen hundred. Just thirteen big blinds with the blind level set to go up in less than ten minutes. Terrible.

"There'll be time enough for countin' when the dealin's done."

Had Kenny been playing with a mountain of debt, a toxic public image, and a $20 million prize? Doubtful. At a minimum, he was probably singing about a cash game, not a multi-table tournament. At this event, for everyone but the victor there would be *nothing* to count after the dealing was completed.

Kyler considered that if he didn't have children, he could just stay abroad after being eliminated. Then he wouldn't have to face all the hatred and mockery and debt collectors that awaited him back home. He could live life off the grid, ignore the online universe, travel from country to country, see the world. Pretend he had a great life, try to enjoy some adventures in far-flung locales, play poker, and take odd jobs to get by. He could die in peace maybe, knowing his life didn't turn out anywhere near how he had hoped but satisfied that it had been interesting and unique.

But no, the demands of fatherhood and being a provider, as

horrible at it as he was, would pull him back home after this was all over. There was no running away from the hell that awaited him. No opportunity to flee, as long as he still lived.

Kyler knew that poker involved making good decisions with incomplete information, and now with very few chips left, he needed to decide when to go all in with almost no knowledge of what he was probably facing. He didn't have time to wait for pocket aces, or kings, or ace-king, or queens. He would be blinded off soon, and it was now desperation time.

But he still needed to be smart. He needed to stay calm. He needed to drown out all the insanity and just make the right poker move on each hand.

As terrifying and stressful as his situation was, the decisions that he had to make were now actually simpler. With so few chips, there was no opportunity or need for nuanced play, calculating correct bet sizes, and deciding what to do post-flop, turn, and river. As he fought to survive, he had only two simple pre-flop options on every hand now: all in or fold.

With non-premium hands he wanted to move all in when no one had yet raised and he was in late position, one of the last players to act. But finding that situation was difficult with Sacha now the table chip leader and bullying the other players with raises on almost every hand. Kyler waited for someone to stand up to him, but the others were almost always folding to his pre-flop raises or his automatic post-flop continuation bets. When a player did finally challenge him and call down the river, Sacha showed the winning hand and put new energy into his aura of invincibility.

Kyler finally moved all in from middle position with ace-nine, and then held his breath as an older guy with a plethora of arm tattoos and a shaved head thought about whether to call. Did he have a pocket pair? Or a bigger ace? Kyler increasingly regretted his play, and then the man finally folded, so Kyler collected the meager small and big blinds to add to his pathetic chip stack.

This continued for a little while, with Kyler stealing the blinds just often enough to stave off elimination while avoiding landmines that were taking down players throughout the tournament. But he was still progressively tilting toward his demise.

Then, Kyler was under the gun, first to act pre-flop, and looked down to see the always very welcome sight of the king of diamonds with his royal brother, the king of clubs.

"All in," he said as he pushed his chips forward.

"Call," came Sacha's voice to his left, as Kyler continued to vacantly look straight ahead.

Then the tattooed opponent: "All in."

This guy was the only one at the table who seemed to have almost as many chips as Sacha, so it was back to Kyler's antagonist to decide whether to call for virtually all his chips.

"Hey man, why'd you do that?" Sacha asked. "I know I have this man beat," he added, pointing to Kyler. He then stared at the bald contestant. "But not sure about you . . ."

At this point, Kyler wanted a call. If Sacha had aces, the only hand better than kings, he would have called by now. He waited as Sacha thought, groaned, and then shrugged as he tossed his cards face down onto the table. Fold.

Kyler turned over his kings and stood, and then was elated to see the remaining opponent show queens.

The flop and turn were all rags, and Kyler just needed to avoid a queen on the river in order to fight on.

Ace of diamonds.

Kyler pumped his right fist and then sat back down. The dealer pushed the chips toward him and Kyler began to stack them.

"Man, I had an ace," Sacha informed the table. "If this dude doesn't re-raise me, I win that pot and this idiot who's threatening to fight me is gone."

Kyler acted as if he didn't hear this. He was still short on chips, but maybe a comeback was beginning, and he was determined not to be distracted.

"You really had an ace?" another player asked.

"Yeah, man," Sacha replied, and then gave a wink.

Did Sacha actually fold an ace? Did Kyler just come that close to being eliminated? Maybe, maybe not. Sacha asserting that he held one was, of course, meaningless.

Kyler looked at his chips and savored the fact that they were still in front of him, not helping to build the stack of some opponent. He was still in it. Too bad Maggie was no longer there—it would have been nice to win that all-in in front of her.

He decided to quickly text her:

"Just tripled up!"

Where had she gone anyway? What was she doing? And had any of the info that Priya threatened to leak been unleashed yet? There was no time to search on his phone as the next hand was being dealt. But he knew she was in a terrible situation, and he wanted to acknowledge that after his exclamation point message. So he quickly added a follow-up:

"I hope ur ok"

33

HOW MANY TIMES had Maggie received a text about a salacious DC news item? And how often had she sent one? Too many. They generally manifested as some version of . . .

"Omg did u see this article bout her? So crazy, had no idea. Wonder what real story is . . ."

Knowing the major and minor players in Washington provided Maggie and her professional and personal contacts a fascinating view of the constant stream of political scandal stories. To most of America, the tales involved titillating details about people in power who they had seen only on television or had maybe never even heard of. To Maggie and her circles, the players caught up in these media frenzies were people they had often known well, or at least interacted with a few times.

Sometimes the names of those starring in the tawdry dramas were a big surprise:

"Lmfao her?? Unbelievable smh. She always seemed like such a prude. Never imagined her doing shit like that but now of course I can't STOP imagining it LOL!"

And with other stories, not a shock at all:

"Bout time this caught up with him, ffs what did he think, no one would ever find out??"

Not every comment was critical. Some were quite sympathetic:

"Ugh I feel so bad for her. Can't imagine what it's like having that all public now."

But others certainly weren't:

"Plz. I think shez just looking for attention fr"

So . . . what were they saying about her now? Before all this, Maggie never seriously considered that it would one day be her turn, but today was her day.

First she looked at the origin of it all—a post from the popular *Washington Confidential* blog, which began with the headline:

"Sources: White House Chief of Staff Sexually Harassed, Threatened Former Aide"

She was still sitting in the booth, unable to move any part of her body except her fingers, which scrolled through the anonymously-sourced item.

"White House Chief of Staff Bryce Kirkwood sexually harassed former staffer Maggie Raster, leading her to resign from her plum position despite having worked there for less than a year, sources told *Washington Confidential.* After Raster quit her dream job, a witness reported seeing her and Kirkwood arguing ferociously in a DC park, with Kirkwood angrily throwing an object at Raster before storming off. Another witness stated that Raster was overheard just days ago in an airport first class lounge bemoaning Kirkwood's '#MeToo' antics, and explaining that Kirkwood was 'definitely not a good guy' and that 'powerful men like Bryce get away with just about anything.' Follow *Washington Confidential* for additional details of this developing story as soon as they are available."

How had this happened? Who, besides Priya of course, was behind it? There were so many untruths in the post, but just enough hooks in reality so that reading it was like watching her own sexual victimization in a horror movie fun house mirror. In a panic, Maggie franticly considered how she could now undo *this.* But as she reviewed the latest DC gossip from the other side of the world, she knew she couldn't. Just as with what Bryce had *actually* done to her, she would have to find the best way to manage the fallout while trying not to get swallowed up and destroyed by fear, anger, and sadness.

Sensing her distress, Jacques sat back down next to her, and she silently turned the bright screen of her phone toward him. His eyes widened slightly as he reviewed the post, and then he reached out to put a comforting hand on her left shoulder, before thinking better of the move and withdrawing it in advance of making contact.

Maggie finally rose, still clutching the phone in her right hand. She wondered how she had so utterly lost control of her own life and what she could do now to gain it back.

"I need to speak with Bryce now," she said firmly over the deafening music. "Securely."

The ambassador gestured for her to follow him toward the door.

As he led her out the exit and into his waiting car, she was barely aware of her surroundings. She experienced a blur of motion as her mind tried to make sense of how this bombshell report had come together. Collapsed onto the back seat of the car as the driver zoomed off toward their destination, Maggie reopened her ceaselessly vibrating phone and found it surreal to see her own name trending.

"Maggie Raster"

And, of course, so was the name of the last man with whom she had had sex.

"Bryce Kirkwood"

#ResignBryce was trending too, as was #KirkwoodMustGo.

She looked at the comments under her own name, and although a few were supportive of her and the claims that she had never actually made, she had only just begun reading them when she saw such tweets as:

"This bitch will do anything for money and attention. First supports dictator who murdered Kinum, now tries to get 15 minutes of fame with bs claim against cos. Ruthless + unethical = dangerous"

And:

"Anyone who saw Raster on tv knows she's fucking out of her mind. If u believe her ur a complete moron #sixofdiamondsontheriver"

Stop, she told herself. *Don't look. Just don't.*

Countless emails, texts, and DMs began to pour in. Some supportive ones from friends, some nasty and borderline threatening words from anonymous trolls.

Meanwhile, when she'd been unsuccessfully trying to promote her failing consulting business by securing opportunities as a political commentator on television, she had sent her bio and contact information to basically every booker she could reach. Now, they were apparently *all* trying to book her as an on-air guest to discuss Bryce. They had all rejected her, and now suddenly she could be on virtually any news show she desired, just as she wanted no part of any of them.

Well, not *all* had rejected her. One hadn't.

"Hey mags omg I'm so so sorry to read what you have gone thru! I'm here for you anytime and would love to have u come on air to talk about what's going on. I know last hit was rocky but will make sure that doesn't happen again. We wud really appreciate it! Pls let me know what wud work for u! xo natalie"

Natalie, her young booker, who Maggie had never actually met—the one who took a chance on her, who got her into this mess, whose career would no doubt get a very nice boost if she booked her now.

But Maggie had no interest in talking on air about a situation that she was still trying to figure out for herself. If she ever spoke publicly, it would have to be her timing, her choice, her terms. She knew she lived in a world dominated by soundbites and spin and social media and viral clips, and she was determined not to get completely sucked into all that. What she experienced with Bryce—so different than what was now being presented to the world—was very painful and real to her, and she wasn't going to trivialize such an upsetting, confusing, and personal encounter by yapping about it on a vapid news show.

She didn't want this to be her life and her identity now. She had feared since Bryce left her apartment that the short-lived interaction might haunt her forever, and now she saw the real likelihood that it would universally define her for eternity. Any job for which she applied, any client for whom she tried to work, the first item to come up in a basic search would be that she was the one who accused a sitting White House chief of staff of sexual harassment. She knew that the fucked up reality was that virtually any man reading that would steer way clear of her professionally. None would ever voluntarily work with her, out of fear that he would be the next target of accusations.

I feel bad for her, the men who considered themselves good guys would think. *What she probably experienced was terrible, reprehensible. God forbid that happen to my sister/daughter/mother. But I just can't be associated with her. I regret that's how it is, but I can't risk a false accusation against me, just in case she's crazy, just in case she's full of shit. It's a shame, because she's probably telling the truth, but what can I do? I can't risk destroying my career, not with my mortgage, my wife, my kids, my reputation at stake . . .*

And when she died, wouldn't this story be the first line of her obituary?

They finally arrived at the front door of the embassy. Somehow they had exited the car and passed the security gate without her being aware of any of it.

"Is Priya Varma still inside?" she asked Jacques.

"I assume so. The Kingdom wants to seize her as soon as she steps out, so she better be here. Either that, or she would be in custody, or dead."

"Well," Maggie replied, "I'm not saying I want her to be dead. But I also don't really want her to be inside . . ."

He steered her through the same entranceway she had visited the night before, through a hall, and to the door of a small, windowless conference room with gray walls and the Canadian flag hanging across from the entrance.

"This is secure?" she asked.

"It's as secure as we have here."

"I was looking for more reassurance."

"It's all I can truthfully give you."

She nodded. "Okay, I need to talk with him alone first."

"I understand. Just knock on the door when you're ready for me to join."

"Will someone connect me with him?"

"It's already been done, Maggie. He's waiting for you inside."

She entered and closed the door behind her, sat at one of the six black high-backed chairs, and looked directly at the tablet that was propped up in the middle of the light wood table. Bryce's face was drained of color, his eyes revealing poorly disguised anger and terror, a small vein in his temple lightly pulsing.

Where was he? Unclear. The background wall was gray, his red tie slightly loose and crooked as it extended behind his blue pinstripe suit jacket.

"You promised me you would never do this," he started. "You promised."

"I didn't say anything!" Maggie quickly snapped back. "This didn't come from me. Please believe me. I want you to know that. It's not from me."

"Well, from where then? I've told you a million times to be careful what you say out loud, what you text. People can manipulate and misinterpret things. People who want to hurt me. Hurt us."

"It's Priya Varma. She leaked this."

"She's locked up in a fucking embassy! How would she know anything?"

"I don't know, Bryce! Maybe next time don't berate me in a park if you want everything on the DL!"

"Maggie, people are calling for my resignation! It's a feeding frenzy. This can destroy me!"

She paused to really look at him. He was so young to have this powerful role, but he had always come off wise beyond his years, graceful and self-assured and strong. Now, for the first time, she saw him as a kid, lost in a park and unable to find his parents, petrified that his wonderful world was vanishing and there was nothing he could do to prevent it.

"This can destroy me, too," she answered.

"Not in the same way," he replied, shaking his head emphatically. "You'll be fine, and I'll be untouchable."

A few seconds of silence followed, during which he must have realized that he needed to sound more supportive of her if he was to get what he wanted, whatever that was.

"I'm sorry you're going through this," he said robotically.

She knew that he was choosing his words carefully. Just as in the park, he was apologizing—sort of, for some unspecified act—without explicitly saying anything in case someone was able to monitor the conversation.

"I need you to tell the truth," he implored. "Publicly. Now. Please."

The truth? What actually was the truth here?

"I don't want to dignify this story," she answered. "I'm not going to feed it more energy."

"Maggie, please. I need you to *please* get out there and tell the truth. Say that it's all untrue."

"I can tweet that this story is false and that I had nothing to do with it," she proposed. And she didn't even want to do *that*.

He looked exasperated, and desperate.

"Maggie . . . I . . . I appreciate that. Yes, that would be helpful, but I need more than that. It has to be on TV. An interview, so people can see you denying it ever happened. People need to *see* you explaining this is all false. Okay? Please."

And this was exactly what she *didn't* want. To return to the overdramatic, simplistic, insane, and inane news world as the subject of an explosive segment that would instantly go viral and live forever.

She thought about how she should respond, how she could get out of this. And one question loomed in her mind.

"Why should I help you, Bryce?" she asked accusingly. "Seriously. Why should I help you?"

"Because it's not true," he said simply.

Their eyes met, and they both went silent.

But you know what is true, her intense stare communicated. *So you have no right to ask me for anything.*

His quiet response jolted her, as a ferocity flashed across his face, like a wounded animal cornered at the end of a hunt, who had no choice but to fight for its life in any and every way possible. Without saying a word, his intimidating stare told her: *If you don't help me as I ask, you'll give me no choice but to use everything at my disposal to defend myself, which means going after your credibility, dissecting your life in public, and tarnishing your reputation beyond repair.*

This is why she had wanted to talk with him, face-to-face, or at least face-to-on-screen-image. Because she knew that if she didn't directly tell him that she wasn't responsible for this story, that she didn't plant it and wasn't encouraging it and wouldn't corroborate it, he and all of his extremely powerful allies in the White House and beyond would come after her with unmitigated fury, the way powerful men had eviscerated their female accusers since forever.

"This is the only way," he said out loud. "The only way to make it go away. Isn't that what we both want?"

"I had nothing to do with this story, Bryce. We need to ignore it and let it die," she instructed.

He shook his head. "It doesn't work that way. Not with this type of allegation. Not these days. I'll be forced to resign before it ever goes away. I won't let that happen. I'm going to fight this as hard as I can, and I need your help."

I'm going to fight this as hard as I can. Translation: *Help me or I'm going to fight you as hard as I can.*

And she felt she wasn't ready for that fight. Not today. She just didn't have it in her. Maybe at another point in her life—in the past, in the future—but not right now. So, when all else fails, argue logistics. "You know where I am, Bryce. How can I do a TV interview? It would start with saying I'm live from the Kingdom, and all the viewers would immediately hate me. You want your defense beginning that way?"

"There's a plane ready to fly you to London right away. You'll do the live interview there today with a friendly journalist who'll be very supportive, and then the plane will take you wherever you want. Except back to the Kingdom."

"Why not back to the Kingdom?" she asked.

"It's not safe. That's all I can say."

"Was it safe when you sent me here as a presidential liaison?"

"We can't discuss that over this. We don't know how secure it is."

"Was that even true, Bryce? Did the president ask me to take that role?"

"I can't talk about that now, and it's not important anymore."

He looked very uncomfortable with this line of questioning. Maybe because she had unearthed that it was all a lie. Possibly because he just wanted to get back to the main topic of their conversation. Likely both. "Why did you tell me that if it wasn't true? Because you wanted to get me out of the country? You wanted me to die here?"

"I'll admit that I liked the idea of you being out of DC for a little while, but I never wanted you to be hurt. You know that. I'm sorry about how I characterized your position—"

"Lied. You lied. And you knew that lie put my life at risk."

"I gave you what you wanted, Maggie. *You* asked *me*! I got the EO stopped for you."

"You stopped it to help me or to get rid of me? I never asked to go to this fucking place. Never."

"Okay, so now I'm getting you out of there. Right now. It's all arranged."

"I need to think about this."

"There's no time!" he barked, and then added in a less confrontational tone, "You know there's no time. Please, Maggie . . . I know this isn't easy, but it's best for both of us, and I'll be forever grateful."

"Who's the 'very supportive' journalist?" she asked, knowing that just uttering this question virtually conceded that she was going to give him what he wanted.

"Tori Kinum."

"Are you fucking kidding me!?" she exploded, leaning into the screen. "What planet are you living on? She despises me. You saw our segment!"

"She's the only journalist I trust. She wants to help."

"She'll tear me apart for coming here. It'll be a disaster."

"No, she won't do that now. I spoke with her, and she has a strong reason not to do that. She'll make sure the interview is fair and goes as we want it to."

"What's the reason?"

He shook his head, showing that he wouldn't provide specifics. "There's no time to debate this, to explain it all. Please . . . you *have* to do this, Maggie."

The tone of the last part was gracious, conciliatory, almost pleading. "You have to do this for *me*," it sounded like he was saying. But she knew the actual message was really more than that. She had to do it for *herself*, for her own well-being, to make sure she wasn't targeted for obliteration. She *had* to do this. "Tori Kinum interviewing *me*? About *this*? Bryce, there's no way it ends well."

"Maggie, please trust me. It's all arranged. Everything will be fine. It's our only option now."

Maggie took a few seconds to consider this plea and then nodded briefly in agreement. In surrender. In defeat.

She then rose, turned and stepped toward the door, and knocked twice. A few seconds later, Jacques entered and they both looked toward the screen. Bryce stared back, not concealing his surprise and annoyance that another individual had now joined the conversation.

"Before I go, the ambassador wants me to help convince you not to start a war. Although I may not be much help because right now I'm fine with a worldwide nuclear apocalypse. The sooner the better."

34

TWENTY MINUTES LATER, Maggie burst out of the conference room and headed swiftly down the hallway toward the front door of the embassy where a car was to be waiting to take her to the airport for her flight to London.

Maybe the plane will crash, she thought. *Then I won't have to do this.*

She took out her phone and, as she walked, fired off a quick text to Kyler.

"R u still alive?"

Hopefully he was still playing, still competing, still edging closer to that colossal prize for them.

As she approached the end of the hallway, she looked up from her phone to note the person standing in front of her. Priya opened her mouth to say something. Maggie had seen her barely in enough time to stop before running into her.

But she decided not to stop. Instead, she did something that she had never before done in her life. She extended both hands in front of her, increased her speed and momentum, and shoved Priya in the chest with all her might. Maggie was shocked at her own physical ferocity, as Priya went flying backwards, landing awkwardly with the back of her head snapping against the hardwood floor as she let out a low moan.

Maggie breathed heavily as she looked down at Priya, unsure what to do next. Continue the attack? Just walk out the door? Say something? Say what?

Priya groaned and rubbed the back of her head with her right hand, as she slowly climbed back to her feet. She then looked at the hand, probably inspecting it for blood, and then trained an intimidating stare at Maggie. "Okay . . . how about you try that again . . . now that I'm ready?" Priya dared her. "And I'll fucking kick your ass."

Maggie stared back in anger, intent to hold her ground. But she hadn't been in a real physical confrontation since that seventh grade soccer game fight. What about Priya? She had a tough demeanor, but how many real altercations occurred while playing online poker in her dorm room? Or while living the life of a global poker and human rights celebrity? She realized that she had no idea what she was up against, but she never felt more of a desire to hit someone in her life.

"This story you leaked is bullshit," Maggie declared. "It's just not true."

"Then what *is* true?"

"Nothing."

"We both know *that's* not true."

"Where did this all come from? Is it from that tweet you sent?"

It was starting to come together . . . a little. When she had been on the air, and Priya had tweeted her request for help.

"We need YOUR help to win this fight. Let our nation's leaders hear your outrage. They are failing us all! Tell them to finally confront these atrocities. DM me any info that will help the cause! Send anything that will take down those appeasing injustice!"

Priya nodded. "I have a lot of supporters. They see a lot of things. In a park. In an airport."

"So you get these random bits of information and that's enough to publicly accuse a guy of sexual harassment?"

Priya shook her head. "No. It wasn't enough. But those tips, plus the fact that you quit your job so soon, so suddenly . . . they gave me enough to ask *you* about it, and whether you admit it or not, you confirmed it last night. Your reaction told me everything. Your response let me know I could proceed."

Now it was Maggie's turn to shake her head, and she did so emphatically. "Going after the White House isn't helpful. Bryce isn't your enemy."

"Innocent people are being *murdered* here while the White House does nothing!" Priya exclaimed. "Protestors are rounded up and tortured. I'm taking down Bryce Kirkwood, the president, anyone who supports this regime. I don't care how powerful they are. Look what happened to Emily Kinum! And our own government won't lift a finger in response."

"You're so wrong. My God, if you only knew how wrong you were."

"Enlighten me, my college best friend . . ."

"I can't. I'm leaving."

She walked straight ahead in the direction of the door, bracing for Priya's counterattack as Maggie's shoulder brushed past hers. But the poker player decided not to physically escalate at the moment and instead verbally admonished her as she headed toward the exit. "Don't defend him. He doesn't deserve it. Be on the right side of history, Maggie!"

Then she was out the door, in the back seat of the car, embarking on the short drive to the airport for her flight to London.

She looked at her phone. The number of missed calls, emails, texts, and other notifications continued to escalate. She anxiously looked for Kyler's line in her text messages to see if he had responded, and momentarily closed her eyes in relief after seeing that he had answered with a thumbs up emoji followed by "still fighting." He had then asked "R u ok?" as a follow-up to his earlier message to which she had never directly responded, "I hope ur ok."

Of course, if she was being honest, she would write back "no"—but this was no time for veracity. She needed him to stay positive. There was too much—*way* too much—at stake.

"Yes. Have to deal w all this bs so sry can't make it back there rn, but I'm fine."

She looked at what she wrote, and over the succeeding few seconds realized that she needed to say more, so she added:

"I believe in u kyler. U can win this! But as soon as tourney is over for u, u need to get out of country immediately. Can't explain but pls just do it."

35

IN REALITY, more than just fear of White House retribution motivated Maggie. Despite what Bryce had done and all the pain it was causing her, she really didn't want his life to be ruined.

Maggie had known Bryce since he was twenty-two, when he was a recent Georgetown grad working grueling hours for basically nothing as a low-level aide to an obscure Pennsylvania congressman on the Hill. She was a year younger and serving as a summer intern for the same representative. Bryce was different than all the others she met at political events and DC happy hours.

The city was full of ambitious young men and women, most of whom would flame out within a few years or get stuck in some dead-end staffer or civil servant job. But just a few minutes with Bryce back then revealed that he was destined to be very successful. He was so hard working, so smart, so wise beyond his years about how it all worked. Bryce was infectiously charismatic and perfectly polished, qualities that in others could appear obnoxious and be off-putting, but with him never came off as too much or insincere.

And it never seemed to be just about his own advancement. His discussions about politics were highly substantive, filled with real issues, complex policy proposals, and plans for actually helping people.

He was so good at what he did, and then a few years later he got really lucky, although it could be argued that he made his own luck.

He picked the right underdog presidential campaign very early and played his cards right as his candidate made it all the way to the White House and asked Bryce to come along.

Although they kept in touch sporadically, Maggie had never gotten to know Bryce very well. But she must have made a positive impression on him because in the middle of the term he reached out to her while she worked in the governor's office in Harrisburg. Bryce asked that she meet with him, and then soon after offered her a prized position in the chief of staff's office. A decision that he no doubt now profoundly regretted, as did she.

Bryce was the deputy chief of staff at the time, and about a year later he was promoted to the big job itself. He was only thirty-one, and those close to him held a celebratory gathering to mark the momentous occasion. By then she had already left the White House, but she attended to support him, to see friends and former colleagues, and to network with the powerful and well-connected on behalf of her fledgling consulting practice.

Their eyes met, they exchanged a flirtatious glance, and that led to this: landing at Heathrow, for the second time in a matter of days. As soon as her plane touched down and the flight attendant announced all the relevant gates for those catching connecting flights to all sorts of interesting cities, it occurred to her that from here she could fly virtually anywhere in the world and escape all this.

Instead she found the driver in a black suit holding an iPad with her name displayed on its screen. He guided her to his vehicle, and they begin the trip on the left side of the road to the designated hotel in Trafalgar Square.

The conversation she had observed between Jacques and Bryce had not gone well. Bryce really didn't want to talk about military planning with the ambassador and certainly didn't want to be lectured by a Canadian diplomat about how to respond to the murder of an American. It seemed pretty clear that a US military assault was going to begin imminently. If the *Washington Confidential* news item hadn't surfaced which made him demand that she fly to London, would Bryce have warned her to leave the country? He wouldn't have let her die there, would he?

And then there was Priya—agitating for action and condemning the US government for appeasement when it was in reality poised to unleash an overwhelming show of force. Although maybe it was the torrid criticism from Priya and her ilk—Tori Kinum and others—that actually compelled the administration to prepare to take lethal measures. The president was being repeatedly condemned as weak and cowering to a third-world dictator, and of course he couldn't let that narrative stand, especially the year before an election. So now there might be war, and she was safely out of the country, and Jacques would soon depart with Priya, too. But what about Kyler? And if the Kingdom really responded with long-range nuclear missiles, was anywhere safe?

She was so, so tired. If this whole chaotic situation could temporarily stop and she could actually sleep for a few hours, then face it all with the focused clarity of being fully alert . . .

As her car pulled up to the hotel, she knew more than ever that she didn't want to do this interview. Maybe it wasn't too late to back out. If she ever ended up talking publicly about the Bryce accusations, those real and imagined, she wanted it to be on her terms, her timing, not coerced like she was now. Bryce had told her to tell "the truth" and she was very well aware that if she took that literally and told "the truth" for real, probably no one would believe her. And if anyone did believe her, it wouldn't be taken seriously. She would be blamed for her role, and any perceived fault of Bryce would be quickly dismissed as insignificant.

So she would tell his "the truth"—but would anyone believe *that*? And no matter what she said, no matter what people ultimately thought was true, just being at the center of a scandal like this was so completely mortifying that she felt entirely debilitated.

A young female media assistant greeted her at the front of the lobby and helped her check in and head up to her room to change into a charcoal gray business suit that had been laid out for her. The room had been reserved for her to quickly prepare physically and mentally for the interview. She didn't know where she would be headed afterward, but she had no intention of spending the night there.

"We're live in forty-five minutes," the woman instructed. There was a knock on the door, and the media assistant welcomed in an older woman who asked Maggie to sit in a chair so she could apply makeup and fix her hair for television. After about fifteen minutes, both women took a long look at her and appeared satisfied.

"The interview will take place in one of the conference rooms downstairs," the younger one informed her. "We'll come back in five minutes to escort you down."

Then Maggie was alone, sitting on the edge of the king-size bed and viewing herself in the mirror on the far wall. She looked so ready for TV, with her perfectly styled hair, makeup, and outfit. She stared at her own reflection and forced an insincere, telegenic smile to complete the picture and then withdrew back into somber brooding.

She stood, walked over to the large window, and watched the cars and people moving around Trafalgar Square. Then she picked up her phone to see if she had an update from Kyler.

About ten minutes earlier, he had texted:

"50 ppl left. Half field eliminated. I'm under chip avg but still here"

This was very good news, but she didn't want to write back now. She needed to concentrate on how she was going to survive this interview. But before she could put the phone away, another text from Kyler popped up:

"Fwiw I know today is really tough for u. Ur a very strong successful person and I know u can handle this and come out better than ever. Thank u so much for believing in me. I believe in u!"

"Thank u kyler," she quickly typed back.

There was a knock on the door. Her escorts were back. One day, maybe she would review the countless messages on her phone. More likely, she would ignore them forever and try to move on with whatever was left of her life and career and reputation when this was all over.

But before she put the phone away to answer the door and head to the guillotine, one new notification caught her eye. If her phone hadn't already been open after she wrote back to Kyler, the message might have been lost amid the flood of words invading her device. Instead, she saw it and couldn't look away. A direct message from someone she'd never heard of.

She read the few lines quickly and then again more slowly. And then a third time, ignoring the repeated knocks on the door that grew louder and more frequent.

"Ms. Raster?" the British voice called out. "Are you ready to proceed to the interview? We're going live shortly. Ms. Raster?"

But she was transfixed on her phone, trying to process this new information.

"Oh, fuck, seriously?" she finally whispered in response, staring at the screen. She sighed in dismay, shook her head slowly, looked again toward the window, and then turned back to see the DM still watching her.

"Whoever you are," she continued quietly, "you have no idea what you've just done to me."

36

ON OTHER DAYS, important meetings of high-powered executives probably took place here. The sizeable room could accommodate about twenty around a large conference table, with an area for drinks and food by a large window.

But today, the venue had been turned into a space for something much different. Lighting stands were strategically arranged, and at least three cameras and several monitors were positioned at precise locations as television professionals adjusted brightness and focus of the instruments. Two black interview chairs had been positioned facing each other.

Maggie took this all in as she was guided inside and then tensed up when she saw Tori Kinum across the room. She looked professional and serious as she talked earnestly with a man wearing a headset. Tori wanted retaliation against the Kingdom, and Maggie fully understood why. If they had been responsible for murdering one of her family members, she, too, would stop at nothing to secure retribution. And now, Bryce and the administration were set to deliver that pound of flesh, and much more, so Tori was willing to do her part to protect them from scandal.

Tori began striding toward her, and Maggie wondered if this greeting would go better than the one in the DC green room 3,600 miles and a week away. Tori extended her hand and Maggie took it, holding the clasp for a few seconds until Tori let go.

"I'm willing to put aside your support for the Kingdom today," Tori stated with an air of benevolent generosity.

Maggie's first instinct was to proclaim that she didn't support it. Of course, she didn't. But then the natural reply would be: What had she been doing there? And why was she still invested in a client who remained on its soil? There was no point in having that conversation now.

So Maggie simply responded, "It's good to see you again, Tori."

"Obviously, we have our differences," the journalist continued, "But right now we have a shared goal. We need to get Bryce past these slanderous accusations. I understand some people who oppose the Kingdom think taking down Bryce and the president is a helpful strategy, so they've spread these disgusting lies. It's just exasperating. Wrong and shortsighted."

"Well, there's a lot of misinformation going around about this whole situation," Maggie answered.

"Yes, absolutely. So thank you for flying here on short notice. And between you and me, now's not the time to be in the Kingdom. The crown prince is going to pay a high price very soon, and you don't want to be near him or his henchmen when that happens."

"When is that happening?" she asked, particularly concerned about Kyler.

"I don't know exactly. You're worried about your client?"

"Yes."

"That's a logical fear. He should get out of there right away. Tell him to head directly for the E-ZPass lane."

Maggie remained stoic as Tori smirked and then headed to her interview chair. A producer guided Maggie to her seat and then mic'd her up.

She wondered how many people would be tuning in for this live broadcast. Maggie had seen online that the network had heavily promoted it, not that it needed to. Social media was all abuzz about this blockbuster interview with the former staffer addressing sexual harassment allegations about the White House chief of staff. Viewership worldwide would easily top tens of millions.

"Live in sixty seconds," a male voice announced in her ear.

I can still walk away, she thought. *I can just get up, tear off this mic, and walk out the door.*

Tori had a stack of papers on her lap, and was carefully perusing the top sheet. It seemed like a lot of content for a straightforward interview. Unlike Tori, Maggie had no notes, no guide. Just her memories, including instructions from Bryce telling her what to do.

"Thirty seconds."

Tori looked back up and Maggie sensed that she, too, was nervous. For Tori, this was about helping Bryce, who was promising to help her get justice for the murder of her sister. But this was also a major career opportunity. A local news reporter who had operated in her world-renowned sibling's shadow, now conducting the interview of the year in front of a massive audience.

The final countdown progressed as Tori and Maggie sat there and looked at each other in seemingly interminable silence.

Five . . . four . . . three . . .

Finally they were live, with Tori staring directly at the camera behind Maggie's right shoulder.

"Good day, I'm Tori Kinum. Thank you for watching. Earlier this morning, in a Washington, DC political blog, serious accusations surfaced against White House chief of staff Bryce Kirkwood. The article alleged, without evidence, that he sexually harassed former White House staffer Maggie Raster. Now, in her first public comments, Maggie Raster joins me *live* to address this growing controversy. Maggie, thank you for talking with me. I'm sure it's been a very difficult day for you."

"That's certainly true, Tori," Maggie responded.

"Maggie, many people watching may not be familiar with you—"

"I would assume that's the case."

"Right, so why don't you tell us . . . what was your role in the White House? How long did you work there?"

"Sure. Well, for almost a year, I worked in the chief of staff's office. I reported directly to the deputy chief of staff, who was Bryce Kirkwood at the time. That was before the president promoted him to chief of staff."

"Your type of position is highly sought after?" Tori asked.

"Absolutely."

"But you left after just under a year? Why was that?"

"Well . . . that's a complicated answer. It was a very difficult decision. I loved a lot of things about that job. Serving my country at the highest levels and trying to make a difference in the lives of everyday Americans. Interacting with brilliant leaders from across our government, and the world. It was often exhilarating. But, as with any position anywhere, there were aspects that I found unpleasant, and I thought it was the right time to leave government and start my own consulting firm."

"And was Bryce Kirkwood's treatment of you one of those 'unpleasant' reasons for leaving?" Tori queried, and Maggie could tell that she was bracing for the answer.

"Not at all," Maggie answered.

Tori nodded in supportive acknowledgment, as her body relaxed a little.

Yet while Tori felt more at ease, Maggie's insides were churning faster and faster. The world was watching, and she was now trying not to sweat under the hot lights, concentrating on not passing out from stress and exhaustion.

"And what was he like as a boss?"

"He was always professional. I never had a problem working for him."

And it was true. Others throughout her career had made her work life awkward, challenging, and at times maddening. Brad Connelly—Mr. Dog Style—for one. But not Bryce. A consummate professional.

"Thank you for clearing that up, Maggie. It's amazing how people can spread lies so easily. How people can lodge serious, career-threatening allegations based on *absolutely nothing.*"

Tori waited a beat for her expected reassuring, confirming response, but Maggie sat there in silence, giving herself one final opportunity to take stock of her world before jumping into the abyss.

Had these public allegations negatively affected her parents' deteriorating health? Had bombs started falling in the Kingdom? Was Kyler still sitting at a poker table, trying to read opponents and win pots and earn them a fortune?

Meanwhile, Tori was clearly concerned about the ongoing dead air, a major television *faux pas*. "You've seen DC from the inside," the journalist prodded. "So you may be familiar with this terrible phenomenon."

So tired. Fuck, I'm so tired of all the manipulation, the calculation, the deception, the spin. So tired of being told what to do. Sick of begging for attention from Bryce or a twenty-two-year-old TV booker or potential clients. So tired of being alone with this secret and wondering if I'm overreacting or crazy or both. So unbelievably tired of not being in control of what's happening to me . . .

"Well," Maggie finally responded. "It wasn't based on 'absolutely nothing' . . ."

The words hung there for a few seconds, as Tori, caught off guard, nevertheless remained poised as she stared at Maggie and tried to assess their significance. "I don't understand," she finally said.

"The argument in the park *did* happen. The article exaggerated what occurred, but it's not a complete fabrication."

"I was a sophomore," the DM had read. *"I was really trashed and somehow got separated from my friends at the bar."*

"Okay, but you've already said you experienced no sexual harassment while working—"

"And the article quotes me saying in an airport that Bryce is not a good person. That part is true. And stating that powerful men like Bryce get away with everything. I didn't directly refer to Bryce when I said that, but I had just been speaking about him and he was on my mind when I made that comment."

"I don't remember how we got to his apartment or where it was, but what happened there was the most humiliating and disrespectful experience of my life."

Tori shifted uncomfortably. "So what are you trying to say?" she finally asked.

Maggie thought back to her outstretched arm reaching into the bedroom's end table drawer. Clasping the foil package, making the handoff to Bryce. Her life full of mounting stress, but in that moment feeling refreshingly exhilarated and safe.

"I could barely stand or speak. I was so disoriented. I couldn't say no to anything he was doing to me because I was so out of it and he didn't care. I woke up hungover and really sore, left in the morning, didn't know his name until Bryce became famous. I stopped attending classes and dropped out the next semester. Finally made it back after two years of therapy, and graduated last spring. Still looking for a job now. Trying my best but it's really tough. I thought you should know."

She looked back at Tori, who was giving her a pensive, disapproving stare. Maggie had no time to verify this new allegation, to even determine whether it was from a real person. If she had received it three weeks earlier, she would have dismissed it as impossible, not the Bryce she knew. But he was a different Bryce now. He was Bryce who had selfishly disrupted and scarred her life, who had clearly been at best indifferent to whether she lived or died. So this message now gave her a final push down the path that part of her had already known and feared was necessary.

"I had sex with Bryce," Maggie finally stated, so uncomfortable with the reality that she was talking about her own sex life in front of the world. Friends. Family. Former colleagues. Complete strangers.

"Consensual?" Tori asked.

"It started that way . . . but I made it clear he needed to use a condom . . . and while having sex with me, he removed it without my knowledge or consent . . . and continued without it . . . continued having sex with me without wearing it . . . and I had no idea until after. When I saw what had happened . . . saw what he had done . . . it was such a feeling of violation. I tried to just forget about it, pretend it never happened. Figured it was one of those unfortunate experiences that just happens to single women sometimes, and I would move on and not tell anyone and take it to my grave. But what Bryce did keeps eating away at me. It's hanging over every aspect of my life. I haven't been the same since, and I'm afraid—terrified—that I never will be. I tried to talk with him about it, and he was so dismissive. So insulting. Treating me like I'm worthless. Even though I know I'm not."

Her heart was beating fast and she worked to keep her breathing steady. Now it was out there, shared with the world, and she braced for the world's wrath. Or at least that of the White House.

Maggie hadn't been sure how she would emotionally and physically respond if she did indeed go through with telling her story. Would she cry? Panic? Crumble inward with embarrassment and shame? She had counted on the fact that if any of that happened, it would be more than mitigated by a flood of relief and satisfaction from knowing that after all the lies and secrets and loneliness, the truth would finally be out and she would be liberated. She would have finally taken back control of her life.

However, she didn't tear up, and with effort she was able to keep her emotions in check. But the anticipated cathartic wave of release from finally being open and assertive about her experience didn't materialize either, at least not yet.

Instead she found herself steeled with unwavering concentration, ready to defend against the inevitable and imminent onslaught from Bryce's "friendly journalist." The one who had flown to London to clear his name. The one to whom Bryce had promised retribution for her family. The one who had detested Maggie and viewed her as unethical from the second they met.

Tori looked at her with skepticism and displeasure, and then turned her attention to re-arranging the papers in her lap, taking a couple of sheets from the bottom of the packet and placing them on top. Tori reviewed their contents for a few seconds as Maggie strained to be able to see for herself, but the words were too small and too far away. Maggie had deviated from what Tori and Bryce had wanted her to say, and it was clear that Tori had not come unprepared for that.

She glanced back up at Maggie and proceeded to talk in an unsettlingly tranquil voice. "So you wanted to have sex with Bryce, correct? It was absolutely consensual?"

"Yes. But I also made it clear that I wanted him—"

"The condom, I know," Tori interrupted forcefully, and then displayed a self-assured, ominous gaze. "We'll definitely get to that. First, answer my question. You wanted to have sex with Bryce, correct?"

"Yes, that's correct," Maggie replied. "I did."

"In fact," Tori added, "Isn't it fair to say that you were the aggressor? You kept pushing him to have sex even though he told you he didn't want to."

"No, that's not true. It was very mutual."

Tori then lifted a finger in the direction of one of the off-camera producers. "Let's roll the clip. Maggie, please look at the monitor."

And then suddenly a middle-aged man appeared on the screen. He wore a striped button shirt and a too-large collar buttoned to the top. His mustache was full but the rest of his face had a couple days' growth.

At the bottom of the screen, the chyron read: "Ruben Perry, Uber Driver."

"Yeah, I remember them," he began in a hoarse voice, which she heard through her earpiece. "She was all over him. And he kept telling her to stop, but she wasn't taking no for an answer. I remember thinking, 'Damn this girl's so hot, can't believe *he's* trying to get *her* to stop,' you know what I mean? But he was! It was really something."

Was that really her Uber driver? She had no recollection of who drove them that night, and Bryce had ordered the car so she possessed no record to check. White House opposition research could be fiercely quick and thorough, so it made sense that they found him so fast. But she had never expected to be watching a clip of the purported driver on live television, trying to figure out how to best respond to this unfair mischaracterization that had no doubt been coached. And maybe rewarded . . .

"I'm pretty sure I remember her repeatedly saying 'I want to F you,'" the man continued. "She kept saying 'I want to F you right here in the car' and stuff like that and I was like 'oh boy this is getting out of control.' But she didn't say 'F'. She said the actual word. You know what I mean? The F word. And he was like saying 'no' and trying to get her to stop."

The video faded to black and Maggie told herself that she needed to remain calm. She wanted to walk off the set and not dignify these and no doubt other upcoming attacks. But ending the interview now would send a message of weakness and a lack of confidence in her own story. She had to stay and fight.

"First of all, what he said is . . . not true. I know it's standard practice when someone is victimized by a powerful person to smear the accuser with falsehoods and distortions, so that's what you're doing here—"

"I'm not smearing anyone," Tori interrupted firmly. "I'm just presenting all available information, and then the viewers can decide for themselves. There are important questions here. Let me ask this: you just used the word 'victimized' . . . so did you report the alleged incident to any authorities?"

"No. I—"

"You could have called the police, right? You know how to call 9-1-1?"

"Look, Tori . . ." Maggie began as she watched her interviewer glance down at her own open left palm.

"It's pretty simple. Nine . . ." Tori said as her right pointer finger slowly tapped the hand that now served as an invisible screen of an imaginary phone. "One . . ." she then added while pressing down again.

"You're making light of something that's serious," Maggie cut in before the final digit. "I can certainly explain the *many* understandable reasons why I didn't involve the police. And as for that ridiculous, highly exaggerated video you just showed, even though I did want to have sex with Bryce, that's totally irrelevant from the fact that without my consent he—"

"Right, the condom thing. Even if that's true, which we have a lot of reason to doubt, don't you think that by making a claim like this you're undermining the experiences of real sexual assault survivors?"

"What do you mean by real?"

"You know what I mean. *Real.*"

"This is real. This happened."

"You're giving us your word about that?

"That's right."

"And the strength of your word is based on your credibility, of course. Correct?"

"Yes," she replied, knowing she was being led somewhere and assuming it was to a place she didn't want to go.

"Watch the monitor again please," Tori directed, and then Maggie was looking uneasily at her own face on the screen.

"I knew her best in college," Maggie saw herself say. "She was an extremely smart, kind, outgoing, witty woman who was very well-liked across campus. Those of us who knew her were not surprised at all that she became such a success. And everyone is hoping and praying that she's okay and somewhere safe, and that we'll hear from her very soon."

"That's you talking five days ago about human rights activist and poker pro Priya Varma, who was missing at the time," Tori explained. "Fortunately, we now know she's alive, although she's unable to safely leave the Canadian embassy in the Kingdom. Maggie, I should probably find a more diplomatic word, but I'll just say it plainly: that was a lie. Wasn't it? She was missing and feared dead, and you went on TV to proclaim yourself a good friend of hers, when that was just a lie."

"Well, let me explain."

"A complete and total lie. Right?"

"Yes! It was. I deeply regret it, and I want to explain."

"Please do."

"I attended the same college at the same time as Priya, but I didn't really know her. The network told me they were looking for people to say personal, positive, non-political things about her. I didn't see harm in doing that. But now I do, and I'm very sorry. I very much regret it, and I apologize. But that's a completely different situation than what we're talking about today with Bryce."

Tori looked back at her and exhibited her expert-level dubious journalist expression, with her head slightly tilted and her eyes narrowed as if she was in deep thought, trying in good faith to reconcile information that just didn't make sense. "Well, it seems to me to be quite the same thing, actually. When it helps you to lie, you lie."

"What I said about Bryce doesn't help me. It's as far from helping me as anything can possibly be."

"Maggie, you're clearly desperate for attention and fame, and you're willing to tell falsehoods to get it. You admit you lied to get yourself a prime time appearance on national television. Now you're getting even more exposure by making yet another big claim. Accusing Bryce Kirkwood has instantly made you very well-known. Anyone can see the pattern here. It's just more of the same."

"No, I don't want this at all. Being here. Talking about what Bryce did to me. Revealing an incredibly upsetting and personal experience, reliving it with millions of people watching. It's horrible. I'm telling the truth about Bryce. This happened. I would never make an allegation like this if it wasn't true. What I said about Priya was wrong, but it was so different. I saw it as just saying a few supportive things about her. At the time I thought it was innocuous. Now I know better."

"Innocuous?" Tori shot back. "She was risking her life for activism against the brutal regime in the Kingdom, and you used your connection to her as a hook to defend it!"

"That's not true. You're conflating different things. And Priya was actually the first person to encourage me to come forward publicly with what Bryce did."

"Oh really? Well, we have no way to know if that's even true. I haven't spoken with her. And based on your track record with claims about her, we have no idea if you really have. And your credibility deficit extends well beyond that. Didn't you have a financial incentive from the Kingdom at the time you went on television which you never revealed? One you still have now as you sit here! How much do you stand to earn from that arrangement?"

"That's confidential and irrelevant."

"It's not irrelevant to your credibility that you have a client who's looking to earn millions from the Kingdom's tyrant crown prince and you hid that when you were posing as a neutral analyst! And that client is Kyler Dawson, right? The poker player who sold out his country and is now banned from most casinos in the United States."

"Stop!" Maggie ordered. "Listen Tori, you're obviously doing whatever you can to discredit me and help Bryce, and we both know why. Whether you believe me, whether people watching believe me, I can't control that. But I want to be really clear about one thing. Bryce sexually assaulted me. I never consented to having sex without a condom. He knew that, and he did it anyway, without my consent. This happened. I'm gaining nothing from saying this. In fact, I'm probably destroying my career by coming forward, and I can only imagine the terrifying harassment and hatred that will be waiting for me when this interview is done. But the main reason I'm speaking out is that I don't want Bryce to harm someone else the way he harmed me. I'm very concerned about that. Because I'm living with this every day, and it's really difficult. Because this happened to me. You can try to distort my life history and attack me, but that will never change the fact that *this happened*."

37

AS SOON AS the interview ended, Maggie raced back to her hotel room, slammed the door, and released a primal scream. She hadn't been sure the key would still work—maybe Bryce and Tori and their allies would have deactivated it—but she hadn't been evicted yet. She cried out again, louder this time, using every ounce of power from her lungs and soul, not caring who could hear.

When she paused, the room was silent except for the buzzing of her phone which she had left on the bed. She looked down as it vibrated and displayed "Bryce" in bright letters. She shook her head and looked away, and in a few seconds it grew still and dark again.

She breathed heavily, wondering what was left of her life, considering where it would be safe to go now that all the allies of the White House and assorted assholes and kooks throughout both the online and real worlds would be ridiculing and targeting her. Where should she head next? What should she do? What were her options? Did she have any?

And then the phone came back to life, once again declaring "Bryce" as it shook with agitation. Against her better judgment—she was doing a lot of things against her better judgment lately—she answered it.

"You're a fucking liar!" came a bellow that forced her to move the phone away from her ear. "You've always been a liar, and now everyone in the world knows it!"

She thought about his usually intense belief in discretion for personal and sensitive conversations. “Bryce, this phone isn’t secure.”

“I don’t care who can fucking hear! Let everyone hear! You promised that you would never do this. You promised! You’re a fucking liar!”

This time, she wasn’t going to back down, and she began screaming right back at him with fury.

“This is not my fault! This is not my fault, Bryce! *You* did this to me. And then you told me to tell the truth, and I did! Maybe no one else knows that I told the truth, but I know . . . and you know. Fuck you, Bryce. You manipulated me into this interview, and before that you sent me to the Kingdom where I could have died. Probably because you *wanted* me to die. Don’t fucking blame me for anything!”

“When you wanted my help, you promised you wouldn’t do this. Just like you always lie when you want something. You’re going to regret this, Maggie,” he told her, and this sent a chill through her body as she already feared that that would be the case.

“So you’re threatening me now?”

“No, I’m telling you a fact. You’re going to regret this. Good luck ever getting a good job in DC again. Good luck ever finding a real client, not some jerkoff poker player. You’re finished, Maggie! You’ve probably destroyed both of us for a fucking lie!”

“I know I’m not the only one you did this to—” she started to say, but then saw that Bryce had ended the call. Her body was shaking and she swallowed hard and then fell onto the bed, burying her face in the comforter. She screamed again, and this time her scream was muffled by the bedding that was partially suffocating her.

When she finally lifted her head and caught a glimpse of herself in the mirror, she observed that her appearance was now a far cry from the pre-interview reflection that had been created with such care. Her brown hair was now disheveled, her makeup smeared, her dress wrinkled, her face haggard from intense discomfort.

It was all public now. So public. Her trauma, her mistakes, her poor decisions, her bad luck. Talking publicly about her last sexual experience had been so embarrassing and every painful aspect of that terrible memory now resurfaced with unprecedented intensity. It was humiliating. Everyone in the world now owning the image in their heads of her getting fucked and taken advantage of. Her ailing parents now stuck with that as possibly one of their final mental pictures of their daughter.

And how was "everyone in the world" now reacting? Despite somewhat implying during the interview that she didn't care about whether people ultimately believed her, she did want to know. Unfortunately, part of her needed to know.

Social media would be the worst place to look for an answer, but it was also the most available, the most immediate. So in the spirit of bad judgment she turned onto her back and lifted her phone, and saw that she and her story were blowing up.

"Anyone actually believe this (media) whore? She'll do anything to get ahead—lie, try to fuck her boss, tell fake story for attention #icallbullshit"

"She's a liar by her own admission! Uber driver proved raster a crazy nympho! Sink kirkwood for this bitch? No way! Raster really should just gtfoh and stop trying to ruin good people #nocredibility #supportkirkwood"

So many of the online commentors didn't even have an opinion on the merits, but were taking advantage of the easy opportunity to provide demeaning snark at her expense.

"Omggg @uber forget trying to sell me uber premium! How do I sign up for an uber with @maggieraster??? That sounds like the kind of ride we all need!"

But there were also supporters out there, and she was intensely grateful for each one, even if some were backing her just for other political motivations.

"What Maggie Raster did today was brave and bold. What she experienced was wrong. I believe her and so should you #ibelievemaggie"

"Never liked kirkwood and now I know why. Fuck him and whole horrible administration. Vote them out next year! #throwthemallout"

And besides the raging social media inferno about whether she told the truth, there was the related debate about whether there was any significance to her claim, considering she had been a willing and enthusiastic sexual partner. Maggie saw that a huge pop culture site she had followed for years, never contemplating that she would be one of its subjects, tried to settle this with a Twitter poll, asking, "Maggie Raster's Allegations: If True, How Big a Deal???" Poll responders were given three options: "Big Deal!"; "Little Deal!"; and "No Deal!"

Currently, "Little Deal!" was winning by a wide margin and for some reason that felt even more disheartening and dismissive than if "No Deal!" was in the lead.

She urgently needed to go for a walk, feel the cool London winter air, leave her phone off, and just be alone and free for a little while.

But before she shut it down, she saw one hashtag that was now trending along with expressions of support for her. Two words that she had repeated to Tori as she pushed back against the aggressive attempts to discredit her:

#thishappened

38

AS THE TOURNAMENT entered a break for the chips to be colored up, the small-value chips replaced by larger denominations, Kyler considered with nervous exhilaration how close he was to taking the whole thing down and fundamentally changing his existence forever. Yet he was also still so far away.

With twelve people left competing for $20 million, part of him wished he could just cash out for a 1/12 share, or about $1.67 million. But this was winner take all. Even if he could walk away now with that prize, Maggie would be entitled to half, and Mia would get half of the remaining half, and then the IRS would charge its rake, and he would be left with not enough to even make a significant dent in his debts.

He yearned to reach the final table of nine, so he could have a breather from the tension hanging over him every second as he fought through nerves and exhaustion and horrible river cards to concentrate and inch closer to winning.

He looked at his phone to see if Maggie had any new info for him. He hoped to read some encouraging, positive text from her, that she was okay and would soon be returning to his rail. Instead, he didn't learn anything about her progress until he saw a pop-up alert from a news app.

"Ex-White House Staffer Claims Chief of Staff 'Sexually Assaulted' Her"

He sped through the article as he wondered whether this was all true. His connection to Maggie told him to back her, to be convinced that she was only making an allegation because what she reported actually did occur. But how well did he really know her? And if he had known Bryce instead, wouldn't he probably believe his denials?

He only had a few minutes until play resumed and wanted to keep his attention on poker, but he couldn't help looking through the social media explosion that her accusation had initiated. Calls for Bryce to resign. Vicious attacks on Maggie as untrustworthy, deceitful, and starving for media attention. And enhanced pummeling of his name because the interviewer apparently referred to him on air as her client.

So for those on social media looking to feast on and devour the reputations and futures of others, there were three big options here for them to choose from—Bryce, Maggie, and Kyler. Now the wolves could select which of them best fit their particular political, social, and culinary tastes.

Then, with his below average chip stack in front of him, he was back sitting at one of two remaining tables of six men.

"All in," a player from Vietnam called out as he pushed his chip stack forward.

Kyler inspected his cards and saw a pair of nines. What should he do? It was so hard to read people in this tournament—these were not top pros, and their moves were often illogical. For the whole tournament he was dealing with this problem: How could he read if someone was strong if that person didn't understand the answer to that question himself? It was like that charity tournament he once played in, to benefit a local animal shelter where a friend worked as a deliveryman. No one knew how to play, and it was a bunch of random bets and all-ins that ultimately knocked him out and over to the cash bar early.

Plus he had the added complication that there was no prize money except for the ultimate winner. Instead of people wanting to survive for a final table pay jump, there was no incentive to play it safe here. Might as well move all the chips in the middle and hope for the best, as there might be no other way to accumulate enough to win it all.

As he contemplated whether to call, he asked for a count and saw that he was covered—if he called and lost, he'd be gone. And then the player added another justification for being extra aggressive with non-premium hands.

"You should just call," he said to Kyler. "One of us will double up. The other can quickly leave before being blown apart by an American missile. Worth risking my life for twenty mil, but once I'm out, I'm *out . . .*"

The man let out a gallows humor chuckle that was definitely *not* appreciated or copied by anyone else. Even Sacha, the chip leader who was constantly talking and responding with attitude to every random comment, glanced uncomfortably at the speaker and then back down at his cards.

Kyler had seen this rumor online, and Maggie had warned him via text to leave as soon as his tournament run ended. But she had written that she couldn't provide details, and until now the topic had been unspoken in this room, at least in his vicinity. Word was that the Canadian ambassador was leaving the country immediately. Some sources said he was going by choice, others said by force. Supposedly the United States was preparing for a retaliatory strike that could happen at any moment. Those playing in the Goodwill Poker Classic might die, and, according to some online, it would be a just end for those immoral enough to participate, especially Kyler Dawson.

Did the guy make this oddly flippant warning because he was really concerned? Or because he had an actual strong hand and wanted to deceive Kyler and/or another player into a call? With just six players at the table, pocket nines weren't terrible. But they weren't worth calling off all his chips with either, so he folded. The last to act was Sacha in the big blind, who flipped over ace-king and called, and then saw he was dominating ace-queen from the original bettor.

The flop was king high, making Sacha's lead even larger and making Kyler feel fortunate for folding. But when the nine of diamonds came out as the turn card—harmless and irrelevant to everyone else at the table—he felt sick and wanted to scream. If he had just stayed in the hand. He would have hit a set. He would have tripled up and won a huge pot. He would have been one of the leaders heading into the final table.

He stood and stepped away, consumed with frustration and agitation. When he returned a few seconds later, the Vietnamese player was gone, just like that. In twenty minutes he might be at the airport. He hated to see Sacha winning another big hand and gaining more chips, but at least he took someone else out. Simultaneously, there was an elimination at the other table, and the tournament was down to ten. One more and they would break for the night, and he could decompress, maybe get some sleep.

Then a small stack moved all in at his table, and Kyler found himself holding pocket kings.

"Call," he declared. His opponent revealed two red jacks, and the dealer began to reveal the flop.

No jack. No jack. No fucking jack. And no misdeal!

Standing once again, and viewing each card with trepidation, he watched as the flop, turn, and river all fell harmlessly. It was 1:30 a.m., and after a marathon session, play for the day was finally over. He had reached the final table.

The remaining players and the approximately two hundred people watching from around the room began to applaud. Nine men competing the next day for $20 million.

One time. Let tomorrow be my one time. Or have I already used it up?

He accepted handshakes from a fellow player and a few uniformed men, and then looked toward the exits, intent on quickly escaping to the elevator that would take him to his hotel room floor so that he could be alone. He took a quick glance at his phone, hoping to see an update from Maggie. But none was there, so he fired off a message to her.

"I made the final table! Nine ppl left. So exhausted. FT starts noon tomorrow. I hope ur ok. Please call if u can."

He put the phone back in his front pocket and, before he could take a step toward the door, he felt a vibration. He removed it, looking to see Maggie's response, but instead read a new text from Priya.

"Kyler I'm at airport with Ambassador Bouchard. We're about to take off and leave the Kingdom. I know you made the final table. Please please please listen to me: don't play tomorrow. Maggie did the right thing today. I know it wasn't easy for her, and it won't be for you. But now it's your turn. Don't play and you'll be a hero."

And then, just as he finished reading, a second message:

"It's also not safe to stay. Don't risk your life for a huge mistake. Just leave and take a stand against tyranny. My offer still stands. I will be v appreciative and will help you rebuild your career! People see so many tragedies and atrocities in the news and feel helpless, like they can't do anything meaningful to really help. But you can! You take this significant stand and the whole world will notice."

Two short years ago, he had known Priya Varma only from poker shows and YouTube videos. As he had watched this popular, celebrated, and seemingly unapproachable rising star, he had never contemplated the inconceivable idea that she would one day personally text him and ask for *anything*. The possibility that she would even acknowledge his existence, that she would actually make a request, and say how "appreciative" she would be—before all this, is there anything he wouldn't have done for her attention and approval?

So much had changed. Just two weeks ago, he could have played in this tournament without being submerged in a highly toxic and volatile situation. Then Emily Kinum was murdered and the whole world was different. Without her death, his participation would have been criticized but not condemned. People would have continued to mock but not detest him. Now he was the global target of intense derision and disgust. Her killing right before this tournament was the biggest fucking bad beat of all time. More for her, of course, but for him, too.

Nevertheless, Kyler recognized that if he was victorious tomorrow, an unsettling argument could be made that he actually *benefited* big time from her murder. If she hadn't died and mass boycotts hadn't occurred, the field here would have included top poker pros, much tougher competition than he was currently facing. Then again, he'd beaten them all once, and maybe he would have done it again.

Now he needed to put that all aside and just think about tomorrow and hope that the cards would fall his way. As he had explained to Maggie, he knew that in poker (and everything else), luck tends to even out over time. But after tomorrow there would be no more time. It was a concept Priya was very familiar with—one day you're calling the exact card to win a tournament, and the next your wildest dreams are in sight as they come abruptly crashing down runner-runner.

#sixofdiamondsontheriver

There were now nine men left, competing for $20 million. Despite Priya's offer to help if he dropped out, there was no way he could walk away at this point. He was too close, and the prize was too enormous.

What good was her word anyway? He had learned from Nolan about the disastrous consequences of giving up millions in return for unenforceable promises. He could quit, take some inconsequential stand against injustice that would accomplish nothing but sentence him and his family to crushing debt for the rest of his life, and Priya would never be there to support him. She was a top poker pro who by definition deceived others for a living, and he was going to rely on her promise? After all he had been through? Absolutely not.

He noticed the camera in the face of another competitor a few feet away, and the woman from the state news service holding a microphone in front of the guy.

"Congratulations on making the final table of this highly prestigious tournament," she said.

"Thank you!" the thin man with a polo shirt exclaimed. "I'm very excited!"

"Please tell us," she followed up, "What does this hugely successful event say about the crown prince and his extraordinary modernization plan?"

He appeared to think about this for a couple of seconds, and then gushed, "It's just fantastic. Spectacular! He's a tremendous leader and a man who wants to improve the lives of his people and create goodwill throughout the world. I'm honored to be a part of this, and I hope those who are throwing hate and threats his way will learn that they are the *real* troublemakers on this planet, not him."

Next the camera turned toward Kyler, and the woman moved the microphone in front of his mouth as she glanced up at him with synthetic joy.

"Congratulations on making the final table of this highly prestigious tournament," she said again.

"Thank you," Kyler said plainly, and she kept her smile but her eyes showed that she was clearly disappointed by his failure to show more enthusiasm.

"And do you have a word for your country regarding its unnecessary militaristic posturing and how it is threatening innocent people in the Kingdom and undermining world peace?"

Kyler was disgusted—at this woman and her question, at himself, at the whole world, at the fact that he was stuck so deep in this thing, so pot committed, that it was impossible to get out now. But no matter what leverage the Kingdom or anyone else had over him because of his past traumas and current desperation, he wasn't going to give her the response she wanted.

I won't be a propaganda tool against my own country. Never. "I'm just here to play poker," he responded brusquely, and then turned and walked away.

As he headed toward the exit, he again remembered Maggie's proposal during their first meeting: *"So why don't we agree that if you win—if we pull this off—we both devote a significant amount of the money to helping people in need. Maybe here, maybe elsewhere. Maybe even in the Kingdom."*

If he could win tomorrow, if he could be victorious without getting killed in the process, he would absolutely do that in a big, big way. Then he could show the world that in reality he was a good man.

He decided not to respond to Priya's texts, but her voice chimed in his head as he reached the door and imagined what she would say: *"You won't be a propaganda tool? Please. That's been my whole point since the beginning. You already are one, Kyler. You are such a tool."*

39

JACQUES'S EYES were fixed on his phone while he cruised at 30,000 feet. His diplomatic career was almost over, but he had one last mission, and it was the most important of his life. He fully believed the crown prince's promises about retaliating with nuclear weapons if America attacked, and Jacques needed to immediately communicate the credibility of this threat to those in power.

He had tried with Bryce—passionately tried with him—but Bryce told him that his lack of compelling, confirmable intelligence made the crown prince's threats unlikely to be taken seriously and that if the United States didn't act now, the nuclear capability might soon become a reality. Then it would be too late to do anything to avenge Emily's death and prevent future atrocities and nuclear blackmail.

Few wanted to get revenge for her death more than Jacques did, but there had to be another way because the current path could result in unprecedented devastation.

"Is that her?" Priya asked from the window seat on his right.

She was looking down at the phone in his right hand, at the photo of Emily and him that Jacques had been staring at as he tried to figure out how to proceed. "Yes," he said sadly. "We had become very close."

He knew immediately that he shouldn't have said that, shouldn't have used those final two words. His time together with Emily had actually been relatively brief, and very possibly she never shared the strong feelings he had for her. What specific actions or words on her part persuasively demonstrated otherwise? He could name none. But he firmly believed that there had been the seeds of a powerful connection, that if she had lived those two words would have had a strong chance of becoming a reality.

Regardless, he couldn't really consider that now. Far too much was at stake. So much was riding on how he and others tried to resolve this highly dangerous international predicament.

The final negotiations with the Kingdom had come together quickly. He needed to get out of the country, and they wanted to end the embarrassment of Priya undermining their regime with social media posts from within their sovereign territory. They would have preferred to have her in custody, but he was intent on preventing her arrest.

"Let me take her directly to the airport, and we'll both leave immediately," he proposed.

"And why would we allow that?"

"Because I'm going to head directly to Washington with the sole mission of convincing them not to attack you. Because I believe your nuclear threats, and I want to stop a war. But I can't leave her behind after what you did to Emily."

So they had an agreement, with one final condition—that Priya make no further public statements critical of the Kingdom until she had left its airspace. Both sides kept their word, and now they were airborne.

He remembered the words that Priya had spoken to him when she first confronted him outside the embassy. *"You need to do more. And I'm here to help and make sure that you do. When this is all over, history will judge you on how you handled this humanitarian crisis, and right now you're failing."*

Since then he had explained at length how much he wanted to help the oppressed people of that nation and how he had been trying to get important information to the international community via

Emily when she had been murdered. He talked with Priya not only about the current "humanitarian crisis" but about the so much larger one that was on the brink of unfolding.

She never stopped believing that he wasn't doing enough, that he needed to take a more public stand against the atrocities around him. Passing information to a journalist while he maintained a public air of diplomatic benevolence was never going to be acceptable to her. She didn't want a war, and that they agreed on, but in her opinion too many people, including the current US administration, were afraid to call out the Kingdom for what it was. He hadn't explicitly told her about the possible American strike or the Kingdom's nuclear capability—that information was too sensitive to reveal, especially with her penchant for inflammatory posts on social media. But enough of that was public now, so she surely had a good idea about the treacherous situation they all faced.

Maybe if he had explained this situation fully to her earlier, she would have been more careful. If she had all the information he had, possibly she wouldn't have pulled that ridiculous stunt with Maggie while he was away from the embassy.

He strongly disapproved of what she had done, but he also recognized that the resulting chain of events now presented them with an important opportunity. He had a strategy for stopping a war for now, while still making the Kingdom pay. But his middle-ground plan would never work with Bryce, who believed that such a proposal was weak and fruitless. Bryce had always seemed rash and viewed decisions in an all-or-nothing framework. That became clearer than ever during their call with Maggie. Bryce wasn't leading the armed forces, but he had powerful sway with the president, and if Bryce favored a military attack and rejected other options, the president would probably follow his recommendations.

But then . . .

"These allegations are completely false," Bryce declared to a scrum of reporters surrounding him outside the White House, as Jacques watched live on his phone shortly before he and Priya headed to the airport. Bryce was clearly rattled as he fought to salvage his reputation, career, and future. "Clearly, Ms. Raster is a dishonest person," Bryce continued as the assembled media representatives captured the moment with video and photos. "She has no credibility. She herself admitted that she's made false public claims in the past. Anything that happened between us was completely consensual. If anyone said 'no' at any point, it was me, not her. You don't need to take my word on that. You heard it from the Uber driver."

"What about this argument in the park?" a reporter asked. "Did that happen?"

"I'm not getting into that now," he responded.

"So it really happened?"

"I didn't say that," he answered with clear frustration. "I don't think it's appropriate to address every random rumor that's thrown out."

"What's your response to the #thishappened hashtag that's trending as a result of Maggie Raster's interview?" another reporter asked.

"You want me to respond to a hashtag? Really? Come on."

"Did you have sex with Ms. Raster?" asked another.

"Look, I'm not discussing those details. Her allegations are completely untrue. That's all I can say right now."

"Did she ask you to wear a condom? And, if so, did you take it off during sex without her knowledge and consent?" came the follow-up question.

He looked increasingly irritated as he replied, "Again, I'm not discussing details of any sexual activity with Ms. Raster. But I will say that what you just described is something I would never, ever do. Ever."

"He's lying, you know," Priya said matter-of-factly, having joined him in his office a few minutes earlier. "So many tells."

But Jacques didn't need the poker player's analysis to tell him this. It was obvious to him, too.

Bryce definitely had some defenders in Washington, in the media, and online. But far too many saw what Priya and Jacques saw. Within an hour, there were online rumors of another sexual misconduct allegation against Bryce about to surface, and then a third. This was getting bigger, not going away, and even though people were divided on whether Bryce should stay in his post, the president just couldn't proceed into a re-election year with his chief of staff engulfed in a growing firestorm.

About a half hour after takeoff, when the plane's spotty Wi-Fi finally kicked in, Jacques read the statement that the White House issued in Bryce's name.

"I hereby resign my position as chief of staff to the president of the United States. Serving the president and my country has been the greatest honor of my life. I am enormously proud of all this administration has accomplished and of its continuing efforts to improve the lives of everyday Americans and people throughout the world. Although the allegations leveled against me are completely false and I will never back down from the fight to clear my name, I do not want to be a distraction to the president and his team's crucial work. Therefore, I regretfully submit my resignation, effective immediately."

An hour later, Jacques received an urgent, encrypted message from Brad Connelly, who had just been promoted from deputy chief of staff to acting chief of staff, asking to meet right away to discuss everything he had learned while in the Kingdom. Jacques had never met or spoken with this man, but he welcomed a new person in the position, someone who already seemed interested in utilizing Jacques's experience and expertise. Bryce had been so rigid, so unreceptive to Jacques's warnings and briefings and pleadings to avoid military action.

This was a new opportunity to avoid war, to prevent nuclear

retaliation. And he had Maggie to thank for that, and then, of course, Priya to thank for forcing Maggie's hand, as much as he strongly disapproved of her tactics and motives.

He wrote to Connelly that he was landing in London in about three hours and would take an immediate flight from there to Washington.

"Thank you. It's essential that we speak in person immediately. Let me know the flight information and I will arrange for transportation from the airport to the WH."

Despite his fears, the window to stop a war wasn't closed yet. There was an unexpected opportunity here, and he needed to seize it. A few minutes later, he received a follow-up message from the acting chief of staff.

"I assume you're traveling with Priya Varma. If possible, please bring her, too. We'd very much like to hear her perspective."

And then:

"Also, off the record, and don't tell her this, but I play poker and have followed her career. Big fan. Would love to meet her."

He was troubled by the frivolousness of this last comment, considering the emergency they needed to defuse. But Jacques knew it was best to accommodate the White House as much as possible. He discreetly turned his phone to Priya and showed her the last few messages, despite Connelly's instruction.

"So," he whispered, "can you come with me to Washington?"

40

IT'S JUST a poker game, Kyler told himself as the Kingdom's militaristic national anthem blared with a steady, defiant drumbeat. *Make smart decisions. Focus. Focus on making the correct play on every hand. Win it all, then get the hell out of here.*

Everyone was standing at attention, with cameras around the room trained on the uniformed musicians and those whose lives, choices, and circumstances had brought them all to this one large reception hall on this frigid January day: the nine final participants, surrounding the table's wood edge and green felt; the hundreds of spectators in the stands that had been erected around the final table overnight; the crown prince himself, hand over heart, dressed as always in a perfectly tailored custom suit. All of it was being broadcast live on state television and streamed online to the world.

Kyler noted that, on the surface, the crown prince displayed his normally self-assured demeanor and charismatic air of benevolent command, exuding in-control leadership while standing among his physically imposing advisers and assistants. But Kyler could tell from looking at the man's unblinking eyes that he was not at all at ease. Inside, Kyler saw fear, disappointment, and frustration. He could sense all this because he knew these sentiments all too well himself. And he recognized something else that was familiar: *determination*—determination to conquer whoever and whatever was responsible for all the obstacles and setbacks he faced.

Or was Kyler just projecting? Possible, but unlikely.

The crown prince had planned this international event for at least two years, with the goal of earning prestige and positive attention for him, his "reform" program, and his nation. For a state languishing on the fringes of the world's economic, political, and cultural power centers, it aspired to be an opportunity to host the planet's greatest players from a game whose popularity was exploding all over the globe. The event could have earned so much pride and yes, *goodwill,* for him and his country. But now that the culmination was finally here, as much as he portrayed it as a victorious celebration, he had to be greatly troubled and disappointed by where he found himself: boycotted by the top pros in the world; condemned throughout the planet for a brutal murder; no longer idolized as a benevolent reformer; potentially moments away from a missile strike from the United States of America.

Why is this taking so long? Let's get started already. Kyler stood in front of Seat 4, facing the dealer. Sacha, the chip leader, was by Seat 8. Seven other men from around the world tensely awaited the start of the biggest competition of their lives. Kyler was seventh in chips, so not in great shape, but he had made it this far and needed to conquer just one more day to win $20 million.

What did Priya expect? That he could just leave? *Now*? Impossible.

The anthem finally, thankfully, ended. The crown prince was at the microphone. "To all the brave, talented, wonderful, brilliant final table participants, I congratulate you and wish you good luck! Now, let's shuffle up and deal!"

Applause rocked the room, and the players took their assigned seats.

Then, a distraction. A big distraction.

By one of the entrance doors, at the far end of the room, away from the poker table, she stepped in tentatively, still wrapped in her blue winter coat, and then caught his eye and hurriedly walked toward him.

Kyler took a few steps away from the table. When Maggie reached him, he threw his arms around her and squeezed in relief. Then he quickly withdrew. "Sorry, that was too much."

"No, it's fine," she answered with the tone of someone who was contending with much bigger problems than his greeting.

"Are you okay?" he asked.

She looked at him with exhausted eyes and responded, "I don't even know how to begin answering that. And you don't have time to listen now." She motioned with her head toward the table.

"Well, I can only imagine how crazy everything is now for you. I'm so glad to see you."

"Listen, Kyler," she said, moving past the pleasantries and lowering her voice, "I don't want to disturb you now, but please understand that you need to get out of the country as soon as you're finished. Win or lose. Immediately."

"I saw the online rumors and your text. I wasn't sure how much was media hype."

"It's not media hype. It's very real. There's a planned, imminent missile attack that the ambassador is trying to stop, and it's not safe to stay here. I'm sorry to tell you right before you start, but you have to know."

"So why did you come back here if it's not safe?"

"To warn you. I came back to make sure you know this is real and that you get out right after. And because I have $10 million riding on this stupid game."

"Thank you," he gushed, concerned about her warning but basking in the warmth of knowing that this remarkable woman cared enough to come back for him.

Kyler seized on the confidence that came from knowing she was there and believed in him. It temporarily replaced all the stress, and he was able to just focus, focus, focus on the cards, the bets, the strategy, the other players. He put aside all the anger and misery that was constantly tearing him apart and instead concentrated on her and all things positive.

The dealer distributed the cards. As Kyler raised pre-flop in middle position with suited connectors, continuation bet, and then hit his flush on the turn, it was just another hand. He wasn't thinking about the huge stakes. In that moment, it was no longer a life or death event. It was just a poker game, and he was playing the rush and stacking chips.

When he took down another pot a few hands later with an aggressive bet while holding a double belly-buster straight draw, he chose to believe his children loved him and nothing he had done had brought them shame. He was on his way to ensuring their comfort for the rest of their lives, to making them proud of him once again.

A few minutes later, another player re-raised him pre-flop, and Kyler four-bet with *absolutely nothing* and took down a nice pot, all the while convincing himself that his wife had never texted him in the middle of the night to mock him with the fact that she had just had sex with two other guys, both of whom were more of a man to her than he ever was. That had never happened now, and the temporary liberation was wonderful.

In this new world he was able to create, he never foolishly settled a lawsuit with Nolan for $2.8 million, only to have his name and reputation defiled in a global act of brutal humiliation. In fact, as he eliminated another player by calling an all-in with ace-king suited and pairing both cards on the flop, he had never needed Nolan's help to buy into that original tournament in the first place. No, he had been able to scrape together the needed $600 himself and had entered and won his WSOP entry all on his own.

As he later expertly called down a huge bluff on the river with second pair, he relished in the fact that neither Priya nor anyone else had any objection to him playing this tournament. It was a prestigious event for top players from around the world, and nobody had any reason to criticize him for participating.

When he flopped a set of tens in a big four-way pot, the people Priya told him about had never been burned alive. The citizens of the Kingdom, led by the crown prince, had a long way to go to reach the wonderful, precious freedoms of the United States, but they were moving in that direction, and there was real reason for hope and optimism in the future. Thankfully, in that moment there was no longer fear of an imminent US attack in which Kyler might soon be collateral damage.

When there were only three men left, Kyler eliminated one of them, his top two pair holding up by dodging all the outs of his opponent's desperation flush draw. In that moment, Emily Kinum had never been murdered. The esteemed journalist, whom Kyler had never heard of as recently as two weeks ago, was diligently writing somewhere, continuing her legendary career, still alive and happy. Just as he was happy. Just as they all were.

And through all this, Sacha wasn't someone who tormented him, who reminded him constantly through his demeaning comments and gestures about what Kyler's life and history were *really* like, *really* about. He no longer taunted Kyler with the reality of his own perennial failures of every kind—moral, family, career, judgment—that no elaborate fantasy could ever really undo.

At this time, Sacha was just another player, and when Kyler eliminated the other man in third place, he was able to turn to Maggie and smile. She was standing fifteen feet away, in front of the stands, having watched in support for the past eight hours as he played the best poker of his life and no missiles fell.

She nodded back to him, appearing apprehensive and fatigued but also hopeful.

You're almost there, her look told him. *We're almost there.*

It was just him and Sacha, heads up for $20 million. Sacha stared at Kyler from across the table and flashed a condescending sneer. And then all of Kyler's positivity vanished, and all the rage and tension and regret and fear came pouring back, as his body became a cauldron of fury.

I absolutely need to beat him. Everything is at stake. I'll never be able to live the rest of my life if I don't defeat him now.

41

JACQUES UNDERSTOOD that as soon as Priya departed the Kingdom with him, it was inevitable that news reports of her leaving the nation would quickly make worldwide headlines, especially after all the coverage of her potential whereabouts when her location had been unknown. She was no longer just a niche celebrity. She challenged *the Kingdom* on its own territory, supported its dissenters, and boldly called for reforms, all on the heels of Emily's murder and the worldwide outrage that no one was truly being held accountable.

But even though enough people knew she was leaving in order for that information to be made public, hardly anyone was aware of her ultimate destination, which had only been decided en route to London. That all changed on the connecting flight to DC, when a young man approached her, leaning over Jacques's seat, and said that he was a huge fan and supporter. The large dark sunglasses she had been wearing hadn't hidden her identity.

Jacques then knew that word would quickly be out. By the time they landed, a throng of media awaited her at Reagan National Airport. Priya had yet to make any public comment since she departed the Kingdom, and they all wanted to get her first reaction to everything that had occurred over the past few days. Fortunately, the White House had arranged for security to move them quickly around the public gathering spaces at the airport and into a waiting SUV, which sped off under an overcast winter sky.

"The president is meeting with the Joint Chiefs right now and will be making a decision shortly," Brad Connelly told them twenty-five minutes later as he sat behind his new desk in the White House chief of staff's office. "He wants me to report to him right away with what you both know. Can we agree that everything we discuss here is confidential?"

The question was presented to both of them, but Jacques had no doubt the real concern was Priya, whom the media was clamoring to interview.

"Of course," he responded.

"Sure," she said. "As long as this is a real discussion. If this is just bullshit posturing, then don't blame me if I later call you out on that."

"No bullshit," Brad responded. "Ambassador, you know that Bryce was pushing hard for a strategic but powerful air strike. He wanted to do it now, quickly, before the Kingdom has the ability to retaliate with ICBMs. The intelligence consensus is that this window is closing rapidly. Once that genie is out of the bottle, we'll be in a horrible situation, at the mercy of their blackmail threats."

"And as I told Bryce, that window is closed, according to the crown prince," Jacques quickly responded. "And I believe him. He says they'll retaliate with a nuclear missile aimed at DC. And another one at New York. I explained this to Bryce, and he rejected everything I told him. I provided alternatives. We have alternatives that must be considered. He didn't care."

"Well, he's gone now. And we're open to other options. We're also very aware that launching a missile strike right after a high-profile scandal will look like an attempt at diverting the world's attention, and many will doubt our credibility and moral authority."

"There's a lot of misinformation out there," Priya interjected. "A lot of decisions being made without all the facts. I saw Bryce and this administration as kowtowing to the crown prince because that's what you all had been doing. So now there's this overcompensation, a potential military attack that may lead to a nuclear response. I can tell you from spending time there, from knowing the real people who have stood up in the Kingdom and died for freedom there, that something massive has to be done to help them. And done now. But a missile attack that will probably kill some of those same freedom fighters and may lead to a catastrophic response is not the way to go."

"The other problem," Jacques added, "is that even if they don't retaliate with nuclear weapons, a military strike may result in their government falling, and there's a high probability that the next government will be even worse. More radical. More repressive. So we could have an even more anti-Western regime with nuclear weapons. Then we've just made this whole situation even more dire."

"So what's your proposal?" the acting chief of staff asked.

"We need a powerful response," Priya replied. "Something that will hurt their government in a real way and the crown prince personally. Something that will inspire those fighting for freedom there, because they will know that they have a powerful ally in the United States. Right now they feel abandoned, but you can change that. We need a response, without military action, that shows that the murder of Emily Kinum will not be ignored. A response that will force the crown prince to consider a different path for the future if he wants to stay in power. And it needs to happen immediately."

Brad nodded. "I know Bryce was never receptive to this, but I am. And I agree with everything you've said. So let's talk specifics and then I'll take it right to the president. He's instructed all of us that our actions need to be tough and comprehensive here because we have important scores to settle."

"Okay," Jacques said, with a sigh of relief. "Based on my experience over there, and my knowledge of how his regime works, here's what I recommend. . . ."

42

HER SISTER'S right eye. Swollen, broken, destroyed. Purple. Black. Unrecognizable except that it must be an eye because that's where a person's right eye belongs.

So many injuries on her poor body. But that was the one that Tori saw in her dreams every night, and the image lingered in her field of vision virtually every waking moment.

True vengeance. Actual revenge. Real justice. Making those responsible pay with their lives.

She had received a promise. A vow that powerful retribution was near.

And then the lies of a publicity hound took that away. In her career, Tori had seen so many like her—yearning to be on television, craving attention, willing to claim anything for the reward of a spotlight.

Tori had exposed her, shown her to be a fraud masquerading as whatever she needed to be to promote herself, undermining women who have suffered actual abuse, uncaring about anyone she callously shattered in the process.

Now tens of millions saw her for all this and more, and that's how they would forever remember her. But unfortunately tens of millions were not enough. Not today. Not with this type of allegation, and with those who threatened to take the opportunity to pile on.

So now Bryce was destroyed, his life and career so suddenly unsalvageable. No due process, no investigation—his existence expeditiously obliterated by uncorroborated allegations. And without his advocacy and support and influence, meaningful, powerful retaliation for Emily was probably gone. Her murder would go virtually unanswered, her killers surviving without meaningful consequence. Or so implied Bryce's replacement, the new acting chief of staff. The one who said that the president was considering options but was looking to "resolve" this crisis peacefully while still sending "a powerful message" that her murder was unacceptable.

She had made clear that she would speak out about all this, that she would condemn their lack of decisive action, now and through the re-election year. And he said that he understood this threat and they hoped she would not take that path, but it was within her rights, of course. But first, could she speak with two individuals who were coming to see him? They would meet with him, and then join her in the conference room she now occupied.

She waited by herself, pacing around the oak table and too agitated to sit. Then, approximately forty-five minutes later, the door opened and the two individuals entered. She immediately recognized both even though she had never met either. She had had so much hope for what they would help accomplish. Instead, they had now each bitterly disappointed.

"I thought you were on our side," Tori uttered with sadness to Priya. "All this time, I thought you were with us. And now look what you did."

Priya didn't answer right away, but instead approached Tori and gave her a warm embrace, putting her arms around her body and leaning her head onto Tori's shoulder.

Tori didn't move, and then Priya looked back up and dropped her hold.

"I am on your side," she said. "I was and always will be. I want justice for Emily. That's what I've been fighting for. That's the main reason I went there in the first place."

"But that woman took down our biggest advocate here. And she said you were the one responsible for that. Why would you do that? You talked this big game of really confronting the Kingdom's leadership, and now you come here and advocate for the opposite."

Priya shook her head sympathetically. "Bryce was not a good man. I believe she was telling the truth—"

"Oh my God. She fooled you, too?" Tori interrupted. "This is beyond belief. Such an injustice. Yet another injustice."

"The military response Bryce was pushing for would have killed many of the people we're trying to help. And the retaliation might have been catastrophic. We just proposed a better way that's real and powerful and will hurt the crown prince badly. And this isn't the end. We're going to make sure he and his men face the consequences of their actions for the rest of their lives."

"That's all just weak, meaningless promises," Tori responded. "*Meaningless.* Besides Bryce, there was always worthless spin from everyone in this building, and now it's coming from you too, Priya. And you, Mr. Ambassador, what do you have to say about this?"

"Well," he began nervously, "For starters, I can say that I greatly admired your sister. I loved your sister. I would never advocate for anything that would dishonor her memory." He pulled out his phone from the left inside pocket of his suit jacket, manipulated it for a couple of seconds, and then held it out toward Tori, who involuntarily whimpered as she viewed the screen. There, off-center and grinning, was her beloved sister, her face next to the smiling ambassador in a poorly taken selfie.

"Emily . . ." she gasped. "When was this taken?"

"Right before . . . before . . ."

She continued to view the photo as she slowly, sadly shook her head.

"I spent a lot of time with her then," he continued. "We talked about a million different topics. I was so fond of her. I was devastated by what they did to her . . . I *am* devastated. Avenging her death, without killing innocent people, is the most important thing in the world to me right now. I swear I would never support or push for anything that undermines that goal."

"It's true," Priya added. "I didn't always believe that, but I definitely do now."

Tori looked at them both. Two supposed allies, who together had probably just saved the lives of her sister's murderers. They had their supposed justifications, but in her heart she knew they were wrong. All of this was so fucking wrong. But she did want to learn more about her sister's last days, and what she said and did with this man who she had spoken with right before her death. "I'd like to hear about your conversations with my sister," she said.

"Certainly. She and I became quite close. It started when we first met—"

"No, not in here. I can't take this place anymore. I know it's pretty cold outside, but would you take a walk with me?"

"Absolutely, Tori. Where I come from, this isn't cold at all."

He reached out and rested his hand on her shoulder as he looked into her eyes in a show of sympathy and support, and she responded with a forlorn but appreciative nod.

Her sister had apparently connected with this man in her final days, and Tori was eager to learn more about their interactions. Of course, she was surprised that her sister had never mentioned him, for she had spoken with Emily regularly about all notable aspects of their lives. But the ambassador possessed one of the last known photos of Emily and said they had become "quite close," so she decided to take him at his word.

43

MAGGIE KNEW she was supposed to be terrified—terrified that at any moment sirens would sound, buildings would shake and crumble, and people would start screaming and running. Or maybe she wouldn't have to observe all that. Possibly it would all be over in a flash without her ever knowing what had happened. After all, she sat just yards away from the primary target of this military operation.

However, while she was petrified of so much else, the fact that she might be incinerated at any moment barely registered. She had gotten into politics and government to help people, to make lives better, and now look where she was. Maybe she deserved to die. Maybe they all did—Kyler, the crown prince, everyone in the room who was part of this spectacle, watching two men play a card game for $20 million as a dictator watched from a stage and a crowd served as supportive props.

Maggie wasn't sure she could continue living with the memory of what Bryce did to her constantly being replayed in her mind. She didn't know how she would function normally as long as she was unable to shut it off, so aware that despite the consequences for Bryce, so many didn't believe her, and those who did largely considered it a "little deal!" Because of the takedown of Bryce and her participation in this entire Kingdom event, millions and millions hated her now, and some of those who despised her were quite powerful allies of Bryce with long memories and a penchant for vindictiveness. They would hound her for the rest of her life, taking every available opportunity to demolish her and any client who retained her. And potential clients would know that. So, there would be none.

Plus, whether what she said was viewed as truth, her overall public image—which was now larger than she'd ever imagined possible—was one of a slutty, dishonest opportunist who had bated Bryce with her evil, seductive powers and then seized on their sexual liaison to enhance her own profile and destroy his. In addition to social media attacks, she was receiving so many vitriolic text messages that she was trying to ignore. And that didn't even include the countless disturbing dick pics that were now regularly streaming into her phone.

Then there was the fact that after all this, Bryce had been replaced by Mr. Dog Style of all people. That Connolly—the poster child for workplace harassment—was now the White House chief of staff because Bryce was deemed morally tainted was beyond dispiriting. Just too much to bear.

She didn't want to die, but she acknowledged that one reason she willingly returned was that if she did pay with her life as this regime was taken down, possibly that would make everything so much easier. Maybe that would be justice. And mercy.

Maggie had never had thoughts like this before, never reflected on death as anything other than something to be feared. Not too long ago, she was a happy person. A fun person. She missed that woman.

And she wanted her back. If she lived, she was going to try with all her might to rebuild her life. Or start a new one. How could she do that? She didn't know. But in the war to regain her former vibrant self, Kyler winning would give her *so much* ammunition.

Money can't buy happiness *yada yada yada* but oh my God she knew recovering her life would be so much more doable if he was successful. Ten million dollars. The security, the comfort, the freedom. Knowing that at least *something* positive, something big, would have come out of everything she had gone through. Being able to do what she needed to heal without simultaneously scrambling to meet her daunting financial obligations.

She had watched as the other final table participants fell one by one over the course of hours. A plump announcer in a tuxedo narrated the action into a microphone, declaring bet amounts, raises, folds, and eliminations. The crowd *oohed* and *aahed* with each escalation in action and clapped politely at the conclusion of each hand.

Maggie really didn't know poker, but it didn't take a poker savant to follow the general action here—she could see when Kyler was getting aggressive, when he was backing down, when he was winning, when he was not. Her emotions rose and fell with each hand, each card. When Kyler bet big, she wondered if he really had a strong hand or was bluffing. Of course, she couldn't tell. And fortunately, it seemed as if the rest of the table couldn't either, as he was winning a lot more pots than he was losing.

Now, there were just two men left—Kyler and the jerk from his first table at the beginning of the tournament. Kyler walked over to her with a nervous, exhausted expression and she rose to greet him.

"Great job," she said. "Just one more left." And she got herself to actually smile a little as she said it. *One more. Just one more . . .*

"This guy's a really good player," Kyler told her quietly.

"Well, obviously so are you," she responded encouragingly.

"I could use some luck here."

"Good luck, Kyler."

They looked at each other, and she sensed that some kind of embrace would be the natural thing to do at this point. But she really didn't want that right now. Not with Kyler, not with anyone. He had already greeted her with one voracious bear hug, and she'd tried to mask how uncomfortable it made her feel. She didn't want to upset him, didn't want to do anything to throw him off his game at this crucial juncture. She had made so many mistakes recently, but the one thing she had done right was that she had fully supported Kyler, her first client, and in part because of her efforts and encouragement, he was close to winning. She wouldn't do anything to undermine their shared cause now.

So if he leaned in for a hug, some final physical contact before stepping away to battle, she would hug him back and pretend she welcomed it. She wouldn't reveal how much she wanted to just sit back down and watch and not have to engage in some ritualistic touching that she wouldn't have thought twice about in the past.

They both stood there for a moment, and she braced for his response, knowing that the time to assert her preferred physical boundaries was certainly not now.

"Thanks Maggie," he finally answered, placing a hand on her arm. "I couldn't have done this without you."

He turned and walked toward the table, which had been positioned in the middle of the room, with a large banner proclaiming "Goodwill Poker Classic" as its backdrop. Sacha had been talking with his supporters nearby and now strolled back to the tournament area. As the two men crossed paths, they were close enough that Maggie was able to see and hear Sacha lean toward his opponent and speak in a low voice.

"Hey EZ, when your wife bangs two guys, how do they decide who gets to be first to . . ."

And she couldn't decipher the rest, or maybe her ears just preemptively shut down. Meanwhile, Kyler didn't even flinch, and just kept moving toward his seat at one end of the poker table, as Sacha took his on the other side.

Next the cash. So much cash. Was that real? Could that actually be $20 million? Real or fake, it looked like US currency, an interesting choice for a nation almost at war with America. It was displayed on a large table a few feet away from the poker felt amidst extensive cheers from the crowd. This was the big moment, so long in the making. No matter who won, so much planning had gone into making sure the crown prince was triumphant in the end, and now that preordained outcome was seriously in doubt.

Cards were dealt, and Maggie watched tensely for two hours as the two men alternated betting, raising, folding, stacking chips, posturing, staring, getting closer to the ultimate goal, and then taking painful steps further away.

As the announcer declared the cards and bet sizes, Maggie tried her best to follow all the action, but this wasn't her game. If this was a political campaign, or a policy debate, she'd be taking charge and able to detect and explain nuances that most others would miss. But she had no experience in this world, so she looked mostly at Kyler to see whether things were going well on any given hand. He did his part by revealing nothing.

"Raise," Sacha declared on the next hand, and Kyler paused before "re-raise" escaped his mouth. Maggie's tired body snapped to attention, as it had during so many earlier hands in which the action had accelerated.

Then Sacha bet even more, and nervous tension swept through her as Kyler called, and the dealer put three cards in the middle of the table. A screen above the action showed them to be a ten, a jack, and a three. Two were hearts. One was clubs. Or spades. What was the difference again?

Kyler tapped the table with his fingertips a couple of times, and then Sacha did the same, both men staring at each other coldly. Another card was dealt, another black card. A six. Almost certainly the six of spades.

And then Kyler pushed forward what seemed like a lot of chips.

"Call," Sacha replied, and the dealer placed a five of diamonds on the board.

So many chips in the middle now. Who had more left in front of him? Hard to tell. Too close. What did Kyler have? What did he need to have? Was he making the correct moves? Or squandering everything?

Kyler tapped the table again. She knew by now that meant he was "checking" or passing to the other person. But what did that *really* mean? Was that a good sign at this point? Or waiving the white flag?

"All in," Sacha announced, and then Kyler appeared as unsettled as Maggie had ever seen him. He glanced down, then leaned back, then sighed and rubbed his right hand over his beard.

"You have two pair?" Kyler asked, probably trying to get a better read on his opponent. But Sacha wasn't playing games anymore. For once, he had decided to just shut the fuck up.

Kyler looked around the room, and for half a second his eyes connected emotionlessly with Maggie. Then he was back staring at Sacha, slowing shaking his head, considering what to do next.

"Call," Kyler finally said, pushing his chips forward, and now it looked like all the chips were in the middle, so whoever lost this hand would be more or less finished.

Sacha stood up and tossed two tens onto the table. So he didn't have two pair. He had three tens, and Maggie knew enough to understand that that was an even stronger hand. But all that really mattered now was what Kyler thought, as his cards were still face down.

She rose too and looked at her client, who stared at the tens as his eyes widened and jaw extended and all life drained out of his face. She saw all this, and how his body sagged weakly. She didn't need to be a poker player to read his agony.

No, please no. Not after all this. Not when we're this close.

Sacha stood over his opponent, looking down from across the table, a smile stretching across his face.

Now. Let the missiles all fall now. Please.

"I just have jacks," Kyler finally uttered meekly, turning over two of the young men and laying them sadly on the table.

And now she was not only devastated but also so confused.

Didn't this mean he had *three* jacks?

And didn't three jacks actually *beat* three tens?

44

"YOU MOTHERFUCKER!" Sacha screamed as he slammed his hand down on the table. "What the fuck was that?!"

His face was crimson and he shook in fury as he began to approach Kyler with a clenched fist. The crowd buzzed as many of them turned to neighbors to try to understand what had just happened, while simultaneously watching the drama that was unfolding in front of them.

Kyler stood up to face him, looking unafraid of a physical attack.

"I'd love for you to try to hit me now," Kyler taunted.

Sacha stopped in his tracks, a few feet from Kyler, and then released a guttural yell and swept his hands across the poker table, sending many of Kyler's chips flying to the floor.

"You fucking classless piece of shit!" he bellowed at Kyler. "You act that way on *this* hand? Like you fucking lost. Disgusting!" He then turned to the crown prince, sitting on his riser overlooking the room. "He doesn't deserve this prize! That was horrible! He dishonored this whole tournament!"

"You did the same thing to me!" Kyler charged.

"On a small pot with one hundred people left! Not on the final hand with $20 million at stake!"

The crown prince had been handed a microphone, and he stood up to address the crowd.

"Remember the name of this event. The *Goodwill* Poker Classic.

I urge all participants to remember that they must show proper sportsmanship. No threats, no improper behavior, no screaming at opponents will be tolerated. Now, Mr. Dawson showed a set of jacks, which obviously defeats a set of tens. Mr. Dealer, does Mr. Dawson have his opponent covered?"

The dealer began stacking chips, including those he and others quickly collected from the floor. He placed Kyler's side by side with Sacha's and carefully inspected that each column was even. Maggie saw tears begin to form in Kyler's eyes as he watched the man finish the count.

"Yes, he does, Prince."

"Then," the crown prince responded, "it is my honor to declare Kyler Dawson the victor in the first Goodwill Poker Classic. A World Champion, now he is also our champion. Congratulations, sir!"

"Yes!" Kyler hollered in triumph as he thrust both arms in the air and tears flooded down his face. While Sacha stood silently incensed, Kyler ecstatically pumped his right fist, so wildly that it almost hit Maggie as she ran up to him.

The crowd cheered and applauded in a deafening standing ovation.

"Oh my God, oh my God, you did it, Kyler!" she yelled at him even though she stood just inches away, and now she was crying, too. "You fucking did it!"

He looked at her and wiped some of the tears off his left cheek.

"*We* did it, Maggie. I can't believe it. It's unbelievable."

"I know," she replied, shaking her head as she tried to soak this all in. "Thank you, Kyler. I'm so grateful. Oh my God."

"No, thank *you*."

She was still trying to process all of this, to understand what had happened and confirm that it was for real. "You realize that when you slow balled him, you also slow balled me, right?"

"Slow rolled."

"Whatever. When you slow *rolled* him you also slow rolled me. You almost fucking killed me."

"Sorry. I just had to. So many assholes never get what they deserve—"

"I know."

"So finally one did."

The audience had died down, and she looked over at the crown prince's row. An adviser was whispering in his right ear, and the crown prince's smile disappeared.

"Something's wrong," she quietly declared to Kyler.

No, not now. This sadist should also get what he deserves, but not right now. It can't happen right now.

The crown prince dashed out a side door, surrounded by a few of his men. Meanwhile, security officers began hurriedly securing and removing the huge pile of cash that had been on display for the past two hours, as patriotic music began playing from a few speakers that were scattered across the room.

"Is that attack starting now?" Kyler asked nervously. "The one you told me about . . ."

"I think we would hear sirens if it was. People would be evacuating. But I don't know. It better not happen before we arrange for payment."

"Oh fuck," he said in a panic. "I don't want to die here. And if we survive, how do we get paid if this whole country is reduced to rubble? They can't do this now. Can you contact the White House?"

She looked at him sternly. "Are you kidding me? The White House would love for me to die here right now."

"I'm sorry, I thought it was just the chief of staff you accused. And he's gone now."

"That's not the way it works." She grabbed her phone to call Jacques, maybe the only person with some influence outside the Kingdom who didn't detest her now. Before she could call him, she saw that he had texted her approximately an hour before.

"Maggie, I believe you stopped a war. You helped prevent a nuclear conflict. POTUS decided there will be no military assault (for now). We are all in your debt."

She felt a wave of relief rush over her body. They had won. And they weren't going to die in a missile strike. And it was relief upon that relief to know that she truly still wanted to live.

She was getting credit here? Crazy. Yes, she had learned that Bryce had been the main advocate for a military assault, and he had simultaneously helped facilitate her presence here, untroubled by and possibly even seeking that she stand in harm's way. Now that she had been instrumental in his removal, and the White House had altered its policy, was this really in part her doing?

"We're okay," she told Kyler as she looked up at him from her phone. "There's not going to be any military action today."

"Oh, thank God," he replied quickly as he ran his right hand over his eyes. "It would be just my luck to get pulverized by a missile right after winning $20 million." He looked around with concern. "But then what's happening? You saw the look on his face. Something's wrong."

Before she could answer, four armed security officers approached them, with one extending a hand in the direction of one of the exits.

"The crown prince wants to speak with both of you," he said. "Right away."

They were quickly ushered out a side door, down a hallway, and into a smaller room where the crown prince stood in conversation with several of his men. He turned as Kyler and Maggie entered the room, his face full of stress, his air of gracious benevolence gone.

"Your country just declared war on me!" he shouted.

"No, that's not right," Maggie quickly responded. "That can't be."

"They've frozen my assets in banks throughout the world. Not just mine, but my whole family's assets, and those of every official in this government. They're trying to cripple us!"

He looked at Maggie and stepped toward her and pointed before continuing angrily, "And what do you know about this?"

Maggie thought about who was speaking to her now, and where she was. He was a tyrant, a murderer, enraged and not rational, and there was no one here to protect her.

"Nothing. I swear. I know nothing about this."

"You were sent here by the United States government. You met with the Canadian ambassador just before he departed to meet with the White House. And you know nothing?"

"He was working to stop a war," Maggie explained, knowing that she was talking with someone who could kill her without consequence, and therefore she better not be caught in a lie. "I spoke with him about that and tried to help. He wanted the US to avoid a military conflict. And I was asking for his assistance with my situation with Bryce Kirkwood, which as you probably know is now very public."

"I never should have allowed him and Varma to leave this country after all they did to undermine my government! They may not be launching missiles, but they're trying to destroy me. They want to starve this government of money. Don't they realize what will happen then? Don't they know the radicals that will take over if I fall? They want *them* to then control our nuclear arsenal? What stupidity!"

"I came here to participate in your tournament when no one else in my country would," Kyler replied. "Maggie helped make that happen. I wouldn't be here without her. We've done nothing to undermine you at all. I just came here to play poker. And I won. Fair and square. Please don't blame us."

Maggie listened to Kyler talk, and noted with trepidation the implied message, an acknowledgment that this enraged despot, now facing a major, possibly debilitating financial crunch, had the power to not only kill them, but to withhold the promised prize money that they had come so far to win. Now that he appeared increasingly delirious with rage and in full blown crisis, what would be their recourse if he refused to pay? A lawsuit? In what court? Ludicrous.

"Unlike your country," the crown prince responded, "I honor my commitments and my word is good. There was a $20 million prize for this event, and you won. I would never renege on that. Don't blame *me* for your inability to collect it."

Maggie's throat went dry and head started pounding as Kyler quickly jumped in, "What inability to collect? What are you talking about?"

"In addition to freezing many of my assets, your country is trying to destabilize my economy. The new executive order's economic sanctions prohibit all financial transactions between American citizens and my government. And between American citizens and any entity or state doing business with my government."

"Well, there has to be a way to still pay!" Kyler called out in panic. "There has to be some way! Maggie?"

She was his consultant, his advisor, his expert on politics and policy. From the beginning, he had retained her to navigate around a proposed executive order, so naturally he was looking for her to help now. But she knew that if the crown prince was accurate, any money they transferred out would be immediately seized, and they would likely both face heavy fines, and probably incarceration. They weren't two individuals gaining a small amount of money while flying under the radar. They were prime targets of the radar.

Her head was throbbing even harder, and her heartbeat quickened and she wanted to vomit. She needed to speak with Jacques. Maybe he could help. Maybe there was some loophole here that he would know about. He was probably the only one who might be able to give her some guidance now, but even that was a long shot.

"I have to make some calls. I need to see what I can find out. But this is my fault," she said, her voice growing increasingly quieter. "I'm so sorry Kyler. This is my fault."

"What are you talking about?" he asked with terrified urgency. "We need to do something. You have to figure this out!"

"Bryce was always opposed to economic sanctions. He wanted a military option instead. He wouldn't have done this. It's only because of what I said about him, what I did, that he's gone and now this is happening. And the timing of this is all intentional. The White House wants to undermine the Kingdom's big propaganda event, and they also want to destroy me. They're extremely vindictive. If they can't kill me with a missile, they're sure as hell not letting me walk out of here with $20 million. I'm so sorry."

"No!" she heard Kyler scream in pain. "No! There has to be a way. I'm not losing this now! I'm not letting that happen!"

Then Maggie had a desperate idea and turned to the crown prince. "What if you give up your nuclear weapons?" she pleaded. "Disarm. Allow inspections. They'll have to unfreeze your assets and cancel the sanctions."

"Are you crazy?" the crown prince answered. "Those weapons are the only thing keeping me alive right now. The only reason your nation hasn't tried to kill me is that the US doesn't want nuclear retaliation. And they don't want me to die yet because radicals would then inherit these weapons. I surrender those weapons, and I'm a dead man."

She was now so full of rage and almost agnostic again about whether she survived. And that made her bold. "Then why did you kill Emily Kinum?! You started this whole crisis. You did this!"

The room went silent as the crown prince's men looked startled and furious as they turned toward him and awaited direction. Their leader was generally feared by anyone in his presence and always spoken to with reverence and supplication. Little chance they had ever witnessed comments like this directed at him, especially from a woman.

Kyler stepped toward Maggie in a fruitless attempt to exude protectiveness. Meanwhile, the crown prince again raised a finger and glared at her, and she stared right back without wavering.

"I'm fighting for my country's life right now," he said. "If our economy is cut off from the world, all my people will suffer greatly, and this government will collapse. So I'm going to give you a chance to make those calls you mentioned. You call your friends back in Washington and you try to undo this, if you want your client here to claim his money."

"And what about my question?" she asked, this time calmer. This time really hoping for an answer.

"I never wanted her to die. But she's just one person. I'm trying to reform this country, to bring us into this century. To give women and girls the freedoms that they have been asking for. Do you know what would have happened if she published what she was writing? If she published what your friend the ambassador encouraged her to write? If she helped bring down my government and made me a pariah and allowed my opponents to seize this nation? The result would have been chaos. Unimaginable chaos. Here. Around the world. Everywhere."

Maggie considered how she should respond. How do you answer someone who just tells you unrepentantly that he is a murderer? When that person has virtually unrestricted power to kill again?

She thought about how Jacques wrote to tell her that she helped prevent a nuclear war. Had she? Or had she just bought this madman more time to build up his stockpile and then later start one or use the threat of one to intimidate the rest of the world with impunity?

45

KYLER WATCHED Maggie pace anxiously around his hotel suite with her phone to her ear, as he simultaneously, frantically, tried to find news on his phone about the sanctions. He alternatingly rose and sat, looked up at her and back to his device, unable to remain in any fixed physical position for more than a few seconds.

He was no expert in analyzing economic sanctions, but it was completely clear from every article that the new sanctions were very real, and they were devastating in their scope and strength.

"He's still not answering," Maggie said again with frustration. And then after a couple of seconds added, "Now he's texting me."

She was trying to reach the Canadian ambassador, who was now the former Canadian ambassador, to get his guidance and insight. What could he really do to help? She said she didn't know, but it was the best place to start.

"He's writing that he can't talk while I'm in the Kingdom. Not secure. Fuck!"

"Who else can you try?" he asked.

"No one in the White House will speak with me. Even my friends. They'll be too terrified to talk to me now. If anyone at the White House found out, they'd lose their jobs."

"Well, there has to be someone you know who can help!"

"Kyler, there's no one," she said mournfully. "No one is undoing this for us. It's done. It can't be undone."

Kyler screamed, grabbed a vase, and threw it against the wall. He forcefully kicked over a coffee table and then shoved a nearby lamp that went crashing to the floor.

"Stop it!" she yelled, and for now he stopped in his tracks.

She collapsed onto the floor, wrapped her arms around her knees, and tucked her head between her legs.

"Bryce never would have done this," she said. "He always said economic sanctions were terrible policy. That they never accomplish anything. This never would have happened if he was still there."

"Then why didn't you wait to do what you did?" Kyler asked. "Why didn't you just wait until this was all over? Just another couple of days . . ."

"You saw how this happened!" she snapped back, lifting her head. "I wasn't in control. This all snowballed so fast, and then I tried to take control before it destroyed me. This was a no-win situation!"

He fell to his knees next to her. "I just can't handle this. I can't! That money is ours."

"I know," she said in despair.

He was miserable, and so was she. So lost, and so was she. He felt so alone and broke with a life destroyed many times over. She was the only person who could probably understand him now, and maybe he could understand her, or at least be supportive, sympathetic. He longed for some comfort, anything to salve this anguish.

She looked at him as if waiting for him to say something. Or do something. To find a few words or make a move that would render this torturous situation just a tiny bit more bearable.

Kyler had been with his wife for so many years. Their marriage had fizzled long ago. He had since kissed one woman in a bar, in a drunken, ridiculous, and sloppy moment. It had been so long since he had *really* kissed someone. Kissed someone with the tenderness and passion and maybe even love that he felt for Maggie now. So unbearably long.

And it had been even longer since he had tried to kiss a woman and she leaned away from him, as Maggie now did. Their shared desolation had recklessly induced him to believe that she too sought this physical connection. But that instinct instantly transformed into the awkward and mortifying realization that he had so absurdly misread her, as she moved her head away in startled surprise. A self-protective withdrawal because she didn't want it to happen, not with him.

"I'm sorry . . ." he gasped. "I thought . . ."

They were still on the floor, still very close and facing each other, collapsed on the luxurious rug of this fancy suite with their lives in tatters.

"We need to get to the airport," she said softly but decisively. "We need to get out of here."

But he couldn't. Not now. He couldn't think, let alone move, let alone really breathe. So he shook his head.

"You go."

"Kyler, we need to get to the airport. I don't know how, but I'm going to try to rebuild my life. You need to try to do the same."

"I can't. Every time I try, it all just gets worse. I can't recover from *this*. This was my last chance . . ."

"You need to keep trying. You need to come to the airport with me now. The first step is leaving here. Right now. And never coming back."

46

Four months later.

"KD FOR one-two Hold'em! KD for one-two Hold'em!"

In the end, the wait list hadn't been that bad. Fifteen minutes, maybe twenty.

During that time, he walked over to the cage and handed over an assortment of wrinkled bills—twenties, tens, fives, and five ones—in return for a rack of chips. Clear plastic rack, with five rows, each capable of holding twenty chips. For the cash he surrendered, he received two full rows of red $5 chips, leaving three rows empty, hopefully to be filled by winnings once he was given a seat in the action.

As he waited for his initials to be called by the poker room manager, he looked at the electronic screens showing the wait lists for all the other available games—Stud, Omaha, and Hold'em with a variety of stakes. Two-five. Ten-twenty. Fifty-one hundred.

He looked around the poker room at the forty or so tables packed with players. Talking, drinking, clinking chips, cheering success, cursing bad beats. Television screens above them showed muted coverage of sports events and a few news programs. At the back of the room, in a raised area, the high-limit section currently offered one table of activity, with seven or eight players winning or losing more on each hand than most players in the room would ever see in their checking accounts.

He had $200 in chips to start. How much would he have when

he cashed out? If he played smart, if he stayed in command of his emotions and didn't go on tilt, potentially hundreds more. Not that a couple of hundred in profit would restore his unsalvageable reputation or make a difference with his staggering debts or help support his children in any meaningful way. But it would be nice to win.

It had also been nice when his phone buzzed an hour earlier while he was getting some food at a burger place near the casino. A while ago he had set up a text alert for Maggie's tweets, and now he had received a notification for the first time. He was excited to see what information made her break her Twitter silence.

They had barely communicated with each other since returning to the United States. Their only interaction had been two months ago when he learned that her mother passed away, and he sent an email saying how sorry he was for her loss and that she and her mother and entire family were in his prayers. A week and a half later, he received a one-word response:

"Thanks."

Such a short answer, and he spent far too much time thinking about what *thanks* meant. Was it appreciative? Dismissive? He wondered why she didn't write "Thank you," or "Thanks, Kyler." And he fantasized about her actually writing "Thank you, Kyler."

He occasionally watched the news and hoped to one day catch her back on the screen as a political analyst, giving her opinion on the big topics of the day. But he never saw her, and as far as he could tell there were no new videos of Maggie's television appearances online.

He saw a commercial for a new reality show in which a bunch of political consultants were locked in a house together for a couple of months. They would have contests to sway the audience on a host of random issues, with viewers voting their opinions each week to determine who was most persuasive and who failed to convince and thus would be eliminated from the house. It was called *Spin Room*, or something like that.

Maggie would be perfect for this, he thought. And he watched the beginning of the first episode, hoping she would be one of the contestants.

But she wasn't.

Now, after several months, she was finally making her first public comments since returning to the United States with two tweets:

"VERY proud to announce that I will be serving as campaign manager for @MeganBlackforCouncil! She will bring much-needed experience, commitment, and common sense to the Mountain Hill City Council!"

And:

"Megan will work tirelessly to strengthen the MH School District and will finally improve the lighting and road conditions on Route 48! #megan4council #reformmountainhillnow"

Kyler quickly clicked the heart icon to "like" both tweets. Then, in the following minutes, he considered whether that was a mistake. Despite the fact that the #thishappened hashtag had now been adopted by other sexual assault survivors, Maggie's own reputation continued to be trashed online, with people attacking her as a dishonest, immoral opportunist. Good for her that she had a new client, something to be excited and hopeful about. Kyler recognized that the last thing she or her candidate needed was to be publicly associated now with him, and all the baggage that he brought along.

So he "unliked" both tweets.

Now his initials were finally being called, and one of the poker room managers pointed him and his tray of chips toward a table in the middle of the room.

"Table 20, Seat 6," he told Kyler.

The casino's corporate owner had officially banned him from its premises, as had other casinos throughout the country in response to the public petitions after his participation in the Goodwill Poker Classic. In reality, that prevented him buying into high-dollar events, which he couldn't afford anyway. And he was far too toxic for anyone to sponsor.

But for low stakes cash games, with $1 and $2 blinds and for which one just had to provide initials, there was generally no problem getting access. He sensed that some of the poker managers even liked having him there. It was a little rebellious, in the spirit of old school, outlaw casino life.

His beard was now longer and he wore a baseball cap today, but that didn't prevent people from recognizing him. As soon as he took his seat and joined the other eight players—seven men and one woman—a middle-aged guy at the corner of the table exclaimed, "Kyler Dawson! World champ Kyler Dawson playing in a 1-2 game? Oh man, the reports must be true. You really *are* broke!"

"Well," Kyler responded calmly, "even if I am, that'll change in a few minutes once I take all your money."

The man chuckled and raised his beer to salute Kyler's answer.

The cards were dealt, and Kyler peered down at three-seven offsuit and promptly folded. He looked around at the various muted televisions around the room and noted that one was previewing the upcoming World Series of Poker. The closed captioning displayed the words on the screen, as a male host interviewed Priya Varma, poker icon and international activist, her star now shining brighter than ever.

"How do you balance your human rights work with your poker career?" the host asked.

Kyler read her response on the screen as he watched her mouth move:

"Well, poker is incredibly important to me, but the most significant thing in my life will always be working to prevent injustice. The history of the world is a brutal one of people exerting power and control over others in terrible ways. It's an extremely cruel history, but it doesn't have to be like that forever. Together we can help oppressed people around the globe. We can change our world for the better."

"Can you imagine?" the man sitting to Kyler's right asked as he also stared up at the screen.

Kyler looked down at ace-king of diamonds and pushed $8 in chips forward. “Imagine what?” he replied.

“Imagine *that*,” the player said, motioning with his head toward Priya’s image on the screen as a smirk crossed his face. “Hitting *that*. So fucking hot. Can you imagine?”

Someone else re-raised to $25, and there were two other callers, so a decent sized pot was building as Kyler decided to call, too, and then the dealer laid down the flop.

“No way,” another guy responded. “She’s always so serious on TV. Zero chance she’s any fun. Bet she’d be super uptight.”

Five of clubs, seven of clubs, jack of hearts. Total whiff. But Kyler placed a decent-sized bet anyway.

“No,” the man to his right answered, insistent on defending his position. “Those activist girls are like *crazy*. Out of control. She’d probably be up for *anything*. It would be awesome.”

One caller. The guy who originally flagged him for being broke. Just the two of them now heading to the turn card. Meanwhile, Priya had been asked about her chances of getting back to the WSOP final table this year.

“That’s my goal. I want to make the final table and win the world championship. But if you look at how many thousands of players are in this tournament, no matter how much success I have, the odds are stacked against going that deep again. That’s why coming in ninth, and the way I got knocked out on that hand, will always haunt me. To come that close to a dream and have it end like that . . .”

“Hey Kyler!” another man who had been following the table conversation called out. “You know her, right? You ever tap that?”

The table rocked with laughter as the ten of spades fell on the turn. He still had nothing, but he bet again and then concealed his disappointment when his opponent paused for a couple of seconds and then called.

Meanwhile, now that the image of him having sex had been introduced to the conversation, he braced for the inevitable E-ZPass comment. But before anyone could go there, the closed captioning provided some new material.

"What's it like to watch that hand?" the host asked Priya.

"I've never watched it."

"Never? Not even once?"

"No. Never. Too heartbreaking."

And now the table exploded with guffaws and cheers directed at Kyler.

"Kyler, you heartbreaker!" one player exclaimed.

Another followed with an equally sarcastic, "Kyler, you mean guy! Breaking that poor girl's heart!" as the surrounding players collapsed into laughter.

"Kyler, you clearly need to throw her one," the man to his right instructed. "Just out of sympathy! Find it in *your* heart!"

But Kyler was too focused on the hand to respond. The river card had brought a third club, putting a possible flush out there. Of course he didn't have it. He had nothing. But he was pretty sure his opponent didn't have much either.

"All in," Kyler proclaimed as he moved his remaining chips forward.

And then he was a statue, as the other man stared him down, trying to figure out what to do.

"Guess you caught your flush," the guy finally said as he folded, pushing his face down cards forward.

"Was there a flush on the board?" Kyler asked slyly.

The dealer shoved a pile of chips toward Kyler, and he began the always exhilarating process of stacking them, feeling all the new chips between his fingers and watching the columns in front of him grow. How much had he won? Probably over $150. Nice start.

But this wasn't the time to count. Right now he needed to post the $2 big blind for the next hand because the dealer was already tossing out the cards.

Acknowledgments

I'D LIKE TO thank everyone at SparkPress, especially Brooke Warner and Samantha Strom, for your guidance, enthusiasm, and skillful editing in connection with this novel. I'm also grateful to Crystal Patriarche, Tabitha Bailey, Maggie Ruf, and Madison Ostrander for your excellent, resourceful publicity efforts.

Thank you to all the great friends who were instrumental in the creation of this book, particularly Cyndi Ferencz and Peggy Wang for reading early drafts and providing vital edits and advice for improving the plot and characters; author Jacqueline Friedland for generously sharing your invaluable expertise about the writing and publishing process; and Austin Krumpfes, Andrew Wong, and Michael King for teaching me poker—I credit you for all the fun and comradery the game has brought me, and I blame you for every agonizing bad beat.

Thank you to my parents Gary and Linda and my brother Steve for your unwavering support, love, encouragement, and inspiration, and for your insightful suggestions for revising this story. Mom, thank you so much for giving me as a child a lifelong love of books and a dream of writing them.

Thank you to Jen Buchwald, the love of my life, for your creative and imaginative ideas and edits as you read and reread this novel. Your enhancements made this book so much stronger than it ever could have been without you. Meeting you was by far the greatest and most unexpected plot twist. You are always my #sixofdiamondsontheriver.

To Samantha and Jake, I can't wait to hear your thoughts on this book when you're old enough to read it. You bring endless joy to my life every day, and my favorite stories in the world are the ones you each create.

About the Author

© Suzanne Claire Photography

DAN SCHORR is a sexual misconduct investigator at his firm, Dan Schorr, LLC, and an adjunct professor at Fordham Law School, where he teaches a course on sexual misconduct and domestic violence. Previously, he served as a New York sex crimes prosecutor, the Inspector General for the City of Yonkers, and an adjunct law professor with Tsinghua University in Beijing, China. He has been a regular television legal analyst for *Good Morning America*, CNN, Fox News Channel, Law & Crime Network, and elsewhere. Schorr holds a BA and MA from the University of Pennsylvania, and a JD from Harvard Law School. He lives in White Plains, New York, with his wife and two children. *Final Table* is his first novel.

SELECTED TITLES FROM SPARKPRESS

SparkPress is an independent boutique publisher delivering high-quality, entertaining, and engaging content that enhances readers' lives, with a special focus on female-driven work. www.gosparkpress.com

Attachments: A Novel, Jeff Arch, $16.95, 9781684630813
What happens when the mistakes we make in the past don't stay in the past? When no amount of running from the things we've done can keep them from catching up to us? When everything depends on what we do next?

Indelible: A Sean McPherson Novel, Book 1, Laurie Buchanan, $16.95, 9781684630714
Murder at a writing retreat in the Pacific Northwest, but this one isn't imaginary. Authors only kill with words. Or do they?

Absolution: A Novel, Regina Buttner, $16.95, 978-1-68463-061-5
A guilt-ridden young wife and mother struggles to keep a long-ago sexual assault and pregnancy a secret from her ambitious husband whose career aspirations depend upon her silence and unswerving loyalty to him.

Firewall: A Novel, Eugenia Lovett West. $16.95, 978-1-68463-010-3
When Emma Streat's rich, socialite godmother is threatened with blackmail, Emma becomes immersed in the dark world of cybercrime—and mounting dangers take her to exclusive places in Europe and contacts with the elite in financial and art collecting circles. Through passion and heartbreak, Emma must fight to save herself and bring a vicious criminal to justice.

Seventh Flag: A Novel, Sid Balman, Jr. $16.95, 978-1-68463-014-1
A sweeping work of historical fiction, *Seventh Flag* is a Micheneresque parable that traces the arc of radicalization in modern Western Civilization—reaffirming what it means to be an American in a dangerously divided nation.

CPSIA information can be obtained
at www.ICGtesting.com
Printed in the USA
FSHW011132280521
81773FS